About the Author

Annie Burrows  was old enough literature. She beyond that, bu those daydream carrying out m pleasure to other women. She was right...and Annie hasn't looked back since. Readers can sign up to Annie's newsletter at annie-burrows.co.uk

Regency Secrets

July 2022
Those Scandalous
Stricklands

August 2022
The Governess Swap

September 2022
Penniless Brides of
Convenience

October 2022
The Cornish Dukes

November 2022
Breaking the Marriage
Rules

December 2022
The Beauchamp Heirs

January 2023
The Wild Warriners

February 2023
Brides for Bachelors

March 2023
Secret Lives of the Ton

April 2023
The Widows of
Westram

May 2023
Saved from Disgrace

June 2023
The Return of the
Rogues

Regency Secrets:

Brides for
Bachelors

ANNIE BURROWS

MILLS & BOON

THE MAJOR MEETS
HIS MATCH

I am really grateful to Aidan for brainstorming with me when I got stuck with this one. And for reminding me what kind of heroine I first imagined in Lady Harriet.

Chapter One

Lady Harriet Inskip tilted back her head and breathed in deeply. She could still smell soot, but at least this early in the day it wasn't completely blotting out the more wholesome odours of dew-damp grass and leather and horse. It didn't matter that it was still barely light enough to see the trees and flowers, or the curve of the Serpentine. She hadn't come here to admire the decorous landscape, after all.

She leaned forward and patted her horse's neck.

'Come on, Shadow, let's have a good gallop, shall we? While there's nobody to tell us we can't.'

Shadow snorted and pawed at the gravel path to indicate she was just as eager for exercise as her mistress. And then, with just the slightest tap of Harriet's heel against Shadow's flank, they were off.

For a few glorious minutes they flew through the dappled dawn, both revelling in Shadow's power and vitality. For those few minutes Harriet was free. Free as any wild creature that lived purely by instinct. Unhindered by the fetters with which society restricted the movements of young ladies.

But then her peaceful communion with nature was shattered by a sound that made the hairs on the back of her neck stand up and Shadow to falter mid-stride. It was the neigh of another horse. From beyond a stand of chestnut trees. A neigh so high pitched in outrage, it was almost a scream.

Harriet slowed Shadow to a canter. 'Easy, girl,' she murmured as her mount twitched her ears and rolled her eyes. But Shadow kept fidgeting nervously. And Harriet could hardly blame her when she reared up at the precise moment a black stallion burst from the cover of the trees as though it had been shot from a cannon.

At first she thought the black horse was a riderless runaway. But as it came closer, she could see a dark shape huddled on its back and a pair of legs flailing along its flanks.

'What an idiot,' she muttered to herself. For the man clinging to the stallion had not put a saddle on it. Perhaps there hadn't been time. Perhaps he was attempting to steal the magnificent, and no doubt very expensive, animal. The horse certainly looked as if it wanted nothing more than to dislodge the impertinent human who'd had the temerity to ride him without following the proper conventions first. The stallion had just galloped through the trees as if it had been an attempt to scrape the interloper from his back, to judge from the way he began to buck and kick the moment he got out into the open.

'The idiot,' said Harriet again, this time a bit louder, as she saw that the runaway stallion was now heading straight for the Cumberland Gate. There wasn't much traffic on the roads at this time of day, but if that horse, and the idiot on board, got out into the streets, who knew what damage they might inflict on innocent passers-by?

'Come on, Shadow,' she said, tapping her mare on the flank with her riding crop. 'We're going to have to head off those two before they get into real trouble.' Shadow didn't need much prompting. She loved racing. However, rather than attempt to pull alongside the snorting, furious stallion, Harriet guided Shadow into a course that would take them across his current path. For one thing, even if they could catch up with the runaway horse, any attempt to snatch at the reins to try to bring him to a halt was bound to end in disaster. Though Harriet took pride in her own skills in the saddle, she couldn't imagine being able to lean over far enough to grab the reins without being unseated. Not whilst mounted side-saddle as she was. In fact, only a trained acrobat would be able to accomplish such a feat with any degree of confidence.

For another thing, she knew that no horse would run directly into another, not unless it was completely maddened with terror. And the black stallion, though furious, did not look to be in that state.

Just as she'd hoped, after only a few yards, the stallion did indeed notice their approach and veered off to the left.

It was just a shame for its rider that it did so rather abruptly, because the man, who'd clung on through all the stallion's attempts to dislodge him thus far, shot over its shoulder and landed with a sickening thump on the grass.

Harriet briefly wondered whether she ought to go to the rider's aid. But the man was lying crumpled like a bundle of washing, so there probably wasn't much she could do for him. She could, however, prevent the magnificent stallion from injuring itself or others, if she could only prevent it from reaching the Gate. To that end, she repeated her manoeuvre, pulling sharply to the left as though about to cut across the stallion's path. Once again, the stallion took evasive action. What was more, since it wasn't anywhere near as angry now that it had unseated its hapless rider, it didn't appear to feel the need to gallop flat out. By dint of continually urging it to veer left, Harriet made the stallion go round in a large, but ever-decreasing circle, with her on the outside. By the time they'd returned to the spot where the man still lay motionless, the stallion had slowed to a brisk trot. It curvetted past him, as though doing a little victory dance, shivered as though being attacked by a swarm of flies and then came to a complete standstill, snorting out clouds of steam.

Harriet dismounted, threw her reins over the nearest shrub and slowly approached the sweating, shivering, snorting stallion, crooning the kind of nonsense words that horses the country over always responded to, when spoken in a confident yet soothing tone. The beast tossed his head in a last act of defiance before permitting her to take its trailing reins.

'There, there,' she said, looping them over the same shrub which served as a tether for Shadow. 'You're safe now.' After tossing his head and snorting again for good measure, the stallion appeared to give her the benefit of the doubt.

Only once she was pretty sure the stallion wouldn't attempt to bolt again did Harriet turn to the man.

He was still lying spread out face down on the grass. Harriet's heart lurched in a way it hadn't when she'd gone after the runaway horse. Horses she could deal with. She spent more time in the stables than anywhere else. People, especially injured people, were another kettle of fish.

Nevertheless, she couldn't just leave him lying there. So she squared her shoulders, looped her train over her arm and walked over to where he lay.

Utterly still.

What did one do for a man who'd been tossed from his horse? A man who might have a broken neck?

Two answers sprang to mind, spoken in two very diverse voices. The first was that of her aunt, Lady Tarbrook.

'Go and fetch help,' it said plaintively, raising a vinaigrette to its nose. *'Ladies do not kneel down on wet grass and touch persons to whom they have not been introduced.'*

She gave a mental snort. According to Lady Tarbrook, Harriet shouldn't be out here at all. Since she'd come to London, Harriet had learned there were hundreds, nay, thousands of things she ought never to do. If Lady Tarbrook had her way, Harriet would do nothing but sit on a sofa doing embroidery or reading fashion magazines all day.

The second voice, coming swiftly after, sounded very much like that of her mother. *'Observe him more closely,'* it said, merely glancing up from the latest scientific journal, *'and find out exactly what his injuries are.'*

Which was the sensible thing to do. *Then* she could go and fetch help, if the man needed it. And what was more, she'd be able to say something to the point about him, rather than voice vague conjectures.

She ran her eyes over him swiftly as she knelt beside him. None of his limbs looked obviously broken. Nor was there any blood that she could see. If she hadn't seen him take a tumble, she might have thought he'd just decided to take a nap there, so relaxed did his body look. His face, at least the part of it that wasn't pressed into the grass, also looked as though he were asleep, rather than unconscious. There was even a slight smile playing about his lips.

She cleared her throat, and then, when he didn't stir, reached out one gloved hand and shook his shoulder gently.

That elicited a mumbled protest.

Encouraged, she shook him again, a bit harder. And his eyes flew open. Eyes of a startlingly deep blue. With deep lines darting from the outer corners, as though he laughed often. Or screwed his eyes up against the sun, perhaps, because, now she came to think of it, the skin of his face was noticeably tanned. Unlike most of the men to whom she was being introduced, of late. He wasn't handsome, in the rather soft way eligible Town-dwellers seemed to be, either. His face was a bit too square and his chin rather too forceful to fit the accepted patrician mould. And yet somehow it was a very attractive face all the same.

And then he smiled at her. As though he recognised her and was pleased to see her. Genuinely pleased. Which puzzled her. As did the funny little jolt that speared her stomach, making her heart lurch.

'I have died and gone to heaven,' he said, wreathing her in sweet fumes which she recognised as emanating, originally, from a brandy bottle.

She recoiled. But not fast enough. Oh, lord, in spite

of appearing extremely foxed, he still managed to get his arms round her and tug her down so she lay sprawled half over him. She then only had time to gasp in shock before he got one hand round the back of her head and pulled her face down to his. At which point he kissed her.

Very masterfully.

Even though Harriet had never been kissed before and was shocked that this drunkard was the first man to want to do any such thing, she suspected he must have a lot of experience. Because instead of feeling disgusted, the sensations shooting through her entire body were rather intriguing. Which she was certain ought not to be the case.

'Open your mouth, sweetheart,' the man said, breaking the spell he'd woven round her.

Naturally, she pressed her lips firmly together and shook her head, remembering, all of a sudden, that she ought to be struggling.

Then he chuckled. And started rolling, as if to reverse their positions. Which changed everything. Allowing curiosity to hold her in place while an attractive man obliged her to taste his lips was one thing. Letting him pin her to the ground and render her powerless was quite another.

So she did what she should have done in the first place. She wriggled her right arm as free as she could and struck at him with her riding crop. Because he was holding her so close to him, it glanced harmlessly off the thick thatch of light brown curls protecting the back of his head. But she had at least succeeded in surprising him.

'Let go of me, you beast,' she said, interjecting as

much affront in her voice as she could. And began to struggle.

To her chagrin, though he looked rather surprised by her demand, he let go of her at once. Even so, it was no easy matter to wriggle off him, hampered as she was by the train of her riding habit, which had become tangled round her legs.

'Ooohh...' he sighed. 'That feels good.' He half closed his eyes and sort of undulated under her. Indicating that all her frantic efforts to get up were only having a very basic effect on his body.

'You...you beast,' she said, swiping at him with her crop again.

He winced and rubbed at his arm where she'd managed to get in a decent hit before overbalancing and landing flat on his chest again.

'I don't enjoy those sorts of games,' he protested. 'I'd much rather we just kissed a bit more and then—'

She shoved her hands hard against his chest, using his rock-solid body as leverage so she could get to her hands and knees.

'Then nothing,' she said, shuffling back a bit before her trailing riding habit became so tangled she had to roll half over and sit on it. 'You clearly aren't injured after your fall from your horse, though you deserve,' she said, kicking and plucking at her skirts until she got her legs free, 'to have your neck broken.'

'I say, that's rather harsh,' he objected, propping himself up on one elbow and watching her struggles sleepily.

'No, it isn't. You are drunk. And you were trying to ride the kind of horse that would be a handful for any man, sober. What were you thinking? You could have injured him!'

'No, I couldn't. I can ride any horse, drunk or sober—'.

'Well, clearly you can't, or he wouldn't have bolted and you wouldn't be lying here—'

'Lucifer wouldn't have thrown me if you hadn't dashed across in front of us and startled him.'

'No, he would have carried you on to a public highway and ridden down some hapless milkmaid instead. And you would definitely have broken your neck if he'd thrown you on the cobbles.'

'I might have known,' he said with a plaintive sigh, 'that you were too good to be true. You might look like an angel and kiss like a siren, and have a fine pair of legs, but you have the disposition of a harpy.'

She gasped. Not at the insult, so much, but at the fact that he was gazing admiringly at her legs while saying it. Making her aware that far too much of them was on show.

'Well, you're an oaf. A drunken oaf at that!' She finally managed to untangle her legs and get to her feet just as three more men came staggering into view.

'Good God, just look at that,' said the first of the trio to reach them, a slender, well-dressed man with cold grey eyes and a cruel mouth. 'Even lying flat on his back in the middle of nowhere, Ulysses can find entertainment to round off the evening.'

Since the man with the cruel mouth was looking at her as though she was about to become his entertainment, Harriet's blood ran cold.

'I have no intention of being anyone's entertainment,' she protested, inching towards Shadow, though how on earth she was to mount up and escape, she had no idea. 'I only came over here to see if I could help.'

'You can certainly help settle the b-bet,' said the second young man to arrive, flicking his long, rather greasy fringe out of his eyes. 'Did he reach the C-Cumberland Gate b-before Lucifer unseated him?'

'It was a wager?' She rounded on the one they'd referred to as Ulysses, the one who was still half-reclining, propped up on one arm, watching them all with a crooked grin on his face. 'You risked injuring that magnificent beast for the sake of a wager?'

'The only risk was to his own fool neck,' said the man with the cold eyes. 'Lucifer can take care of himself,' he said, going across to the stallion and patting his neck proudly. From the way the stallion lowered his head and butted his chest, it was clear he was Lucifer's master.

Harriet stooped to gather her train over one arm, her heart hammering. At no point had she felt afraid of the man they called Ulysses, even when he'd been trying to roll her over on to her back. There was something about his square, good-natured face that put her at ease. Or perhaps it had been that twinkle in his eyes.

But the way the one with the cruel mouth was looking at her was a different matter. There was something…dark about him. Predatory. Even if he was fond of his horse and the horse clearly adored him in return, that didn't make him a decent man.

He then confirmed all her suspicions about his nature by turning to her with a mocking smile on his face. 'It is hardly fair of you to reward Ulysses with a kiss,' he said, taking a purposeful step closer, 'when it is I who won the wager.'

She lashed out with her riding crop and would have caught him across his face had he not flinched out of her way with a dexterity that both amazed and alarmed her. Even in a state of inebriation, this man could still pose a very real threat to a lone female.

Keeping her eyes on him, she inched sideways to where she'd tethered Shadow. And collided with what felt like a brick wall.

'Oof!' said the wall, which turned out to be the third of Ulysses's companions, a veritable giant of a man.

'You got off lightly,' remarked Mr Cold-Eyes to the giant, who was rubbing his mid-section ruefully. 'She made a *deliberate* attempt to injure me.'

'That's prob'ly 'cos you're fright'ning her,' slurred the giant. 'Clearly not a lightskirt.'

'Then what is she doing in the park, at this hour, kissing stray men she finds lying about the place?' Cold-Eyes gave her a look of such derision it sent a flicker of shame coiling through her insides.

'She couldn't resist me,' said Ulysses, grinning at her.

'She d-don't seem to like you, th-though, Zeus,' said the one with the greasy, floppy fringe.

'Archie, you wound me,' said Zeus, as she got her fingers, finally, on Shadow's reins. Though how on earth she was to mount up, she couldn't think. There was no mounting block. No groom to help her reach the stirrup.

Just as she'd resigned herself to walking home leading her mount, she felt a pair of hands fasten round her waist. On a reflex, she lashed out at her would-be assailant, catching him on the crown of his head.

'Ouch,' said the drunken giant of a man, as he launched her up and on to Shadow's saddle. 'There was no call for that.' He backed away, rubbing his head with a puzzled air.

No, there hadn't been any call for it. But how could she have guessed the giant had only been intending to help her?

'Then I beg *your* pardon,' she said through gritted teeth as she fumbled her foot into the stirrup.

'As for the rest of you,' she said as she got her knee over the pommel and adjusted her skirts, 'you ought… all of you…to be ashamed of yourselves.'

She did her best to toss her head as though she held them all in disdain. As though her heart wasn't hammering like a wild, frightened bird within the bars of her rib cage. To ride off with dignity, rather than hammering her heels into Shadow's flank, and urging her mare to head for home at a full gallop.

She wouldn't give them the satisfaction.

Chapter Two

⊱∽⧸∾⊰

Harriet urged Shadow into a gallop, as soon as she was out of their sight. They'd thought she was a light-skirt. That was why *Ulysses* had kissed her, and the one with the cold eyes—*Zeus*—had looked at her as though she was nothing.

That was why the giant had lifted her on to the horse without asking her permission, too. Even though he'd meant well, he hadn't treated her with the respect due to a lady.

Because she'd stepped outside the bounds set for the behaviour of ladies.

Damn her aunt for being right! She dashed a tear away from her cheek. A tear humiliation had wrung from her. She wasn't afraid. Just angry. So angry. At the men, for treating her so…casually. For manhandling her, and mocking her and insinuating she was…

Oh, how she wished she'd struck them *all* with her crop. Men who went about the park, getting drunk and frightening decent females…

Although they hadn't thought she *was* decent, had they? They'd thought she was out there drumming up custom.

She shuddered.

And no wonder. She'd melted into *Ulysses*'s kiss like butter on to toasted bread. And then been so flustered she'd forgotten to conceal her legs when untangling them from her skirts, giving him a view of them right up to her knees, like as not.

Oh, but she wished she could hit something now. Though she was more to blame than anyone and she couldn't hit herself. Because it turned out that sometimes, just sometimes, Aunt Susan might just be right. Ladies *couldn't* go about on their own, in London. Because if they did, drunken idiots assumed they were fair game.

Why hadn't Aunt Susan explained that some of the rules were for her own good, though? If she'd only warned Harriet that men could behave that badly, when they were intoxicated, then…

Honesty compelled her to admit that she knew how idiotic men became when they drank too much. Didn't she see it every week back home in Donnywich? By the end of market day, men came rolling out of the tavern, wits so addled with drink they had to rely on their horses to find their way home.

And men were men, whether they lived in the country and wore smocks, or in Town and dressed in the height of fashion. So she should have known. Because the rules were made by men, for the convenience of men. So, rather than expect men to behave properly, at all times, women just had to stay out of their way, or go around with guards, just in case they felt like being beastly.

She slowed Shadow to a walk as she left the park via the Stanhope Gate, her heart sinking. She'd so enjoyed escaping to the park at first light. It had been the only thing making her stay in London bearable of late. But now, because men rolled home from their clubs in drunken packs and…and *pounced* on any female foolish enough to cross their path, she would never be able to do so again. She'd have to take a groom. Which would mean waiting until one was awake and willing to take her without first checking with Aunt Susan that she had permission.

And Aunt Susan wouldn't give it, like as not.

Oh, it was all so…vexing!

London was turning out to be such a disappointment that she was even starting to see the advantages of the kind of life she'd lived at home. At least nobody there had ever so much as raised an eyebrow if she'd gone out riding on her own. Not even when she'd worn some of her brothers' cast-offs, for comfort. Even the times she'd stayed out all day, nobody had ever appeared to notice. Mama was always too engrossed in some scientific tome or other to bother about what her only daughter was getting up to. And Papa had never once criticised her, no matter how bitterly Aunt Susan might complain she was turning into a hoyden.

Nobody who lived for miles around Stone Court would ever have dreamed of molesting her, either, since everyone knew she was Lord and Lady Balderstone's youngest child.

She sighed as Shadow picked her way daintily along Curzon Street. She'd been in the habit of feeling aggrieved when nobody commented on her absence, or even appeared to care if she missed meals. But the alternative, of having her aunt watching her like a hawk, practically every waking moment, was beginning to feel like being laced into someone else's corset, then shut in a room with no windows.

She reached the end of Curzon Street and crossed Charles Street, her heart sinking still further. The nearer she got to Tarbrook House, the more it felt as though she was putting her head under a velvet cushion and inviting her aunt and uncle to smother her with it.

If only she'd known what a London Season would be like, she would have thanked Aunt Susan politely for offering her the chance to make her debut alongside her younger cousin, Kitty, and made some excuse to stay away. She could easily have said that Papa relied on her to keep the household running smoothly, what with Mama being mostly too preoccupied to bother with anything so mundane as paying servants or ordering meals. Aunt Susan would have understood and accepted the excuse that *somebody* had to approve the menus and go over the household accounts on a regular basis. For it was one of the things that had always caused dissension between the sisters, whenever Aunt Susan had come on a visit. Mama had resented the notion that she ought to entertain visitors, saying that it interfered with her studies. Aunt Susan would retort that she ought to venture out of her workshop at least once a day, to enquire how her guests were faring, even if she didn't really care. The sniping would escalate until, in the end, everyone was very relieved when the family duty visit came to an end.

Except for Harriet. For it was only when Aunt Susan was paying one of her annual visits, en route to her own country estate after yet another glittering London Season, that she felt as if anyone saw her. Really saw her.

And had the temerity to raise concerns about the way her own mother and father neglected her.

But, oh, what Harriet wouldn't give for a little of that sort of neglect right now. For, from the moment she'd arrived, Aunt Susan hadn't ceased complaining about her behaviour, her posture, her hair, her clothes, and even the expression on her face from time to time. Even shopping for clothes, which Harriet had been looking forward to with such high hopes, had not lived up to her expectations. She didn't know why it was, but though she bought exactly the same sorts of things as Kitty, she never looked as good in them. To be honest, she suspected she looked a perfect fright in one or two of the fussier dresses, to judge from the way men eyed her up and down with looks verging from disbelief to amusement. She couldn't understand why Aunt Susan had let her out in public in one of them, when she'd gone home and looked at herself, with critical eyes, in the mirror. At her*self*, rather than the delicacy of the lace, or the sparkle of the spangled trimmings.

Worse, on the few occasions she'd attended balls so far, Aunt Susan had not granted any of the men who'd asked her to dance the permission to do so. The first few refusals had stemmed from Aunt Susan's conviction that Harriet had not fully mastered the complexities of the steps. And after that, she simply found fault with the men who were then doing the asking. But what did it matter if her dance partners were not good *ton*? Surely it would be more fun to skip round the room with somebody, even if he was a desperate fortune-hunter, rather than sit wilting on the sidelines? Every blessed night.

Yes, she sighed, catching her first glimpse of Tarbrook House, the longer she stayed in Town, the more appealing Stone Court was beginning to look. At least at home she'd started to carve out a niche for herself. After being of no consequence for so many years, she'd found a great deal of consolation in taking over the duties her mother habitually neglected.

But in Town she was truly a fish out of water, she reflected glumly as Shadow trotted through the arch leading to the mews at the back of Tarbrook House. Instead of dancing every night at glittering balls, with a succession of handsome men, one of whom was going to fall madly in love with her and whisk her away to his estate where he'd treat her like a queen, she was actually turning out to be a social failure.

The only time she felt like herself recently had been on these secret forays into the park, before anyone else was awake. And now, because of those…*beasts*, she wasn't even going to be able to have that any longer.

She dismounted, and led Shadow to her stall, where a groom darted forward with a scowl on his face.

'I know,' she said. 'I should not have gone out riding on my own. But you need not report this to Lady Tarbrook. For I shall not be doing so again, you may be certain.'

The groom ran his eyes over her. His gaze paused once or twice. Over the grass stains on her riding habit, for example. At which his mouth twisted in derision.

He thought she'd taken a tumble and had now lost her nerve, the fool. She gripped her crop tightly as she warred with the urge to defend her skill as a horsewoman. But if she admitted she'd dismounted through choice, he'd wonder where the grass stains had come from. And since she was not in the habit of telling lies, she'd probably blush and stammer, and look so guilty that he'd go straight to Aunt Susan and tell her that her hoyden of a niece had been up to no good.

And Aunt Susan would extract the truth out of her in no time flat.

And she would die rather than have to confess she'd let a man kiss her. A strange man. A strange drunken man.

And worse, that she'd liked it. Because, for a few brief moments, he'd made her feel attractive. Interesting. When for most of her life—until she'd taken to giving the servants directions, that was—nobody had thought her of any value at all. She'd just been an afterthought. A girl, what was worse. A girl that nobody knew quite what to do with.

So she lifted her chin and simply stalked away, her reputation as a horsewoman ruined in the eyes of the head groom.

Jack Hesketh sat up slowly, his head spinning, and watched the virago galloping away.

'Do you know,' he mused, 'I think we may have just insulted a lady.'

Zeus snorted. 'If she were a lady, she would not have been out here unattended at this hour, flirting with a pack of drunken bucks.'

Jack shook his head. He couldn't believe Zeus—who'd pursued women with such fervour and conquered so many of them while he, and Archie, and Atlas had still been too pimply and awkward to do anything but stand back in awe—had become the kind of man who could now speak of such a lovely one with so much contempt.

If he were to meet Zeus now, for the first time, he didn't think he'd want to be his friend.

In fact, after the way he'd behaved tonight, he'd steer well clear of such a man. Zeus had always been a bit full of himself, which was only to be expected when he was of such high rank and swimming in lard to boot. But there had been a basic sort of decency about him, too. He'd had a sense of humour, anyway.

But now…it was as if a sort of malaise had infected him, rendering him incapable of seeing any good in anyone or anything.

And Archie—well, he'd turned into a sort of…tame hound, trotting along behind Zeus like a spaniel at his master's heels.

While Atlas…oh, dear God, Atlas. He winced as he turned his head rather too quickly, to peer into the gloom at the wreck of the man who'd been his boyhood idol.

Though, hadn't they all been his heroes, one way or another? Which was, perhaps, where he'd gone wrong. In keeping his schoolboy reverence for them firm in his heart during all his years of active service, like a talisman, he'd sort of pickled their images, like flies set in amber. That would certainly explain why it had come as such a shock to see how much they'd all changed.

Especially Atlas. Imprisonment at the hands of the French, and illness, had reduced him to an emaciated ruin of his former self. In fact, he looked such a wreck that Jack had been a bit surprised he'd managed to lift the virago on to her horse at all. Though at least it proved he was still the same man, inside, where it mattered. They hadn't given him the nickname of Atlas only because of his immense size and strength compared to the rest of them, but because of his habit of always trying to take everyone else's burdens on his own shoulders. Rescuing that girl from Zeus was exactly the kind of thing he'd always been doing. Atlas had always hated seeing anyone weak or vulnerable being tormented.

Which was what they'd been doing to that poor girl, Jack thought, his stomach turning over in shame. The four of them, making sport of her. No—make that three. Atlas had been the only one of them to behave like a perfect gentleman even though he was as drunk as the rest of them.

Or was he? He'd barely touched any of the drink Zeus had so lavishly supplied, at what was supposed to be a celebration of not only the Peace, but also his return to England. Of the fact that for the first time in years, all four of them had the liberty to meet up. As though the poor fellow felt he couldn't trust himself to hold it down. Nobody had said anything, though. They'd all been too shocked at the sight of him to do more than squirm a bit as they drank his health. Health? Hah! The best that anyone could say of the gaunt and yellow-skinned Atlas was that he was alive.

'I tell you what, though,' he said aloud. 'You are still my hero, Atlas'

Atlas started, looking taken aback.

'No, really. After all this time, you are still the best of us. Always was.'

'You paid too much attention to the letters I wrote when I first went to sea,' he said, looking uncomfortable. 'I made it sound far more exciting than it was. Didn't want you all to…pity me, for having to leave. Didn't want to admit that I was seasick, and homesick and utterly wretched.'

'B-but,' said Archie, looking shocked, 'you *were* a hero. Read ab-bout your exp-ploits in the *Gazette*.'

Atlas made a dismissive motion with his hand, as though banishing the *Gazette* and all that was printed in it to perdition.

'Just did my duty. No choice, when you're in the thick of action. You either fight like a demon, or...well, you know how it is, Jack. Same in the army, I dare say.' He sent Jack a beseeching look, as though begging him to divert attention from him.

'Only too well,' he therefore said. 'Which is why your homecoming is worth celebrating. Glad you're alive. Glad I'm alive. Even glad Zeus is alive,' he said, shooting his godship a wry grin. 'Since he got us all together again, for the first time since...what year was it when you left school, Atlas?'

'You are foxed,' said Zeus with exasperation, before Atlas had a chance to make his response. 'If I'd realised quite how badly foxed, I would never have let you attempt to ride Lucifer.'

'Attempt? Pah! I *did* ride Lucifer.'

'Not very far.'

'Far enough to prove your boast about being the only man to be able to do it was patently false.' God, how he'd wanted to knock the sneering expression from Zeus's face when he'd made that claim. Which was why he'd declared there wasn't a horse he couldn't ride, drunk or sober.

Zeus shook his head this time as he stood over Jack where he lay sprawled.

But Jack didn't care. For a few minutes, directly after he'd made the wager, all four of them had shaken off the gloom that had been hanging over them like a pall.

They'd even laughed and started calling each other by the silly names they'd given each other at school as they staggered round to the stables. They'd sobered slightly when Lucifer had rolled his eyes at them and snorted indignantly when they'd approached his stall. Archie had even suggested, albeit timidly, that he was sure nobody would mind if Jack withdrew his claim.

'Draw back from a bet? What kind of man do you think I am?' Jack had retorted. And Zeus had grabbed the stallion's halter and led the animal out into the streets before anyone could talk sense into either of them.

Good God. Zeus had been as intent on carrying through on the wager as Jack himself. Did that mean…?

Was there still something of the old Zeus left? Deep under all that sarcasm and sneering? He'd certainly been the one to arrange this reunion. And he'd also made sure they'd been given a chance to laugh at Jack's antics, the way they'd done so many times at school. They'd certainly all been roaring with laughter as Lucifer had shot off, with Jack clinging to his mane. And so sweet had been that sound that Jack hadn't cared that the beast had unseated him before he'd managed one circuit of the park.

'I still maintain that girl was not flirting with us,' he said defiantly. Was he imagining it, or was there an answering gleam in Zeus's eyes? As though he was relishing having someone refusing to lie down and roll over at his bidding.

Ah.

Was that why he'd become so jaded? Because nobody challenged him any more? It would explain why he'd jumped at the wager, ridiculous though it was. Why he'd whisked Lucifer out of his stall before the sleepy groom had a chance to fling a saddle on his back.

Perhaps, even, why he'd gathered them all together in the first place.

'She may not have been a lady, precisely,' Jack continued. 'But I stick to my guns about her not flirting with us. Else why would she have set about us with her riding crop?'

That had come as a shock, too, he had to admit. One moment she'd been melting into his arms, the next she was fighting him off. And she'd been kissing him so sweetly, after that initial hesitation, so shyly yet…hang on…shyly. With hesitation. As though she didn't know quite what to do, but couldn't help herself. As if she was catching fire, just as he'd been.

One moment she was with him, and then…it was as if she'd come to her senses. As though she realised it was a stranger with whom she was rolling about on the grass.

'I would wager,' he said, a smile tugging at his lips as he recalled and re-examined her every reaction, 'that not only was she not flirting, but that she was an innocent, to boot.'

That would explain it all. That gasp of shock when he'd first started kissing her. Her inexpert, almost clumsy, yet uninhibited response. Until the very moment when she'd hauled up the drawbridge and slammed down the portcullis. The moment when she remembered she was dabbling in sin.

'And I don't care what you think, Zeus,' he said with determination. 'We owe that girl an apology. Well, I do, anyway. Shouldn't have kissed her.'

'She shouldn't have put her face in the way of your lips, then,' retorted Zeus.

'No, no, the girl was only trying to see if I was injured.' Which had been remarkably brave of her. Not many females would have come rushing to the aid of a stranger like that. Nor would they have been able to bring Zeus's bad-tempered stallion under control, either.

'Which is more than any of you have done,' he finished pointedly.

'You are not injured,' said Zeus pithily. 'You are indestructible. And I have that on the best authority.'

'Must have been speaking to m'father.'

'Your brother,' Zeus corrected him.

'Oh? Which one?'

'I forget,' said Zeus with a wave of his hand. 'He did tell me he was Viscount Becconsall when he walked up to me in White's and presumed friendship with me because of my friendship with you.' His mouth twisted in distaste.

'Could have been either of them, then,' said Jack, who'd recently acquired the title himself. 'Poor sod,' he said, and not only because both his brothers were now dead, but because he could picture the reception such behaviour would have gained them. They hadn't started calling him Zeus without good reason. From the very first day he'd attended school, he'd looked down on all the other boys from a very lofty height. He didn't require an education, he'd informed anyone who would listen. He'd had perfectly good tutors at home. It was just that his father, who had suddenly developed radical tendencies, had decided the next Marquis of Rawcliffe ought to get to know how the lower orders lived.

Jack chuckled at the vision of his bumptious brother

attempting to take such a liberty with Zeus. 'I can just see it. You gave him one of your freezing stares and raised your eyebrow at him.'

'Not only my eyebrow, but also my quizzing glass,' said Zeus, leaning down to offer him a hand, as though deciding Jack had been cluttering up the ground for long enough. 'It had no effect. The man kept wittering on about what a charmed life you led. How you came through the bloodiest battles unscathed. As though you had some kind of lucky charm keeping you safe, instead of being willing to acknowledge that you owed your successes on the battlefield to your skill as a strategist, as well as personal valour.'

Jack gasped as Zeus pulled him to his feet. That was the thing about him. He might be the most arrogant, conceited fellow he'd ever met, but he'd also been the first person to look beyond the way Jack clowned around to distract the bullies who'd been hounding Archie at school. The only person to take one look at him and see the intelligence he'd been at such pains to disguise.

To believe in him.

'Didn't come through this tussle unscathed,' he said, rubbing his posterior to explain his involuntary gasp. Zeus gave him one of his looks. The kind that told Jack he knew he was avoiding an issue, but was magnanimous enough to permit him to do so.

'Which brings me back to the girl. Did you notice the way she spoke? And the horse? Expensive bit of blood and bone, that dappled grey.'

'Hmmph,' said Zeus. 'I grant you that she may have been gently reared, but just because she speaks well and rides an expensive horse does not mean she is an innocent now.'

'No, truly, I would stake my life on it.'

'Since n-none of us know who she is,' said Archie. 'There is n-no way for us to v-verify your conc-clusion.'

No, there wasn't.

Which was a horrible thought. In fact, the prospect of never seeing her again gave him a queer, almost painful feeling in his chest. And not only because she'd melted into his arms as if she belonged there. It was more than that. It was…it was…well, out of all the disappointments the night had brought, those few moments kissing her, holding her, and, yes, even fighting with her, had been…a breath of fresh air. No, he shook his head. More like a…well, the way the night had been going, he'd felt as if he was sinking deeper and deeper into a dark well of disappointment. And then, all of a sudden, she'd been in the centre of the one bright spot of the whole night. And that kiss…well, it had revived him, the way the sight of a lighthouse would revive a storm-tossed mariner, he suspected.

Hope, that was what she'd brought him. Somehow.

Was it a coincidence that right after meeting her, he'd seen that Atlas was still the same man, deep down, where it mattered? That there was even hope for Zeus, too?

Hope. That was the name he'd give her, then, while he searched for her. And why not? Why not remember the one bright spot of the evening as a glimmer of hope in what was, of late, a life that contained anything but?

And another thing. Hope was always worth pursuing.

'Right then,' said Jack, rubbing his hands together. 'We'll just have to search London until we find her.'

Zeus's eyes narrowed with interest. 'And then?'

'And then, we will know which one of us is right.'

'Another wager?' Atlas shook his head in mock re-proof. Though nobody had said anything about a wager. 'At this rate, you will beggar me.'

'Not I,' said Jack, his heart lifting. Because Atlas was clearly doing his best to raise morale amongst his friends. He must have seen the effect the wager over Lucifer had on Zeus, the way Jack had. 'You and Archie will just act as witnesses,' he therefore informed Atlas. 'This wager, just like the one over Lucifer, is be-tween me and Zeus.'

'And the stakes?' Zeus had gone all narrow-eyed and sneering again, as though he suspected Jack of trading on their long-ago connections to take advantage of him.

What the hell had happened to him, since school, to turn him into such a suspicious devil?

'Why, the usual, naturally,' said Jack. Which was al-most as good as drawing his cork, since his head reared back in momentary surprise.

'The...the usual?'

'Yes. The usual between the four of us, that is.'

'You...' For a moment, Zeus looked as though he was about to express one of the softer emotions. But only for a moment.

'Which reminds me,' he drawled in that ghastly, af-fected way that set Jack's teeth on edge. 'You have al-ready lost one wager.'

'Are you demanding payment?' Jack planted his fists on his hips and scowled. 'Are you accusing me of at-tempting to welch on the bet?'

'No,' he said softly. 'I was only going to suggest... double or quits?'

For a moment the four of them all stood in stunned silence.

And then Archie began to giggle. Atlas snorted. And soon, all four of them were laughing like the schoolboys they had once been.

Chapter Three

'Nobody is going to ask you to dance if you don't sit up straight and take that scowl off your face,' said Aunt Susan, sternly.

They might if Aunt Susan hadn't already repulsed the young men who'd shown an interest in her when she'd first come to Town, on the grounds that they were all fortune-hunters or scoundrels.

Nevertheless, Harriet obediently squared her shoulders and attempted the social smile her aunt had made her practise in the mirror every day for half an hour since she'd come to Town.

'That's better,' said Aunt Susan out of the corner of her mouth which was also pulled into a similarly insincere rictus. 'I know it must chafe that Kitty is having so much more success than you, but you must remember that you are no longer in the first flush of youth.'

Harriet only just managed to stop herself rolling her eyes. She was only twenty, for heaven's sake. But eligible gentlemen looking for brides, her aunt had informed her, with a rueful shake of her head, wanted much younger girls. 'It's perfectly natural,' she'd explained. 'Gels usually make their debut when they are seventeen, or eighteen, unless there's been a death in the family, or something of a similar nature. So everyone is bound to wonder why any girl who looks much older hasn't appeared in society before. And,' she'd added with a grimace of distaste, 'draw their own conclusions.'

'Please, dear,' she was saying now, 'do try to look as if you are enjoying yourself. Gentlemen are much more likely to ask you to dance if you appear to be good-natured.'

Harriet was beginning to suspect that actually she was not the slightest bit good-natured. She'd always thought of herself as being fairly placid before she'd come to Town. But ever since her aunt had descended on Stone Court like a fairy godmother to take her to the ball, she'd been see-sawing from one wild emotion to another. At first she'd been in a froth of excitement. But then had come the painful discovery that no amount of fine clothes could make her compare with her prettier, younger, more sociable cousin Kitty. After that, in spite of her aunt's best efforts to bring her up to scratch in the short time they had, had come the discovery that actually, she didn't want to conform to society's notions of how a young lady should behave. And now she just felt as if she had a stone permanently lodged in her shoe.

'Now, *there* is a young man with whom you might safely dance,' said Lady Tarbrook, nudging Harriet in the ribs. And drawing her attention to the slender young man who'd just come into the ballroom. A man she'd been dreading coming across for the last two weeks. Ever since he'd fallen off his horse and tricked her into kissing him.

'Though I shouldn't like to raise your hopes too

much. He hasn't asked any eligible female to dance
since he came to Town. Not that he's actually attended
many balls, to my knowledge. Well, not this sort of
ball,' Lady Tarbrook was muttering darkly. 'Not his
style. Not his style at all.'

No, his style was roistering all night with a pack
of reprobates, then taking part in reckless wagers that
ended up with him almost breaking his stupid neck. To
say nothing of molesting people who went to help him.

And yet Aunt Susan was prepared to give her permission to dance with him. In the unlikely event he
were to ask her.

It beggared belief.

'Still, nothing ventured, nothing gained,' said Aunt
Susan, fluttering her fan wildly and smiling for all she
was worth in his direction.

While Harriet did her best to shrink into the meagre
upholstery of the chair upon which she was sitting. Oh,
where was a potted plant, or a fire screen, or…a hole in
the ground when she needed one?

Ulysses—for that was the only name she knew him
by—ran his eyes round the ballroom as though searching for someone before setting off in the direction of a
group of military men gathered in the doorway to the
refreshment room.

'Oh, I see,' said Lady Tarbrook with resignation. 'He
must have wanted to speak to one of his…associates. I
don't suppose he will stay long.' She folded her fan as
though consigning him to history.

While Harriet fumed. The…the beast! He'd looked
right through her, as though she wasn't there. Without
the slightest sign he recognised her.

Well, he probably didn't. He probably kissed random

women senseless every day of the week. The kiss that she'd spent so many nights recalling, in great detail, before she went to sleep, and at odd moments during the day as well, had obviously completely slipped his mind.

Because it had meant nothing to him.

Because *she* meant nothing to him.

Well—he meant nothing to her, either. And nor did that kiss. Just because it was her first and still had the power to make her toes curl if she dwelt on it for too long, did not mean that…that…

Oh, bother him for getting her thoughts into a tangle.

A loud burst of laughter gave her the excuse she needed to let her eyes stray to the doorway of the refreshment room and the group of men who'd opened up to admit him to their company.

She couldn't help noticing several other women turning their heads in his direction, too. And eyeing him with great interest. Which came as no surprise, seeing the way he moved. There was a vitality about him that naturally drew the eye, for it was so very different from the languid stroll affected by the other men present tonight. And in the candlelight his hair, which had just looked a sort of dull brown in the shade of that chestnut tree, gleamed with traces of gold.

She flicked her fan open and plied it vigorously before her face. Which she turned away from the part of the room in which he was standing. She would not stare at him. She would do nothing to attract his attention, either, in case he did have a dim recollection of her. You could sometimes get even quite stupid people to remember things if you constantly reminded them of it, or so Aunt Susan had told her, when she'd despaired of

ever grasping the myriad rules of etiquette that seemed
to come naturally to Kitty.

But then Kitty had been drilled into good behaviour
from the moment she was born.

'I don't know what your mother was thinking, to
leave you to run wild the way she has,' Aunt Susan
had said upon discovering that Harriet had only the
vaguest notion of how deeply to curtsy to people of
various ranks.

'She didn't let me run wild, precisely,' Harriet had
countered, because there had definitely been times
when Mama had applied the birch. When she'd used
phrases she'd picked up in the stables at the dinner table,
for instance. 'It's just that she doesn't think things like
teaching me to curtsy are terribly important.' Nor having a Season, come to that. In fact, she was beginning
to think her mother might have a point. How on earth
could anyone pick a life partner this way? Nobody really talked to anyone. Not about anything important.
Everyone in Town seemed to Harriet to behave like a
swarm of giddy mayflies, flitting above the surface of
a glittering pond.

'Clearly,' Aunt Susan had said frostily. 'But even
if she couldn't prise herself away from her books and
bottles to do it herself, she could have engaged a sensible woman to take over that side of your education.
In fact,' she'd said, shifting in her seat as though she
was itching to get up and stride about the room to make
her point, 'for a woman who goes on so about how important the life of the mind is to her, you'd think she
would have wanted you to have had the same education as her sons. Instead of no education at all. Why, if
it hadn't been for me sending you that Person to teach

you how to read and write you could have ended up as ignorant as a savage!'

Harriet had hung her head at that reminder of how much she owed to Aunt Susan, stifling the flare of resentment she'd been experiencing at being forced to curtsy over and over again until she got it right. Because the truth was that Mama *had* been too interested in her books and bottles, as Aunt Susan had so scathingly referred to Mama's laboratory, to concern herself with something as mundane as the education of her daughter. Papa had arranged for the education of his sons. But a girl's education, he'd said, was the province of her mother.

Between Papa's focus on his three fine sons and Mama's absorption with her hobbies, Harriet had been forgotten entirely.

And if her own parents could forget her existence for weeks at a time, it stood to reason that Ulysses would do the same.

Although perhaps it was just as well. Far better that, than that he should come over and start talking to her as if she was an old acquaintance, or something. Which would make Aunt Susan ask questions. All sorts of awkward questions.

At which point, naturally, he sauntered over to where they were sitting and bowed punctiliously to her aunt.

'Good evening, Lady Tarbrook,' he said in a voice that struck like a dart to her midriff.

'Lord Becconsall, how delightful to see you,' simpered her aunt.

Lord Becconsall?

Well, obviously, Ulysses couldn't be his real name, but she was still surprised he had a title.

Though perhaps she shouldn't have been. The kind of men who were out in the park after a long night of drinking could only be men who didn't have jobs to go to in the morning. She should have known he was titled, really, now she came to think of it.

And for all she knew, Ulysses *was* his real name. She had an Uncle Agamemnon, after all. And a distant cousin by marriage by the name of Priam. The craze for all things classical seemed to have affected a lot of parents with the strangest urges to name their children after ancient Greeks lately.

She snapped back to attention when she heard her aunt say, 'And you must allow me to present my niece, Lady Harriet Inskip.'

'*Lady* Harriet?'

Though he bowed, he did so with the air of a man who wasn't sure he should be doing any such thing. How did he do that? Inject such…mockery into the mere act of bowing?

'Oh, you have not heard of her, I dare say, because she has lived such a secluded life, in the country. This is her first visit to London.'

Harriet gritted her teeth. For this was the excuse Aunt Susan was always trotting out, whenever some society matron quizzed her over some defect or other. Or a gentleman drew down his brows when she made an observation that ran counter to some opinion he'd just expressed. '*Oh, fresh up from the country, you know,*' her aunt would say airily. '*Quite unspoiled and natural in her manners.*' Which invariably alerted her to the fact she must have just committed a terrible faux pas for which she'd be reprimanded later, in private. Though the worst, the very worst fault she had, apparently, was speaking her mind. Young ladies did not do such things, Aunt Susan insisted. Which shouldn't have come as such a surprise, really. She should have known that females, and their opinions, were of less value than males. Hadn't that fact been demonstrated to her, in no uncertain terms, all her life?

Except when it came to Mama. Papa never found fault with anything she ever said, or did. Even when he didn't agree with it.

'That would account for it,' said Ulysses, with a knowing smile. And though Aunt Susan heard nothing amiss, Harriet could tell that he was remembering their last encounter. And decrying her behaviour. The way those society matrons had done. Though at least this time she knew exactly what she'd done to earn his scorn.

'You might know one of her older brothers,' Aunt Susan was persisting, valiantly. 'George Inskip? Major the Honourable George Inskip? He's a Light Dragoon.'

'Sadly, no,' said Ulysses, though he didn't look the least bit sad. 'The cavalry rarely fraternises with the infantry, you know. We are far, far, beneath their notice, as a rule.'

So he was in the army. No—had been in the army. He was not wearing uniform, whereas men who still held commissions, like the group still milling around in the doorway to the refreshment room, flaunted their scarlet jackets and gold braid at every opportunity.

So, that would account for the tanned face. And the lines fanning out from his eyes. And the energy he put into the mere act of walking across a room. And the hardness of his body. And the...

'Oh, I'm sure you are no such thing,' simpered Aunt

Susan. Making Harriet's gorge rise. Why on earth was she gushing all over the very last man she wished to encourage, when so far she'd done her level best to repulse every other man who'd shown the slightest bit of interest in her?

'And probably too far beneath Lady Harriet to presume to request the pleasure of a dance,' he said. Placing a slight emphasis on the word beneath. Which sent her mind back to the moments he had been lying beneath her, his arms clamped round her body as he ravaged her mouth.

Which made her blush. To her absolute fury. Because Aunt Susan gave her a knowing look.

'But of course you may dance with Lady Harriet, Lord Becconsall,' trilled Aunt Susan, who clearly saw this as a coup. For a man notorious for not dancing with debutantes was asking her protégée to do just that. 'She would love to dance with you, would you not, my dear?'

Ulysses cocked his head to one side and observed her mutinous face with evident amusement. Just as she'd suspected. He was planning on having a great deal of fun at her expense.

'I do not think she wishes to dance with me at all,' he said ruefully. 'In fact, she looks as though she would rather lay about me with a riding crop to make me go away.'

Harriet was not normally given to temper. But right at this moment she could feel it coming to the fore. How she wished she were not in a ballroom, so that she could slap that mocking smile from his face.

'Oh, no, not at all! She is just a little…awkward, in her manners. Being brought up so…in such a very… that is, Harriet,' said Aunt Susan rather sharply, 'I know you are very shy, but you really must take that scowl off your face and tell Lord Becconsall that you would love above all things to dance with him.'

Ulysses schooled his features into the approximation of a man who had endless patience with awkward young females who needed coaxing out of their modest disinclination to so much as dance with a man to whom she had only just been introduced.

While the twinkle in his eyes told her that, inside, he was laughing at her. That he was enjoying taunting her with those oblique references to their previous meeting. And, she suspected, that he was going to enjoy holding that episode over her head every time they met from this time forth.

Oh, lord, what was she to do? What would happen if Aunt Susan found out she'd been caught, in the Park, by a group of drunken bucks and kissed breathless by this particular one? When she should have been in her room, in her bed, recovering from the exertions of the ball the night before?

Disgrace, that was what. Humiliation. All sorts of unpleasantness.

If she found out.

Therefore, Aunt Susan had better not find out. Had better not suspect anything was amiss. Or she would start digging.

That prospect was enough to make her draw on all those hours she'd spent in front of the mirror, perfecting that insincere smile. And plastering it on to her face.

'Lord Becconsall,' she said through gritted teeth. 'I would love above all things to dance with you.'

With a triumphant grin, he held out his hand, took hers and led her on to the dance floor.

Chapter Four

'*Lady* Harriet,' he said, raising one eyebrow.

'*Lord* Becconsall,' she replied tartly.

He grinned. Because addressing him by his title had not managed to convey the same degree of censure at all. But then, as she very well knew, lords could get away with staggering around the park, drunk. Or riding horses bareback for wagers.

Whereas ladies could not.

Not that she'd been doing either, but still.

'I suppose you expect me to feel flattered by your invitation to dance,' she said, 'when you are notorious for not doing so.'

'Flattered?' He raised one eyebrow. And then the corner of his mouth, as though he was biting back a laugh. 'No, I didn't expect that.'

'Do you want me to ask what you did expect?'

'Well, if we are about to delve into my motives for asking you, then perhaps I should warn you that you might not like mine.'

'I'm quite sure I won't.'

'But would you like me to be completely honest?'

'Yes, why not,' she said with a defiant toss of her head. 'It will be a…a refreshing change.' At least, in comparison with all the other encounters she'd had in Town, where people only talked about trivialities, in what sounded, to her countrified ears, like a series of stock, accepted phrases they'd learned by rote.

'Well then, if you must know, I felt so sorry for you that I felt compelled to swoop in to your rescue.'

'My rescue?' That was the very last motive she would have attributed to him.

'Yes.' He looked at her with a perfectly straight face. 'You looked so miserable, sitting there all hunched up as though you were trying to shrink away from the silly clothes and hairstyle you are affecting tonight. And I recalled the impulsive way you dropped to your knees beside my prone body, to give what succour you could. And I thought that one good turn deserved another.'

Harriet sucked in a short, shocked breath. Though it was more in keeping with what she knew of him so far to fling insults at her, under cover of escorting her to the dance floor, than to *swoop in to her rescue.*

He would definitely never say anything so…rude to any other lady to whom he'd just been introduced. It just wasn't done. Even she knew that.

But then, since he held her reputation in the palm of his hand, he clearly felt he could get away with saying anything he liked.

'Well, if we are being *honest* with one another,' she said, since what was sauce for the goose was sauce for the gander, 'I have to say I agree with you.' There, that should take the wind from his sails.

'Surely not. Or—' A frown flitted across his face.

'Is your duenna compelling you to wear gowns of her choosing?'

'I wish I could say you were correct. But this display of poor taste is entirely my own doing,' she said.

'You are deliberately making yourself look ridiculous?'

Far from looking shocked, or disapproving, Lord Becconsall only appeared intrigued.

But the necessity of taking her place in line, and dipping a curtsy as the first strains of music blared, prevented either of them from saying anything further. Which made her grind her teeth. Because of course she had not been deliberately trying to make herself look ridiculous. She'd just never had the chance to spend whatever she wanted on clothes, that was all. And it was only with hindsight that she'd seen that modelling her wardrobe so slavishly on Kitty's, who had always looked so fashionable and pretty whenever she'd come to visit, had been a mistake.

But from now on, she was going to ask the modiste, and her aunt—and, yes, even Kitty—if the styles and fabrics she was choosing actually suited *her*.

For some time the intricacies of the dance meant that he could only take jabs at her during the few seconds during which they passed or circled each other. Jabs which she could deflect by looking blank, then twirling away as though she hadn't heard them.

'You are supposed to smile at your partner, just occasionally, you know,' he informed her at one point.

'I might do so were I dancing with someone I liked,' she snapped back.

'Tut, tut, Lady Harriet,' he said dolefully. 'You gave

me to believe you wished above all things to dance
with me.'

'You know very well I had to say that,' she hissed
at him.

'Do I?' He looked thoughtful for a few measures.
And then, with a devilish gleam in his eyes, asked her,
'Would you mind explaining why?'

'You know why.'

He widened his eyes in a look of puzzled innocence.
'But…how can you have changed your opinion of me
so completely? Last time we met, you flung yourself
into my arms—'

'I did no such thing,' she hissed at him. 'You…
grabbed me—'

'You put up no resistance, however. And you appeared to be enjoying the interlude as much as I did.'

Well, what could she say to that? Though he was
wicked to remind her that she'd behaved with dreadful
impropriety, he'd also admitted to enjoying kissing her.
Which went a good way to soothing the sting imparted
by his taunts. As well as doing something to her insides.

The same sort of something his kiss had done to
them, actually.

'No riposte?' He sighed, looking almost disappointed. 'I was so sure you would waste no opportunity to give me a tongue lashing.'

Since he looked at her mouth with a wistful expression as he said this, she couldn't help licking her lips.
And recalling the way his own tongue had probed at
them, seeking entrance. Which made her unable to tear
her eyes away from *his* mouth.

She cannoned into the lady to her right.

This was a disaster! Almost the first time she'd actually got on to a dance floor and he was ruining it by saying things that made her forget where she was, or which direction she was supposed to be hopping in.

'You are determined to humiliate me, aren't you?' she said, next time they drew close enough for him to hear her.

'I have no need.' He chuckled. 'You are doing an admirable job of it all on your own, what with the clothes and the scowls, and the growls and the missteps.' He shook his head. 'I cannot believe you are related to Major Inskip.'

Her head flew up. 'You know George? But you just said you didn't.'

He shrugged as he whirled away from her to promenade up the outside of the set. By the time she reached the head of it on the ladies' side, she was seething with impatience.

'Well?'

'I only said cavalry officers don't normally hob-nob with the infantry. I didn't say I didn't know him. Though, to be precise, I only know him by sight.' He eyed her with amusement before adding, 'And what a sight he is to behold.'

She flushed angrily. George was, indeed, very often a sight to behold. For he had his uniforms made by a top tailor, out of the finest fabrics, and never looked better than when mounted on one of his extremely expensive horses. From which he did tend to look down his aristocratic nose at the rest of the world. Including her. And to her chagrin, although he'd always used to concede she was a bruising rider when they'd been much younger, the last few times he'd come home there had been a touch of disdain about his lips whenever his eyes had rested on her. Which had also, she now saw, influenced her decision to buy the most elaborate and costly gowns she could.

'What, no pithy retort?' Ulysses shook his head in mock reproof. 'I am disappointed.'

'Yes, well, that's the thing with swooping to someone's rescue, isn't it? They do tend to do things you didn't expect and make you wish you hadn't bothered.'

He threw back his head and laughed.

'Touché!'

She glowered at him. Far from showing the slightest sign of contrition, he was clearly thoroughly enjoying himself. At her expense.

'Come, come, don't look at me like that,' he said. 'I conceded the point. And far from being sorry I swooped, I have to admit I am glad I did so. No, truly,' he said, just as he whirled away from her.

'Well, I'm not,' she said as the interminable music finally gasped its last and everyone bowed or curtsied to everyone else in their set. 'I'm tired of being baited.' At least, she would very soon be if he kept this up for any length of time. It was just one more vexation she was going to have to endure. On top of everything else she was struggling with, it felt like the last straw. 'Why don't you just get it over with? Hmm? Go on. Tell Lady Tarbrook where you found me, two weeks ago, and what we were doing. And then...'

Her mind raced over Aunt Susan's inevitable disappointment and her tears, and the scolding and the punishment. Which might well, if Uncle Hugo had anything to do with it, involve being sent back to Stone Court.

Which would mean her ordeal by London society would come to an end.

Which would be a relief, in a way.

At first. But then she'd have to live, for the rest of her life, with the knowledge that she'd failed. Which she most emphatically did not wish to do.

She lifted her head to stare at Lord Becconsall who, though being thoroughly annoying, had at least made her see that she was nowhere near ready to throw in the towel.

He was shaking his head. 'I don't know what I have done to make you think I would behave in such a scaly fashion,' he said.

'What do you mean?'

'Only that I would never betray a lady's secrets.'

'Not if it didn't suit your schemes, no,' she said uncharitably.

Which made him look a bit cross.

'It wouldn't be in *either* of our interests for anyone else to hear about that kiss,' he snapped. And then went very still. And then he turned a devilish grin in her direction.

'I'm beginning to wonder,' he said, leaning close and lowering his voice to a murmur, 'if you aren't playing a similar kind of game to mine.'

'Game?'

'Oh, very nicely done. That touch of baffled innocence would have fooled most men. But I met you under, shall we say, very different circumstances. Revealing circumstances.'

'Revealing?' Her heart was hammering. What had she revealed? Apart from rather too much of her legs. And what game was it he suspected her of playing?

'Oh, yes. You are a rebel, aren't you?'

Well, that much was true. She had rebelled against

Mama and Papa's wishes to come to London for this Season.

And since she'd been here, she'd been rebelling against all the strictures imposed upon her behaviour.

'Ha! I knew it. Your guilty expression has given it away. You are merely pretending to go along with all this...' He waved his hand to include not only the ballroom, but by extension, the whole society it represented. 'But the fact that you felt the need to go galloping round the park at dawn, unfettered by all the restrictions society would impose on you, coupled with the dreadful way you are dressed, hints at a cunning scheme to avoid falling into the trap of matrimony.'

'Absolutely not,' she retorted, stung by his continuing references to her poor choice of clothing. 'If you must know...' she drew herself to her full height, which meant she only had to tilt her head the slightest bit to look him straight in the eyes '...I dressed like this because...because...'

She paused, wondering why on earth Aunt Susan had permitted her to buy so many things that didn't suit her. When she was doing so much to make her a social success.

And it came to her in a flash.

'This is the first time I have ever been anywhere near a fashionable dressmaker and my aunt didn't want to ruin the pleasure of being able to feel satin against my skin, or picking out lace and ribbons and feathers by objecting to every single gaudy thing I set my heart upon.'

'But—'

'And I *do* want to get married. That is why I've come to London. To find somebody who will...value me and...admire me and talk to me as if what I have to say is...not a joke!'

He flinched.

'Oh, there is no need to worry that I will ever set my sights on you,' she said with a curl of her lip. And, as a fleeting look of relief flitted across his face, she had another flash of insight. 'That is what you meant, isn't it, about playing a game? You are avoiding matrimony. Like the plague.'

He started and the wary look that came across his face told her she'd hit the nail on the head.

And then, because he'd had so much fun baiting her, she couldn't resist taking the opportunity to turn the tables on him. It wouldn't take much. He'd practically handed her all the ammunition she needed.

'What devilish schemes,' he said in alarm, 'are running through that pretty head of yours?'

Pretty? She looked up at him sharply.

And met his eyes, squarely, for the first time that night.

And felt something arc between them, something that flared through all the places that he'd set ablaze when he'd crushed her to his chest and kissed her.

'You think I'm pretty?'

What a stupid thing to say. Of all the things she might have said, all the clever responses she could have flung at him, she'd had to focus on that.

Fortunately, it seemed to amuse him.

'In spite of those hideous clothes, and the ridiculous feathers in your hair, yes, Lady Harriet, you know full well you are vastly pretty.'

The words, and the way he said them, felt like being stroked all the way down her spine with a velvet glove.

Even though they weren't true. She'd had no idea anyone might think she was pretty. Let alone vastly pretty.

Even so, she wasn't going to let him off the hook that easily.

'You are not going to turn me up sweet by saying things like that,' she said sternly. 'One word from me, just one, about that kiss in the park and my outraged family will be dragging you to the altar so fast it will make your head spin.'

'What? You wouldn't!'

'Oh, wouldn't I?'

'No, now look here, Lady Harriet—'

'Oh, don't worry. The ordeal of being shackled to you for the rest of my life does not appeal. In the *slightest*. I'm just reminding you that I have as much on you as you have on me.'

At that point, they reached the chair upon which Aunt Susan was sitting, beaming at them.

'Your niece, Lady Tarbrook,' said Lord Becconsall, letting go of her hand as though it was red hot and making his bow rather stiffly. He then gave her a look which seemed two parts frustration and one part irritation, before turning and marching away, his back ramrod stiff.

'Harriet, I despair of you,' said her aunt as Harriet sank to the chair at her side, her knees shaking, her palms sweating and her insides feeling as if they were performing acrobatics.

'There you had the chance of making a conquest of one of the most elusive bachelors in Town, and what must you do but frighten the poor man off. Whatever did you say to him on the dance floor to make him run away like that?'

She considered for a moment.

'Only that I had no wish to marry him, when he raised the subject,' she said daringly.

'What!' Aunt Susan looked aghast. 'You turned down a proposal from Lord Becconsall? Not that I can believe he really did propose. Although,' she mused, fanning herself rapidly, 'he really is such a very harum-scarum young man it is probably exactly the sort of thing he would do. To fall in love at first sight and propose in the middle of Astley's Hornpipe.'

Of course he hadn't fallen in love at first sight. Nor had he proposed. But something inside her softened towards her aunt for believing he could easily have done both.

However, 'You cannot wish me to marry a…harum-scarum young man, can you?'

'What can that matter when it would be such a triumph for you? Oh, I know he is only a viscount and one would, in the normal way of things, hope for a much better match for a girl of your background, but the way your training has been neglected one cannot expect a man with very nice tastes to look twice at you.'

The soft feeling chilled into the more usual wedge of inferiority and loneliness with which Harriet was familiar.

'Not once he's seen your performance on the dance floor,' Aunt Susan continued. 'My dear, what were you thinking, to collide with Lady Vosborough in that clumsy way? Unless Lord Becconsall had just that moment proposed. Yes, I suppose that would have shocked you enough to make a misstep completely understandable.'

'Well, yes, it would,' said Harriet, deciding that this had gone far enough. 'But—'

'If he proposes again, or if *any* gentleman proposes to you again,' continued Aunt Susan as though she hadn't spoken, 'you are not to turn him down out of hand. You are to tell him you will reflect upon the matter and come to me, and I will advise you. I know all there is to know about any gentleman who might propose, you may be sure.'

Although Harriet really had no intention of marrying Lord Becconsall, even if he ever did propose, which he'd just informed her he wouldn't, she couldn't help indulging her curiosity.

'What should I know about Lord Becconsall, then?' she said in as meek a tone as she could muster. Whilst looking down at her fingers as they played with the struts of her fan.

'Oh, so it is like that, is it?' Aunt Susan smiled. 'Well, in that case, we might still be able to repair the damage. I can drop a word in his ear,' she said, patting her hand.

'What? No! I mean, I'm sure that is very kind of you, Aunt, but—'

But Aunt Susan had got the bit between her teeth.

'Lord Becconsall has a very handsome fortune, my dear, and a couple of really lovely estates. All kept in immaculate condition by his family for generations. I admit, since he has come into the title, he has not behaved with—that is, he has gained a reputation for being something of a…wastrel, let us say, but then what can you expect? I mean, he never expected to inherit anything, I shouldn't think, what with having two such strapping older brothers.'

'Oh?' It felt strange to think he, like her, was the

youngest out of a handful of brothers. 'What happened to them?'

'Oh, you need not worry about any sort of hereditary weakness that might carry him off the same way,' said Aunt Susan, completely missing the point. 'No, the eldest fell from his horse and broke his neck.'

Harriet winced.

'And the next in line contracted…well, a most unpleasant illness which was the scourge of the district at the time. Which came as a very great shock to everyone. Particularly him, I should think. Why, he probably assumed he would spend the rest of his life in the army. Where, I must say, he did at least acquit himself with honours. Though he only came out with the rank of major,' she mused. 'Although that was probably as much to do with finances as anything,' she added, brightening up. 'As the third son, I don't suppose he had much in the way of money to buy promotions. Oh. It has just occurred to me—yes, it probably went to his head, suddenly having so much money and the title as well. Is it any wonder he went just a little…wild? Just at first. I am sure he will settle down and do his duty to his family. Perhaps he is already starting to think along those lines. Yes,' she said, brightening up. 'Perhaps that is why he asked you to dance.'

Harriet swallowed, knowing it was no such thing.

But Aunt Susan was sitting there, plotting and planning ways and means of getting him to propose to her.

Because, deep down, she thought her niece only good enough to marry a…wastrel.

Worse, said wastrel had no intention of marrying her. Had indeed scuttled away with his tail between his legs at the merest threat he might have to do something so abhorrent should their kiss become common knowledge.

She was still seething by the time they called for their carriage. Which was an utterly stupid thing to do, since their own house was not two hundred yards away. They could have walked home far quicker. But, no, in London, ladies waited for the horses to be put to and the carriage to be brought round, rather than do anything as prosaic as walk home.

Oh, how she hated London tonight. Why had she listened to Aunt Susan's tales of balls and picnics and beaux? Why had she allowed herself to get swept along on the tide of Kitty's enthusiasm at the prospect of them making their come-out together?

Because, she answered herself as she clambered into the coach behind her two female relatives, Aunt Susan and Kitty had made her feel wanted, that was why. It would never have occurred to either of her parents that it was high time their only daughter made her social debut. And if it had, neither of them would have wanted to oversee it. Papa hated London and Mama considered it all a ridiculous waste of time and expense.

She sighed, and in the darkness of the coach, reached out and took Aunt Susan's gloved hand. It was not her fault Harriet had not, so far, found her feet in society. Her aunt had done all she could.

Nor could Harriet blame her for believing she was only fit to marry a wastrel. Not when she was so awkward, and…yes, rebellious, as Lord Becconsall had pointed out.

As the coach rumbled through the darkened streets, and Kitty prattled on about the many and various partners with whom she'd danced, Harriet wondered how she was going to break it to Aunt Susan that not even the wastrel looked on her as a potential bride.

Though time would probably take care of that. Since, after the way they'd just parted, he'd probably take good care not to come anywhere near her, ever again.

Chapter Five

Jack couldn't face returning to Becconsall House, the town house that now belonged to him. It was too full of ghosts.

Besides, he was still too unsettled after his encounter with Hope. Who'd turned out to be…of all things, the daughter of an earl. He certainly hadn't expected that. To think that the owner of those sparkling blue eyes, that tart tongue, and those lush lips, was not only a lady, but a *lady*.

He shook his head as he strolled aimlessly along the street. What had she been thinking, going out at that hour of the day without an escort? If she'd run into anyone but him, in the park, she would have ended up getting far more than just a kiss.

She was so…naive, that was the word. And she had no idea of the effect she had on men.

Although, to be frank, if he'd seen her for the first time tonight, he wouldn't have looked at her twice. If he hadn't seen the other side of her, in the park, he would never have suspected she possessed anything to take a man's interest, except for her rank. The silly gown, and the even sillier hairstyle, completely distracted a man from noticing the subtle curve of her mouth, or the determined set of her chin, or the intelligence and wit lurking in the depths of her eyes. Not to mention the lush curves of her body.

Lush curves he'd held against his own body and would very much like to feel pressed closely to him again. The urge to do something about it had taken him by surprise, several times, while they'd been dancing. Even though she'd been doing nothing to attempt to interest him. On the contrary, she'd been all bristles and spikes.

Which had soon stopped him from feeling sorry for her. Nobody could possibly feel sorry for a girl with as much spirit as that, not for long.

A reminiscent smile played about his lips. He'd really enjoyed the thrust and parry of the verbal fencing match they'd fought as they'd danced round the events of their first meeting. Right up to the end, that was, he thought, his smile fading, when she'd lashed out rather too cruelly.

Not that he could blame her, he supposed. He'd been unforgivably rude. Or so she must have thought. It was just that he'd thought he'd glimpsed the same sort of… hurt and rebellion, and desire to shock that he had lurking in his own heart, in her behaviour. Had thought he'd found a kindred soul. That she was doing what he was doing. Pretending to do as he'd been told, whilst making damn sure everyone thought he was completely ineligible.

He'd thought the way she dressed was due to a rebellion against what society expected of her. The way he'd rebelled when the lawyers had told him his best course of action would be to come to Town and find a respectable bride as quickly as he could, to ensure the succession. As if there was no worth in him apart from the blood which they wanted him to pass on to the next generation.

Instead of which, she'd admitted she just had no clue about fashion. Or taste.

He groaned as he thought of the sheen of tears he'd told himself he'd imagined, at one point during the evening. She'd made a swift recovery, but there was no doubt in his mind now that he'd hurt her. Rather badly, to judge from the way she'd lashed out at him towards the end.

He couldn't blame her. Not when his own jibes must have seemed so cruel, to her.

Which left him no choice.

He was going to have to swallow his pride and tender an apology.

And so, the next day, he presented himself at Tarbrook House at the correct hour for paying visits, armed with a posy of spring flowers.

Though the room was full of visitors, Lady Harriet was sitting on her own, on a chair by the window, from which she was looking out on to whatever it was that was at the rear of the house. The other gentlemen who'd called were all clustering round another girl, who was wearing a gown almost identical to Lady Harriet's. Only wearing it rather better. And the aunt, Lady Tarbrook, was keeping her beady eye on her own daughter's visitors.

Lady Harriet gave a start when he stopped by her

chair, so engrossed had she been by whatever she'd been watching through the window.

He craned his neck to follow her line of sight. But all he could see was a courtyard containing an ornamental fountain which sprayed water a few inches into the air.

So, she had been lost in thought, rather than admiring the view.

'A penny for them? Your thoughts?'

'They are not worth that much,' she replied tartly. 'And anyway—'

'You would rather walk barefoot along Piccadilly than share them with me,' he finished for her.

Her face turned a charming shade of pink.

Which was, to his way of thinking, the perfect moment to present her with the posy.

'Oh,' she said looking down at them with surprise. And then up at him with a touch of suspicion. And then, being the girl she was, she asked the question no other delicately nurtured female would ask.

'Why have you brought me these? Why have you come at all, for that matter?'

'Well,' he said, reaching for a nearby chair and placing it closer to hers, 'it is the done thing, you know, for a gentleman to pay a morning call upon a lady with whom he has danced the night before.'

'Yes, I know that,' she snapped.

'But you did not think that *I* would pay any attention to the conventions,' he said, flicking aside his coat tails as he sat down. 'I can see why you might think that, given the way we have…dealt with each other up to now. But the truth is…' He shifted, suddenly finding the chair rather hard and unforgiving.

'Oh, yes, by all means, let us always speak the truth to one another,' she said waspishly.

'The truth is,' he continued, leaning in closer, 'that I owe you an apology.'

She couldn't have looked more surprised if he'd leaned in and kissed her. Which he could easily do, since nobody was paying them any attention. The focus of the other visitors was all on the insipid, younger, paler copy of Lady Harriet.

'I was rude and hurtful to you last night, about your—' His eyes flicked to her gown. Back up to her hair.

'But truthful,' she said. 'And completely correct.'

'But it wasn't kind of me to say so—'

'No,' she said, holding up one hand to stop him. 'It made me see that I needed to do something, instead of wondering why Kitty always looks so much better than me. Your criticism made me go to my aunt and ask her, outright, what I was doing wrong. And why she hadn't stopped me before. And it was...' She paused and rolled her lips together as though trying hard to find the right words.

'Yes, I did wonder why your sponsor would let you go about looking so...' He trailed off. 'If she really cared about you, that is.'

'Oh, she does,' said Lady Harriet with some vehemence. 'More than anybody else. But since she brought me to London she has had to be so strict with me about so many other things that she had not the heart, she told me, to ruin the one pleasure I had left. That is, shopping. And anyway, she said that since I have rank and fortune on my side she didn't think it would matter if I looked just a little eccentric in my own choice of clothes, just to start with. And besides...'

'Besides,' he urged her, when she appeared to realise that she ought not to be rattling on in such an indiscreet fashion with a man she hardly knew. 'Go on, you might as well tell me the besides, now that I know the rest.'

'I don't suppose there is any harm in it,' she admitted. 'Since it's only that my aunt was so touched that I was trying to model myself on Kitty, because I have always thought her so pretty and feminine, that she could never quite bring herself to stop me.'

'She is not that pretty,' he said, glancing just once at Lady Harriet's cousin.

'I thought you promised to be truthful,' said Lady Harriet with a frown.

'I am being truthful.'

'No, you are not. Because Kitty is pretty. Even Papa notices and tells her so whenever she visits. When he has never said—'

She broke off, and looked down at the posy she was clutching tightly in her lap.

'Well, he should have done,' he said irritably. 'Because you are *much* prettier than her.'

Her head flew up, her eyes widening in what might have been shock, which was swiftly changing to annoyance.

'No, truthfully,' he said, laying his hands just briefly over hers. 'She is just… Whereas you are…'

'Yes?' She tilted her head on one side, her eyes narrowing in challenge.

'That is, she looks to me the kind of girl who blushes and simpers and giggles when a man asks her to dance,' he said with derision. 'And you should not be trying to emulate either her looks, or her behaviour.'

'That is your opinion, is it?'

'Yes. You are...well, when I think of the way you looked in the park, bringing Lucifer under control, and then dashing to my side to see if I was hurt...that is how I wish you could look all the time. You ought to be wearing vibrant colours, to go with your vibrant character. And you should positively never crimp your lovely hair into silly curls that dangle round your face like this.' He reached out and flicked one ringlet.

'You are abominable.'

'To tell you how to make the most of yourself? When nobody else will?'

'I have already told you, Aunt Susan and I have had a little chat and, when next we go shopping, things are going to be different.'

'No more dresses that belong on a frippery little schoolgirl, I hope. No more of those silly frills and flounces.'

'For two pins,' she said, her eyes flashing fire, 'I would deck myself from head to toe in frills, just to annoy you.'

'If only you didn't have too much sense,' he reminded her.

'Well, yes, there is that. No sense in cutting off my nose to spite my face, is there?'

'None whatever. It is far too charming a nose. And anyway, I'm really not worth it.'

A frown flitted across her face.

'Oh, come now. Surely your aunt has already warned you not to set your sights on me.'

A rather mulish look came to her mouth.

'Actually, she thinks you might do very well for me. Seeing as how I'm not likely to attract a man with higher standards.'

'I thought you said she cared for you.'

'Oh, she does. But then…' She shrugged, as though the action was self-explanatory.

'And you said your own father never once told you that you are pretty,' he growled. 'What is wrong with them all?'

Lady Harriet shrugged again. 'My parents were content with the three sons they already had, I suppose. They didn't really know what to do with a daughter.'

'That's family for you,' he said with feeling. 'My own father never had a good word to say about me, either.'

A stricken look came across her face. She reached out and touched his hand, just briefly, as though understanding, completely, what it felt like to be the runt of the litter.

For a moment, they sat there in silence. For some reason, he couldn't take his eyes from her hand, though she had withdrawn it and tucked it underneath the posy now, as though she couldn't believe she had lost control of it so far as to reach out and touch him.

He glanced up at her face.

'I suppose,' he said, 'I should take my leave, now. I have said what I came to say.'

'And a sight more.'

He grinned at her. 'Yes. You do seem to have the knack of provoking me into saying more than I should. More than I intended.'

'I do not! Provoke you, that is.'

'You do. You are the most provoking creature I have ever met.'

They smiled at each other, then. For a moment it felt as if they were in perfect accord.

He got to his feet. 'Time I was going.'

'Yes, indeed,' she said, getting to her feet as well. 'Are you going to Lady Wiscombe's ball tonight?'

'I had not intended to.'

Her face fell. Which gave him a peculiar feeling. But then nobody had ever appeared disappointed when he'd said he wasn't going to be somewhere. So it wasn't any wonder he was a touch surprised. Particularly since she did nothing but snipe at him.

'I suppose, I might be persuaded to attend...' he began slowly.

'Oh, no, really, it doesn't matter,' she said, blushing fiery red.

And the delight of teasing her took over his common sense.

'Well, do you know, I rather think it does.'

'No,' she said, her eyes narrowing in annoyance, 'it really, really doesn't.'

'Yes, it does. Because I rather think you ought to demonstrate that you have forgiven me for my appalling rudeness last night, by dancing with me again.'

'What?'

'Yes, and this time, I think you ought to try being polite.'

'You could try it yourself,' she snapped.

He laughed. 'Yes, I suppose I could, only,' he said, taking her hand to bow over it in farewell, 'where would be the fun in that?'

Though Harriet knew she ought not to keep on doing it, she couldn't help looking at the door. So that she'd know the moment he arrived.

She couldn't wait to see what he thought of the dress she was wearing tonight. The dressmaker had wrought a miracle with it, considering the short notice Aunt Susan had given her. It no longer had a single frill and only the one flounce was at the hem, and that only because Madame Grenoir had told them point blank they'd have to choose between removing the flounce or doing something about the sleeves and the neckline.

Harriet had chosen to do something about the sleeves and the neckline. To her way of thinking, that was two alterations, rather than just one. And it felt more important to remove the fuss from her upper half, than her lower, somehow.

She'd had her hair done differently, too. The man who'd come to do their hair for the ball was adamant about creating a row of tiny curls across her forehead, but he had agreed that she need not have bunches of ringlets hanging round her face as well. He'd pulled most of it up on to the crown of her head, leaving only a few curls trailing about her neck. Which tickled, a bit, but that was a price worth paying, when even Kitty had clapped her hands and said how much the new style suited her.

A group of men eyed her as they went past. And didn't give her that look she'd been getting from men so far. The one of mingled pity and amusement.

Not that she cared what they thought. It was Lord Becconsall's opinion that counted.

Oh, if only he weren't so abominably rude and so determined not to marry anyone, he would be perfect. He was so handsome and witty. And in spite of having a reputation for being a bit wild, he was eligible, just, in Aunt Susan's opinion. Even the way they had first met had been rather romantic, now she came to think of it. And as for the way he kissed…

Oh, well. At least he had said he would dance with her tonight. If he could be bothered to come to the ball at all.

And then, at last, there he was. Standing in the doorway glancing round at the assembled throng. Only this time, when his eyes finally quartered her corner of the room, they paused. And he smiled. And walked straight over.

'Good evening, Lady Tarbrook,' he said, bowing to Aunt Susan.

'Why, good evening, Lord Becconsall,' she gushed. 'So lovely to see you again. At a ball. Again.'

Lord Becconsall coloured, faintly, his lips compressing in what looked like irritation.

Oh, dear. She hoped Aunt Susan wasn't going to frighten him off by saying anything about him falling for her on the spot, or something equally embarrassing. And since the best way to prevent her from doing so would be to get Lord Becconsall out of her orbit, she got to her feet.

'Yes, thank you, I would love to dance,' she said.

Lord Becconsall raised one eyebrow.

'You really should wait to be asked.'

'But you asked me this afternoon.'

'Did I?' He feigned confusion.

'Well, you promised you would dance with me if you came tonight, which is the same thing. Practically the same thing.'

'Harriet, really,' protested Aunt Susan, in a scandalised voice. Fortunately. Because it gave Lord Becconsall the very prod he needed.

'Yes, and it has just occurred to me that as soon as

I get this dance with you out of the way, I shall be able to leave.'

Aunt Susan made a sort of strangled noise, as Harriet smiled and laid her hand upon Lord Becconsall's outstretched arm.

'Please, don't say anything about the way I look, until after we've danced,' said Harriet.

'Not even if it is flattering?'

'Oh.' She pretended to think about it. 'That might be agreeable, I suppose.' She darted a look at him from under her lashes.

'In that case, I shall say that you look fine as fivepence.'

'Do you mean that?' She ought not to let one throwaway comment, from a man she hardly knew matter so much. But she couldn't prevent her heart from giving a little skip.

'You know I never say anything I don't mean.'

'No. You are abominably rude,' she agreed cheerfully. 'Which is why it's so comfortable being with you, I suppose.'

'Really?'

'Yes. Because I don't have to mind my manners either, do I? And honestly, you cannot imagine what a relief it is to be able to speak my mind. Most men don't seem to like it.'

'I cannot think why,' he said gravely.

'No, nor can I. And the trouble is I have such a struggle not to say exactly what I think. Even when it doesn't defer to the opinion of a man.'

'How shocking,' he said, with a twitch to his lips as though he was trying not to laugh.

'Well I did think it was, which was rather stupid of me.'

'Er, dare I enquire in what way?'

'In that I should have known that females, and their views, are of less value, in society, than men. Given the difference in the way my parents treated me and my brothers.'

'At least they had the excuse that you were a girl,' he said. And then grimaced. 'That is, my own father never had a good word to say about me. Whereas my brothers could apparently do no wrong.'

'How horrid for you. Why do you think that was?'

'It may have been,' he said drily, 'because they were big and strong and handsome, whereas I was small and sickly and bookish.'

'And yet,' she said, 'you are the only man I have ever met who has not been frightened when I speak my mind.'

'Frightened? Good God, no, why should I be frightened of a slip of a thing like you?' he said with amusement. 'I was a soldier for many years. I faced massed French troops. Not to mention the cut-throat band of ruffians I was supposed to be leading into battle myself.'

'Yes, and you were very brave on lots of occasions, weren't you?'

'What do you mean by that?'

'Oh, nothing much,' she said with a shrug, not liking to admit that she'd asked about his career in the army. 'It's just that I'm convinced that a few ideas, expressed by an impertinent female, are never going to make you quake in your boots, are they?'

He laughed outright at that. 'Never.'

Oh, what a pity it was that he was so set against

marriage. He was exactly the sort of man she would love being married to. He wouldn't defer to her in everything, the way Papa deferred to Mama for being so clever. Nor would he lay down the law the way Uncle Hugo did, expecting unquestioning obedience from the females around him.

Lord Becconsall would be more like a partner. A friend with whom she could discuss anything she liked.

Ah well. Perhaps she would meet someone else just like him.

Except, she didn't think there *was* anyone else just like him.

'Your father must have been a very stupid man,' she said, just as they took their place alongside the other two couples in their set.

'No, not all that stupid,' said Lord Becconsall. 'He just regarded me as the runt of the litter.'

After they'd performed the first change of place, he said, 'Did your brothers bully you?'

'No. They just ignored me, for the most part. Excluded me from their male pursuits. That sort of thing. Did yours…?' She didn't like to think of him being bullied. Nor did she want to say the word out loud, on a dance floor, even though the music would probably prevent her words from carrying very far and the other couples were concentrating on the intricacies of their steps.

Besides, he had the sort of look on his face that indicated he might be regretting speaking so frankly. Men didn't, as a rule, like to confess to any weakness whatever. At least, her brothers hadn't.

After that, he confined himself to the sort of commonplace remarks that everyone else was making as they danced.

Only when it was over did he draw close, his expression serious.

'Do you think you tried to become…less feminine in order to fit in? Is that why you had no idea of how to dress yourself to advantage, when you first came to Town?'

She thought it over. 'I don't think that was it. I just… Actually, Mama always said I should not be forced into some kind of mould, just because of my sex. That I should be free to act exactly as I wished.' It had never occurred to her before that Mama might have meant it. She'd always thought it was an excuse for not paying her any attention at all. But since she'd come to Town, and learned just how many rules there seemed to be that applied to girls, she was beginning to wonder if Mama might have a point.

'And anyway, didn't you accuse me of being a rebel? You will have to make up your mind,' she teased as he started leading her back to where Aunt Susan was sitting. 'Am I a rebel, or trying desperately to fit in?'

He gave her a thoughtful look. 'I think you are doing both. Trying to fit in, but not managing it because you cannot quite quench your rebellious tendencies.'

They were almost there. And once he'd thanked her for the dance, he would leave. And she couldn't face the thought she might never see him, or speak to him again.

'I don't suppose you have an invitation to Lady Lensborough's picnic outing tomorrow, do you?'

'As a matter of fact, I do. On account of the fact that her younger son is a friend of mine.'

'Oh,' she said, her heart lifting. 'Then I shall look forward to seeing you there.'

'What?' He gave her a strange look. 'No, I...I never said I was going.'

'But what possible excuse can you give for not going?'

Now the look was no longer indecipherable. It was plain irritation. 'I won't have to give an excuse. Nobody will expect me to go. And don't ask why they *did* send me an invitation. I get dozens of them. Mostly from matchmaking mothers attempting to foist their branfaced daughters into my arms.'

She gasped, feeling as though he'd just slapped her. In fact, she did raise just one hand to her face, which had a smattering of the very freckles he'd just spoken of with such disdain.

'Lady Lensborough doesn't have a daughter,' she pointed out. 'Don't you think she might have invited you thinking you might actually enjoy yourself?'

'If she did, she must have windmills in her head,' he muttered grimly, before releasing her hand, giving Aunt Susan a brief bow and marching straight out of the ballroom.

Chapter Six

It was a lovely day. The sun was shining. A few white clouds were scudding across the sky on the wings of a light breeze. Perfect weather, in fact, for driving into the countryside for a picnic.

Good grief. He was actually considering going. Just for the pleasure of seeing her face light up at the sight of him, the way it had done last night.

And savouring the way she kept on looking at his mouth as though she was remembering their kiss. Fondly.

Oh, the way she talked. The way she danced. The way she smiled. The way that tendril of hair caressed her neck, the way he'd like to caress it with his tongue.

Oh, hell! He whisked his hat from his head and rammed it on to the peg on the wall. If he was not careful he was going to fall for Lady Harriet. And would start trying to become the kind of man she wanted him to be. Some kind of… Prince Charming to her Cinderella.

And he wasn't that man. He'd told her to her face he wasn't that man. Warned her that nobody thought him worth a rap.

But she hadn't cared. That was what got to him. That was what was tempting him to go on a stupid picnic, where he'd have to sit on damp grass and consume soggy sandwiches and drink flat champagne. Because she actually seemed to enjoy being with him. No matter how…frank he was. Because it meant she could be frank, too.

A chill trickled down his spine. How had it got this far? How had he reached the stage where they were being *frank* with one another? As though they were *intimate*?

And why the hell hadn't he gone straight to Zeus, and Atlas, and Archie, the moment he'd found her, so that he could claim his winnings, come to that? Why was he prolonging this period of…getting to know her?

When it couldn't lead anywhere.

Because he was damned if he was going to marry anyone this Season.

Not even her.

He slammed into his study and spent several hours excluding her from his thoughts by concentrating on the mountain of paperwork that he'd inherited along with the title.

When the light started to fade, he stalked round to Zeus's club. To do what he should have done straight away. Tell him he'd found…damn it, if he thought of her as Hope, he'd weaken and keep her to himself.

Gritting his teeth, he mounted the steps. It would be better for his peace of mind to stay away from her altogether. But he would have to see her at least once more. To settle the wager. They all had to see her and agree she was indeed the girl who'd set about them with her riding crop and concede that he'd been the one to track her down. Or Zeus would think he'd won. Which was unthinkable.

Yes, at least he was going to enjoy the look on the know-it-all's face when Zeus learned that all his assumptions about Lady Harriet were completely wrong.

What was more, the next time he saw her, with the others at his back and his attitude fixed on the wager, she wouldn't have the same effect upon him. She couldn't have.

Taking comfort from those two things, he tossed his hat and gloves to the doorman.

'Lord Rawcliffe in?'

'Yes, my lord. He and his guests have just dined and are taking coffee in the lounge.'

Jack could hazard a guess at the identity of Rawcliffe's guests. And was proved correct when he entered the lounge a few moments later to see Archie and Atlas flanking the Marquis of Rawcliffe, Atlas with a despondent air and Archie with an abstracted one.

'You really know how to entertain your guests, eh, Zeus,' said Jack, approaching the gloomy trio. 'Anyone would think someone had died.'

'My g-grandmother d-did,' said Archie.

'Oh? Well, in that case, I beg pardon. When did that happen?'

'Six months ago,' said Zeus laconically.

'Six months?' Archie looked puzzled. 'As long ago as that?'

Zeus met Jack's gaze and rolled his eyes.

'Dare say you have had other things on your mind,' said Jack soothingly. 'Nevertheless, my condolences.'

'Yes, it was all very unpleasant,' said Archie. 'Things

c-came out about her that none of my family ever suspected.'

Jack pulled up a fourth chair, summoned a waiter and ordered a drink.

'That's the thing with family,' he said affably. 'Always doing the damnedest things and leaving you totally spifflicated. But that's not what I came here to discuss,' he said, as he sat down.

'Oh?' Zeus raised one eyebrow. 'You have come here to have a discussion, have you?'

Jack grinned. 'Not that either. Astute of you to guess.'

'It was not a guess. In all the years that I have known you, you have never once shown any interest in starting a discussion for its own sake.'

'I think I detect a slur upon my character in there somewhere. But I shall let it pass. Because I've come to tell you that I have won the wager.'

'You've found the girl?' Atlas sat up a bit straighter.

'Yes. And you'll never guess who she is.'

'No, I won't,' said Zeus. 'You will spare me the effort of doing anything so tedious by informing me instead.'

'Her name is Lady Harriet Inskip. She's the daughter of the Earl and Countess of Balderstone.'

'Is that so?' Zeus didn't look convinced. 'I was not aware they had a daughter. Three sons, yes, but…' He spread his hands wide.

'She's never been up to Town, according to her aunt. Kept in seclusion in the countryside, apparently.'

'That accounts for the rustic manners, then.'

Not for the first time in recent weeks, Jack felt a very strong urge to knock a couple of Zeus's teeth down his throat. Even though he'd teased her along the same lines himself, it was vastly different hearing the words come from Zeus's mouth, larded as they were with a hefty dose of contempt.

'How ever d-did you manage it?' Archie was looking at him, for once, in something like the way he inevitably looked at Zeus. As though he had some kind of divine wisdom.

'I did not give him the nickname Ulysses for nothing,' Zeus drawled. 'He does have a cunning, low-down sort of intelligence.'

Jack grinned at him. 'That's me,' he said, promptly forgiving Zeus for his apparent ill humour.

He leaned back in his chair, crossing his legs. That was the thing about Zeus. Deep down, beneath the camouflage of unpleasant manners and cutting barbs, Zeus actually rated him fairly highly. Or at least, as highly as he rated any other mortal who crossed his orbit.

And not many men did.

'And for another thing,' said Zeus as though Jack had not spoken, '*he* was actually looking.'

'Meaning you were not?'

'I confess,' said Zeus with a shrug, 'that I did not have as much interest as you. Besides—' He pulled up short, with what might, in any other man, have passed for an apologetic shrug.

'What you mean is that you have more important things to do than run round Town hunting down mystery females, I take it?'

Zeus managed to look down his thin, aristocratic nose at Jack, even though they were sitting on a level. 'I could point out that you also have more important things to do than run round Town hunting down mystery females. Or making wagers which are likely to end up with you breaking your neck, come to that.'

'You could, but you would not do so, lest I take it as an insult and decide to draw your cork.'

'I am surprised you do not simply do it, since you are clearly spoiling for a fight and have been doing so ever since you sold out.'

At some time during this interchange, Jack had actually clenched his fists. Though he only realised he'd done so when the waiter came over with his brandy, obliging him to unclench them.

Zeus watched him pour and down his drink, with what looked to Jack like a trace of disappointment. Almost as though he was spoiling for a fight, too. Though he couldn't imagine why. There were no estate managers telling *him* he didn't know what he was talking about and had better leave matters to the men his father and older brothers had trusted. *He* hadn't rushed home from a life that had suited him down to the ground, hoping for a deathbed reconciliation with his dying father, only to have the man weep at the cruelty of a fate which had seen his two splendidly brawny sons precede him to the grave, leaving everything in the hands of what he termed the runt of the litter.

Atlas cleared his throat. 'Gentlemen, don't you think there is enough fighting in this world without friends turning upon one another over the question of a wager? Or a woman?' He frowned. 'Or whatever this is about.'

Both Jack and Zeus turned to glare at him.

'What will you do, knock our heads together? The way you used to do at school?'

'I'd like to see him try,' said Zeus scornfully. 'In his present state, I think even Archie could overpower him.'

'What?' Archie blinked in a bewildered fashion at the other three, having clearly drifted off again and missed the swirling undercurrents that had brought them close to the brink of quarrelling.

'I was just saying,' said Zeus, 'that you could overpower Atlas these days, if you put your mind to it.'

'Yes, of c-course I c-could,' said Archie. 'Under the right c-conditions. Or if I had a weapon that meant I would not have to c-come within reach of his fists. Though why should I wish to? Atlas is my friend.'

'We are all your friends, Archie,' said Jack. Though he wondered how long their friendships with each other would last, now they were grown men who had little in common beyond their shared past.

'Just because Zeus is the only one who has been in a position to do anything for you,' put in Atlas bitterly, 'that does not mean that we wouldn't have done so. Wouldn't do anything in our power to help you, that is, should you need it.'

'Well, I know that...' said Archie, looking baffled. 'I really d-don't know why—'

'Enough!' Zeus bit out the one word with savagery. 'It is clear that we all have...difficulties in our lives, which are making us resent what we see as the good fortune of the others. Let us...cease dwelling on them. For tonight, at least. And...'

This time, when he ran out of words, it was Jack who felt obliged to come to the rescue.

'And tomorrow night, let us all meet again at Miss Roke's come-out ball. I am sure you have an invitation, Zeus?'

'I have no idea. My secretary deals with the flood of invitations I get to those kinds of events at this time of year. I generally avoid them wherever possible.'

'Yes, but tomorrow night, you will delight Miss Roke by making an appearance. And bring these two along with you,' he finished, waving in the direction of Archie and Atlas.

'And why, pray,' said Zeus, pokering up the way he invariably did when anyone else had the temerity to attempt to take the initiative when he was in the room, 'should I do any such thing?'

'Why, because that is where Lady Harriet will be.' At least, he was fairly sure that was where she would be. It was the most exclusive of the balls being held, that he knew of. The kind where all the better-born debutantes would be doing their utmost to attract a husband from the highest echelons of society. 'And you all need to see her. To verify my claim that she is the same woman who came galloping to my rescue, then thought better of it and let us all feel the force of her displeasure. With her riding crop.'

'And then this thing between the pair of you will be settled,' said Atlas hopefully.

Jack very much doubted it. It had been a long time, a very long time, since he'd hung on Zeus's every word. He'd become an officer. Grown accustomed to command. Had led men into battle. And could no longer go back to the attitude of hero-worship which Zeus still seemed to feel was his due.

'The *wager* will be settled,' said Zeus, confirming Jack's suspicions. 'But what ails Ulysses, I fear, will not be remedied until he returns home and deals with the usurpers attempting to keep him from his kingdom.'

Jack sucked in a sharp breath as the dart went home.

Damned if Zeus wasn't right.

As always.

Chapter Seven

On the face of it, the picnic had been a success. It hadn't rained, the food had been delicious and only one person had been stung by a bee.

And yet it would have been so much more enjoyable if Lord Becconsall had been there.

In the coach, on the way home, Aunt Susan took her to task for looking bored.

'I should not need to remind you that a lady must always be charming in public. She must never let anyone suspect she is not perfectly content with things as they are.'

At which point Kitty giggled.

'Yes, well, dear,' said Aunt Susan, pursing her lips, 'you did behave much better than some of the girls present, I have to admit. So we will say no more.'

And she hadn't. They'd all travelled home in perfect amity, Harriet with the sensation of having been given a great accolade. She'd behaved *much better* than some of the other girls at the picnic. Girls who'd had years and years of coaching in correct behaviour. And who should have known better.

She was smiling to herself as their coach pulled up outside the imposing mansion in Berkeley Square known to all and sundry as Tarbrook House. And kept on smiling as they gathered their shawls, reticules and skirts in preparation for alighting.

The footman let down the steps, Keeble, the butler, pulled the front door wide and stood to one side.

To reveal Lord Tarbrook, standing with his fists on his hips, glaring out at them.

Oh, dear. What had she done now? She racked her brains, but could come up with nothing.

'You,' he snarled, pointing not at Harriet, but at Aunt Susan. 'My study. Now.'

Though Aunt Susan looked puzzled, she only hesitated for a moment before doing as she'd been told, following her husband along the corridor and through the door which he was holding open.

Before it had even shut on the pair of them, he started bellowing. Harriet was too shocked to register the exact words, but between his hectoring tone and Aunt Susan's protestations, it was clear he was accusing her of something which she was strenuously denying.

And before she could start to strain her ears, Kitty took her arm and propelled her at breakneck speed to the staircase.

'It's best to steer well clear of Papa when he's, um, in a bit of a taking,' she explained apologetically, thrusting Harriet into her room and scurrying off in the direction of her own.

A bit of a taking?

If ever she did get married, she vowed as she closed the bedroom door, it would be to a man of an even temperament. Not one who flew up into the boughs over every little thing.

Someone more like Papa, who was contented pottering about in his stables, and kennels, and seeing to estate business. Who was happy to let his wife spend all her time on what he considered her hobbies. Who didn't demand anything…

Well, except heirs, naturally. And he'd always told Mama, and anyone else who cared to listen, how very grateful he'd been to her for presenting him with three such strapping sons in rapid succession in the early days of their marriage.

He'd never said what he thought of the way she'd inexplicably given birth to Harriet—after such a lengthy gap she looked like an afterthought—or if he had, she'd never heard about it.

She supposed that was one point in Uncle Hugo's favour. He really did seem to dote on Kitty. Even though she was merely a girl.

She shook off the contrary thought and applied herself to the task of making herself presentable for the evening's outing. It was another ball. This one to celebrate the betrothal of a pretty young heiress to an elderly earl. At last she had a truly lovely gown to wear, of white satin with a white crape overdress which made it look deliciously filmy. Best of all, though, the bodice was of rich green satin, decorated only with touches of silver at the waist and neckline. No more pure white for her, Aunt Susan had agreed. With a bandeau of pearls twisted into her upswept hair, and pearls at her throat, Harriet felt as pretty as she was ever likely to look.

* * *

When it was time to go out, Aunt Susan gave a splendid demonstration of her earlier advice about how a lady ought to behave. From her calm demeanour nobody would ever guess she'd just spent a couple of hours being scolded. Nor did Kitty betray any curiosity about the way her parents had been arguing.

Though Harriet tried to emulate them, she couldn't help glancing at the doorway rather more often than she ought. But she also kept a smile pasted to her face, even when Kitty's admirers made the most fatuous comments, and pretended to be interested in what they had to say. And to her surprise, she reaped the rewards at once. One of Kitty's more bashful admirers, a Mr Swaffham, who'd been thrust to the back of the queue by his rivals, gave Harriet a rueful smile when Kitty informed him that she regretted being unable to dance with him and asked if she wouldn't mind standing up with him instead.

Mr Swaffham did not give any sign that she was a less acceptable partner than Kitty. Even though he would much rather have been dancing with her cousin. He was unfailingly polite. And yet by the end of the dance, she couldn't say she'd enjoyed it half so much as she had done when Lord Becconsall had been so rude he'd goaded her into colliding with another lady in her set.

Not that she gave Mr Swaffham the slightest hint how she felt. This time she could see the point in disguising her true feelings. After all, Mr Swaffham had concealed his, so that he wouldn't hurt her. The least she could do would be to return the favour.

* * *

She must have done so convincingly, because later on another of Kitty's admirers, a Lord Frensham, also asked her to dance and appeared to be perfectly content with the arrangement until the very moment he returned her to Aunt Susan's side and abandoned Harriet to return to the pursuit of her cousin.

On their return home, Aunt Susan gave Harriet the first completely unqualified compliment she'd received since the Season had begun.

'You are finding your feet in society at last,' she said, with a satisfied smile. 'I am proud of you.'

Harriet basked in that compliment all the way home.

But all her pleasure evaporated the moment they set foot in Tarbrook House, to find Uncle Hugo once again pacing the hallway, waiting for them to come back.

'Hugo, surely, not now,' Aunt Susan protested, indicating the girls.

'Right now, madam,' he replied.

'But, I've already told you—'

'My study,' he said implacably.

And far from voicing any more objections, Aunt Susan trudged wearily in his wake. And Kitty hustled Harriet up the stairs.

Poor Aunt Susan must have been exhausted already, after a full day out in the countryside, then a good hour's scolding before hastily preparing for a ball where she'd sat watching over both her young charges all night.

Yet Uncle Hugo had no pity.

In fact, she could still hear him shouting at her the next morning, the moment she emerged from her bedroom. The only difference was that now his angry voice was filtering through Aunt Susan's bedroom door, rather than through the one to his study.

Good grief, had he been shouting at her all night? No, surely not. Even Uncle Hugo would have needed to sleep at some point.

Though Harriet could just imagine him leaving his study and marching Aunt Susan up the stairs so that he could continue accusing her of whatever it was she was still insisting she hadn't done, in more comfort.

She was just passing Aunt Susan's closed bedroom door, on her way to the staircase, when something shattered against its other side. She flinched, before scurrying along the corridor to the head of the stairs, out of range. If Uncle Hugo had opened the door at the moment Aunt Susan had thrown whatever it was at his head, she might have been struck by a flying porcelain shepherdess.

That was another thing to be said for her own parents. They might not have what she would describe as an ideal marriage, she reflected as she reached the stairs, down which she needed to go to arrive at the breakfast parlour, but each was content to let the other go their own way. There were never any scenes such as the one Uncle Hugo had enacted last night and Harriet had certainly never felt the need to run and hide from Papa at any time, the way Kitty had advised her to do from Uncle Hugo.

Nor did Mama ever reach the stage where she felt her only recourse was to throw breakables about.

But then…oh, good heavens! Harriet came to a standstill in the doorway to the breakfast parlour, wondering if it was possible to conjure someone up just by thinking about them. For there sat her mother, scattering toast crumbs in all directions from behind the pages of whatever obscure publication she'd brought to the breakfast table with her.

'Good Lor...I mean, good heavens, Mama? When did you arrive? I had no idea you were coming to stay.'

'Hmm?' Mama peered up at her with a distracted air, as though she couldn't quite recall who she was.

'She got here late last night,' said Kitty, who was standing by the sideboard, where a gargantuan breakfast lay spread out.

Since Mama was engrossed in her paper once more, Harriet went over to her cousin.

'Was that,' whispered Harriet, since Peter, the second footman, was standing close to the sideboard, in case anyone had need of him, 'what started the...um...*discussion*? Between your father and mother?' What a silly question. Harriet felt like kicking herself the moment she'd asked it. Kitty couldn't possibly have heard what the argument had been about. But instead of pointing that out, Kitty shook her head, and leaned close, lowering her voice.

'Not directly. Though Papa did say something about it being the last straw. Though I have to say your mother was absolutely splendid in the face of his accusations,' she said, darting her mother a glowing look.

'Mama was?'

'Oh, yes, she said that if it was a question of him being in the basket,' said Kitty, clattering the dome over a dish of eggs, in order, Harriet supposed, to prevent the nearby footman from overhearing, 'he ought to send all the bills for our come-out to your father, who was ready to stand the nonsense. Which practically sent him off into an apoplexy on the spot.'

Golly. It sounded as though, having advised Harriet to steer well clear of Lord Tarbrook, Kitty had crept back downstairs and put her ear to the keyhole.

'I cannot quite see why,' Harriet began. 'I mean, if your father is having money troubles, why on earth did your mother insist on sponsoring me for a Season?'

'Because he isn't having money troubles at all,' hissed Kitty indignantly. 'It is just that Mama,' she breathed, her eyes suddenly lighting up with excitement, 'seems to have pawned off a lot of jewellery and had it copied. Papa found out when he took an old family heirloom to the jewellers to be re-set for my engagement ball.'

'Your engagement ball? I didn't even know you had received a proposal. When did that happen?'

'It hasn't happened yet, silly,' said Kitty with a giggle. 'But when it does, I was dreading being weighted down by the hideous parure that has been worn by all the Tarbrook daughters for the past two centuries. And Papa knows how much I detest it. So he sent it off to be put into new settings. As a surprise for me when I do finally choose a husband.'

'My…my goodness,' said Harriet, absentmindedly scooping a spoonful of scrambled eggs on to the plate Kitty had just pressed into her hand.

'Yes, and now everyone is whispering about Mama,' said Kitty, glaring round the room at the wooden-faced servants. 'They must have all heard Papa shouting at her last night.'

'And this morning,' said Harriet. 'I heard him myself as I was coming down.'

'What, still?'

Apparently not. For at that moment, the door opened and Aunt Susan herself came in, red-eyed but straight-backed as she swished to her place at the foot of the table. Even before she sat down the butler snapped his fingers and Fred, the first footman, brought her tea and a plate of toast cut into fingers, the breakfast which she habitually consumed every morning.

Harriet's mother peered at her sister over the top of her paper, frowned and laid it aside.

'Never say the brute is still refusing to listen to sense?'

Aunt Susan stuck out her chin, her cheeks quivering as though with the effort of not bursting into tears again.

'I cannot comprehend why he should think you would rob your own daughter,' said Mama with ex-asperation. 'You have no need of the money, after all. He gives you a very generous allowance, doesn't he?'

'He won't believe a word I say,' said Aunt Susan in-dignantly. 'Not one word. After all these years.'

Well, that explained the sound of shattering crock-ery. Or at least, it was probably one of those funny little statue things that Lady Tarbrook kept handy on every available surface. If someone had accused *her* of theft, Harriet thought she might very well be inclined to throw something at her accuser's fat head.

'It would serve him right if you did start going to gaming hells and taking heavy losses,' said Mama, star-tling Harriet so much she put her thumb in her eggs. 'In fact, if it was me in your shoes, that is exactly what I'd do.'

'Not all husbands are as easy to tame as yours,' said Aunt Susan bitterly, as Peter deftly took Harriet's plate from her, walked to the table, set it at her place and pulled out her chair.

'To think of all the years I have been the perfect wife…'

Harriet and Kitty crept to the table while Aunt Susan began enumerating the dozens of ways in which she'd borne with her husband's odd tempers over the years. The servants all adopted carefully bland expressions as they went about their work, though some of the tales about Uncle Hugo's doings were so risqué they made Harriet's cheeks burn. It wasn't long before she started to wonder whether she ought to send the servants from the room. But then she remembered what Kitty had said and reasoned that not only was it too late to prevent them learning more than they should, but also that it wasn't her place.

'And now,' Aunt Susan was complaining, 'the first time something inexplicable occurs, instead of trusting me, he accuses me of…of…' Her lower lip wobbled. She raised her napkin to her eyes and hid her face for a moment.

By the time she lowered it, Mama was looking thoroughly annoyed.

'Do you know what you should do?'

'I feel sure…' Aunt Susan sighed '…you are about to tell me.'

'Well, in your place, I think I might get some Bow Street Runners on the case. To see if they can find out what happened to the rubies.'

Aunt Susan froze, a finger of toast halfway to her mouth. But then she shook her head and sighed.

'I would not know how to go about hiring them. Do you?'

Harriet's mother shook her head. 'It is a great pity James did not wish to come to Town with me. He may be a bit of a dunderhead, but it is the sort of thing even he would know, I dare say. Or if he didn't, he could find out.'

Harriet grabbed a piece of toast and slapped it on to her plate. Then hacked off a slice of butter to spread on it, wishing Mama would not speak of Papa in such a derogatory fashion all the time. Why couldn't she appreciate what an absolute lamb he was? In comparison with the tyrannical Uncle Hugo, particularly?

'I don't think Hugo would like that,' said Aunt Susan, confirming Harriet's opinion of him. 'He might regard it as interference in his private business.'

Harriet's mother curled her lip in scorn at what Aunt Susan believed her husband might think.

'If anyone could find out how to hire such a person,' said Aunt Susan, reaching across and patting her sister's hand, 'I feel sure it is *you*, Mary.'

'Me? Oh, but I only came to Town to—'

'Attend some important lecture and speak to some genius who has written some paper that has a bearing on what you yourself are looking into at the moment, I know, dear, you told me all that last night. But don't you think you might find the time to…'

Mama withdrew her hand swiftly. 'You know I won't. I told you, that is why I didn't even have Stone House opened up. I don't have time for distractions of that sort. My work is important,' she said firmly. 'Not that I expect you to understand…'

'Oh, I understand perfectly,' snapped Aunt Susan, the brief moment of harmony between the sisters shattering. 'If your work is more important to you than your own daughter's future, not to say well-being, then naturally the troubles of a mere sister must fade into insignificance.'

'There is no need to take that attitude—'

'You were always a selfish little girl,' said Aunt Susan, her blood clearly up. 'But after I've gone to all the effort of making up for your neglect, teaching your daughter all the things you should have done, dressing her, taking her about and all the rest of it, and you will not even—'

'Well, nobody asked you to do any of those things,' replied Mama, unperturbed. 'She—' she glanced across the table at Harriet, who promptly buried her face in the cup of tea which had been sitting beside her place '—was perfectly content living quietly in the country.'

'And what would have happened to her when Charles took a bride and brought her home? What would she do then with another woman taking the reins of Stone Court? Where would her place have been then?'

It felt as if someone had just jabbed a knife into Harriet's gut. She'd never looked that far into her future. She'd never wondered what her role would be, once a woman came to live at Stone Court who would be entitled to take on the duties her mother shirked.

But Aunt Susan had.

Harriet lowered her half-empty cup to its saucer with a snap. Once again, Aunt Susan was the only person who'd considered Harriet's welfare.

The scraping of the chair next to her alerted her to the fact that Kitty was getting to her feet.

'If you will excuse us, Mama, Aunt Mary,' she said, dropping a curtsy as both women's heads whipped round and treated her to almost identical glares. 'But we need to attend to some, um, mending.'

Harriet gave her half-eaten plate of eggs and toast just one rueful glance before getting to her feet as well. Because she would rather go without breakfast than be a witness to any more quarrelling. Let alone revelations about what went on within such a stormy marriage as her aunt and uncle were conducting. It had been the most uncomfortable mealtime she'd ever endured. No wonder Kitty had suggested a way of escape.

Aunt Susan gave a wave of her hand, dismissing them, and the girls scuttled out of the room, their breakfast abandoned.

Fred darted before them to open the door, and, as they heard their respective mothers take up the cudgels once again, followed them out into the hall.

'Shall I send some fresh tea and toast to the drawing room, Miss Kitty?'

'Yes, thank you, Fred,' said Kitty as though it was the most natural thing in the world to resume breakfast in another location. Which, in this house, it probably was, Harriet reflected as Kitty took her by the elbow and steered her across to the stairs.

'Your poor mother,' said Harriet as they started up the stairs. So far, though she'd been grateful for all the things Aunt Susan had tried to do for her, she rather thought she'd taken her for granted. To start with she'd seen her, she realised, in the light of a fairy godmother creature, who existed only to grant her wishes. But since coming to London she was coming to know her as a real woman, who, though having plenty of troubles of her own, had a heart big enough to constantly look out for her lonely, socially awkward niece. And take practical steps to ensure she had a comfortable future.

Aunt Susan had never once counted the cost. Neither financially nor in terms of the potential for embarrassment.

Whereas Mama had done nothing to prepare her for life outside Stone Court. Which she *would* have to leave when Charles found a bride. At least, once Papa left the place to Charles, that was. Which would hopefully be a long way off. But…ugh. The thought of lingering in the place, with no real function, once Charles brought a wife in to run the place the way she saw fit. It was bad enough as it was, feeling as though she had to earn her place to win anyone's notice by running the household, rather than just taking it for granted, the way Kitty did. But once they no longer needed her to stand in for Mama, she would be nothing. Worse than nothing—an encumbrance, that's what she'd be. Hanging about the place with no real purpose and no value.

It would be unbearable.

'Come on, Harriet, this way,' said Kitty, making her realise she'd come to a standstill at the head of the stairs.

'Beg pardon,' she said, setting off again along the landing in the direction of the drawing room. She only wished she could beg Aunt Susan's pardon so easily. For all the times she'd let her down. For rebelling against the strictures, even if she'd only done it inwardly. For wasting the chance Aunt Susan was giving her by comparing perfectly eligible men to Lord Becconsall, who'd told her outright he didn't want to get married at all.

Well, no longer. From now on she would stop mooning about, wishing for Lord Becconsall, or some other man, to come into her life and turn it into something that only existed in the pages of a storybook. She would focus on the things that mattered. On making it up to Aunt Susan, somehow, for what she was going through. Because it was terribly unfair that all she was getting, in return for her generosity, was half-hearted compliance from her niece, and indifference from her sister, whilst enduring such persecution from her husband.

'Kitty, we have to do something,' she said, penitence for being so self-centred in the face of her aunt's unhappiness making her stomach squirm.

'Yes. I know. I only said that about sewing to get us out of the breakfast parlour because I couldn't think of anything better. What would you like to do?'

'No.' Harriet felt like stamping her foot. 'I mean, to help your mama.'

Kitty frowned. 'Like…rubbing her temples with lavender water, do you mean?'

'No. Though I suppose we could. Would she like that? But, no, actually, what I meant was finding out what really happened to those rubies and clearing her name.'

'Oh, but we can't possibly! I mean…' she dropped on to the nearest chair '…how?'

'Well, we can start by talking to the servants about it.'

'The servants?' Kitty clapped her hand to her breast in shock. 'But, one should never discuss family matters with them.'

Harriet pursed her lips. 'Look, Kitty, the way my mother and yours were arguing at the breakfast table, the servants already know all about it.'

'That's different.'

'I don't see how.'

Kitty sighed and rolled her eyes. 'That's the thing about you, Harriet. You just do not grasp the subtler points of governing a household such as this.'

No. And she didn't want to, either. It all seemed to consist of one set of people pretending they didn't know what they knew, while the other set expected them to keep their mouths shut about it. Instead of everyone just being open and honest.

'Well, since I am so...lacking in subtlety, nobody will be surprised when I start blundering about asking awkward questions then, will they? Besides which,' she put in hastily when Kitty opened her mouth to make another objection, 'as you pointed out, the servants overhear everything. If anything suspicious has happened inside your household, ten to one, most of the servants will know all about it.'

'Well, then, why didn't one of them come forward?'

Harriet felt like running her fingers through her hair. Except that would dislodge the pins which were holding it in place and ruin the style which had taken longer to create than the so-called *fussy* ringlets to which Lord Becconsall had objected.

'Because,' she said slowly, 'they aren't in the habit of speaking to the family openly, are they? And anyway, all this about the jewels has only just come to light, from what I can gather?'

Kitty nodded.

'Well then, let's give them a bit of time to talk about it and start to speculate about what must have really happened to the parure. And then I shall start asking them if they can recall... I don't know...the last time anyone saw them before your father took them to the jewellers. I take it they don't get an airing very often, if they're so hideous?'

Kitty shook her head. 'As I said, it is tradition for the ladies of the family to wear them for their betrothal ball and new brides usually wear them when they have their portrait painted, but other than that, they tend to stay locked away.'

'So they might have been copied years ago?'

Kitty nodded, slowly. 'Yes, I suppose so. But then… if that is the case, who is likely to remember anything helpful?'

'I don't know. But one thing I do know,' she said with resolution, 'I am not going to rest until I have cleared your mother's name.'

Chapter Eight

'**P**apa!' Kitty could not conceal her surprise when, that night, Lord Tarbrook climbed into the carriage which was taking them to Miss Roke's come-out ball. He'd never bothered to attend any of the events of the Season thus far, claiming they were insipid affairs which bored him to death.

'Clearly, your mother is not to be trusted to put your welfare first,' he grumbled as he took the seat beside his wife, 'so what choice do I have but to keep a closer watch on her doings?'

Aunt Susan gasped as though he had slapped her. Harriet did not know where to look. It was hard to avoid catching anyone's eye in the confines of a small carriage, but by putting her mind to it, she managed to do so all the way to the ball.

'It is of no use putting on that martyred air,' snapped Uncle Hugo as they drew up outside the brightly lit house, causing everyone to start guiltily and look up. He was glaring at his wife, which relieved Harriet and probably Kitty, too, by the look of it. 'What can you expect,' he snarled, 'after letting your daughter down so badly?'

Aunt Susan gave his back, as he pushed open the carriage door rather than wait for one of their footmen to perform the task, a wounded look. Though she replaced it with an emotionless mask almost instantly.

Harriet couldn't help admiring the way Aunt Susan wrapped her dignity round her like a mantle as she climbed out of the carriage. And the way she held up her head as she placed her hand on her toad of a husband's sleeve as they mounted the steps was nothing short of regal. This was exactly the way she was always encouraging Harriet to behave. And if Aunt Susan could do it, under the strain of such unfair accusations, then so could she.

Harriet took a deep breath, mentally renewing her vow to do all in her power to show support for her poor beleaguered aunt. She had not made much progress with questioning the servants so far. But anyway, what Aunt Susan seemed to want most, from Harriet, was to see her married off to someone *suitable*.

With that in mind, Harriet vowed that for tonight at least, she would behave impeccably. She could certainly *try* to recall all the advice Aunt Susan had given her and apply it diligently. She would not slouch in her chair, or pick at her gloves, or sigh, or fidget, or any of the things she was not supposed to do. And when some man did happen to ask her to dance, she would act as though she was thrilled, no matter who he was, if her aunt appeared to approve of him. What was more, she would treat him as though she thought he was amazingly handsome and witty, for the entire duration of the dance, no matter how dull and stupid he was. She would bite her tongue, if necessary, to prevent herself from speaking her mind.

And even if she didn't get asked to dance, at least Aunt Susan would see she was doing her best, for once. It was not much to do for her, but at least Aunt Susan would feel she'd made a success out of transforming Harriet from a country bumpkin to a society miss.

The moment they entered the ballroom Kitty's usual crowd of admirers began to gather round, asking for various dances throughout the evening. And since Kitty couldn't possibly dance with all of them at once, Harriet managed to snare one or two of her leftovers, by the simple ruse of smiling hopefully up at them.

Mr Swaffham was the first to lead her on to the dance floor. This time, instead of merely concentrating on getting through the steps without mishap, she put herself out to make sure he enjoyed himself, paying rapt attention to everything he said and smiling at him frequently. She felt drained by the time he returned her to Aunt Susan's side at the end of the dance, but at least he didn't look as though dancing with her was a poor substitute for standing up with the girl he really admired.

On any other night, Aunt Susan would probably have congratulated her for making so much effort. But tonight, it was Aunt Susan who was fidgeting, and sighing, and generally looking thoroughly miserable. It was probably due to the fact that Uncle Hugo was nowhere in sight. The moment both she and Kitty had secured partners, he'd taken himself off in the direction of the refreshment room. Taking all Aunt Susan's self-esteem with him, by the looks of things.

What her aunt needed was something to put the heart back in her. Though Harriet could not think what.

But then she spotted the perfect opportunity, in the person of Lord Becconsall.

'Oh, look,' she said, in a desperate attempt to dispel the cloud of despondency hanging over her aunt like a greasy grey cloud. 'It is Lord Becconsall, just come in.'

'Hmm?' Lady Tarbrook brought her attention back to the ballroom with a visible effort. 'Oh, yes. That handsome young wastrel who has been showing an interest in you.'

'The one who spoke of matrimony the first time we danced,' Harriet reminded her shamelessly. 'The one you said has not danced with anyone else this Season.'

'The one,' said Aunt Susan drily, 'for whom you have been looking everywhere we've been these past few days. Unless I am very much mistaken.'

'Um, yes.' Well, there was no point in denying it. Even though it would probably mean a lecture for wearing her heart too much on her sleeve.

'Is your heart fixed on him, then?'

What sort of a question was that? Usually, Aunt Susan's first concern was with a gentleman's pedigree and fortune. Whether Harriet liked him or not was an irrelevancy when it came to his matrimonial worth.

'I...well, that is...' No, she couldn't admit that she still tingled all over whenever she dwelled on his kiss. Even the thought of it was making her go hot.

'Your blush is answer enough. Attract him, if you wish, then,' said Aunt Susan gloomily. 'Better a husband who makes your heart flutter to start with, than one who is chosen for you by your parents, who you have done your best to like, and to please, for years, and for what? To discover he never trusted you!'

Harriet winced. She had no idea how to cope with moods of this sort. Nobody ever had them at Stone Court. They just…got on with life. Even when she'd been a very little girl, nobody had ever bothered to cajole her into a good mood if she was ill or out of sorts, so she had absolutely no idea how to do the same for someone else. Why, even when her pony had put its foot down a rabbit hole, tossing her over his head with such force she'd broken her arm, nobody had done more than chuck her under the chin and say they were proud of her for not making a fuss when the groom who was with her set the bone.

She twisted her fan between her fingers, wishing she could say, or do, something to cheer her aunt up. And found herself looking, beseechingly, in the direction of Lord Becconsall.

As if in answer to her silent plea for help, he made his way across the increasingly crowded ballroom to where they were sitting.

'Good evening, Lady Tarbrook, Lady Harriet,' said Lord Becconsall, bowing from the waist.

Instead of simpering and gushing, Aunt Susan looked him up and down, as though she wasn't sure what to make of him.

'Have I,' he said, looking a touch uncomfortable, 'offended you in some way?'

'Oh, not at all, my lord,' said Harriet. And then almost shuddered. Because, to her utter disgust, what had just emerged from her lips could only be described as a simper. 'Whatever gave you that idea?' And with the feeling of in for a penny, in for a pound, she lowered her head and darted a look up at him from beneath her eyelashes, in the prescribed manner to indicate modesty, yet interest, at the same time.

He blinked.

'Ah, um. What was I about to say?'

'That you feared you had offended me in some way and was about to explain what gave you that idea,' she said. And then, from nowhere but her own desperation, she hit upon what could be the very thing.

'Though, of course, I was terribly disappointed you did not come on the picnic.'

And then she blushed. Because that sounded rather too desperate and she didn't want to scare him off.

'I fear the prospect of sitting on damp ground and eating stale sandwiches did not appeal,' he said.

'Oh, but the sandwiches were not stale. All the food was positively delicious,' she gushed. Oh, lord, she was sounding like a complete ninny. Fortunately, her attempts to behave exactly the way a debutante should appeared to amuse Lord Becconsall. At least, his eyes were twinkling now and his lips relaxing from the rather grim line in which he'd been holding them when he first approached.

'I hope you are not about to reprimand me for dereliction of duty,' he said playfully.

Which was a sort of quip. She was supposed to laugh at a man's attempts at humour, no matter how feeble.

And so she did. At least, she tittered. To her shame. The sound emerging from her mouth was such an artificial, brittle sound she was sure even Aunt Susan would say she'd gone too far. But, having darted a look at her from the corner of her eye, it was to see her aunt was gazing into space, her mouth pinched up in very obvious bitterness.

Harriet gave up.

'The truth is we are all a bit out of sorts this evening. We have had a…that is…' She racked her brains for a plausible excuse to give him which would account for Aunt Susan's mood, without giving away any family secrets.

'We had an unexpected visitor,' she said, finally hitting on an excuse that was near enough to the truth to be useful. 'It set us all at sixes and sevens.'

'A visitor?'

'Yes. My mother.'

He cocked his head to one side, eyeing her as though he wasn't sure what to expect from her next. 'I beg your pardon, but I fail to see…'

'Oh, for heaven's sake,' she said crossly. 'Are you going to ask me to dance, or not?'

On any other night, such a comment would have shocked Aunt Susan to the core. Tonight she didn't even seem to notice.

But Lord Becconsall did. His eyes flicked from her, to her aunt, and back again, thoughtfully.

'I think I should ask you to dance.'

'Thank you,' she said, leaping to her feet and placing her hand on his forearm, before he'd even had the chance to extend it in her direction.

'I sense a mystery,' he said softly as they made their way to the dance floor.

'Oh, very observant of you,' she said sarcastically. And then mentally kicked herself. Hadn't she vowed she would be all sweetness and light tonight? To prove that Aunt Susan's lessons in how to behave around eligible men were bearing fruit?

'I mean, yes, how observant of you,' she said, shooting him what she hoped was a worshipful smile.

'Oho! Now my curiosity is really roused. What on earth can have happened to dull the edge of that sharp tongue of yours? And were you actually attempting to flirt with me just now?'

Attempting? She *had* flirted. She'd given him the benefit of a coy look, and a simper, and a titter, and had rounded it all off by fluttering her eyelashes.

'Absolutely not,' she snapped back. 'I never flirt. And if I was to start, you may be sure I would not waste my time flirting with *you*.'

'That's better,' he said affably. 'I was beginning to worry that the strain of being polite to me might give you the headache.'

The beast! He'd deliberately goaded her into losing her temper.

Making sport of her, to be precise. If only it wouldn't cause a scene, she'd march right back to her chair and leave him standing on the dance floor alone.

But it would. And her aunt had enough on her plate without that. So she had to satisfy herself with shooting him a daggers look as they took their places in the set forming.

The only effect it had on him was to make his grin a touch triumphant.

But at least during the dance she didn't have to speak to him again. And as she concentrated on performing her steps correctly, she also, almost, regained control over her annoyance.

* * *

When the dance ended, instead of leading her directly back to where Aunt Susan was sitting, Lord Becconsall steered her in the opposite direction.

'Um, what are you doing?'

'I thought you would benefit from a short turn on the terrace,' he replied.

'What?' She whipped her hand from his sleeve as though it had burned her.

Far from looking offended, he looked at her with respect.

'You have learned your lesson, I see, since the last time I got you alone.'

'Yes, and—'

'But if you come out on to the terrace with me, we shall not be alone. I have already observed several other couples going out to take the air.'

'Oh.' What game was he playing now? She'd assumed he'd been sending her a message by not attending the picnic. Which she'd interpreted as a declaration that she must not look upon him as a prospective suitor. But now he was behaving just like a man who was determined to fix his interest with her.

'Look, there is even a maid, waiting to hand out shawls to protect the shoulders of young ladies from the night air. I wouldn't be surprised to find a footman out there, serving refreshments,' he said as a final inducement.

Why he wanted to take her outside was a mystery, but if she were truly serious about wanting to discover whether or not she could consider marrying him, then she'd leap at the chance to spend a little time in relative privacy. And it would be just what Aunt Susan would expect.

'Oh, very well,' she said, far from graciously. 'But don't…try anything.'

'Try anything?' He looked at her in mock surprise. With just a dash of innocence thrown in for good measure. 'Whatever do you mean?'

She heard a noise well up in her throat which was rather like a growl. Which appeared to amuse him immensely. Because he was chuckling as he took the proffered shawl from the maid stationed by the double doors, and draped it round her shoulders himself.

'There,' he said with what sounded like satisfaction. And took his time removing his hands from her person.

And just like that, she was reliving the moment they'd been lying together on the grass. He with his arms wrapped tightly round her, and she…melting into him.

She sucked in a short, shocked breath and inhaled the scent of him, since he was standing so close to her. And it was just like smelling the kiss. Or The Kiss, as she was coming to think of it.

Until this moment, she hadn't known that she'd remembered what The Kiss had smelled like. Or that a kiss could even be said to have a smell. Only now, breathing in the scent of his clothes, and his…well, she supposed it was his body, too…did her nostrils detect the absence of crushed grass, and horse, and even the brandy fumes that had sweetened his breath.

He frowned at her. 'What is it? What is troubling you?'

'Wh-what?' She had to give herself a mental shake. Now was not the time to wish she was in the park, or in a stable, or some other location suitable for snatched kisses.

He took her by the arm and steered her away from the door.

'I can see you are deeply troubled, Lady Harriet,' he said, setting up a pace that anyone watching them would describe as a casual stroll. 'About your aunt, at a guess.'

'What makes you think that?'

He chuckled. 'Lady Harriet, you are practically doing cartwheels in the attempt to restore her to her normal frame of mind.'

'I don't know what you mean.'

'Yes, you do. Nothing but the direst need would have induced you to come outside with me like this. Not after the…er…lesson you received in the park that morning.'

She glowered up at him as he described what she was starting to regard as one of the most pleasant experiences of her life as a lesson.

'But we are not alone. As you pointed out, there are several other couples taking the air. As well as a brace of single gentlemen poisoning their lungs with cigar smoke.'

He drew her to a halt and turned her to face him.

'If you don't want to tell me, I can understand that. But don't take me for a fool, Lady Harriet.'

She didn't. Lord Becconsall, for all his playfulness, was nobody's fool. He was the only man tonight who had noticed that anything was amiss with her aunt. The only man who'd bothered to enquire about it. The only one to seem to care.

Oh, how she wished she could tell him all about it. That they could revert to the easy way they'd got into, albeit briefly, of talking about all sorts of personal things. Like his odious brothers and her inability to choose clothes wisely. But she couldn't. He'd made a strategic withdrawal when she'd asked him if he was going on that picnic. She'd seen it in his eyes. She supposed she should be glad he was doing what he could not to raise false hope in her heart. It was honourable of him. If he were a different sort of man he could very well use the easy way they'd got into of speaking to each other to take advantage. Right now he could be luring her into a darkened corner and kissing her again. She wouldn't resist. And he knew it.

She whirled away from him, clasping her hands to her breast.

He followed, her, laid his hands on her shoulders, and turned her round, a questioning expression in his eyes.

'Lady Harriet?'

'I...I cannot!' She gulped. 'Ask me about something else, instead. Or let me tell you all about the picnic.'

'The picnic?'

'Yes. You would have enjoyed it immensely, you know. Some of the girls there behaved really badly. First of all Miss Angstrom got stung by a bee and let loose a screech that set all the dogs for miles around howling. And then, when Miss Jeavons saw that it made certain gentlemen take notice, she pretended to faint.'

For a moment, it looked as if he was going to object to her conversational choice. But then he half-shrugged, as though giving in.

'How do you know she was only pretending?'

'Because she sort of slid all the way down Lord Lensborough's front, then landed in a graceful pose right at his feet.'

'Did she?' He almost smiled at that.

'Yes, and then his younger brother, Captain Challinor, dashed a cup of water in her face. Which brought her round in a twinkling.'

'Water has a tendency to do that. I wonder you didn't try that remedy on me when you found me in a similar condition.'

'Oh, well, there wasn't a river nearby to fetch it from. Or any empty glasses to hand.'

He gave her a look.

'I know what you are doing, Lady Harriet,' he said.

'Isn't it for the best?'

He turned away from her and leant his hands on the balustrade bordering the terrace. 'Yes,' he said grimly. Causing something inside her to curl up and whimper.

Until that moment, she hadn't realised just how lonely she was. Only now that he was agreeing with her, that it was best they maintain a distance from each other, did she understand just how badly she wanted to confide in him. To unburden herself. Even ask him for help.

'It…it really isn't my secret to tell.'

'I understand,' he said, turning to look at her over his shoulder. 'And I commend your loyalty.'

'You…you do?'

'Yes, and, Lady Harriet, should there be any way in which I may be of service…'

'There isn't,' she said more sharply than she'd intended. 'And don't ask about it any more.'

He raised his hands as if in surrender. 'I wouldn't dream of it.'

And now she was angry with him for giving in so easily.

'You had better take me back to my aunt now.'

'Very well,' he said, without even making a token protest.

Well, naturally not. Because he didn't really care. This was all some kind of game to him. He'd told her so. She wasn't sure yet what part he wanted her to play in his game, but the one thing she did know was that she couldn't rely on him.

No matter how much she wished she could.

Oh, how she wished she'd never come out here. Well, that was one thing that was easily remedied. All she had to do was go back inside.

And so, giving him one last look which she hoped revealed how disappointed in him she was, she whirled away from him and marched across the terrace with her fists clenched.

Chapter Nine

'Lady Harriet, wait!'

Lord Becconsall grabbed her hand before she'd gone more than a couple of paces from him and placed it on his sleeve, matching his own pace to her stride.

'It needs to look as if I am leading you,' he warned her out of the corner of his mouth. Which brought her to a standstill. It was things like this that made her like him so much. Oh, how could he do this to her?

Injecting every ounce of disdain she could muster into her movement, she removed her hand from his arm.

'Don't think you can bully me,' she hissed.

'What? I say, that's a bit extreme, even for you. Especially when I was only trying to observe the conventions which—'

'Stuff conventions!'

To her irritation, he grinned. 'Well, most of the time I'd agree with you, but if I just let you flounce back into the ballroom with your fists clenched, after everyone saw us going outside together, it would create the kind of speculation that your aunt wouldn't like, even if you don't care what anyone thinks of you.'

Having delivered that little homily, he extended his arm to her in the correct manner.

Giving her the choice whether to lay her hand on it and behave correctly, or resume her headlong flight from the terrace.

She didn't have to think it over for long. She'd come here tonight vowing to support her aunt by behaving impeccably. Creating gossip by making it look as though Lord Becconsall had insulted her in some way, after she'd strayed out of sight of her chaperon, was the exact opposite. And it was a good job Lord Becconsall had reminded her in time.

'I apologise for implying that you are a bully,' she said grudgingly as she laid her hand on his sleeve.

'Was that what you did? I assumed,' he said as they stepped back into the ballroom, 'that it was the equivalent of kicking the cat.'

'Cat? What cat?'

'The metaphorical one that takes the brunt of your anger when whatever it is that has made you angry isn't in reach.'

'Oh, that cat.' Goodness, but he was perceptive. It was Uncle Hugo with whom she was really angry. Lord Becconsall was…she darted him a glance…incredibly endearing, actually. Even though he'd teased her rather a lot, there had never been any malicious intent to it. He'd warned her how he felt about marriage and stayed away rather than raise false hope in her breast. He'd even taken steps to prevent her from creating a scene—though he had been the one to goad her into losing her temper in the first place.

She was just starting to wish she hadn't been quite so sharp with him when she noticed that Lady Tarbrook was no longer sitting by herself. Lord Becconsall's three friends, from the park, were standing all round her.

She felt his arm tense beneath her hand and darted him a look. Hadn't he known they were going to be here? Was he as embarrassed to see them, with her clinging to his arm, as she was going to be, to have to acknowledge them in front of Aunt Susan? Unwittingly, her fingers gripped Lord Becconsall's sleeve rather tightly, which was excessively stupid, since he was at the root of her potential humiliation.

But, as if sensing she needed reassurance, he patted her hand and kept his own resting over hers when they drew to a halt before her aunt's chair.

'Lady Harriet,' he said, 'permit me to introduce you to my friends. Lord Rawcliffe…' he indicated the one they'd called Zeus in the park '…Captain Bretherton of his Majesty's navy…' who was the skeletal giant '…and Mr Thomas Kellett.'

She let out a relieved breath as she curtsied to them all in turn. For he'd made it sound as though they had only just met for the first time tonight.

They all bowed in their turn and muttered suitable responses. Though each of them stared at her rather harder than absolutely necessary. And in the case of the one they called Zeus, with so much contempt in his eyes that he made her feel like some kind of…insect that he dearly wished to flick from his friend's sleeve and crush under his heel.

'Lady Tarbrook,' said Lord Becconsall, 'I can see they have already made themselves known to you.'

'Oh, I have known this scamp ever since he was in short coats,' she said, reducing Zeus from god to toddler with one offhand remark and a dismissive motion with her fan. The look on his face was priceless. Oh, how she admired her aunt.

'He has introduced me to his two friends,' said Aunt Susan. 'And yours, I now learn, Lord Becconsall.'

'Yes. We were all at school together.'

'Oh, that accounts for it,' said Lady Tarbrook, casting Mr Kellett a rather scathing look. As though he had no business hobnobbing with titled gentlemen. Or captains in his Majesty's navy.

Harriet felt indignant on his behalf. She hated to see anyone dismissed as being of no account, knowing exactly how it felt. For she'd been of no account pretty much all her life.

'I have heard of you, I think,' she said to the man she could have sworn they'd called Archie.

'Have you?' He peered at her through the fringe flopping into his puzzled brown eyes, putting her in mind of a shortsighted spaniel. 'C-can't think why you should have.'

'Lady Harriet is, perchance, a follower of all the latest scientific investigations,' said Lord Rawcliffe sarcastically, 'and has been impressed by the brilliance of your latest publication regarding your theories concerning the properties of dephlogisticated air.'

If there was one thing Harriet knew about, thanks to her mother's obsession with all things scientific, it was the vast range of theories currently being hotly debated regarding various gases.

'Not at all,' she said, flinging up her chin mutinously. 'There is nothing the least bit impressive about suffocating mice under glass domes.'

All three men changed the way they were looking at her.

Aunt Susan sighed. As if to say, *that is the end of that*. For she firmly believed that if there was one thing more detrimental to a girl's chances of success in the matrimonial stakes than being too old, it was being too clever.

But Lord Becconsall chuckled.

'You have underestimated her, Rawcliffe,' he said. 'She clearly knows all about the experiments to determine what it is in the air that sustains life.'

Something flashed between the two men. Something that looked suspiciously like rivalry. And for some reason she didn't understand, she felt like confirming the confidence Lord Becconsall had shown in her, whilst taking the odiously cynical Rawcliffe down a peg or two at the same time. She reached into the deepest recesses of her memory for anything her mother might have said, which she could fling at him.

'Well, who could fail to be interested by the experiments of the British Pneumatic Institution to attempt to treat disease by the inhalation of various gases,' she said, hoping she'd recalled the name of the society correctly.

'Science being put to a practical use, rather than merely for its own sake,' said Lord Becconsall at once, approvingly.

'Exactly,' she said without a qualm. Although she had no idea what gases were inhaled, or for what purpose, she didn't think she'd been too far from saying something vaguely intelligent, because Mr Kellett was nodding eagerly.

'It is a great p-pity Mr Davy d-did not pursue his initial experiments with factitious airs,' he said. 'I think he might have b-been on to something there. My own work—'

'For the lord's sake, do not start boring the present assembly with an exposition of your current experiments,' said Rawcliffe scathingly.

To her fury, Mr Kellett subsided at once, with the air of a spaniel who'd just been kicked by its master.

The naval officer patted Kellett's drooping shoulders in a sympathetic manner, which made her rather like him. He'd been the one to put a stop to the teasing in the park, too, now she came to think of it. That he'd done it by flinging her up into the saddle had infuriated her at the time, but at least he had enabled her to escape a situation that had been becoming downright unnerving.

'That's the trouble with being a genius, Archie,' said Lord Becconsall. 'You leave the rest of us floundering in the wake of your brilliance. We wouldn't understand the half of what you are saying.'

'Yes,' said Mr Kellett. 'Not the t-topic for a b-ballroom.' He shot Rawcliffe an abject look. 'Forgot.'

'No matter,' said Rawcliffe, his expression mellowing a touch. 'That is what you employ me for, is it not?'

'Employ you?' Aunt Susan's eyes rounded. 'But—you are one of the wealthiest men in England.'

So why wasn't she attempting to get him to notice Harriet? she wondered. Or, more to the point, Kitty? It could only mean there was something seriously wrong with him as a prospective husband. She'd have to ask her what it was later.

'It was my little joke, my lady,' said Rawcliffe with a sardonic smile. 'For, although my friend is, nominally, employed by me in the capacity of, ah, chaplain, is it not—' he gave Kellett a wry look '—I have long since learned that, when in pursuit of some new theory, he will give me orders for raw materials and equipment as though I am merely his assistant, whilst shamelessly poaching my staff to act in various menial capacities.'

Mr Kellett hung his head. 'Forget, sometimes. Sorry.'

'No need. When you make the discovery that will rock the scientific world, my name, too, will go down in history. As your sponsor and benefactor.'

'And indeed, I am sure it is very generous of you,' said Aunt Susan. Although she didn't look the slightest bit impressed. 'But, look, Harriet my dear. Here is Mr Swaffham come to claim his dance. If you will excuse her, my lords, Captain, Mr Kellett?'

Harriet had never been so glad to see someone coming over with the intention of asking her to dance. There was something about Lord Becconsall and his three friends that made her extremely uncomfortable. And it wasn't just the way she reacted, physically, to him. It was…the way they spoke as if each word had a hidden meaning, known only to the four of them. As if there were undercurrents beneath their behaviour that only they understood. Which effectively shut out the rest of the world.

And she'd had quite enough of being made to feel like an outsider by her own family. She had no desire to suffer the same kind of exclusion from people who were practically strangers.

Chapter Ten

Poor Mr Swaffham did not receive anything like the attention she'd bestowed upon him during their previous dances together. Because Harriet couldn't stop watching Lord Becconsall and his three friends, in spite of having told herself she wanted nothing to do with a group of men who'd first witnessed her behaving badly, then given her a bit of a scare and finally just made her feel excluded.

She watched them making their excuses to Aunt Susan and leaving her side almost as soon as Harriet had taken her place in the set. She watched them strolling round the room, greeting acquaintances or, in the case of the odious Lord Rawcliffe, cutting people he clearly regarded as impertinent for daring to accost him. And she watched them making their way, inexorably, in the direction of the exit.

She was glad they were leaving. She had no wish to speak to Lord Becconsall again. Or, heaven forbid, dance with him. No, twice in one night was entirely too much. People would start to link her name with his if she danced with him twice.

Oh. Would they do that with Mr Swaffham? She shot him a speculative glance as the dance came to an end. Thankfully, he was looking rather disgruntled, which meant that any speculation in that quarter was likely to be short-lived.

She smiled at him apologetically as he extended his arm to lead her back to her aunt. But from the cool way he took his leave of her it was highly unlikely he would be asking her to dance with him any time soon.

Oh, dear. Aunt Susan would be so disappointed.

In an effort to mitigate her offence Harriet sat up straight and drew her shoulders back. Not that Aunt Susan had admonished her for slouching. In fact, she wasn't watching Harriet at all. She was simply staring off into space and fanning herself rapidly. And, Harriet noticed with alarm, looking a most unhealthy colour.

'Aunt Susan, are you feeling quite well?'

Her aunt turned her head very slowly. And gulped.

It was all the answer Harriet needed.

'Come along, Aunt Susan,' she said, taking her by the elbow to encourage her to her feet. 'We'll go in search of fresh air, shall we?'

'Fresh air,' her aunt repeated in a weak voice. 'Yes, just the thing. It is very hot in here.' From the way the older woman was leaning on her, and the slight trembling she could feel through her limbs, Harriet thought her aunt might be perilously close to a faint. A *real* faint.

She glanced to right and left, desperately trying to recall the layout of the house. She'd been to the ladies' retiring room when she came in, of course, to leave her cloak and change into her dancing shoes. She was pretty certain that once they left the ballroom, they had to turn right and it would be down the stairs and just along the corridor.

She found a room exactly where she thought the retiring room should be, but the moment they went in, she realised her mistake.

'Oh, dear, I am so sorry,' she said, gazing round the empty room in consternation. 'I have lost my way.'

'It doesn't matter,' said Aunt Susan wearily. 'In fact, I would as soon sit in here quietly for a few minutes as have some gossipy maid fussing round me in the retiring room.' She tottered to the solitary sofa positioned before empty hearth and sank on to it. 'It is cooler in here, anyway, which is the main thing.'

'Is there something I can get for you? A glass of water?' There would have been all that sort of thing if only she'd got her aunt to the correct place. And although she'd said she didn't want a maid fussing, at least there would have been one who knew the layout of the house and who could fetch…she didn't know…a vinaigrette, or something.

'A glass of water?' Aunt Susan looked at her sharply. And then closed her eyes. 'That is it. That is why I came over all peculiar. With all the…fuss…today, I quite forgot to eat. I am feeling faint, that is what it is.'

'Well, then, shall I go and fetch you something to eat?'

Aunt Susan lay her head against the back of the sofa. 'Yes, please, if you wouldn't mind, dear. Just something light.'

Harriet backed out of the room, concern for her aunt chasing every other concern from her mind. But…where was the refreshment room? Back through the ballroom, unfortunately. She didn't want to go there, get a plate of food and a glass of water, and carry it back through the ballroom to her aunt. That would be such unusual behaviour it was bound to attract exactly the kind of attention her aunt wanted least. She racked her brains. Oh, if only Lord Becconsall *were* a proper suitor, she could go to him and ask him for help. As it was, she'd just have to find a footman to do the fetching and carrying for her.

She retraced her steps to the ballroom, aided by the sound of music, hoping there would be a servant free to see to her needs. And who could be persuaded to employ discretion.

The doors to the ballroom opened outwards and had been left open so that people could come and go with ease. But they had not been pushed quite flat to the wall. There was a slight gap behind which she could easily squeeze and from that vantage point she could peep in through the crack between the hinges and the wall, and locate a servant without anyone seeing her searching.

She was really glad she'd ducked behind the door out of sight of the other guests when not two seconds after she'd put her eye to the crack, Lord Becconsall and his three friends came strolling in her direction.

It was the shock of seeing them when she'd thought them long gone that made her watch them, rather than begin to search for a footman, she told herself the moment she realised what she was doing. It *wasn't* because there was something about Lord Becconsall that drew her gaze like iron filings to a magnet.

Although she couldn't deny he was a feast for the eyes. It was something about the way he carried himself. With that brisk, upright bearing that was in such stark contrast to the languid slouch of men who'd never done anything with their lives but drink and gamble and amuse themselves. The neat way his clothes moulded his muscular frame, without the slightest hint of flamboyance about his attire was pleasing, too. As was the way he looked as though he was never far from laughing.

Though the laughter was very often at her expense, the beast.

By the time she'd reached this stage in her cogitation, the four of them had drawn close enough to her hiding place for her to hear snatches of their conversation over the background noise of a ball in full progress.

'So, you agree then,' Lord Becconsall was saying. 'Lady Harriet and the girl in the park are one and the same person?'

She froze. Well, she'd been standing still anyway, but the mention of her name on his lips, in that context, made even the blood stop swirling through her veins.

'If you insist,' Zeus said, in a bored tone.

'No, come on, old chap, that is no way to treat such an important subject,' said Lord Becconsall, though he was grinning.

'The wager was only important to you,' said Zeus. 'I have genuinely important things on my mind.'

Wager? Lord Becconsall had made her the topic of a wager?

Harriet flattened herself against the wall as they passed on the other side of the door.

Lord Becconsall was laughing. 'You mean, that is what you are going to claim as the excuse for not finding her first,' he said. Quite clearly. 'That you were too busy to bother. And then say, when you pay up, that if you had more time, you would have beaten me...'

She didn't hear any more. They'd strolled past her and were heading for the stairs. Besides, there was a roaring sound in her ears that was drowning out everything else.

She'd thought…no, she'd hoped he'd been…fascinated by her. That he'd sought her out in the ballroom and brought her flowers because he…liked her. That he'd taken her out on to the terrace because he was concerned about her. That he'd prevented her from causing a scene because he felt protective of her. Even if he didn't want to actually marry her, she'd thought he *liked* her.

Oh, what an idiot she was! She was nothing more to him than the object of a bet. By the sound of it, whoever discovered her true identity first, out of the four of them, would win a tidy sum of money.

He'd probably kept her out on the terrace until he could see that his friends were all gathered round Aunt Susan's chair. Aunt Susan, who had, she now saw, confirmed her identity for them.

She clenched her fists against the pain that was tearing at her insides. The rage that felt as if it was clawing its way out of the same spot.

She would never speak to him again.

And as for pressing one of the flowers he'd given her as a keepsake, that felt like the height of absurdity now.

To think she'd actually…

There was the sound of someone clearing his throat.

'Excuse me, miss, may I be of assistance?'

She whirled round to see a wigged and powdered footman eyeing her as though she was some kind of lunatic.

She supposed she must look like one, leaning against

the wall behind the door, with her fists clenched and her mouth twitching with suppressed rage.

She uncurled her fists, lifted her chin and looked the footman in the eye.

'Yes, you may. My aunt, Lady Tarbrook, has been taken unwell.'

The moment she claimed Lady Tarbrook as a relative, the footman's demeanour became far more respectful.

'Do you wish me to call for your carriage?'

'No, thank you. She does not want to…to leave early, or…do anything to spoil the evening for my cousin. Her daughter.' Well, it must certainly be true, even though Aunt Susan had not said so. 'I have taken her to a little room downstairs, where it is cool and quiet. The one with the mirrors in the alcoves just outside?'

The footman nodded to indicate he knew exactly which room she meant.

'But…could you possibly bring us some refreshments? A glass of water. And some sandwiches and cake, too…' She bit down on her lower lip for a second, as it struck her that her aunt would not want even a servant to know she'd turned faint from forgetting to eat.

'I am going to sit with her, you see, which means we might well miss supper,' she said, hoping the explanation would throw him off the scent. She blushed though, not being used to telling fibs.

'Dancing does have a powerful effect on the appetite, doesn't it, miss,' said the footman, with a wink.

Well, it did, so she could nod, bashfully, and hope it made her look exactly like a maiden who was embarrassed to own up to having a healthy appetite. In public, gently reared girls were only supposed to pick at their food, as though they were merely being polite to their hostess. That was one of the tests she'd passed at the picnic, actually—refraining from showing too great an appreciation of all the dainties on offer, when she could easily have wolfed down three times the amount.

Once the smirking footman had gone about his business, she hurried back down the stairs, heading for the little room where she'd left her aunt, her mind whirling.

She should have known a handsome, experienced man like Lord Becconsall would not find her as interesting as she found him. She might have known there would be an ulterior motive behind the attention he'd paid her. After all, the only other men who'd sought her out had only done so because of her rank and fortune, or because Kitty hadn't time for them. But...to make her the subject of a wager!

She paused at the foot of the stairs as she caught sight of her reflection in both the mirrors hanging on either side of the door to her aunt's sanctuary. She'd always known she was nothing much to look at. She had a square face and nondescript brown hair. Ordinary eyes and a squashed-up-looking nose. Why on earth had she suddenly forgotten how very plain and ordinary she was? How completely lacking in personality, too. She'd never mastered the art of sparkling repartee. Well, nobody had taught her how to sparkle. Actually, nobody had taught her anything very much at all. If it hadn't been for the governess Aunt Susan had sent, cajoling her to run her fingers along the words as she'd read to her from all those books of fairy stories, she might never have learned to so much as read and write. And it had only been because the housekeeper had reached her wits' end over Mama's lack of interest in running Stone Court, and had started training Harriet to do what was necessary, that she knew the first thing about domestic economy, either.

The images in the mirrors blurred at the reminder of the haphazard way she'd been educated, if you could call it an education. She'd been of so little account that neither of her parents had even bothered to hire another governess for her, once the one Aunt Susan had sent had left to go and care for an elderly relative, let alone think of sending her to school. Most people in London already made her feel like a complete country bumpkin. But, actually, she was little better than a savage.

No wonder Lord Becconsall and his friends had no compunction about wagering on her the way they'd wager on a horse, or a dog.

She blinked rapidly to clear her vision. She'd been of no account to anyone, all her life. So why should it hurt so much to find she was still of no account, now she'd come to London? She had never expected anything else, had she?

But, oh, once Lord Becconsall had kissed her, and then turned up at a ball and asked her to dance, she'd...

She'd started to fall for him, that's what she'd done. In her head, she'd turned him into something like one of those handsome princes from the fairy tales she'd loved so much as a little girl. Because he was the first handsome, eligible man to speak to her as though she had something about her to interest him.

But it had all been a hum.

Of course it had.

The only person to ever really look out for her, and consider her future, and do something about it, was Aunt Susan.

Poor Aunt Susan, who was sitting alone, in a dark

little room, waiting for her glass of water and cake. Because she'd been too upset by her husband's refusal to believe in her innocence to eat today, when normally it was one of her greatest pleasures in life.

Casting her unimpressive reflections one last glance of loathing, Harriet headed for the room where she'd left her aunt.

Since Aunt Susan was the only person who'd ever put herself out for her, the least Harriet could do was find out what had really happened to the rubies she'd been falsely accused of pawning.

She'd spend the rest of this evening taking the very best care of the only person in the whole world who'd ever put themselves out for her, and then, first thing tomorrow, she'd resume investigations with a vengeance.

Chapter Eleven

It was all very well deciding she was never going to speak to Lord Beconsall again. But she soon discovered that it was not so simple putting that decision into practice.

Her first attempt to administer a resounding snub ran aground the moment she asked the butler not to admit him to the house.

Keeble raised his left eyebrow an infinitesimal fraction and gave her the kind of look she wished she could perfect herself so that she could use it on Lord Becconsall.

'You are passing on a message from Lady Tarbrook,' he suggested.

'Well, no.'

The eyebrow went up a further fraction.

'I just don't want to bother her with my, um, that is, she has troubles enough at the moment without…' She dried up, then, as Keeble's expression turned positively arctic.

'I could not possibly take it upon myself to deny admittance to a gentleman of Lord Becconsall's rank,' he said repressively, 'without direct orders from either his lordship or her ladyship.'

Harriet had found herself wrapping her arms about her waist. 'Oh, oh, well then, never mind,' she'd said lamely. And decided she would just have to give him the cold shoulder when he came to call. Which he was bound to do. Even if he had only danced with her for low, nefarious reasons he would still observe the proprieties the day after. All gentlemen did so. Even Mr Swaffham, who'd only asked her to dance because Kitty hadn't had time for him, had paid his duty call the day after. True, he'd spent the entire half-hour gazing across the room at Kitty rather than attempting to make conversation with her, but he'd come.

And today was no different. Mr Swaffham made his bow, sat next to Harriet on the sofa which Aunt Susan had decreed she occupy and accepted his cup of tea politely. But then his glances across the room to where Kitty was sitting, accepting compliments, very prettily, from a bevy of gentlemen who *had* managed to secure her hand for dances the previous night increased in frequency until they merged into one continuous stare.

He started as badly as Harriet when Keeble announced the arrival of Lord Becconsall and got to his feet at once.

Which left the spot on the sofa beside her perilously vacant.

When Lord Becconsall sat down she didn't know where to look. Or what to say. She knew what she wanted to say, of course, but she didn't have the courage to spit it out. Not in Aunt Susan's drawing room. Not after vowing she was going to do all in her power to defend and support her.

'This is pleasant,' said Lord Becconsall, glancing with amusement at the two gentlemen currently attempting to outshine each other with the wittiness and gallantry of their compliments to Kitty. 'I do so enjoy watching other men making complete cakes of themselves.'

Harriet grappled with the urge to ignore him. But then, she suspected that if she did so, he would carry on goading her and goading her until she…flew at him and slapped his impudent face.

So she schooled her features into what she hoped looked more like mild disdain than what she was really feeling and put on a voice that was frigidly polite.

'Are you implying that Mr Congleton and Lord Frensham are fools for paying court to Kitty in particular, or for taking any woman at all seriously?'

He leaned back and ran his eyes over her, one of his most annoyingly amused grins playing about his lips.

'Got out of bed the wrong side, did you? Or,' he said, leaning closer and lowering his voice, 'are you just jealous that she is having so much more success than you?'

She turned to face him, her blood boiling. Oh, how she wanted to slap him. Or…pull his nose, or tweak his ears or…simply poke him in the eye. Anything to wipe that horrid smirk from his face.

But if she did any of those things, it would create a scene. Which would wound Aunt Susan far more than it would hurt Lord Becconsall. In fact, he would probably find the whole thing vastly amusing.

He would be impervious to anything she could do.

Because he thought she was a joke. A huge joke.

Just then, the door to the drawing room opened again. But instead of Keeble announcing another visi-

tor, it was her uncle standing in the doorway. Which
caused all conversation in the room to falter, for he so
very rarely strayed into this room when it was full of
callers.

'Lady Harriet,' he said, beckoning to her in a perremp-
tory manner. 'A word, if you please.'

It felt like a reprieve. If she'd stayed sitting next to
Lord Becconsall one second longer, who knew what
she might have done next?

She got to her feet at once. Dropped Lord Becconsall
a perfunctory curtsy, since that was what Aunt Susan
would expect of her, and hurried over to her uncle.

He stepped out into the hall, inviting her to follow.
As soon as he'd closed the door on the drawing room,
her anger with Lord Becconsall faded to the back of
her mind. What on earth could have induced her uncle
to summon her this way? Surely, only some dire emergency would have him obliging her to leave the room
like this, in front of everyone. Could there be bad news
from home?

Papa? Oh, no. Her heart began to pound sickly in
her chest as she followed her uncle down the stairs and
along the hall to his study, which lay towards the back
of the house. She'd only ever been in here once before,
on the first night she'd arrived. She'd thought what a
lovely room it was then and had spent most of the time
he'd been telling her what he expected of her while she
was staying in his house admiring the view out of the
window, which overlooked a pleasant courtyard with
an ornamental fountain.

Today, however, she couldn't drag her eyes from her
uncle as, having indicated with a brusque gesture that

she should sit in the chair before his desk, he went round it to sit down himself.

He huffed. Frowned. Leaned back, making the chair creak. Leaned forward, folding his hands on the desk.

Harriet swallowed.

'I have had…something in the nature of a complaint,' he finally said. 'About your behaviour.'

'Oh?' Not Papa, then. Thank heaven. But…had somebody told him about her tussle on the grass with Lord Becconsall? How typical that would be, to be found out now she'd vowed never to speak to him again. Knowing her uncle, he'd insist it was grounds for marriage. And the only person who would be more appalled at the prospect would be Lord Becconsall himself.

It wouldn't surprise her if he was so appalled that he sought out a regiment that was serving overseas and joined up at once.

But what if he was wounded? Killed? Her stomach turned over.

'It pains me to have to be the one to say this,' said Uncle Hugo, breaking through the chaos raging inside her head. 'But as things stand, I cannot trust Lady Tarbrook to set you to rights.' He scowled.

She said nothing. What was there to say? That she'd already learned her lesson, in the worst way possible? To confess that at some time just after dawn, having been unable to sleep, she'd seen that most people would say she'd probably deserved for Lord Becconsall to treat her as a joke, because of the way she'd behaved. That she shouldn't have been out in the park, unattended. And that, therefore, whatever had happened since was entirely her own fault.

That on the whole, she could see their point.

'It is one thing ordering my staff to refuse admittance to my house to certain gentlemen,' he began. 'Though really, if you find some suitor unacceptable, you should have spoken to your aunt and explained why, and then she would have taken care of it.'

She hung her head to conceal any expression of relief that might have flitted across her face. It didn't sound as if he'd found out about her escapade in the park. Or he would have opened with that. Besides which she was a bit ashamed of having tried to go round the problem of Lord Becconsall instead of facing it head on. She knew it wasn't her place to give such orders to Lord and Lady Tarbrook's staff, but if she'd gone to her aunt in the regular way, she'd have wanted to know what her objection was to Lord Becconsall. And she simply couldn't face telling her.

'But as for questioning them about the fate of the Tarbrook parure...' he breathed very loudly through his nostrils, which were pinched and white, she noticed as she raised her head in surprise '...that, I have to tell you, young lady, is going beyond what is acceptable. My staff,' he said, getting to his feet, 'have been for the most part with me since I was a boy. I trust them all implicitly. And to have them all upset by accusations of...theft, is something I will not have. Do you understand me?'

By the time he spoke the last words he was standing right over her, his brows drawn down. If he hadn't been, she might have blurted out that it was a great pity he didn't feel the same about upsetting his wife with similar accusations.

'I...I didn't accuse anyone of anything,' she said mulishly. 'I only asked if anyone had any suspicions. The servants are, after all, the best people to know what goes on in a big household—'

She flinched as Uncle Hugo slammed his fist down on his desk.

'Enough! I will not have you answer me back in that insolent fashion. A mere chit of a girl like you. It would serve you right if I packed you back off to the country, where you clearly belong if you are so ungrateful for this chance my wife has seen fit to give you, that you go round upsetting the household by making the servants fear they are about to be accused of something that is a hanging offence!'

Only a few days ago, she'd thought the threat of being sent back to the country might have come as a relief. Because it was where she belonged. London, and London society, was like a foreign country to her. She scarcely spoke the same language as the natives. And their customs and habits made very little sense to her.

But at that time she hadn't fully appreciated just how much she owed Aunt Susan. To abandon her, now, would be an appalling act of selfishness. Even if it would be a means of escaping Lord Becconsall.

So she hung her head and attempted to look repentant.

Actually, she *was* a bit repentant now that Uncle Hugo had told her how she'd made the staff feel. She hadn't considered the fact that theft of such precious items was a hanging offence.

'I never meant to frighten anyone,' she said with genuine remorse. She lifted her head to look her uncle straight in the eye, to show him that she was being completely honest. 'I just thought that one of the staff might have seen something suspicious. Or at least been able to say exactly when the last time the genuine stones had been seen…'

'You are not to plague any of my staff with any more of your impertinent questions about this matter, do you hear me?'

She nodded. For just about everyone in the house must have heard. When Uncle Hugo got angry, his voice carried.

'Because if you do, I shall most certainly send you back where you came from. And that will be the end of any chance some decent man might marry you. Though why on earth any man of sense would wish to…' He looked at her as though she was a worm. 'I believe there is a certain type who would overlook your lack of address because of your fortune, but what man could stomach a woman who…meddles in things that don't concern her? That answers back?'

'I…' She bit down on the retort that she hadn't answered back, since that would have been answering back.

'Go to your room and stay there,' he bellowed. 'And think about the consequences of your actions this day.'

She didn't hesitate. She got out of her chair and scurried to the door. Oh, not because her uncle frightened her. Although it was a bit disconcerting to have a grown man standing over her, shouting right into her face. It was Harriet's guilty conscience that was making her so uncomfortable. Because it really was unforgivable to upset the servants so badly. Badly enough for them to break with all the etiquette that appeared to govern them and make a complaint about her.

As if that weren't bad enough, worse was to come. Just as she reached the foot of the stairs, who should she see descending them but Lord Becconsall.

He was frowning. And his eyes were flicking from where she was standing clutching at the newel post for support to the door of her uncle's study.

He must have seen her coming out. He'd probably heard her uncle shouting. And he'd definitely seen her being hauled unceremoniously out of the drawing room.

Not that he cared. Not about her. That frown, that expression of concern, couldn't possibly be concern on her behalf. For a man like that cared only about himself. And his stupid friends. And their stupid wagers.

So he was probably wondering if somehow, someone had told her uncle what she'd been up to in the park. Or, more likely, told tales about her going out on to the terrace with him last night.

Yes, he was probably scared that her warning about him having to marry her if anyone should find out he'd kissed her was about to come true.

Well, he need not be. She would rather spend the rest of her days…well…*anywhere* than married to him when it was clearly the last thing he wanted. In the hopes of conveying her determination to do anything rather than be dragged down the aisle to marry him, she lifted her chin, prised her fingers from the newel post, urged her feet into motion and began to mount the stairs.

'Lady Harriet…' he began in an urgent undertone as she drew level with him.

She shot him a scathing glance, tossing her head for good measure, and kept right on climbing the stairs.

And then she strode along the corridor to her room with her head held high. Without looking back to see his reaction to her snub.

Not even once.

Chapter Twelve

She didn't slam the door to her room behind her. But she did attempt to relieve her feelings by marching across to the dressing table and kicking the stool. Which hurt like blazes.

Cursing under her breath, she hopped over to her bed and sat down quickly. As she sat there cradling her foot, wondering if she'd broken a bone, she listened to callers leaving and callers arriving. Eventually the hour for paying such calls came to an end and the house fell quiet. Relatively quiet. She heard Kitty's footsteps hurry past her room and then the sound of her bedroom door open and close. Her little bedroom clock struck the hour twice, but it wasn't until she heard the family making their way to the dining room that she began to wonder if she was not only confined to her room, but also going to be deprived of food and drink.

Which made her get up and start pacing the room angrily. That she was able to do so came as some relief in regard to her toe. At least she had only bruised, rather than broken, it.

Nevertheless, she didn't kick any other item of furniture, even when she heard evidence that the family had not only dined without her, but were also getting ready to go out, without a single one of them deigning to see if there was anything she might need.

She'd just flung herself on to her bed, with her poor injured foot at the head so that she could treat it to the softness of half-a-dozen pillows, when the door opened to reveal her aunt, all dressed up ready to go out, but looking far from well enough to do so.

'Aunt Susan, I am so sorry,' said Harriet, instantly struck with remorse for having spent the day thinking of nobody but herself. Uncle Hugo had probably used her behaviour as yet another stick to beat Aunt Susan with. Metaphorically, that was.

'I didn't mean to cause you any trouble,' she said, scrambling to sit up. 'Or upset the servants. I just couldn't bear to think of you bearing the blame any longer. I hoped to find out...'

'Oh, my dear,' said Aunt Susan, glancing over her shoulder guiltily before coming in and shutting the door behind her. 'It is better, really, that the world should believe that I sold the jewels to pay gambling debts and had the stones copied, than that a serious enquiry should be made.'

'What? No! Surely—'

'Hush.' She came across the room and sat down on the bed, next to Harriet. 'Let me explain something to you,' she said, taking hold of her hands. 'It will help you to understand your uncle's attitude over this. I know you think he is being harsh and unforgiving, but it is not the case. You see,' she went on hurriedly when Harriet took a breath to protest that it *was* the case and she would *never* forgive him. 'When he was a boy, his mother...

lost a string of pearls. She accused a servant, who hadn't been with the family for very long, of stealing them. The maid swore she was innocent, but his mother insisted it must have been her, since nobody else had access to them. She was found guilty and hanged. And then… the pearls turned up.'

'What? How dreadful!'

'Yes. His mother never forgave herself. She'd sent an innocent woman to the gallows. You can imagine the effect it must have had upon him. Which is why, though it has upset me, I…I can forgive Lord Tarbrook for being so insistent on blaming me, when he must know…' Her lower lip trembled.

'Well, anyway, enough of that. You are not to be permitted to come out with us tonight. Though, I take it, that will not concern you too much?' She tilted her head and looked Harriet in the eye. 'Since you seem determined to avoid a certain…gentleman?'

'Oh, dear. Yes, that is something else I need to apologise for. Uncle Hugo told me I had no right to have your butler refuse admittance to any of his guests. It was just that—'

'You have taken him in strong aversion.'

'Yes.' She found she couldn't look her aunt in the eye. Instead she gazed down at where her own hands were being held between her aunt's bejewelled fingers as she braced herself to face some awkward questions.

But her aunt only sighed.

'Well, no matter. He is not exactly a splendid catch. Although he comes from a good family and has a comfortable income, his reputation is that he is not all that… steady. Had I been thinking more clearly I might have given him a hint he was wasting his time in the first place. However, you appeared to like him, so…'

'Yes, I did, at first. It is just that…' She swallowed, wondering how to continue that sentence without owning up to what she'd done, or what he'd done, or what she'd subsequently overheard.

'First impressions can be deceptive. And I don't forget that he was the first man of any real consequence to pay you attention. However, I am sure he won't be the last, so we will say no more.'

She was sure he wouldn't be the last? Harriet lifted her head to stare in astonishment at her aunt. That definitely wasn't what Uncle Hugo thought. He'd told her she was so worthless and unattractive that only a desperate fortune-hunter would be prepared to overlook her faults. He'd been so cutting and cruel that if she'd been a sensitive sort of girl she would have been devastated. Fortunately, he'd already revealed his true colours by the way he'd treated his own wife. Her lovely, lovely Aunt Susan, who was trying to make her feel better instead of crushing her when she was already down.

'I shall tell your uncle that I have found you suitably penitent,' said Aunt Susan. 'And not mention your obvious relief that you don't have to face the ordeal of yet another ball. It would quite spoil his conviction that he is being extremely strict with you,' she said, much to Harriet's amazement. In the space of three minutes, Aunt Susan had not only expressed an opinion which was the very opposite of the man she normally deferred to on all matters, but now she was proposing to actually hoodwink him!

'I shall have Maud bring you up some supper the

moment we have gone out. You can manage until then? You are not too hungry?'

'No, thank you Aunt Susan,' she said, wishing there was some way to express the sudden surge of affection she felt for her brave, kindly and compassionate aunt. Who was always trying to see the good in people, even when experience must have taught her that there wasn't all that much, all that often.

'I will also select a few journals and books for you to read. I see no reason why you should be deprived of all forms of entertainment, just because you are not allowed to leave your room. Especially since...' She trailed off, looking guilty. Leaving Harriet wondering what she'd been about to say. She hoped that Aunt Susan might have thought about saying she was touched by Harriet's belief in her innocence. Or that she didn't think the things she'd done warranted confinement in her room. But to do either would have meant openly declaring that she no longer believed her husband was infallible. And she clearly wasn't yet ready to commit such open sacrilege.

It wasn't long after Aunt Susan left her room that Harriet heard everyone going downstairs. She went to the window to watch the family get into the coach and go out. She folded her arms as the coach merged with the traffic going around the square and shook her head over the tale Aunt Susan had told her, about the innocent servant going to the gallows. She'd done it to try to make her believe that Uncle Hugo wasn't a complete ogre, of course. But, well, it had given her food for thought.

For one thing, she could see that Uncle Hugo did have a good reason for behaving the way he'd done.

For another, if she'd known about the awful fate of that poor servant girl in his childhood, she would never have asked the servants so many questions about Aunt Susan's rubies. They must all be terrified the same kind of thing might be going to happen all over again.

Which made it impossible to ask them anything else.

Which meant poor Aunt Susan was just going to have to bear the blame.

Which wasn't fair! She couldn't have had the jewels copied. She just wouldn't do such a thing.

She leaned her head against the cool panes of glass. And it was just as if some of its clarity seeped right into her head. Because she could suddenly see that although the horrid fate of that serving girl had come as a complete surprise to her, there must be plenty of other people who knew all about it. A story that shocking was bound to have been broadcast far and wide at the time. You couldn't keep a story like that hushed up, no matter how hard a family tried to do so.

She straightened up. Anyone who knew about it would also know how reluctant Uncle Hugo would be to question his servants very closely. That he'd be much more likely to pretend nothing had happened rather than risk sending another innocent to the gallows.

And if they knew the family well enough to have heard about that old scandal, then they'd probably also know how infrequently Aunt Susan got the rubies out of the…well, wherever it was she kept them.

Oh, how she wished she hadn't promised she wouldn't ask the servants any more questions. Because now Aunt Susan had told her all about those pearls, it had shone light on the mystery of the fake rubies in a whole new way. She no longer needed to look for the

kind of thief who'd climb in through a window. Someone like…a close friend of the family would have had
far more opportunity to effect the swap. Someone who
could walk into the house as though they had every
right to be there.

She'd just reached that conclusion when someone
scratched at the door, then came straight in. It was
Maud, with her supper, and Peter with a bundle of magazines and a couple of novels.

Neither of them looked at her, but simply set their
burdens down on the nearest surface.

'Please,' said Harriet, darting forward, her hand outstretched. 'Would you be so kind as to convey my heart-
felt apologies to all the staff? I never meant to frighten
anyone. I never imagined I *could* frighten anyone. It
is just that my aunt has been so good to me and, seeing her so upset over being accused of something I just
know she couldn't have done, well, I wanted to clear
her name. It never occurred to me that clearing her
name might mean casting suspicion on any of you. I
am sure none of you would do anything so disloyal. I
just thought you might have some suspicion of…well,
how an intruder might have got in. Or something,' she
finished, her heart sinking as both maid and footman
regarded her with identically stony faces.

'Will that be all?'

'Yes,' said Harriet, on a sigh. She'd done what she
could. It was up to them whether they chose to forgive
her or not.

The next morning, when Maud came in to open her
curtains and set out her wash water, Harriet could barely
resist the temptation to pull her quilt up over her ears

and pretend she was still asleep. *Still* asleep? She didn't feel as if she'd slept for more than brief snatches all night. If it wasn't her guilt over the mess she'd made of trying to question the servants that had kept sleep at bay, it was cringing reminders of the way she'd started to feel about Lord Becconsall. In spite of him warning her not to.

Whenever she did drop off to sleep, the dreams that plagued her were so uncomfortable she jerked out of them as soon as she could. Either Lord Becconsall and his friends were lurking behind some bushes, all pointing and laughing at her. Or he was holding her in his arms and kissing her breathless. And in the dreams where he was kissing her, he sometimes had the rubies held behind his back. Whenever she woke up she puzzled over that, because she didn't really believe he had anything to do with the theft. Eventually she worked out that it was just her mind jumbling up the one fraud— the switch of the jewels for fakes—with his deceptive appearance of friendship. Or whatever it was that she'd thought had been growing between them.

In any case, all the dreams told her the same thing. She was a fool. A gullible, clumsy, ridiculous fool. And now it was morning and her eyes were gritty and her head felt as if it was full of sponge. Sponge that had soaked up too much unpleasantness and was consequently pressing at the inside of her skull.

But Maud, once she'd seen to her chores, seemed to be in no hurry to leave her in peace to mope. In fact, she stood at the foot of the bed, her hands clasped at her waist, and cleared her throat.

Repressing a moan, Harriet sat up, hugged her knees to her chest and looked the maid in the eye.

'Yes?'

Maud cleared her throat again. 'Well, Miss Harriet, it's like this. We, all of us, want to say that we're that sorry about the way Lord Tarbrook has taken our complaint. We never dreamed he'd haul you out of the drawing room like that, not when it was chock full of visitors. Especially not when that nice Lord Becconsall what is just starting to show an interest in you was there.'

Harriet made a dismissive wave of her hand at the mention of Lord Becconsall.

'We just wanted you to stop asking so many questions,' persisted Maud. 'For the older ones, see, it brought back so many bad memories.'

'I know,' said Harriet. 'That is, Lady Tarbrook explained it to me last night. It must have been dreadful.'

'Oh, yes it was, miss. I mean, my lady,' Maud corrected herself, dropping a curtsy.

'And as I said last night, I wasn't trying to point the finger of blame at any of you. I just thought that someone might have come into the house while you were all away. Or out for the evening, or something of the sort.'

'What, and broke in again another time to put the fakes back in place?' Maud shook her head. 'Couldn't have been done.'

'No, I quite see that,' said Harriet, her breath quickening a bit. Because she was technically breaking her word about not talking to the servants about the rubies.

Or was she? After all, it had been Maud who'd brought the subject up.

'Couldn't have been done when we were all away at a house party, neither,' Maud continued of her own volition. 'Her ladyship takes all her gewgaws along with her, rather than leave them behind in an empty house.

Even the ones she has no intention of wearing.' Maud frowned as if in confusion.

And Harriet racked her brains to remember the exact wording of what she'd promised her uncle. She was pretty sure she'd only promised not to ask the servants any more questions. Not to refrain from speaking about the topic at all. Especially not if they were the ones who brought it up.

Having squared it with her conscience, Harriet made a statement that could in no way be interpreted as a question.

'It's…it's a puzzle, isn't it?'

'That it is. But we none of us can believe her ladyship done it. What his lordship suggested. Only if she didn't, then it must have been one of us, that's what they'd say.'

By the sound of it, overnight the servants had been discussing not only whether to accept Harriet's apology, but also the mystery of the fake rubies as well.

If she subtly dropped her own ideas into the conversation, they might go away and discuss it some more. That wasn't actually asking them questions, was it?

'I was thinking,' she said tentatively, 'that if it wasn't any of you, and it wasn't my aunt, and it wasn't a burglar who broke in, then that only leaves…'

'Yes?' Maud leaned forward, clearly eager to hear Harriet's theory.

'Well, a close family friend. Or at least, someone who could come and go without rousing suspicion.'

'Yes, but I still don't see how they *could* have done it. Her ladyship would know straight off if those rubies had been missing long enough to have them copied.'

'Oh.' Harriet sank back on to her pillows. 'Well, I suppose that's that then. Lord Tarbrook,' she said airily, 'will no doubt hold this over my aunt's head for the rest of their married lives.'

Maud's face fell. She clearly didn't like that outcome any more than Harriet did.

'Will that be all, my lady?'

'Yes, thank you, Maud,' said Harriet. 'And thank everyone below stairs, won't you, for understanding why I was so…well, tactless.'

'Oh, we understand that right enough,' said Maud, with a shy smile. 'You didn't mean no harm. Not one of us has ever thought that.'

'Thank you,' said Harriet, blushing.

Maud curtsied, turned away and had just reached the door when she suddenly paused. And stiffened.

'What is it?' Harriet sat bolt upright again. 'You have thought of something, haven't you?'

'Well, it's probably nothing,' said Maud, turning slowly. 'It's just, now I'm not so angry about you accusing us, and thinking about it a bit more clear, like, about what you said about some outsider coming in…' She shook her head again. 'No, I still don't see how…'

'What? Please tell me. After all,' she said with a hollow laugh, 'it isn't as if I can do anything, can I?'

The maid shook her head again. 'Even if you could, I'm not the sort to go casting blame on those who can't defend themselves. But, well, I think I shall just ask Mr Keeble what he thinks.'

And having delivered that tantalising hint that she did, finally, have a suspect in mind, she whisked out of the room, closing the door firmly behind her.

Harriet flung herself back on to the bed with a shriek of frustration. The maid knew something. Or suspected something. But she didn't trust Harriet enough to confide in her.

Still, at least the servants were all talking about it. Which was all she'd wanted them to do. If anyone could work out what had really happened to those rubies, it was bound to be one of them.

So all she had to do now was wait until they'd done so. And hope that they had the courage to confront Uncle Hugo with their conclusions.

And in the meantime, she might as well get up and get washed and dressed. It would give her *something* constructive to do. Because she could see that it was going to be a long, long day.

Chapter Thirteen

Once Harriet was dressed there didn't seem to be anything to do but go and lay back down on the bed again. Where she stared up at the ruched canopy. For about five minutes. It was just too hard to stay here, with nothing to do, when she so badly ached to *do* something.

She strode to the window and imagined going out there and...

Doing what?

She whirled away in frustration. She had no idea where to start, that was the trouble. Because she was so ignorant.

An ignorant, naive country miss, that was all she was. A girl who was no good for anything in London but to serve as the butt of jokes made by sophisticated, heartless males with nothing better to do with themselves than make sport of ignorant, country...

She was going round in circles. On the carpet as well as in her head.

Though at least she hadn't yet yielded to the temptation to kick anything. She'd learned her lesson on the dressing-table stool.

See? She wasn't a *complete* idiot. She could learn some things. When it came to the hardness of dressing-table stools or men's hearts, that was.

From then on, her day followed pretty much the same pattern. For hour after hour, it seemed to Harriet, she either lay on the bed staring at the ruched canopy, or paced up and down, glaring at the carpet. She had just reached the stage where she was cursing the canopy for its inability to inspire her with a clever plan of campaign and the carpet for being entirely too frivolous with its stupid swirly patterns that only encouraged her mind to go round and round in circles, when the door flew open.

'I cannot believe Hugo could be such a tyrant,' said her mother, stalking across to the bed on which Harriet was currently lying. 'Besides which he has no right to confine you to your room. He is not your father.'

Goodness. Harriet sat up, slowly, stunned to see her mother so worked up on her behalf.

'Get up and get your hat on. You are coming out with me.'

'With you?' Golly. Mama had never invited her to go anywhere with her before. Not even to church. Although that was because Mama frequently forgot what day it was when she was deep in some piece of experimentation and so rarely attended Saint Martin's herself.

As her mother disappeared into the dressing room, Harriet swung her legs to the floor.

'The things he said,' Harriet heard her mother exclaim, although in a rather muffled voice since she'd just opened the door to the armoire and stuck her head inside. 'As if it was my fault you have an enquiring mind and have been asking awkward questions.'

Ah. That explained Mama's sudden interest in her

daughter. Uncle Hugo must have declared his conviction that Harriet took after her and said it as though it was an insult, and Mama had obviously taken it personally.

'This will do,' she said, thrusting a relatively plain bonnet at her. 'I am not off to some foolish *ton*nish event, so there is no need to make any work for one of Hugo's precious servants, since he appears to hold them in higher regard than his own family.'

Oh, dear. Uncle Hugo must have told Mama exactly why Harriet had been confined to her room.

'And the dress you are wearing,' she said, flicking her eyes over Harriet's crumpled gown, 'is perfectly acceptable for a lecture at the Royal Institution. Besides which you will put on a coat to cover it up,' she declared, turning to rummage in the armoire again.

'The Royal Institution?' Harriet gulped. 'You are actually taking *me* to a public lecture? With you?'

'Why should I not? It will be an educational experience for you. Mr Babbage, who is giving the lecture today, is one of the greatest minds of our age.'

Wonderful. Harriet pictured an elderly man with unkempt hair and less than pristine clothing droning on about some subject she knew absolutely nothing about. Possibly in Latin.

'And there is no need to look like that. It will be most interesting, I promise you.'

That wasn't likely. But it was certainly better than staying here staring at either the canopy or the carpet.

And going out would feel as though she was thumbing her nose at Uncle Hugo, a prospect that cheered her up to no end.

Besides which, this was the first time her mother had taken up the cudgels on her behalf about anything. And though it had more to do with her long-standing feud with Uncle Hugo than genuine affection for her daughter, it was still a sort of milestone in their relationship. And deserved acknowledging.

'Thank you, Mama,' she therefore said meekly, setting the bonnet on her head and tying the ribbons under her chin.

Mama nodded and set off at a brisk pace along the landing, obliging Harriet to trot to keep up with her. She then sailed down the stairs and across the hall with her nose in the air. Harriet wasn't at all sure the footman on duty would have opened the door and let them out, when he'd seen her trailing behind her mother, but fortunately for all concerned, just as they reached the door, somebody knocked on it. So when Peter opened it to admit an afternoon caller, he could not be blamed when the two houseguests made use of the fact to escape.

'Ah, good afternoon, Lady Balderstone,' said the plump matron panting her way up the front steps as they were descending.

'Is it?' said Mama frostily, carrying on her way without so much as a pause to nod a greeting.

Harriet eyed her mother with grudging admiration. Wouldn't it be wonderful to be able to get away with ignoring people to whom one didn't wish to talk? Especially women who were only trying to push their noses into your private business.

'We can catch a hackney cab at the corner,' said Mama, setting off in that direction, 'if memory serves me correctly.'

Harriet scurried off after her. 'Shouldn't we have,' she began hesitantly, 'a footman to procure one for us?' Or a maid to go with them.

Mama made a noise Harriet was sure no lady ought to make, being something less than a snort, but very much more than a sniff. 'If you think I am going to send Hugo's servants on errands, when he has made it quite clear he thinks their sensibilities are of more importance than the welfare of any member of the Inskip family, then he is very much mistaken.'

'It isn't that,' panted Harriet. 'It is just that Aunt Susan said I was not to go anywhere in Town without a maid or a footman.' She didn't mind flouting Uncle Hugo's edicts, but it was a different matter to appear to disregard everything her aunt had been trying to teach her.

'As your mother I am a perfectly adequate chaperon, *wherever* I choose to take you,' she said, waving her umbrella in a militant fashion at the first cab she saw.

'Yes, of course you are, Mama, I didn't mean—'

'Although I must say that the rules that apply to girls are completely unfair. They are designed to restrict the freedoms of an entire sex,' she said, causing the jarvey to stare and fumble the reins, just as they were attempting to climb into his vehicle, 'whilst bolstering the mastery of the other. The world would be a better place,' she said, taking her seat, 'if such rules did not exist and mankind lived in a state of intellectual, spiritual and legal harmony.'

Goodness. She'd never expected to hear her own views pouring from the lips of her own mother. But then, when had Mama ever bothered to sit down and have a conversation with her?

'Why are you pulling that face,' said Mama peering at her across the narrow space between the seats. 'I sincerely hope that my sister and her tyrannical husband have not managed to indoctrinate you with their views, in so short a space of time.'

'Goodness, no, Mama,' said Harriet. 'On the contrary, I was just thinking that I am more like you than I ever suspected.'

'Oh?' Now it was Mama's turn to look surprised. 'Are you become interested in the natural sciences, then?'

How was that likely to have happened, when Harriet had never had the kind of education that would have made it possible?

'No,' she said coldly. 'I was referring to my temperament.'

'Oh, that, yes. Tarbrook did mention something about the apple not falling far from the tree. He has never liked me,' she finished with a curl of her lip, indicating the feeling was mutual. 'He prefers his women meek and submissive. I sometimes wonder if he does not have a great deal of confidence in himself, that he has to browbeat all those around him to such a degree.'

Harriet tried to imagine her uncle feeling insecure about himself and failed. If anything, she suspected the opposite of what her mother had suggested. That he believed in himself so completely that he couldn't understand why anyone could possibly have an opinion that ran counter to his own.

Much like Mama.

No wonder they clashed.

'Ah, here we are,' said Mama unnecessarily as the cab jerked to a halt. It had taken such a short time to reach Albemarle Street that, once again, Harriet wondered why they had taken a cab at all. Why was it such a crime to use one's own legs to get wherever you wanted to go in Town?

Mama clambered out first and, while she was paying the driver, Harriet studied the large colonnaded building in which she was about to endure several hours of boredom. She was rather surprised by the number of other carriages drawing up along the street and the many people heading their way. She would never have guessed, from the way Aunt Susan behaved, that so many people of the *ton* would willingly spend an afternoon attending something educational. But there was no disputing the quality of many of the carriages coming and going, or the stylish clothing of their occupants.

Inside the lecture hall the benches were arranged in a vast semi-circle that reminded her of a Roman amphitheatre and looked as though they could seat several hundred people. Most people who were already there had taken seats at the front, near a central sort of pit in which stood a table loaded with books. Those who hadn't, nodded greetings to Mama as she stalked past them, though she didn't pause to make any introductions.

She learned why as they took their seats.

'Only just made it in time,' said Mama. 'I should have been most displeased if my detour to fetch you had caused me to miss the opening statements.'

Having neatly put Harriet in her place, Mama then gave her full attention to the talk that followed.

To Harriet's surprise, it was not about gases—which she'd thought was Mama's latest field of enquiry—but stars. And she could actually understand some of it.

Still, it wasn't long before her attention began to stray. There was only so much science a girl could stomach. Which made her wonder why there were so many females present. And some of them dressed, contrary to what Mama had said, with what could only be described as flamboyance.

She was just wondering what on earth had prompted an extremely thin young lady to wear a turban with feathers in, unless it was to annoy the gentlemen seated behind her, when she noticed that the gentleman in question was Lord Becconsall. And far from seeming annoyed by the feathers, he had his eyes closed. And his arms folded across his chest. As though he was taking a nap.

Which was just typical. While everyone else was hanging on every word uttered by Mr...she frowned as she tried to recall the name and only came up with Cabbage, though she wasn't convinced that was correct... Ulysses—that was, Lord Becconsall—was gently snoring.

She sniffed and turned her head away. What kind of man attended a lecture only to fall asleep during its course? A man who would...make a girl think he found her attractive, intriguing, only to...dash her hopes by... well, to be honest he had no idea he'd dashed any hopes. Because he didn't know she'd discovered he was only interested in her as the subject of a wager.

But if he thought she was going to dance with him again, let alone speak to him, then he'd very soon discover his mistake.

For the next few minutes Harriet amused herself by constructing several speeches in her head, all of them designed to annihilate his considerable self-esteem with the eloquence of her witheringly crushing wit. And was therefore rather surprised when suddenly everyone around her began to applaud. And the man at the central desk bowed. Then people began to get to their feet.

'Well,' said Mama. 'What did you think of that?'

'Um…' said Harriet, desperately trying to think of a polite response.

Mama sighed. 'If I had brought William *he* would have found it most instructive.'

Harriet flinched at the mention of Mama's favourite child and, since her head was already full of pithy rejoinders, she found herself uttering one.

'Well, since William is several thousand miles away, hunting for plants, you could not very well have done so, could you, Mama?'

Instead of slapping her down for her impertinence, though, Mama just shook her head. 'The only one of you to take after me,' she said morosely. 'Or so I have always believed.' She looked at Harriet. Really looked at her, instead of through her. 'But there is more of my temper about you than I had thought. Perhaps,' she said, gathering her reticule as though in preparation for standing up, 'though you do not show any signs of great intellect, it might be worth my while spending more time with you.'

What? All it had taken for Mama to wish to spend more time with her was for her to be rude? She wished she'd known that years ago.

Or perhaps not. Spending time with Mama would mean sitting through more lectures like this one, only to be told at the end that she was a disappointment for not having much in the way of intellect. She preferred going round the shops with her aunt. At least at the end of what Mama would condemn as an afternoon frittered away, she had some new clothes to show for the experience. Which had been purchased from motives of generosity, even if they hadn't, so far, been exactly a success.

'Good afternoon, Lady Harriet,' said a voice close to her ear. The voice of Lord Becconsall.

For a moment she contemplated cutting him. But before she could sniff, or turn her head away, or anything like that, he'd turned his attention to her mother.

'And you must be Lady Balderstone.' He bowed over Mama's hand.

'Indeed,' said Mama. 'A friend of Harriet's, are you?'

'I like to think so,' said Lord Becconsall provocatively. To Harriet's mind. Since he was nothing of the kind. And then he stepped slightly to one side to reveal Archie. 'Allow me to introduce my friend, Mr Kellett,' he said to Mama.

'Kellett?' Mama practically thrust Harriet aside to seize the young man's hand. 'Not Thomas Kellett? *The* Thomas Kellett?'

'Ah,' said Archie, going rather red in the face.

'The Thomas Kellett who has been doing such splendid work with the isolation of the essential elements?'

'Ah, well, you know,' he said, his face lighting up, 'nothing like the strides being made by Nicholson and Carlisle with natronium and kallium, but I am hoping, now that I have constructed my own voltaic pile...'

Harriet stifled a sigh. Once people began to pepper their sentences with words ending in -*ium* there would be no understanding the half of it.

'So now I know where you have acquired your knowledge of all things scientific,' said Lord Becconsall, with a mocking smile. Which set her teeth on edge all the way down her spine. 'Your mother is, according to Archie, something of a phenomenon.'

'And I suppose he wouldn't let you rest until he had been introduced,' she said acidly.

'Correct,' said Lord Becconsall, oblivious to her dig about him sleeping through the lecture. Clearly she was going to have to speak more bluntly if she was going to succeed in insulting him.

'You managed to get quite a bit of sleep, none the less, though, didn't you?'

'Lady Harriet,' said Lord Becconsall with a mocking smile. 'Never say you were watching me, rather than attending to the lecture?' He laid his hand upon his heart. 'I am touched. Deeply touched.'

'I was not watching you rather than attending—'

'No? Then, you will be able to fill me in on the salient points. Archie is bound to want to talk about them on the way home and I should not wish to disappoint him by being unable to contribute to the conversation.'

'First of all, I very much doubt that. I think you are far more likely to tell him, to his face, without the slightest hint of shame, that you slept through pretty much the whole lecture. And second...'

'Second?' His smile twisted into a grin. 'Let me guess. Knowing you, I suspect you were about to admit that your mind wandered far too often for you to be able to so much as tell anyone even one thing Mr Babbage said.'

Babbage, that was it, not Cabbage.

'But you do not know me,' she retorted, despite the fact that he'd just described *exactly* what she'd been doing.

'Then I shall look forward to that particular pleasure,' he said, leaning close and lowering his voice.

Which sent a velvet caress all the way down to the places he'd previously set on edge with his mockery.

'You will do no such thing,' she replied.

'Oh, but I shall. Bound to, during the course of the Season, since we will be going to the same balls and lectures…and parks.'

The way he said that, all low, and sort of meaningfully, turned the velvet molten. How did he do that? Make her remember the kiss, that was? And the feel of his body, pressed up against hers? Just by saying the word *parks*, with a slightly different tone to his voice and a certain sort of glint in his eye?

'We will not!' She was never going to go to the park again. Not on her own anyway. Not when it was such a dangerous thing to do.

'One outing to the Royal Institution enough for you, was it?' He chuckled. 'Cannot say I blame you. All I have gained from coming here is a crick in my neck.'

'I was not referring to this lecture hall.'

'No?' He shook his head. 'Well, since it cannot be the balls I was mentioning, you must mean…'

'That is just where you are wrong. I did mean the balls.'

'Oh? You are giving up dancing then, are you?'

'With you, yes.'

'Come, come, just because we got off on the wrong foot…'

'It has nothing to do with our feet,' she said, stupidly. But then that was what happened when she got cross. Her words came out half-wrong. 'I mean, it wasn't to do with the way we met. It is what I have learned about you since.'

The laughter died from his eyes.

'Oh? And what, pray have you learned?'

'You know very well what it is,' she said, although she knew he probably didn't. 'So don't bother asking me to dance. And don't come calling again. I shall not receive you.'

'Is that so?' His face had set into an expression that looked as though she'd just handed him a challenge. 'We'll see,' he said softly.

And with just a hint of menace.

Chapter Fourteen

It stung.

He didn't know why it should, but when she'd flung her chin up like that and told him she would never dance with him again, nor admit him to her home, it had most definitely stung.

'I s-say,' Archie suddenly panted, from somewhere behind him. 'C-could you slow d-down a t-touch?'

'What? Oh, sorry, old friend, I was miles away.' And had started walking much faster as irritation had gone fizzing through his veins.

'Alm-most literally,' said Archie with a smile. 'Civilians like me aren't used to c-covering the miles on f-foot like you military men.'

And that was when it struck him. He'd felt the same, when she'd rebuffed him just now, as he'd felt every time he'd been passed over for promotion. When the credit had gone to someone who didn't *play the fool*. In other words, to some stiff and starchy booby who had no imagination and stuck to the rules like glue.

Was that what she wanted, then? Some stickler for propriety, with no sense of humour, who probably voted

Tory and sent tenants to the gallows when they had the temerity to poach from his land instead of meekly lying down and starving?

He hadn't thought so. He'd thought she was...

He couldn't put it into words. It was just as though he'd recognised her, somehow. The way she struggled to fit in. The way she...

Hang it. What did it matter anyway? It wasn't as if he was in love with her.

He clapped Archie on the back and smiled. The devil-may-care smile that was his armour against all of life's setbacks.

'Enjoy the lecture, did you?'

'Very much. Although the highlight of this afternoon had to be meeting Lady Balderstone. Never usually stirs from her estate, you know, and one c-can't simply ride out there and visit.'

Something stirred in the labyrinths of Jack's mind. Something mischievous.

'You...ah...keen to see her again, then, are you, old man?'

Archie nodded, his eyes gleaming through the hair that Jack itched to set about with a pair of scissors.

'Then we must definitely call upon her.'

'We?'

'Yes.' Archie had just handed him the perfect way to exact revenge on Lady Harriet. Because he would not be calling upon *her* again. Oh, no. He would be calling upon the fascinating Lady Balderstone instead, in the company of one of her most fervent admirers.

He might even set up a flirtation with her, while he was at it. See how Lady Harriet liked *that*.

'B-but you must have b-better things to do,' said Archie.

'Well, that's just it, I haven't.' The old army cronies with whom he'd spent the first few weeks in Town, drinking and going over old battles, only reminded him of what he'd lost. Oh, he wouldn't have had a brilliant career in the army, he was too apt to ignore orders from superiors when they were stupid, or worse, downright dangerous. But he'd been good at what he did. And he knew it. And his men had known it. Even some of his brother officers had admitted they wished they had his knack of getting their men to follow them the way his men followed him.

But being Lord Becconsall—that was something he had no idea how to do. And nobody on his estates expected him to make so much as even a token effort to be him, either.

All they'd asked of him was to do the Season and go back with a wife.

Set up his nursery.

Ensure the succession.

Which was another reason why he'd been at such pains to avoid society events. He might have come to Town, but that didn't mean he was going to meekly obey orders to find a wife.

On the contrary.

Which was why the moment his fascination with Lady Harriet had begun to alarm him, he'd gone into full retreat. She was only supposed to have been a minor and pleasant diversion. Once he'd satisfied his curiosity about her, he was supposed to have reported straight back to Zeus and consigned her to his past. Instead of which he hadn't told any of them anything about her.

And he'd been drawn to any event where she might be, like iron filings to a magnet.

Even now, when she'd given him the perfect excuse to walk away and forget about her, he just couldn't do it.

Not at *her* bidding, anyway.

No, because she had no right to forbid him to do anything or go anywhere. She was going to find that wherever she went, he would be there.

Flirting with every other woman in the place. Showing her that she meant *nothing* to him.

'I really think,' said Archie plaintively, 'that I c-could manage to get myself to a house in Grosvenor Square on my own without…g-getting lost, or c-committing some social solecism.'

'I'm sure you could.'

'Then, you don't need to come with me, do you?'

'What's this, Archie? Want the lady scientist all to yourself, do you? Afraid I'll queer your pitch?'

'No.' Archie went a bit pink in the face. 'It's just that…well, I don't see why you all spend so much time p-pretending an interest in the things I am interested in, when—'

'You aren't going to upbraid me for catching forty winks during that lecture, are you?' Jack cut in before Archie could really get going.

'N-no, but see—'

'Look, if you must know, I wasn't asleep at all. I was just pretending.'

'P-pretending? Why?'

'Because I'd seen Lady Harriet come in, with her mother and…' He'd been afraid he wouldn't be able to keep his eyes off her. That she'd catch him staring at her, and think…well, he hadn't been prepared to let her start thinking anything. 'She was too distracting, if you must know,' he admitted. Which was true. He'd hoped that once he'd told his friends who she was, that her identity was out in the open, she'd lose some of the fascination she held for him. It hadn't worked. When her uncle had hauled her out of the drawing room, in a way that presaged trouble for her, he'd scarcely managed to stop himself from going with her. Because he wanted to defend her from whatever was about to happen. And when he'd seen her face, after the thundering scold she'd received for who knew what crime, he'd wanted to gather her into his arms and comfort her.

And to crown it all, when he'd seen her earlier, all he'd wanted to do was drink in the sight of her like some...brainless, infatuated sapskull.

Of course he'd shut his eyes and pretended she wasn't there. What other defence did a man have?

'Thank you for t-telling me. I wouldn't have thought...' He trailed off, his face flushing slightly.

'What?'

'Oh, nothing. A...thought I had. That's all. A stupid thought, I c-can see. B-but then...truth is, I've b-been a b-bit b-blue-devilled of late.'

Jack darted him a glance. Why hadn't he noticed the way his friend had been walking, with his head bowed as though weighted down with invisible burdens?

'Want to tell me what ails you? I know I ain't as clever as you, but you didn't all start calling me Ulysses for nothing.'

Archie glanced up, and smiled sadly. 'You are out, there, I'm afraid.'

'In what way?'

'In the way of thinking you are not as c-clever as I

am. You are a master tactician. Couldn't have led so many men into battle, and lost so few of them without having k-kind of mind that c-can implement c-complex strategies. And what you have done actually matters. To the outcome of the c-campaign as well as the men you k-kept alive. Whereas I...' He sighed again. 'Lady B-Balderstone reminded me of it, inadvertently of course, when she spoke of the discoveries being made of late in the field of isolating the elements. It feels as if every time I get to the point of a b-breakthrough, someone else b-beats me to it.' He sighed again. 'I am starting to feel like an imp-postor. That I ought to stop leeching off Zeus and go to t-teach in a school or some-thing.'

'I say, that's a bit drastic, isn't it?' Schoolboys would eat Archie alive.

'P-possibly, but at least I would feel as if I was earn-ing my living. Instead of sponging off Zeus.'

'You aren't sponging off him. He employs you as his chaplain, doesn't he?'

Archie made an impatient movement with his hand. 'It's a n-nominal appointment. Designed to give me p-pin money. I have never p-presided over a single ser-vice whilst living in K-Kelsham Park.'

'Well, I don't think you need to let that side of things bother you. Zeus didn't employ you to say prayers for him. He ain't the slightest bit bothered about his soul. Since he thinks he's God already.'

Archie let out a surprised bark of laughter.

'D-don't be impious, Ulysses,' he said. 'Else he'll strike you down with a b-bolt of lightning.'

'I'd dodge it,' said Jack, relieved to see that Archie's mood was lifting. 'That's why he named me Ulysses.

I'm adept at wriggling my way out of what look like impossible situations, by dint of my low cunning.' He waggled his eyebrows theatrically.

Archie smiled again. Briefly. 'Seriously, though, I do wonder how much longer he will tolerate my c-constant stream of failures to discover anything that will make him famous as a sponsor of the sciences. The way he has b-been looking at me, of late…'

Ah. 'Well, you know what, Archie? If he does turn you out of your comfortable quarters, you can come to me. Now that I'm a lord, I am swimming in lard and have all sorts of gifts and benefits at my disposal. And if,' he said quickly, when it looked as if Archie was going to voice an objection, 'you don't want to carry on researching any longer, why don't you just come for a prolonged stay? Spend some time thinking about what you really do want to do with your life?'

'Th-that's good of you, but…'

'Just think about it, that's all. Take some time.'

'Yes, that is just what Zeus said when I raised my c-concerns with him.'

'What? You've already told Zeus how you feel?'

Archie nodded. 'That is why we c-came up to London, when we heard that Atlas was ashore again.'

'Not because I'd sold out and was kicking my heels in Town?' Which was *his* problem in a nutshell. His friends were prepared to disrupt their routines and travel up to Town to celebrate the fact that Atlas had returned safe from the wars. But not him.

Archie shrugged. 'There is no telling why he chooses to do anything. That is the one way in which he does resemble G-God, actually.' He shot Jack a challenging look.

'Ah, yes,' said Jack, remembering. 'Because he moves in mysterious ways.'

'And so do you,' said Archie, his brows drawing down. 'I thought you only ran the g-girl from the p-park to earth out of some sort of...'

'Well, so did I, at first,' said Jack. 'But the thing is...' He trailed off as they finally reached the front door of their club, where they'd arranged to meet Zeus himself. 'To be honest, I'm dashed if I know what the thing is,' he said, with what he hoped was a disarming smile.

'But you hope that you might find out, if you c-call on her again?'

'Indeed I do,' he said and jogged up the steps before Archie could ask any more questions about his intentions with regard to Lady Harriet, which might mean not being completely straight with the fellow. Because he had no wish to embroil Archie in his schemes, which were not the slightest bit honourable. Especially not when it sounded as if Archie had enough troubles as it was.

Besides which, he couldn't trust Archie not to blurt out the truth, if he learned it. Because, clever though Archie was, when it came to subterfuge and cunning, he was the veriest babe.

Chapter Fifteen

The moment Keeble opened the front door of Tarbrook House, Harriet could tell there was going to be trouble.

'His lordship has requested that you attend him in his study, as soon as you return,' he said sternly.

'Does he?' said Mama, undoing the strings of her bonnet and handing it to him, neatly reminding him of his place. 'I shall bear that in mind,' she said, turning in the direction of the staircase and making as if to ascend.

She had not climbed up more than two steps before the door to Uncle Hugo's study burst open and the man himself erupted.

'I might have known you would ignore a civil request,' he said, striding across the hall. How on earth he'd known that Mama was not heading in the direction of his study, Harriet had no idea. Unless he had some sort of telescopic contraption mounted in there somewhere, through which he could observe the comings and goings that went on in his hallway. Which wouldn't surprise her, now she came to think of it.

'So why,' said Mama, turning to look down at him over her shoulder, 'did you bother to make it?'

'It is all of a piece with the rest of your behaviour,' he said from the foot of the staircase. 'You undermine me at every turn.'

'If you did not make so many foolish decisions, there would be no need to flout them.'

Mama's statement was like a red rag to a bull.

'May I remind you,' seethed Uncle Hugo through his nostrils 'that the reason I confined your daughter,' he said, pointing an accusing finger in her direction as she attempted to sidle up the stairs past Mama, 'to her room is that she turned my household...' he slapped his hand to his chest to emphasise exactly whose house it was '...upside down with her outrageous accusations of theft and skulduggery. She needed to learn a lesson. And you took her out of her room, nay, out of the very house,' he cried, pointing to the front door, 'against my express orders.'

Mama, from her vantage point on the stairs, looked down on him with disdain and clucked her tongue. 'It has come to a pretty pass if a woman cannot take her own daughter out whenever she pleases.'

'Well, that is it, in a nutshell, is it not? You only think of her when it pleases you to use her to make a point. May I remind you that it has been *my* wife who has gone to all the trouble of launching that graceless daughter of *yours* into society. And what thanks do we get? From either of you?'

The sound of a muffled sob, emanating from the half-open door to the drawing room, drew Harriet's attention to her aunt, whom she could just see, sitting on a sofa with her head bowed. And a handkerchief to her face.

'Nobody asked Susan to bring Harriet up to Town,'

said Mama, oblivious to everything but her quarrel with Uncle Hugo. 'She knew exactly what my objections were and chose to override them.'

'That was because they were foolhardy.'

'No, they were not. Do you think I had any wish to see my own flesh and blood laced into the constraints that made me so unhappy as a girl and paraded about Town like some brood mare for idiot men to appraise? I brought her up to be completely free of all restraints normally imposed on the behaviour of females so she wouldn't be stunted and Susan planned to undo it all in the space of two short months!'

Goodness. Harriet would never have guessed that Mama's treatment of her stemmed from anything more than indifference. But now it sounded as though, all along, Mama had been following some radical approach to rearing her, so that she wouldn't end up...well, as unhappy she'd been as a girl, by the sound of it.

'She was perfectly happy at Stone Court,' Mama was continuing, a touch inaccurately. 'Bringing her to Town has been like shutting a wild bird into a tiny gilded cage.'

'Then you will have no objection to taking her back there, then, will you, when you leave.'

'None whatever,' said Mama cheerfully.

'Which you will be doing this very night,' he finished.

'Tonight? Oh, no. I have no intention of leaving Town just yet. I have not finished—'

'Whatever it is you have not finished, madam, I give leave to inform you, you will not be doing from under my roof. To be blunt, you are no longer welcome to stay here. And neither is your daughter.'

'That's not fair, Hugo! Your quarrel is with me. Banish me if you like, but don't vent your spleen on Harriet.'

Good grief. Now Mama was actually trying to defend her.

'I thought you said she was like a wild bird in a gilded cage. Should I not, then, free her?'

'Oh, don't throw that in my face. You know as well as I do that she doesn't see it like that. She *wanted* to come to Town, or nothing Susan said would ever have convinced me to give in.'

'Nevertheless,' he said, his face turning an interesting shade of puce, 'you will both leave. As soon as I can have the carriage brought round.'

'Don't bother,' Mama hissed, whilst moving between Uncle Hugo and Harriet as though to put up a shield between her daughter and this man's anger. 'We are perfectly capable of hiring a hack—'

'If you think I am about to permit you to remove from my house in a hired hack and cause every Tom, Dick and Harry to speculate about what might have prompted such unprecedented behaviour,' he bellowed, 'you are very much mistaken.'

'Still more concerned about appearances,' Mama sneered, 'than the welfare of your family.' Having rendered him speechless with rage, Mama stuck her nose in the air and stalked up the stairs.

There was nothing Harriet could do but trot obediently up the stairs behind her mother. Though, when they reached the landing, she did not make for her own room, but followed Mama to hers.

'Mama…'

'Not one word, Harriet. If you think I will stay one moment longer in the house of a man who can lock girls in their rooms simply for asking a few innocent questions, then—'

'Yes, Mama, I quite see that you have no choice, but to leave here...' Indeed, Uncle Hugo had given them none. 'It is just that I was wondering where we are to go. Isn't it a bit late in the day to be thinking of returning to Stone Court? Even if Uncle Hugo is lending us his carriage for the journey?'

'Did you not hear? I have no intention of leaving Town until I am good and ready. We shall only be going as far as St James's Square.' Which was where their London residence was situated.

'But we haven't written to have Stone House opened up. Everything will be under holland covers.'

Mama waved a hand, airily. 'Then the staff will just have to remove them.'

'What staff?'

Mama's brow wrinkled. 'There are some people there whose job it is to keep an eye on the place and forward any mail, aren't there?'

'Yes, but I think you will find there are only two of them. And they are quite elderly.'

'Really, Harriet, I don't see why you are throwing so many obstacles in the way. Unless it is that you wish to stay here. Is that it? Well,' she continued before Harriet had a chance to answer, 'I am afraid that is out of the question. You heard your uncle.'

Yes. And she was fairly sure everyone in the house had heard him as well. 'I do not wish to stay here, no,' she said, suddenly realising that it was the truth. She was sorry to be causing her aunt even more distress by the manner of her leaving, but there would be certain compensations. Mama would soon be so wrapped up in whatever she was doing that she would not care what Harriet did as long as the household ran smoothly. In fact, to judge from that impassioned speech earlier, Mama would positively encourage Harriet to do exactly as she pleased. At any rate, Mama would most certainly not expect her to attend any more balls where she would be ignored by decent men, hounded by fortune-hunters and made a game of by scoundrels like Lord Becconsall.

She would, in short, have far more freedom than she ever would have in a more conventionally run household. And she could use that freedom to investigate what had happened to Aunt Susan's rubies. Which would be a far better way of showing her gratitude than simpering at so-called eligible men and learning to do embroidery.

'I am just thinking of the practical details, that is all,' said Harriet. 'Like getting meals on the table and freshly laundered sheets on the beds. That sort of thing.'

'You were born to be a housewife,' said Mama, scornfully. 'Whereas I, if I found the place not to be habitable, would merely remove to a hotel until—'

'Until I have managed to engage enough staff to make our lives comfortable at Stone House' said Harriet with an acid smile. She might have misjudged Mama's motives for treating her the way she had done so far, but she hadn't suddenly turned into someone else.

'Precisely,' said Mama, the insult gliding right off her impenetrable self-consequence. Leaving Harriet understanding exactly why Uncle Hugo found Mama so infuriating.

She whirled away before she said something she might later regret and went to her own room to pack.

She hadn't been in there for long before someone

scratched at the door and came in. She looked over her shoulder to see Maud.

'I'm come to help you pack, miss,' she said, looking apologetic. 'Leastways, that's what Mrs Trimble said I was to say.'

'Are you not, then, going to help me to pack?' Harriet looked in frustration at the armoire stuffed with ball gowns, walking dresses, carriage dresses, pelisses and spencers, and shook her head. 'It will take me a week to do a competent job of it, Aunt Susan has bought me so many things.' And it wasn't just the armoire. There were two dressers and a chest full of stockings and shawls and gloves and dancing pumps dyed the exact shade of the trimmings on her ball gowns, not to mention various other accessories she hadn't possessed when she first came to London. 'I am never going to fit everything in my trunk, anyway.' Not that she wanted to, actually. Not considering how many of her earliest purchases had been such disasters.

'Mrs Trimble is having Fred fetch down a couple of bags from the attics you can use to put your essential items in, then we'll pack the rest of it and bring it on later.'

'Oh, yes. Very practical.'

'No, don't go looking at me like that, my lady, we are all that sorry you are having to leave like this. It ain't—I mean,' she said, flushing, 'it isn't right, turning you out along with your mother, when you didn't have any choice in things.'

'I had already angered his lordship,' said Harriet, pulling open a drawer and wondering what she ought to consider essentials and put in the bags being brought to her for that purpose. 'He was just looking for an excuse to evict me.'

'Yes, and that's the other thing,' said Maud, coming to her side and pulling out a selection of undergarments that Harriet could see were exactly what she should have thought of herself. 'Once you leave this house, he won't be able to stop you asking about the theft of her ladyship's jewels, will he?'

'No.' Harriet lifted her chin. 'And if you've come to plead with me to stop, then I have to tell you—'

'No, it's just the opposite,' said Maud, rolling up a pair of stockings and reaching for another. 'We've been talking, below stairs, and have reached the same conclusion. We know it weren't any of us, but someone must have switched her ladyship's jewels, 'cos we can't none of us believe it was her. And, like you, we'd like to see her name cleared.'

'What?'

'You heard,' said Maud, with unusual pertness. 'Now, listen, miss, 'cos we mayn't have much time. I'm to tell you our suspicions and what we've worked out so far, and then it's up to you. We can trust you not to lay any blame on any of us, can't we?'

'Yes!' Harriet's heart was beating so fast she felt a little shaky. She hadn't dreamed her renewed determination to clear Aunt Susan's name would have borne fruit so swiftly.

'Well, a few years back, in 1812, to be precise, 'cos Mrs Trimble looked it up in her journal, there was this girl come to work as lady's maid. Ever such a quiet little thing, she was. Would barely talk to any of us. Well, at the time, we all thought she was just shy. But now...'

Maud shook her head, lips pursed. 'Even the way she left was suspicious, now we come to look back on it.'

'Suspicious? In what way?'

'Well, she *said* she was leaving on account of she got a better offer. But she wouldn't tell us where she was going. Nor she didn't ask for references neither. At the time, as I was saying, we just thought it was all of a piece with the way she was. But the thing is,' said Maud, going to the armoire and taking a rapid inventory of its contents before lifting down one of the day dresses with the fewest ruffles and bows, and laying it on the bed. 'Thing is, there's been no sign of her anywhere, ever since. Like she vanished off the face of the earth,' Maud finished as though she was reading aloud from some sensational story.

'We *did* think she must have gone back to Bogholt, the village where she said she come from, 'cos she certainly hasn't got work with anyone in London.'

'Do you mean that—have you in fact been looking for her?' Harriet lifted down her riding habit and tossed it on to the bed with the selection Maud was choosing for her.

'No, but see, footmen get together for a heavy wet down now and then. And butlers have their own watering holes. And they talk about...' She blushed and shrugged her shoulders. 'Well, what I mean is, if they get a new girl come to work for them, they talk about her. Whether she will...um...' Maud blushed.

'Let them kiss her?'

Maud nodded, clearly relieved not to have to explain the way footmen gossiped about the female staff they worked alongside. 'And if they are pretty, and so on. Now Jenny—that's the girl who come up from Norfolk—the footmen from here had all been talking about what a cold, starchy kind of girl she was. She gave Peter a real sharp set-down once or twice, apparently. And he reckons, if she'd gone to work anywhere else and someone else tried to flirt with her—not serious, mind, just in the way of having a bit of a laugh, for Mrs Trimble won't permit anything of that sort below stairs,' Maud put in hastily, as though Harriet might suspect the staff of doing nothing but flirting all day long, 'well, they'd have got the same reception. And they would have laughed about it over a heavy wet of an evening.'

Now *that* Harriet could believe. Young men, of whatever station, seemed to delight in making sport of young females and sharing their exploits with their peers appeared to be all part of it.

'So, you think she might have gone home? To Norfolk, was it you said?'

'Well, if she did that, why did she say she had got a better place? No,' Maud shook her head vigorously. 'We think she's gone to ground somewhere. With the proceeds from Lady Tarbrook's rubies. And you, miss, are the likeliest one to be able to find out where that somewhere is.'

Chapter Sixteen

Jack did a complete circuit of the ballroom on the pretext of exchanging a few pleasantries with all his old army cronies, as well as every single member of his club that he could spy. But eventually he could see he had no choice but to surrender to the necessity of approaching Lady Tarbrook. Who looked about as eager to speak to him as he had been to have to ask her the one question uppermost on his mind.

'Good evening,' he said, bowing over her hand. And coming straight to the point. 'Lady Harriet not here tonight? I was so hoping to be able to dance with her again.' Or, to be more precise, to *making* her dance with him again. It wasn't going to be enough, he'd decided about the time he was putting the finishing touches to his neckcloth earlier that evening, to simply flirt with other women. Or dance with other women. Since that was what she'd indicated she wanted. No, what would be a far more fitting revenge would be to challenge her and force her to choose. The rules governing the behaviour of young ladies were incredibly strict. If she refused to dance with a perfectly eligible man, then she could not dance with anyone else for the rest of the ball. Which would put her in bad odour with her aunt.

He'd been hoping to pitch her into a maelstrom somewhere between the devil and the deep blue sea. And now he felt cheated. How was he going to plague the life out of her if he couldn't even find her?

'Now that her own mother is in Town,' Lady Tarbrook said, with what looked like a forced smile, 'naturally she will be taking her about.'

'Yes, I noticed that she wasn't sitting with you. But surely you must have some idea whether she will be attending tonight? Did she not say?'

'I should perhaps explain,' she'd said, her smile growing even more strained, 'that my sister and niece have removed to Stone House. So I am no longer aware of what their plans may be.'

That all sounded plausible. And yet there was a touch of desperation lurking in Lady Tarbrook's eyes which convinced him she was not telling him the complete truth. And he recalled the way Harriet's uncle had called her out of the drawing room, with a face like an offended prune, for the purpose of giving her a trimming, if all the shouting he'd subsequently heard was any indication.

Whatever had the little minx been up to? Well, if she could sneak out of the house alone, at dawn, to indulge in an orgy of forbidden galloping, what other crimes might she not have contrived to commit?

He bowed over Lady Tarbrook's hand, murmuring all that was necessary to convince her that he accepted her version of events at face value. But inside he was whistling a jaunty air as he quit the ballroom, which no longer contained anything to hold his interest. He couldn't wait to find out what she'd done to provoke her uncle to wash his sanctimonious hands of her. Because that, he suspected, was what the old rascal had done.

So, next morning, early, he headed north towards Grosvenor Square where Archie was currently putting up with Zeus—probably in more ways than one.

'And to what,' said Zeus, laconically, 'do we owe the pleasure of your company?'

'I've come to collect Archie,' he said, with complete honesty. 'He said he wanted to call upon Lady Balderstone. The famous lady scientist.'

Zeus had, predictably, pulled a face and claimed a prior commitment. So it was only he and Archie who set off, on foot, for St James's Square a few minutes later.

'Now, you just give the butler your name and tell him you met her ladyship at that lecture we went to, and that she asked you to call whenever you liked.'

'B-but she didn't...'

'She meant to. I could tell from the way she was talking to you that she'd be glad to welcome you into her house whenever you chose to pay a visit.'

With any luck, she'd be so excited to hear Archie's name that she wouldn't bother enquiring who his friend was. So that Jack would be able to get into the house without Harriet hearing about it. It would be like a kind of ambush.

His heart beat in anticipation throughout the short walk to Stone House. For once they'd gained admittance to the drawing room, the two scientists would naturally draw apart from any other callers, as they launched into the kind of conversation that nobody outside the scientific community would understand. They would

become so engrossed in their talk that they wouldn't notice anything going on around them, short of a grenade
exploding, he shouldn't wonder. Archie would, in short,
provide perfect cover for his sortie upon Lady Harriet.

His plans met with a check when they mounted the
front steps only to find there was no knocker on the
door.

'Are you sure Lady T-Tarbrook told you they'd
c-come here?' Archie stepped back from under the
roomy portico to peer up at the white-stuccoed façade.
'Don't look to m-me as though anyone is in residence.'

Jack's heart sank as he followed Archie's gaze and
saw that all the blinds were half-drawn.

'Are you sure she didn't m-mean they'd gone b-back
to the c-country?'

'No!' He rejected the notion with every fibre of his
being. She couldn't have gone back to the country. Not
before he'd had a chance to…to…

His stomach turning over, Jack stepped smartly
up the front steps and pounded on the door with his
clenched fist.

The sound echoed through what sounded like an
empty hallway beyond. And, no matter how hard he
pounded, there were no answering footsteps. No sign
that anyone was coming to let him in.

No sign of anyone at all.

'So that's that, then,' said Archie gloomily.

It appeared so. For some reason, Lady Balderstone
had not informed Lady Tarbrook of her plans. Or Lady
Tarbrook might have said Stone House, when she meant
Stone Court, he supposed. In either case, the result was
the same. Lady Harriet was out of his reach. He could
no longer pursue her.

Worse, he might never see her again.

In brooding silence, he escorted Archie back to Grosvenor Square where they parted company. And then he wandered the streets aimlessly for some time. Though part of him wanted to go to ground somewhere, somewhere quiet where he could lick his wounds in peace. However, the part of him that had seen him through so much of his life thus far refused to even admit that he *was* wounded. It made him greet every acquaintance with a cheerful smile and crack puerile jokes, and generally behave as though he hadn't a care in the world.

That evening, his determination to prove he had no interest at all in Lady Harriet's whereabouts saw him presiding over the most riotous table at Limmer's.

'Never a dull moment since you came to Town,' said Captain Challinor, clapping him on the back. 'What say you we repair to the Guards Club? Liven them up a bit?'

With a grin, he agreed. There was nothing he'd rather do, he decided on the spur of the moment, than shake up some of the stuffy set that presided over that place. He staggered along Bruton Street arm in arm with Captain Challinor, plotting various ways he could wreak havoc on the men who'd written him off as a clown and a fool, and a wastrel.

And then they reached Berkeley Square. And there was Tarbrook House. Where Lady Harriet wasn't living any longer. Lady Harriet, who also thought he was a clown and a fool, and a wastrel, he shouldn't wonder, else why would she have rebuffed him so forcefully?

And suddenly he no longer saw the point in making a nuisance of himself with the military set. It wasn't them he wanted to…shake.

'Just remembered, something I need to do,' he said.

Captain Challinor shrugged and set off south along the square, while Jack, having glared one last time at Tarbrook House, set off in a northerly direction.

The sun was just crawling sluggishly out of a bed of purplish clouds as he entered Hyde Park. He didn't know what good it would do to come and stand by the very tree under which he'd kissed her. Before he'd even known her name. And yet that was where he found himself standing. Gazing down at the ground. Remembering the taste of her. The feel of her coming alive in his arms. The moments he'd spent with her since. The way her little face came alive after only a moment or so of his teasing. The way her eyes flashed up at him as she sent him a stinging riposte.

'You really fell for her, didn't you?'

'Good God!' He whirled round at the sound of Zeus's laconic voice, emanating not five feet from behind him. 'Did you follow me here?' He hadn't noticed anyone following him. He hadn't thought there was anyone in the park at all, apart from a couple of sleepy park-keepers, either.

He clenched his fists. This was what his aimless existence had brought him to. This state of…dulled wits that rendered him vulnerable to ambush. If this had been northern Spain, he could well be dead.

'No. I did not follow you.'

'Then what the devil are you doing prowling around the park at this hour?'

'I could well ask you the same question,' said Zeus, glancing briefly at the spot on the grass where Lucifer had deposited him. 'But in your case, there is no

need, is there?' He sighed. 'It is obvious that you are…
in need of a friend.'

'Is it?' Jack gave a bitter laugh. 'I have it on good
authority that there is never a dull moment while I am
in Town.'

'That's as may be, but that doesn't mean you don't…
hurt all the same.'

Hurt? He didn't hurt. He might be a touch disappointed that this…whatever it was with Lady Harriet
had been nipped in the bud. But that was *all*.

'Damn you, Zeus!' Jack struggled with the urge to
take a swing at him. 'You think you know everything…'

'No. Not everything,' he said with infuriating calm.
'But I do know what I saw when you were with her. You
reminded me of a twelve-year-old boy, pulling the pigtails of a girl you liked, to try to get her attention. And
now she's gone, perhaps *only* now she's gone, you are
having to face the fact that she meant more to you than
you knew. And also that your tactics were the worst
you could possibly have employed.' He turned his head
to gaze across the park, as though watching someone
walking along the path, though Jack couldn't see anyone through the mist. 'Because the way you made her
feel about you, the last time you spoke to her, means
that you have no valid excuse for following after her
and admitting what is really in your heart.' He uttered
a strange, bitter kind of laugh. 'Even if you were to
admit it, she now regards you with such suspicion that
she won't believe a word you say. Not even should you
demean yourself by grovelling. All you would do would
be to make a complete cake of yourself.'

What? 'It's not as bad as that. Lady Harriet—'

'Who?' Zeus raised one hand to his head. It was only

at this point that Jack began to wonder if Zeus was as foxed as himself. Only thing to account for him wandering about the park at this hour.

'Oh, her,' said Zeus. 'Yes, we were speaking of Lady Harriet, were we not?'

Jack wasn't at all sure any longer.

'You know what? You don't look quite the thing. I think you should go home.'

'Home. Hah.' His face contorted into a sneer. 'A great big house, that's all it is. Not a home.'

'Nevertheless, that's where I'm going to take you,' said Jack, going up to Zeus and taking him by the arm. He'd never seen his old friend reduced to such a state. Perversely, it made him feel a touch better to see proof that Zeus wasn't invincible after all. That a woman had managed to pierce what he'd thought was unshakeable belief in himself.

That Jack wasn't alone in his misery.

Jack slept most of the next day away. Awoke with gritty eyes and a sore head, and a determination to pull himself together. He could forgive himself one night of excess. But he was never going to get so drunk that people could creep up on him unawares again. Besides, it was ludicrous to permit one failed love affair to drive him to drink in the first place. If you could even classify it *as* a love affair. He hadn't actually declared himself to Lady Harriet and been repulsed, or anything near.

It was just that Lady Harriet's disappearance, coming on top of all the other blows he'd sustained of late, had been the last straw, that was all, he told himself as he went down to his study.

He was, slowly, making inroads into the mountain of

paperwork he'd inherited from his supposedly magnificent predecessor. He glanced askance at himself as he passed the mirror placed strategically close to the desk. From what he'd been able to gather, George had caused it to be hung there when his father had first started looking as though he'd been given notice to quit. He must have imagined checking his appearance in it, before admitting callers. He could just see him standing there, stroking those magnificent moustaches, and giving a final flick to his neckcloth. Though not actually sitting behind the desk. Not to judge from the utter chaos he'd found in here when he'd first inherited.

His father had put all his effort into training his oldest son, William. That was what had gone wrong. And George had spent most of his time hunting or whoring.

Jack resisted the urge to turn the mirror to the wall before sitting down at the desk. It was a good job he'd acquired a good training in administration during his time in the army. The success of campaigns depended on officers getting through a mountain of paperwork every single day. He might not cut an impressive figure swaggering about the estates, or leading the field in a hunt, but by God he could certainly keep the paperwork in order.

After a few minutes at work, he leaned back in his chair, and yielded to the temptation to put his feet up on the desk, twirling the pen in his ink-stained fingers. Perhaps it was time to return to Shropshire and throw his weight about a bit. Show them he wasn't the timid boy who'd gone, shivering, into the army the moment he left school. The tone of correspondence he was receiving from his father's steward was certainly becoming more respectful of late. Timmins no longer expressed surprise that he actually signed and returned the most urgent documents, anyway. Perhaps he should do as Zeus suggested and go down there, and take up the reins of his new life.

Zeus.

He growled, took his feet off the desk and pulled another document from the stack awaiting his attention. He was not going to do anything because Zeus bid him do it. He would go to Shropshire when he was good and ready.

And not a moment sooner.

The next morning he woke early, thanks to the fact that he'd spent so much of the previous day sleeping and had then passed the night entirely sober. Drinking to excess had never solved anyone's problems. It only dulled the brain, so that they no longer cared so much.

However, the prospect of spending the best part of the day indoors did not appeal. And even though this was only London, rather than somewhere more scenic, he decided to go out for a walk.

He could have gone in any direction. It must have been some perverse kind of desire to punish himself that sent him to St James's Square. Where he stood gazing forlornly up at the shuttered façade of Stone House for several minutes before shaking himself and striking out towards the Strand.

He'd walked along for several minutes before it struck him that the female hurrying along, several yards ahead of him, bore a marked resemblance to Lady Harriet.

Was it just wishful thinking? Was he so far gone that he was conjuring up likenesses to her in every stray woman he saw? Or did he actually recognise that bonnet? His heart speeded up. Surely, no two women in London could possibly have the same shade of hair as that single strand which had escaped from the confines of her bonnet and was trailing over her collar? And would any other woman manage to have all the pedestrians walking in the opposite direction move so swiftly out of her path?

Though she was walking very swiftly, his legs were longer. Nor was he hampered by skirts. Yet, for a few more minutes, he simply relished the sight of her. The way her hips swayed seductively with every step she took. The determined way she was gripping her umbrella in one hand and her reticule in the other, which made a fond smile kick up the corners of his mouth. If he'd been on horseback, at that moment, he would have clapped his heels into its flanks, and yelled 'View Halloo!'

Lady Harriet was still in London. And he had a second chance. This time, knowing what it felt like to imagine a life without her in it, he was going to be more careful with her. He was not going to let her slip through his fingers again.

Chapter Seventeen

The sun came out.

Or maybe it had already been shining and Jack simply hadn't noticed it before.

It took him but a moment to dodge his way through the traffic and reach a point on the pavement past which she'd have to go. And take up a position directly in her path.

'Why, Lady Harriet,' he said, risking the cut direct. 'What a pleasure to run across you today.'

'Is it?' She looked down her nose at him and made as if to step past him. He mirrored her move, blocking her way.

'Indeed it is,' he said. Had he ever seen anything so lovely as her narrowed, furious eyes? 'I was convinced you had left Town altogether and that I would never see you again.'

'And that would have been a tragedy, naturally,' she said in withering tones.

'It would indeed,' he said, smiting his breast. 'I do not know how I would have survived the loss.'

'Oh, I'm sure you would have found some other poor unfortunate female to make the butt of your jokes.'

He almost flinched. Zeus had been correct. He had *'pulled her pigtails'* once too often.

Time to rectify his error.

'I have no interest in any other lady,' he said with complete sincerity.

She made a very strange noise, for a lady. Something between a snarl and a mew.

'Kindly step aside,' she said, in a haughty voice quite unlike her own. 'I have pressing business to attend to.'

He stepped aside. But only to fall into step beside her when she set off again.

'What do you think you are doing?'

'Escorting you.'

'I have no need of your escort.'

'Tut, tut, Lady Harriet. Have you forgotten already how unwise it is to walk about without protection?'

'No, I haven't,' she said bitterly. 'London seems to be full of men who will take advantage of females who are out on their own.'

'Then what are you doing repeating your error? I took you for an intelligent female.'

'It is not a question of intelligence, but necessity. I no longer possess a footman and maid I can spare to traipse round after me when I'm out doing errands.'

'Indeed?' He looked down at her in concern. 'Has some misfortune befallen you? May I be of assistance in any way?'

'You?' She laughed.

He clenched his jaw on what had felt like a direct hit.

'You may think of me as a fool, but I can assure you, Lady Harriet, I am no such thing—'

'I don't think you are a fool,' she interrupted. He would have felt pleased to hear her say that, except that he had a feeling she had something else equally derogatory to say instead.

'You are too full of cunning and trickery to ever be mistaken for a fool.'

'Trickery? Whatever can you mean?'

'Oh, don't give me that. You told me yourself you are playing some kind of devious game. So why don't you go back to it rather than following me around?'

'Because I cannot leave you to wander about the streets, without protection. Since you say you have no footman, I can very easily fulfil that function for you today.'

'I cannot believe you wish to do any such thing. You must have better things to do with your time than…follow round after me, just to annoy me.'

He almost said that he didn't and that, anyway, annoying her was much more fun than anything else he could be doing. But though it was true, telling her that wasn't going to produce the result he wanted. So he sighed. Adopted a mournful air.

'I'm afraid not. I have nothing better to do than loiter about the taverns and clubs, drinking my days away. Or gambling my fortune away. Don't you think it is positively your duty to save me from myself? Because at least if I was affording you some protection, I couldn't be getting into any mischief, now could I?'

'What utter nonsense! Besides, I have no need of your protection. See?' She lifted her umbrella and waved it under his nose. 'If anyone should importune me, I can defend myself.'

He demonstrated that she was in error, by taking it from her hand in a move so swift that she gasped. Then scowled.

'Hmmm,' he said, smacking the handle of it against his gloved palm. 'Yes, you could indeed do someone a nasty injury with this, should they have the effrontery to accost you. And having seen how well able you are to defend yourself, even when armed only with a riding crop, I have no doubt that you would set any number of villains running for their lives. But,' he said, handing her back the umbrella with an ironic bow, 'if I am at your side, the villains would not bother you in the first place. So I will be saving you from an embarrassing and possibly unpleasant scene.'

She made the noise again and started walking a bit faster.

'May I enquire where you are going?'

'What business is it of yours?'

'None whatsoever. I am just curious. We have already passed Ackermann's, which is the only place any person of fashion might consider visiting, along here.'

'Perhaps,' she said with a good deal of resentment, 'I am going to…to an employment agency, to hire a big, burly footman and a maid who enjoys going for walks.'

'Very sensible,' he said soothingly. And then, when she did no more than dart him a look loaded with resentment, saw that it was up to him to keep the conversation going. 'You mentioned lack of staff. Does that explain why there was nobody to answer the door when I called upon you yesterday?'

'You called upon me?'

'Yes. At least, I accompanied Archie, who was wishing to talk with your mother. I had planned to smile at you across the room as you refused to speak to me, just for the pleasure of baiting you.'

'Now that I can believe.'

'Archie and I were most disappointed to find the knocker removed from the door. We assumed you had gone back to the country.'

'No. We…' Lady Harriet paused at the corner of Catherine Street, looking distinctly harassed. 'I believe the, er…employment office is just up here,' she said. 'Please, I would rather you did not come any further.'

'If I didn't know any better, I would think you were intending to visit Bow Street!' He laughed as he made the suggestion, but Lady Harriet flinched and looked downright guilty. 'Good, God! You *are* heading for Bow Street.' A feeling came over him very similar to the one that had overtaken him when he'd seen her hangdog expression on emerging from her uncle's study. A rush of concern that was this time so overwhelming that he turned and, forgetting all notions of propriety, took hold of her by both shoulders. 'Are you in some sort of trouble? Are you sure hiring a Runner is the best course of action? Have you nobody else to advise you? Dammit, what is your mother thinking of, letting you run loose in London on such an errand?'

'Mama does not know I have come,' she said, swiping to left and right with her umbrella to remove his hands from her shoulders.

'Yes, but the Runners? Really? Are you sure?'

She chewed on her lower lip, suddenly looking very unsure and very vulnerable.

'Lady Harriet, if you are in some sort of fix, you'd do much better to let me help you out of it than trying to battle on alone. I didn't get the nickname of Ulysses at school for nothing.'

She looked up at him, as though perplexed. And then her expression closed up completely. 'You will have to forgive me, but I have not the slightest idea what you are talking about. I know nothing about Ulysses except that he was some character out of Ancient Greece.'

'Oh. Right.' He scratched his nose. 'Well, Ulysses was the most wily and...er...cunning of the generals fighting in the Trojan War. But it wasn't until he was on his way back from the wars that his talent for using those two weapons, against apparently insurmountable odds, were really put to the test. For instance once, according to legend, he and his men were imprisoned in a cave by a one-eyed giant.'

'A giant?'

'Yes. And every night, this giant would eat one of his men for his supper.'

'Eurgh!' said Lady Harriet.

'Yes, but then one night Ulysses got the giant drunk and while he was asleep blinded him by poking him in the eye with a sharp stick.'

'He sounds perfectly horrid,' said Lady Harriet, wrinkling her nose.

'Well, it was a desperate situation. He couldn't sit back and let that giant eat his men, one by one, could he?'

She shrugged with one shoulder. 'I suppose not.'

'Well, the giant bellowed and his brothers came to find out what was the matter, and he shouted out—oh, I should perhaps have mentioned that Ulysses had already told the giant that his name was Nemo. Which means nobody, in Latin, do you see? So when the giant shouted, *"Nobody has blinded me"*, they all thought he'd got windmills in his head, and wandered off without helping him.'

'They must have been incredibly stupid.'

'Well, big fellows often are, I've found. But back to Ulysses and his men. The giant went off out to work, as he always did each day. He was a shepherd. And being a giant, his sheep were huge. Since he was blind, he ran his hands over the back of each sheep as he let it out of the cave to make sure it was a sheep and not one of the men who were getting out. But Ulysses got his men to cling to the underside of the sheep and so they all escaped.'

Lady Harriet frowned up at him. 'So your school friends named you after a man who told lies and blinded people?'

'You are missing the point. Ulysses used his brains instead of brute force to save both his own life and that of his men. And that was what I did, when I was at school. Used my brains to escape the attention of bullies, since I was too puny to fight back.'

'Puny?' She looked up at him. Glanced at his shoulders. Back up to his face.

'No,' he admitted, completely unable to stem a flush of pride at her assessment of his physique, 'I'm not puny now. But I was the youngest, and weakest, of three brothers. And the older two got a lot of pleasure from holding me face down in the mud, or by the ankles off a bridge, or what have you.'

'How very nasty of them.'

'They were brutes,' he agreed. 'And it was through them that I learned to dodge and weave my way through life. Or, if all else failed, when cornered, to come up with enough jokes or antics that they got more amusement from making me play the clown than roasting me over a fire. But this,' he said when she gasped, 'is getting beside the point. We are not here to discuss my past, but my ability to help you out of what I suspect is a fix. And don't give me that look,' he said when she pulled her lips into a mutinous line. 'You wouldn't be going to the Runners, all on your own, if you didn't need *somebody*'s help. And see here, Lady Harriet, I served in the army for the best part of ten years, after serving my apprenticeship in dodging trouble first at home and then at Eton. I know I appear in society like a bit of a…wastrel, but you have already told me you've seen through my disguise. The disguise I adopted when I was a boy, to make bullies think I didn't care, so there was no sport to be had from tormenting me.'

'Oh, are you in torment, then?'

She looked concerned. So he decided to strike while the iron was hot.

'I was, when I thought you had left Town and I might never see you again,' he said candidly. 'However,' he continued when she blushed and frowned, and looked as though she was about to voice an objection, 'we are not speaking of me. But you. And why you feel it necessary to visit the offices of Bow Street. Which, I give leave to inform you, is not at all the sort of place a virtuous young lady should venture, even with a footman in tow.'

'It is not,' she said, shifting from one foot to the other, 'something I can tell you.'

'Then it is something that is going on within your family.'

She gasped again. Telling him he'd hit the nail on the head.

'Hmm, well, that explains Lady Tarbrook's reluctance to speak of why your mother removed you from her care.'

She screwed her mouth up into a tight, resentful line.

'I was there, too, that day Lord Tarbrook stormed into the drawing room and hauled you out, in front of all the visitors, to give you a dressing down. At least, I heard him shouting and then saw your face when you came out of his study. Although I cannot see that a rift within your family circle would warrant a trip to Bow Street. Nor how you come to be at the centre of it.'

'Will you just stop this? This is not a guessing game. It is a very serious…' She pulled herself up. To her full height. And glared at him.

'Surely you know you can trust me,' he said gently. 'After all, I kept what happened between us, in the park, a secret, did I not?'

'Only because it was to your advantage,' she said mulishly. 'If anyone had known about it, you might have had to marry me.'

'Nonsense. I have told you that I am adept at escaping tricky situations. If I hadn't wanted to marry you, no amount of threats would have prevailed. I would have found a way to wriggle out of that particular snare, you may be sure. The reason I kept your secret was because…'

She looked up at him. Right in the eye. Which made him swallow.

'You are an innocent, that's why. If anyone had heard what you'd done, they might have placed an entirely different interpretation on events. And you didn't deserve that.'

'You maintain that you were protecting me?'

'I *was* protecting you.'

She didn't look convinced. So he stepped back and folded his arms across his chest.

'Now, look here Lady Harriet. You might as well accept the fact that I am going to find out what you are about, one way or another. Either you tell me, right now. Or I will come with you right into the offices and learn what is going on when you inform one of the Runners. Which is it to be?'

Chapter Eighteen

He wasn't going to budge. She could see it in his stance, in the set of his jaw, in the determined glint in his eyes.

So why didn't Harriet feel furious? Why was she instead tempted to unburden herself? To this man, of all people? The man who'd proved he could take nothing seriously?

It was partly because, the moment she'd set out that morning, she'd fallen prey to all sorts of disturbing thoughts. What if the men at Bow Street didn't believe her? What if they did believe her, but ignored her request for discretion and blundered in, frightening the servants again? After they'd *trusted* her to do the right thing. Or, worst of all, what if they discovered it was Uncle Hugo himself who'd had the jewels copied, because of amassing huge debts, somehow? That made so much sense, since she'd never believed a man so self-absorbed could really have been *that* concerned about the servants, that she then spent several minutes agonising over the consequences, should that prove to be the case.

She foresaw Kitty's Season coming to an ignominious end. The town house having to be sold. The entire family having to retreat to the countryside, which both Kitty *and* Aunt Susan would hate. And they'd hate her, too, for bringing it all down upon their heads. Because the one thing they would not do was blame Uncle Hugo, who, although it was his fault, had been taking steps to secure their future before anyone found out—

'Lady Harriet!'

She blinked out of her tangled web of conjecture to see Lord Becconsall still standing in her path, arms folded, expression stern.

'It…it isn't really my tale to tell,' she said, passing her umbrella from one hand to the other. 'Oh, dear, I really don't know what to do.'

'Is there nobody you can turn to for help?'

She shook her head. Mama didn't care. Papa was too far away. And nothing but the direst emergency would induce him to come up to Town anyway, since it was a place he heartily detested.

'Lady Harriet, I am here.' He spread his hands wide. 'Both willing and able to help you, no matter what it is that is troubling you so deeply.'

He looked so sincere. For a moment the temptation to unburden herself was so strong she almost confided in him.

But then she remembered why doing any such thing would be foolish in the extreme.

'Typical,' she said. 'The only person who has taken any notice of what I planned to do today had to be you.' She jabbed him in the stomach with her umbrella for emphasis. 'The one man I cannot trust with this… business.'

He rubbed his midsection ruefully.

'Of course you can trust me Lady Harriet. I swear, on my honour—'

'Honour? Hah!'

'That I will hold whatever you tell me in the strictest confidence.'

She wanted so badly to believe him it was almost enough to make her weep with vexation.

'Do you take me for a complete idiot? When you've just boasted about your cunning and your love of telling lies in one breath, you then ask me to trust you in the next. As if it were some kind of test of my gullibility. When I know full well that you already regard me as a joke.'

'What? How on earth do you come to that conclusion? Look, I may have teased you a bit, but—'

She stamped her foot. 'Don't think you can wriggle out of this one, *Ulysses*,' she spat out. 'I heard you with my own ears.' As though she could hear with anyone else's. This was what he'd reduced her to. Stamping her foot like a toddler and talking gibberish. 'You were laughing about me with your friends. About the wager you'd made.'

'You misunderstood—'

'No, I didn't.'

'Yes, you did.' He stepped forward. Leaned close and lowered his voice. 'I've just told you how I cover up my feelings by playing the fool. And that was what I did, after you'd left the park. When all I could think about was finding you again. But I didn't want to admit to my friends how much. So I made it seem like something I didn't care about at all.'

She'd planted her hands on her hips the moment he stepped forward. And it suddenly struck her how peculiar they must look, standing toe to toe the way they were. Right in the middle of the pavement so that other pedestrians were having to weave round them, like a stream of water dividing round a pile of rocks.

If anyone her aunt knew were to see her like this…

Only that wasn't very likely. Nobody from her aunt's circle was in the habit of getting up this early, she shouldn't think. Nor would fashionable people stray to this part of Town even if they did.

'I needed to find you, Harriet,' said Lord Becconsall. 'Needed to find out if, once I was sober, you were as perfect as you'd seemed when I was foxed. That the kiss we shared was as magical as I recalled, or merely a combination of drink and a blow to the head.'

Magical? He'd thought that kiss magical as well? She could feel herself leaning into him. Gazing at his mouth.

His lying, deceitful mouth.

She pulled herself up to her full height.

'Except that you didn't.'

'Didn't what?'

'Kiss me again. Nor even attempt to. Not at any point.'

He grabbed her by the upper arms. 'I can rectify *that* error right here, right now,' he said, leaning in and looking intently at her mouth.

'In the street?' Her voice came out as an indignant squeak. And she *was* indignant. Because that wasn't what she'd meant to say. What she ought to have said. Not at all. Because questioning the venue, rather than the action, would make him think that she wanted him to kiss her. And look, see? He was leaning in even closer. If she didn't do something, right now, then he would kiss her. And he was too close already for her to be able to jab him in the stomach with her umbrella again.

All she could do was pull her upper body as far back as she could and bring her umbrella down sharply on to his foot.

It had the desired effect. His face stopped looming inexorably closer. And he winced.

But he didn't let go of her arms.

'Your umbrella isn't going to keep me off,' he growled. 'I'm not a shower of rain.'

'But if you kiss me, here, in the street, it would cause a shocking scandal. You might even end up having to marry me.' There, if anything could frighten him off, the threat of marriage should do it.

Or so she would have thought. But to her surprise, it only made him smile, in a rather grim sort of way.

'At least if we were to marry I'd gain the right to come to your aid when you were in trouble. And you'd never have to walk about the streets unprotected, at the mercy of every rogue and rake in Town.'

'I…' Her breath seized in her throat. He really didn't seem that concerned about the prospect of marrying her. On the contrary, it was almost as though he'd relish the opportunity of getting more involved with her. She felt something melt inside. Something that had always been wound up tight, and hard, in the very centre of her being.

'It is a bit extreme,' she said breathily, 'don't you think? Marrying me, just to find out…what the difficulty is that I'm trying to solve?'

'That wouldn't be the only reason.'

'Oh?' The melty feeling expanded. Fluttered. Almost took on the shape of hope trying to spread its wings.

'What…what other reasons could there possibly be?' Her heart began to beat really fast.

'When I thought you'd left Town, when I thought I'd never see you again…' His hands were no longer gripping her hard. They were sliding up and down her arms in a positively caressing manner. 'I realised something.'

'Did you?'

'Yes, I—'

At that moment, a hawker carrying a massive pile of wicker baskets jostled them as he failed to find enough room on the pavement to avoid them, knocking Lord Becconsall's hat askew. Lord Becconsall scowled at him. Then straightened his hat. Then looked down at her as though he couldn't quite recall what he'd been about to say.

'This is not the place for this kind of discussion,' he said. With such a look in his eye that Harriet's burgeoning hope withered and died on the spot.

'Devil take it,' he snarled. Making her sure that he regretted all the soft words. All the hints that marrying her might not be such a dreadful fate after all.

'Where can a man and a woman go to discuss matters of this sort, without an audience?'

As he scowled at the ever-increasing stream of pedestrians going about their business, Harriet's spirits revived. Because he wanted to talk to her some more. About marriage.

'I know,' he said, seizing her hand and setting off back in the direction from which they'd come.

'Where are you taking me?' And why wasn't she putting up the slightest bit of a struggle?

'A coffee house,' he said, as he plunged down a side street. 'I know it isn't exactly the right place for a respectable young lady to go, on her own, with a young man. But can you imagine what would happen if we were to head for somewhere like Gunther's?'

She shuddered. Gunther's was practically on Aunt Susan's doorstep. Plenty of society people went in there. Possibly even at this hour of the day. Someone would be bound to see them and carry the tale back to her aunt. And make it sound as scurrilous as they could, while they were at it.

'It isn't all that far,' said Lord Becconsall. 'But I suggest that you use the time until then thinking about how much you wish to tell me about your problem.'

Her problem? So...he wasn't taking her somewhere out of the way so he could speak to her about marriage?

Of course he wasn't. Foolish, hopeless, Harriet. He just couldn't stand being kept in the dark over a mystery.

'What,' she said with a touch of resentment, 'if I decide not to tell you anything about it?'

'Then I shall at least have had the pleasure of escorting you along the street and spending time with you, tête-à-tête, in a dark and private nook. But I give you fair warning...' He darted her a look loaded with laughter. 'Now that I know you are in some sort of trouble I shall be dogging your footsteps.'

'Must you?'

'I must. I would never forgive myself, you see, if any harm were to befall you.'

Something warm unfurled inside Harriet once more. Because nobody had ever cared enough to even say that they'd be unable to forgive themselves if something bad happened to her, even if they didn't really mean it.

He towed her across the narrow street and down an even narrower alley, before ducking into the doorway of an oak-beamed building that looked as though it really ought to have fallen down just after the Great Fire.

A couple of men were sitting at tables by the street windows, poring intently over newspapers. It was too dark, further in, for anyone to be able to see clearly enough to read. The place smelled of a mixture of roasting coffee, and stale tobacco smoke, and, strangely enough, something that reminded her of her father's hacking jacket when he'd been out in the rain.

Lord Becconsall strode without hesitation to a table stationed just behind one of the massive, blackened, oak pillars holding up the sooty ceiling.

'Now,' he said, removing his gloves and tossing them on to the table. 'Are you going to tell me how I can employ my low cunning to solve the problem you were considering taking to the Runners?'

She supposed she ought not to feel so disappointed that he looked so eager to talk about that, rather than continuing with the other thread of their conversation. The one that dealt with magical kisses and the world being empty when he thought she'd left Town. Or at least, that was what she hoped he'd been about to say before the basket seller had jostled him.

'It's not really my story to tell,' she began, leaning her umbrella against the table rim and laying her reticule in her lap.

He gave her a look that she thought might have been full of respect. Unless it was just yet more wishful thinking. Or a shadow flitting across his face from when the waiter had gone hurrying past.

'I tell you what,' he said, tilting his hat back to a ridiculous angle. 'Why don't you tell it to me as though it was…a story you have read in a book?'

'A what?'

'You do know what books are, don't you? Small square things, made of paper—'

She kicked him under the table.

He flinched, laughing. 'Come on. I've told you a legend from Ancient Greece. You could at least repay me by telling me a…fairy tale I've never heard before. And then, if anyone was to ask you what we were talking about all morning—if anyone should find out we've been together—you can tell them, with all honesty, that we told each other our favourite nursery tales. Because I have to say, Lady Harriet, that you don't look to me as though you are much good at telling lies.'

'I am not,' she said, lifting her chin.

'There you go, then.'

She sighed. Even now he was thinking of ways to explain away their meeting, ways that would get him out of a tight spot.

'My word, you are tricky,' she said resentfully. 'The inside of your head must be so tangled up with the intricate strategies you have to employ, just to get through a single day, that it must be like a nest of rats' tails.'

He made no reply to that. Because the waiter came over to take their order.

Even though she was sure the fellow couldn't possibly know her, Harriet ducked her head under the pretext of rummaging for something in her reticule. And didn't lift it again until he'd gone.

At which point Lord Becconsall cleared his throat.

'At the very least, if you tell the whole tale out loud, it might help you to get your thoughts clear and then you might know what line to take. Because at the moment, I have to say, you do not look at all as though you do.'

Which was perfectly true.

And anyway, she'd already pretty much made up her mind to tell him as much as she could. And his suggestion of presenting the facts as though they were a story out of a book was the perfect way of unburdening herself without actually breaking any of the promises she'd made about not speaking at all.

'And…and you will not tell anyone what I have told you?'

'I shall not.'

She wasn't sure whether it was because of the expression in his eyes, or simply because she so badly needed to confide in someone, but anyway, she decided to give him a chance. She was never going to find out if she could trust him, unless she took a leap of faith, was she? And if he did let her down, then at least she'd know she'd *tried*.

Chapter Nineteen

'Once upon a time...'

His face, never far from laughter, lit up as though she'd just given him a precious gift. 'Thank you,' he said. And then, after a glance round the murky room, as though to check whether anyone was attempting to eavesdrop, said in a louder voice, 'That's how all the best stories start.'

'There was a...a princess,' she continued, slowly removing her gloves. 'Who was going to a ball, where she was to choose a handsome prince to marry.'

'Did it have to be a prince?'

'I beg your pardon?'

'Couldn't it have been someone of more humble origin? A...viscount, say?'

'Absolutely not. Her father would not want her to marry anyone who wasn't of royal blood.'

His smile dimmed. He frowned at her hands.

'I had no idea he was so high in the instep.'

'Stop interrupting. Anyway, as I was saying, she was going to this ball and wanted to wear her finest jewels. Only when her father went to the...er...royal vault to fetch them, he discovered that they had been stolen. And glass beads left in the place where they were kept.'

'They'd been copied?'

'Yes. And the King was furious. So furious that he forbade anyone to speak of it, on pain of death.'

'That was a bit harsh.'

'He was a tyrant,' she said with feeling. 'I believe kings in fairy tales often are.'

Harriet had to pause in her narrative at that point since the waiter returned with their order and spent some time setting out the pots and cups on the surprisingly clean table.

Once he'd gone, Lord Becconsall leaned forward and murmured, 'Go on. I have a notion you are just getting to the interesting part.'

'Well, I don't know that it was more interesting than having the rubies switched for glass beads. But anyway, the King decided that it must have been the Queen who was guilty and had her put in the pillory! Which, of course, made the Princess very unhappy. And angered some of the courtiers, who loved the Queen and didn't like to see her humiliated in that fashion. So, anyway, one of them, who owed the Queen a very great debt,' she said, lowering her gaze and fiddling with the strings of her reticule, 'decided she would find out who had really stolen the rubies, so she could clear the Queen's name. The King was furious.' She glanced back up at Lord Becconsall. 'When he found out she had been asking questions, first of all he locked her in her room—'

Lord Becconsall stiffened. 'Locked you—I mean, her, in her room? How could he?'

'I did say he was a tyrant.'

'Yes, but—'

'And it wasn't as bad as all that. She only missed one meal. And the Queen brought her some books and things to read. And, actually, it did some good, you know, because it won her some favour with the servants. I mean,' she hastily corrected herself, 'the other courtiers. And it made them all want to help her clear the Queen's name.

'But then, when he found out that people were starting to flout his orders he—the King—um...banished her from court, and sent her to...er... Well, anyway, she found a place where she was safe from the King's wrath. Only...she still wanted to find out who had stolen those jewels, so she thought she'd hire some...er...'

'Wizards?' said Lord Becconsall, helpfully.

'Well, she did think they might be sort of magicians,' she admitted, thinking about the reputation of the Bow Street Runners. 'Only she wasn't sure if she could trust them. And she was a bit...' She lifted her spoon and stirred her chocolate, which Lord Becconsall had ordered for her. And how he'd managed to correctly guess exactly what she'd wanted, without even asking, was beyond her. 'A bit afraid of them, to be honest,' she admitted, fumbling her spoon into her saucer with a clatter.

'Well, those wizards probably lived in an enchanted forest, into which it was perilous to enter.'

'Yes, it was,' she said, grateful that he'd understood.

'What she needed was to find a soldier.'

'Did she?'

'Yes.' He reached across the table and laid his hand on top of the one that had just been occupied with her spoon. 'You know very often in those kinds of stories, the Princess comes across a ragged soldier, who turns out to be able to complete the quest on her behalf.'

'She isn't a princess,' Harriet pointed out.

'She looks like one to the raggedy soldier,' he said, running his fingers over the back of her knuckles.

Harriet flushed. All the way to her toes. It was a very strange feeling, having a man's bare hand caress her own bare hand. She couldn't think why it should be so, but it was having almost as much effect upon her as being held in his arms had done. 'Are we still talking about the...the story?'

'Do you want us to be?'

To her surprise, she rather did. It was far easier to talk about that, than what his light touch was doing to her insides. To admit she wished he would kiss her, the way he'd kissed her that morning. Besides, now that she'd started to tell him about the missing rubies, and what had been happening since she'd decided to find out where they'd gone, it was as though a great weight was sliding from her shoulders. And telling it half-concealed in the language of fairy tales was making it easier still.

However, her life was not a fairy tale. And if she wanted to get anywhere with her investigation, she was going to need practical help, not the laughing eyes of a born flirt distracting her from her purpose.

She pulled her hand out from under his and tucked it safely in her lap.

Lord Becconsall let her do so, but pushed his cup to one side, laid both elbows on the table, and leaned as far across the table as he could.

'Do you—I mean did the lady who was loyal to the Queen have any clues, perchance? It would make the soldier's quest much easier if she could give him, say, a map...'

'And a bottle of magic potion with which to send the dragons to sleep?'

Lord Becconsall chuckled. 'Just a map would be a start. With a map, and his own cunning, I reckon that soldier could find out who'd taken the jewels.'

'Oh, you do, do you? You are very sure of yourself.'

He quirked one eyebrow at her.

'I meant to say, of course, the soldier was very sure of himself. But, as it happens, I do have—I mean to say, the lady did have one clue, given to her by...the keeper of the royal vault.'

She couldn't have said that he moved, exactly, but something came over him. A sort of watchfulness. As though he was fully alert to whatever she might say next.

'Go on,' he said, when she paused.

'Yes, just as I, that is *she*, the courtier, was leaving the castle, the...um...keeper of the vault managed to whisper a name in her ear. It was the name of a person who had worked, for a very brief time, in the Queen's own chamber. And the name of the village from whence she came. And actually,' she said, putting her hand to the reticule in which she'd put the paper on which she'd written down everything Maud had told her, 'the name of the person who'd given her the reference to get the job in the first place. I would have thought, wouldn't you, that the person who'd sent Jenny to work for...um... the Queen, would be the one who now had the jewels, wouldn't you? The only problem is...'

'Is?'

'Well, she appears to be beyond reproach. I've already asked, discreetly, what kind of person she is,' she said, forgetting to hide the events behind the cloak of her fairy tale, 'and according to Mama she is an elderly recluse.'

'Don't you mean, a witch living in the centre of an enchanted forest?'

'No,' she said irritably. 'I can't keep up with all these fairy-tale analogies. And besides, haven't we already had an enchanted forest in this story?'

He chuckled. 'Indeed we have. So, would you prefer to let me give you time to think up a more original scenario? Or...'

'Or?'

'Or would you rather just forget all about kings and wizards and enchanted forests, and just tell me what is really going on?'

She sighed. 'I suppose I might as well. You've probably already worked out who the major characters in the story are.'

'They weren't exactly in heavy disguise.'

'No, well, I've never had to try to make my life sound like some kind of fairy tale before. And you didn't exactly give me much time to do so, did you? So...' She shrugged. 'Do you think you might be able to help me?'

'I'm sure I shall,' he said, boldly taking hold of both her hands this time. For a moment, she experienced a very strong urge to turn them over and cling to him. And never let go.

Which would be really stupid. She hardly knew him. And what she did know didn't encourage her to put her faith in him. Not in *that* way.

Oh, she could easily believe that he was intrigued by the notion of investigating a crime. His mind was so devious, and he had so little else to do, that she could see him finding unravelling what had gone on in Tarbrook

House as entertaining as most people would find...
doing an acrostic, say.

But as for truly wishing to marry her? No, she
couldn't believe in that. He hadn't mentioned it at all
once she'd got started on the mystery of the fake rubies.
And so for the second time, she slid her hands out from
beneath his and placed them on her lap.

He gave a wry smile. 'It's too soon, isn't it? I need to
prove my worth. Demonstrate that I'm not just a cunning trickster, but a man upon whom you can depend.
Will you permit me to do that, Harriet? Will you entrust me with this...quest?'

All of a sudden she felt breathless. Almost as though
she'd been running. Because his words had answered
her doubts with such uncanny accuracy. And it would
help her to believe he was in earnest about her, if she
allowed him to deal with the mystery of the missing
rubies.

'Yes,' she admitted. 'I think...I rather think I will.'

His smile lit up his whole face. 'And you will tell me
everything you've discovered now? In plain English?'

She nodded. Found she had to lower her head for
just a second or two, because his delight was almost too
much for her to resist. Only once she'd overcome the
urge to grin back at him, like a besotted tavern wench
when one of her striking brothers strode into view, did
she raise her head and look at him again.

'Just before I left my uncle's house,' she said, 'one
of the maids came to me and told me who the servants
suspected had been the culprit. Although, I have to say,
it would be very hard on that girl to have a Bow Street
Runner set on her, if the worst she was guilty of was
being rather shy and not very talkative. Or if she left

service because she had an…ailing mother, or something of the sort.'

'There, you see? Hiring a Bow Street Runner would be the very worst thing to do. I can be far more discreet. I can go and investigate this servant's movements under pretext of…um, well of course that depends where she lives.'

'Well, the reference she gave says she comes from a village called Bogholt, which is in Norfolk.'

'Never heard of it. But I can soon locate it, if it exists.'

'Oh, it exists. I found it on the map. Though it took hours and hours.' But that was one of the benefits of not having to go to balls and pay morning calls or go shopping for fripperies she didn't need. It left her hours and hours and *hours* free to pore over maps. 'It is a tiny hamlet in Thetford Forest.'

'Thetford? Well, then, all I have to do is say I'm going to Newmarket for the races, next time there's a meet, and spend a day or so poking around in Thetford Forest to see what I can dig up. And there's no need to frown at me like that. I know how to reconnoitre behind enemy lines. Nobody will guess why I'm there, or what I'm about.'

'Then I fail to see how you will find out anything at all.'

'You do not need to see. Nor do I want you to see, because it will necessitate employing all sorts of underhanded methods which would no doubt give you a disgust of me. Which would rather defeat the object.'

'Would it?'

'You know it would,' he said with such a heated look

that Harriet took refuge in taking a sip of her rapidly cooling chocolate.

'Now, you said you wanted to investigate the person who wrote the reference as well? But that you changed your mind, because she is beyond reproach.'

'So Mama informed me,' said Harriet, setting down her cup now that they were safely back to discussing crime, rather than his intention to impress her. 'The lady is, or was, at least, very well known at one time, although lately she seems to have become something of a recluse.'

'And where has she become a recluse? Somewhere in Norfolk, I take it?'

'No.' And then she gasped at what Lord Becconsall was implying. Just by looking at her in a particular manner. 'Dorset.'

He leaned back in his chair and grinned.

'So, how on earth did this shy little maidservant from a hamlet buried in the Forest of Thetford get a reference from an elderly recluse from Dorset?'

'I...I suppose there could be a perfectly innocent explanation...'

'You don't believe that any more than I do. No, what we need to do,' he said, sitting forward, placing both elbows on the table and clasping his hands over his coffee cup, 'is to look into that connection.'

'But that will take for ever!'

'Is time of the essence?'

'Yes. Because I have no idea how long Mama plans to stay in London. And once we go back to Stone Court I won't be able to...' She waved her hands in his direction. Then at herself.

'To direct operations,' he finished for her.

'Yes. That,' she agreed. Because there was no way she was going to admit she'd been about to say she'd no longer be able to meet with him like this. That there were no handy little coffee houses in Donnywich where nobody knew who she was. There was only the Black Swan. Into which she never ventured. And would never be able to come up with a plausible excuse for suddenly doing so to meet up with what they'd consider a fine London beau. For that's what they would think of Lord Becconsall, if he strolled into the public bar, dressed in the beautifully tailored, highly fashionable kind of outfit he was wearing today.

Actually, there was no plausible excuse for her to be sitting with him here, either, without any chaperon at all. If anyone she knew were to walk in and see her leaning over the table to hold a conversation with a man to whom she was not related, in heated whispers, they'd be bound to draw the worst conclusion.

She sat back, blushing. Lord Becconsall barely seemed to notice. He was frowning off into the distance, as though his mind was already fully occupied with the conundrum she'd set him, rather than proprieties.

'There's nothing for it,' he said after a moment or two, during which Harriet's levels of guilt grew to such a pitch that she couldn't help looking over her shoulder just in case one of the other customers might be someone she knew. 'We'll have to call in reinforcements.'

'What?'

'Get someone else to go to Dorset, while I'm prowling round Thetford Forest.'

'But you promised you wouldn't tell anyone!'

'I did. And I won't tell anyone without your permission. But you have to face facts, Lady Harriet. If you'd gone to Bow Street, you would have had to tell your tale to a lot of people. The mission might have been shared between many operatives, none of whom you would have known. Whereas if I enlist a couple of my friends, you may be sure they would handle your predicament with the utmost tact and discretion.'

'Your friends?' A solid lump of ice formed in her stomach as she saw what he intended. 'You mean, I take it, the ones I met in the park that morning?'

'That's it, you see—'

'The ones who have already made me the subject of a wager?'

'Ah.'

'Yes. Ah, indeed! If you think I am going to have them…interfering in my family business, after they've already made a…game of me…then I…' She got to her feet. Snatched up her gloves. Then her umbrella. 'This was a mistake. I should never have confided in you.' The moment she'd started to trust him, to believe he meant what he'd said, he'd shown his true colours. He saw nothing wrong with breaking a promise if it was expedient to do so. He saw nothing wrong with sharing what she'd told him, in the strictest confidence, with a group of men he must know were the very last people in the world she wished to know anything about her business at all.

'Lady Harriet—'

'Good day to you,' she said, turning on her heel and marching out of the shop.

Leaving him to pick up the bill.

Chapter Twenty

She hated him. Eight hours it had been since she'd stormed out of the coffee house and stalked home, alone, and during that time her initial hurt and mistrust had steadily grown to the point where it felt as if it was going to burst from her very fingertips in sheets of flame.

She wasn't quite sure how she managed to lay down her knife and fork so neatly across her plate when she'd finished eating dinner, rather than fling the plate across the room just for the pleasure of hearing breaking crockery, or stabbing the fork into the table so hard it stood upright, quivering.

'You are quite sure you do not wish to come with me, Harriet?'

Harriet met her mother's enquiry with a cold stare. There was nothing Mama wished for less than for her to suddenly change her mind and say that, yes, actually, she would love to come to the meeting at wherever it was to discuss whatever it was that had Mama so full of anticipation that she could hardly wait to get out the door. The very last thing Mama wanted was an unmarried daughter trailing round behind her, or worse, sitting in a secluded corner where she'd be at the mercy of every importunate rake—if indeed rakes attended meetings where scientists gathered to discuss the latest findings. Mama was just not cut out to take on the onerous duties of chaperon.

She patted her mouth with her napkin before putting Mama out of her misery by saying, 'No, thank you, Mama.'

True to form, Mama smiled at her in undisguised relief as she got to her feet and scurried across the room, leaving Harriet to thank Mrs Smethurst for providing the meal when the elderly woman eventually shuffled in to clear the table.

Mrs Smethurst grunted something that Harriet didn't quite catch above the noise of cutlery scraping and dishes rattling, but it didn't sound any more cheerful than Harriet felt.

She drifted out of the room, across the hall and into the drawing room, though why on earth she'd done so she couldn't imagine. The furniture was still shrouded in holland covers, and the grate stood empty. As empty as she'd felt when, contrary to all his protestations, Lord Becconsall had not pursued her from the coffee house. Not that she'd wanted him to. It was just that, if he'd been sincere, he would surely have attempted to explain. Or apologise. But, no. He hadn't. Which meant he didn't care about her. Not really.

He cared about his friends, though. So much that he'd attempted to conceal his interest in her from them by making it all out to be some kind of joke.

She rubbed her arms vigorously. If only she'd actually gone to an employment bureau this morning, while she'd been out, she might at least have been able to hire someone to light a few fires about the place. Though how hard could it be? The scullery maid who'd performed that office at Stone Court had been very young. As had the girl who'd come in to her room first thing at Tarbrook House. And right at the bottom of the hierarchy. If lighting a fire was such a menial task, she ought to be able to learn how to do it.

She went to the grate, gave the pile of dusty kindling and the empty coal scuttle a brief inspection, before deciding to go up to her room instead. There had been a fire in there earlier on, so that it wouldn't be so damp and smell so musty as it did down here. It wasn't as if she was expecting to receive visitors at this time of night. She could plan out her next move just as well at her dressing table, or curled up on her bed.

As she made her way up the stairs, she gave herself a stern talking-to. Running into Lord Becconsall earlier might have ended up being an infuriating and humiliating experience, but talking things through with him had given her a few ideas. To start with, if he could go to Thetford and make enquiries, then why shouldn't she? She could saddle her horse and...

Actually, no, she couldn't. Shadow was still stabled in the mews behind Tarbrook House. Uncle Hugo had drawn the line at condemning an innocent horse to potential neglect when he'd washed his hands of his female relatives. And she couldn't see him, or his head groom, releasing her mare to her without first making sure the animal was going to be properly cared for.

Besides, a girl couldn't turn up in a remote village, on horseback, without attendants, and expect locals to answer her questions in a helpful, or even respectful, manner. They'd think she was not a respectable person.

She strode to her bed and picked up the shawl she'd left lying there. Bother the rules that restricted the movements of females! Even a married woman couldn't get away with jumping on a horse and taking off like that, without raising eyebrows.

She wrapped the shawl round her shoulders and went to sit at her dressing table. Very well, it wouldn't be feasible to go to Thetford. But there was nothing to prevent her going to pay a visit to an elderly, female recluse, was there? She just had to come up with some pretext for the visit. To that end, she was going to have to—

At that point, her thoughts were interrupted by the sound of someone knocking on her bedroom door. Puzzled, she went to open it to see Mr Smethurst standing there, looking most put out.

'You have visitors, my lady,' he said accusingly.

'Visitors? I didn't hear anyone knock on the front door.'

'They didn't. Come round the back, they did,' he said indignantly, 'and was inside before I could rightly stop 'em.'

Once again Harriet felt guilty for not seeing to the hiring of extra staff to help the elderly couple who had been living here as caretakers. Especially as Mama had warned her, on the way here, that it was going to be her responsibility to see to the running of the house.

'Now, I am not going to berate you for falling foul of Hugo,' she'd said. 'For what woman of spirit could fail to irritate a man with his tyrannical disposition? But you must see that though I support your stand against him, you cannot expect me to suddenly become domesticated. I had no intention of opening up Stone House when I came to London. And getting us thrown out of my sister's house is most inconvenient. You do see?'

'Yes, Mama,' she'd said meekly. And had vowed to see to everything. But first she'd spent those hours poring over maps to find out where Bogholt was and then had decided to visit Bow Street before the employment bureau. And finally, she'd been ambushed by Lord Becconsall. Which had left her so angry that she'd been in no fit state to do anything of a practical nature for the rest of the day.

With the result that she had no trained butler to deal with unexpected visitors, nor a burly footman to evict the kind that barged right in.

'Never mind, Smethurst,' she said. 'I'm sure you did your best.' Poor Mr Smethurst was only supposed to have the light duties of forwarding the mail and reporting to her father should the roof develop a leak, or something of that nature.

His expression became less troubled. 'Put 'em in the drawing room,' he said with a hint of malice. 'Told 'em it would be warmer in the kitchen, but they insisted they wanted somewhere more fitting.'

'You did quite right,' she said, thinking of the empty grate and the holland covers and the general air of disuse. They were not in a fit state to receive callers and if people insisted on coming in then it served them right.

'Who are they?'

Mr Smethurst looked blank.

'Didn't give no names.'

'Did they not give you their cards, either?'

He shook his head.

'Well, I'd better go and see what they want, I suppose. And...and you don't know who they are?'

He shook his head again.

She couldn't imagine what type of person would call at this hour of the night, unless it was someone looking for Mama. Oh, dear. She hadn't been paying very much attention earlier. Had she gone to the Institute of Enquiry into the Natural Sciences, or the Scientific Society of the...something else? The trouble with Mama's societies was that they all had names that used virtually the same words but in different orders. She was going to have to beg everyone's pardon and confess that she had no real idea where Mama was this evening, and invite them to return on another day. By which time she would have made the drawing room a bit more habitable. She descended the stairs with the sense of dread that always went before a potentially humiliating encounter, squared her shoulders as she crossed the hall and opened the door of the drawing room with her chin up.

Only to halt on the threshold in astonishment. For the callers who'd broken with convention by ignoring the lack of the knocker, going round to the back of the house and pushing past poor defenceless Mr Smethurst were none other than Lord Becconsall, Lord Rawcliffe, Captain Bretherton and Mr Kellett.

She might have known it. They were just the sort of men to dispense with decent manners and do exactly as they pleased.

'Very well, Mr Smethurst,' she said to the faithful man, who was still hovering nervously behind her. 'I can deal with this.' Looking relieved, Mr Smethurst turned away and ambled off in the direction of his nice warm kitchen.

Harriet stepped into the drawing room and shut the door behind her.

'You really ought not to be here at all, the four of you, not at this time of the evening,' she said.

'Yes, we know the proper time for paying calls is far earlier in the day,' said Lord Becconsall, 'but this is not exactly a social call, is it?'

And they were here now. And she couldn't very well throw them all out.

Besides, part of her was intrigued by the fact that they'd all come. That Lord Becconsall had obliged them all to come. Even though she'd told him she didn't want them involved. And had walked away from him.

She'd been angry with him all day for not being persistent, but it looked as though his notion of persistency merely differed from hers. Which shouldn't have surprised her, given the complicated way his mind seemed to work.

'Very well,' she said. Because there was just the chance that he'd come here to plead for forgiveness. And more to the point, she'd have no peace if she turned him away without a hearing. 'Say what you have to say,' she said and folded her arms across her chest.

'Could we not sit somewhere where there is a fire? It is like an icehouse in here.'

He glanced at Atlas, then back at her, with a pleading expression.

'It is entirely your own fault. You would insist on coming in here.'

'Then it is clearly up to us to make the place more habitable,' said Lord Becconsall, going over to the fireplace, kneeling down, pulling a tinder box from a pocket and setting about lighting the fire.

'May I?' Captain Bretherton didn't await her reply before yanking the covers off a couple of chairs, rolling them up and tossing them into a corner.

Lord Rawcliffe prodded the upholstery of one of the uncovered chairs with the silver ferrule of his cane.

'Lord Becconsall informs us that we owe you an apology,' he said, turning to the other chair that Captain Bretherton had uncovered and giving it similar treatment. 'Over the matter of the wager.'

'Oh.' So that was why he'd brought them here.

'Yes. He is very angry with us. We have all, naturally, sworn that none of us have spoken out of turn, but he has remained adamant that we must all tender our apologies.' He shot Lord Becconsall's back a look of resentment.

'I don't see it is the slightest bit necessary for all of you to come here,' she said, becoming aware, suddenly, that there was a good deal of tension flickering between all four men.

'No, Ulysses is right,' said Captain Bretherton, his face creasing in concern. 'If you feel we have insulted you, then we do owe you an apology.'

'*If?*' She took a couple of paces into the room. 'You jolly well did insult me. Mocked me. I overheard you laughing about me. At Miss Roke—I think it was—her ball.'

'There, you see, Becconsall?' Lord Rawcliffe turned to where he was crouched on the hearthrug, blowing on to the wisps of kindling he'd managed so far to coax into sputtering out smoke. 'It was not one of us who spoke out of turn.'

'I never said it was,' said Lord Becconsall, between puffs. 'Can't you see, that's not the point,' he said, getting to his feet and wiping his hands on his coat tails.

'Then, what is the p-point?' asked Archie, looking totally bewildered.

'The point is,' said Lord Becconsall, approaching her with his hands held out as though in supplication, 'I need you to trust them all, Lady Harriet. You need help and I have no truer, finer friends than these three men.'

'Is that some kind of joke?' She took a step back. How dare he bring them here and practically demand she spill confidential family information to them, when he'd just confirmed the fact that they'd made a joke of the last predicament they'd found her in?

'The very last people I would trust with confidential family information is a bunch of men who make sport of defenceless females...'

'Hardly defenceless,' put in Lord Rawcliffe. 'I seem to recall you gave a very good account of yourself with that riding crop.'

'Nevertheless, you none of you behaved like gentlemen.'

'I helped you remount your horse,' Captain Bretherton objected.

'And then you made me the topic of a wager!'

'You know,' Lord Rawcliffe drawled, 'I believe Ulysses only did so as a pretext for tracking you down. He has been smitten from the very first.'

'Smitten? Hah!' Harriet tossed her head. Though even as she did so, she wondered if the gesture might be lacking in conviction. Because Lord Becconsall had already told her the very same thing, in the coffee house. 'A man who is smitten,' she continued, putting every ounce of indignation into her voice that she could muster, 'does not…hold the threat of exposure over a lady's head. And torment her with her less than exemplary conduct every time he meets her.'

'He does if he is behaving with the finesse of a boy of the age of twelve, who thinks the best way to attract the attention of a girl he likes is to pull her pigtails,' said Lord Becconsall, ruefully.

Was that what he'd been doing? Oh. Come to think of it, even when she'd warned him she would not admit him to her house, nor dance with him, he hadn't given up that teasing. On the contrary, he'd shown every indication of stepping up his campaign to annoy her.

There was a beat of silence while everyone stared at him. In varying degrees of shock. Well, everyone except Lord Rawcliffe, who wore his usual knowing, and faintly mocking expression.

'While you are setting the record straight, Ulysses,' said Lord Rawcliffe in a sarcastic drawl, 'why don't you explain the nature of the wager? She may well feel differently about the whole episode if she hears what the stakes were.'

'The stakes?' Lord Becconsall frowned. 'What difference will that make? It was not the stakes, but the fact that we were, apparently, bandying her name about as though we had no respect for her that she objected to.'

Harriet's heart leapt. He really did understand the nature of his offence. *That* was why he'd brought all his friends here. He could tell how badly he'd hurt her—how they'd all hurt her by treating her so lightly—and was genuinely sorry for doing something that had left her feeling humiliated. He also knew she needed to hear them *all* apologise.

And cared enough about her to make them do it.

He had broken the invisible bonds of male camaraderie that had made her feel so excluded when she'd seen them together before. To put her feelings first. To put *her* first.

'Just tell her,' Lord Rawcliffe insisted.

Lord Becconsall turned to her, looking shamefaced. 'You have to understand, we were all rather castaway. And I was trying to...'

She pulled herself up as tall as she could and looked down her nose at him, the way Mama was in the habit of looking at Uncle Hugo. She might be on the verge of forgiving him, but she had no intention of letting him off easily. He deserved to squirm, for the misery he'd put her through. 'You were trying to?'

'Well, never mind what I was trying to do. The point is, that night was the first time all four of us had been together since our schooldays. And we...well...' He ran his fingers through his hair. 'I think it was because we all started using the nicknames we had for each other at school. It made us all sort of slip back into the roles we had then. Zeus ordering us all around as though he was a god.' He shot Lord Rawcliffe a look of resentment. 'Atlas taking the burdens of the world on his shoulders...' He glanced over to where Atlas had just slumped into one of the chairs he'd uncovered, looking like the last man able to shoulder any kind of burden. 'And Archie...'

'They called me Archimedes because they all thought I was so much cleverer than them,' said Mr Kellett mournfully. And subsided into the other chair, next to Atlas, even though she was still standing and hadn't given anyone permission to sit down. In other men, she would consider this a display of rank bad manners. And it was. But in the case of Atlas, he looked as though, if he hadn't sat down when he did, he might have fallen down. And Archie was just typical of the sort of men Mama often consorted with, who frequently forgot about inconsequential matters like etiquette when they were all fired up with weightier matters.

'Anyway, we argued about you,' Lord Becconsall continued, having shot Archie one exasperated glance. 'I maintained you were an innocent, who had no idea you were behaving improperly. Zeus swore you were no such thing. I wanted to clear your name,' he said, holding out his hands to her again, in that gesture of appeal for understanding.

And in a way, she did understand. After all, hadn't she infuriated Uncle Hugo, by the way she'd gone about trying to clear Aunt Susan's name? She'd been clumsy, and trampled all over lots of people's feelings. With the best of intentions.

'But at the same time, I'd only just found these fellows again, after years abroad, and…and other things, and it was so…' He spread his hands wide, as though lacking the words to explain himself properly. 'I didn't want to risk losing them again by letting it descend into a real quarrel. And so…'

'He turned it into a joke,' put in Lord Rawcliffe, giving Lord Becconsall a thoughtful look. 'The way he always did when he found himself in a tight corner.'

'A joke? I was a joke, then?'

'No! Not you. The wager. The wager was the joke. I declared that the stake should be what it always had been between us. It was an attempt to remind…all of us that we shared…well…' He floundered to a halt.

'Tell her what the stake was,' Lord Rawcliffe, insisted.

'It was a cream bun,' said Lord Becconsall in a voice barely above a whisper. 'That was what we always used to stake, at school.'

'You…made my reputation the topic of a wager? The winner to be bought a cream bun?'

'Yes.' Lord Becconsall hung his head.

For a moment Harriet stared at the four of them. Lord Rawcliffe somewhat defiant, his hands clasped tightly over the silver handle of his cane. Atlas slumped on one chair, looking too fragile to get up. Archie looking at her like a spaniel who'd been threatened with a bath after rolling in the midden. And Lord Becconsall, flushed, and staring at her with a mixture of defiance and embarrassment.

'Actually, if you want the whole truth,' said Lord Rawcliffe, 'by this stage we already had one wager behind us. Regarding Lucifer, my stallion, which he'd lost spectacularly.'

Lord Becconsall sighed. 'Yes. So we raised the stakes to double or quits.'

She stared at the defiant way Lord Rawcliffe was standing, the silver-topped cane clutched in his elegant fingers. And imagined him sitting down and happily devouring not one, but two cream buns. Like a greedy little schoolboy. The image was so incongruous that she started to giggle.

'C-cream b-buns. Oh, oh, lord!'

Well, she need no longer fear any of these four men would spill her family secrets. If it ever got out that Lord Rawcliffe, who, according to Aunt Susan, was just about the most elegant, hardened, philandering, sophisticated male of his generation, had taken part in a wager to win a cream bun, at the advanced age of thirty-five or whatever he was, he would never live it down.

And he knew it.

'So, now you know my deepest, darkest shame, Lady Harriet,' said Lord Rawcliffe, 'you can have no fear of trusting us with whatever it is that Ulysses wishes us to help you with. Our lips are, perforce, sealed.'

It was as though he'd been reading her mind.

'Yes. I qu-quite see th-that.' She giggled.

'Then you will let us help you?' Lord Becconsall took a pace towards her. 'You can see that they are men you can trust, can you not? After all, they never spoke a word about what you got up to in the park.'

'How ungentlemanly of you to remind me of that,' she said, pretending to be cross.

'Lady Harriet,' he said in a pleading tone.

'Well,' she said, pretending to think about it. 'I suppose…if they can keep the scandalous affair of the cream buns a secret, then they might very well be the type of men to entrust with the solving of the mystery of the fake rubies.'

Chapter Twenty-One

'Fake rubies?' Archie sprang to his feet as though he'd been jerked by invisible strings. 'Someone in your family has discovered they've g-got fake rubies, instead of the genuine article?'

'Yes,' said Harriet.

'By G-G-G...' He shook his head and swallowed. 'S-Same thing happened to us. That is m-my mother. That is, when she inherited g-g...' He swallowed again.

Lord Becconsall went to his side. 'Take a deep breath, Archie,' he said soothingly. 'No need to get so agitated,' he continued while Archie breathed in deeply a couple of times. 'I recall you telling us that your grandmother died recently and that you then discovered something disturbing about her that none of you had ever dreamed. Is this connected to Lady Harriet's case?'

'M-might be coincidence. B-but, see, her j-jewels—at least the rubies—t-turned out to be p-paste. C-Couldn't understand why she'd want to have them c-copied. No gaming habits. No d-debts my father c-could discover.'

'Oh!' Harriet sat down on a sofa that was still covered by a dusty dustsheet. 'And now everyone in your family is trying to keep it a secret, to protect her reputation.'

'That's ab-bout the size of it.'

'That is just what has happened to my aunt. At least…' she rubbed her brow with one finger as she tried to assemble the facts in an intelligible order '…it was Lord Tarbrook who discovered the rubies had been copied. When he took them to the jewellers for cleaning and re-setting against the day when Kitty would wear them at her betrothal ball. It's a sort of family tradition, apparently. And they were in such a horridly old-fashioned setting, Kitty said, that she wasn't surprised nobody wore them except when tradition demanded it. Anyway, when the jeweller told my uncle that the rubies were paste, he immediately assumed that my aunt had got into debt and raised the money to pay it off by having the rubies secretly copied, rather than owning up. And he still believes it, even though she swears she did no such thing.'

'And he didn't try to find out the truth?' Lord Becconsall came to sit beside her on the sofa. Lord Rawcliffe chose to remain standing.

'No. He was determined to blame Aunt Susan,' she said indignantly. 'He was as mad as fire when I started to question the servants. Although, Aunt Susan said she could understand his attitude, because, you see, when he was a boy, his mother had accused a servant of stealing some of her jewellery, falsely, as it turned out, because the missing jewels turned up. But only after the servant had been condemned and hanged.'

Captain Bretherton and Archie both muttered imprecations. Lord Rawcliffe looked grim. Lord Becconsall shook his head.

'I know, it must have been terrible for him. But—' she turned to Lord Becconsall '—that would have given him the perfect reason for claiming he didn't want any sort of investigation if he'd been the one to have them copied, wouldn't it?'

'What makes you think he might have done that?'

'Well, he did cut up rough about some of the expenses Aunt Susan was running up this Season. And complained bitterly about bringing me out alongside her own daughter. So when he went all...medieval about the whole affair, I wondered if some of the bluster wasn't a sort of smokescreen to cover up his own guilt.'

'No, I don't think that's it,' said Lord Becconsall at once. 'For one thing, if he was the one who'd had the jewels copied, he wouldn't have needed to say anything about it, would he?'

'Oh,' said Harriet, crestfallen. 'No, I suppose not.'

'Besides, now we know of a similar thing happening within Archie's family, it sounds much more like the work of a very sophisticated, highly organised, criminal gang.'

'Does it?'

'Yes—it's almost a perfect crime, isn't it?' His face took on a tinge of admiration. 'If jewels are just stolen, someone will raise a hue and cry at once. But stealing them this way, replacing them with good copies so that the crime isn't even noticed for some considerable time, makes tracing the people responsible almost impossible.'

'Oh.' Her spirits sank. 'You mean we are not going

to be able to find out who took the rubies? And clear Aunt Susan's name?'

'I didn't say it was impossible. I said *almost* impossible. But look about you, Lady Harriet. We have here in this room four of the most capable men in England, each in their own way. If anyone can unmask the criminals, we can.'

Lady Harriet looked at his three friends in turn, trying to see what he could see in them. He'd kept insisting that Captain Bretherton was strong, but his sallow complexion and slightly shaky hands told a different tale. Likewise, Mr Kellett was supposed to be the cleverest man in England, but when agitated he could scarcely utter one intelligible word. And then there was Lord Rawcliffe, who believed in himself to such a degree that his friends referred to him as Zeus.

'Well, Ulysses, where do you suggest we start?'

To Harriet's surprise, it was Lord Rawcliffe who had spoken. He'd actually asked Lord Becconsall's opinion. She glanced from Lord Rawcliffe, to Lord Becconsall, who grinned at her expression of amazement. Lord Rawcliffe sniffed.

'I didn't give him the name of Ulysses for nothing. He has the kind of quick brain just suited to this kind of task. Even at school I could tell that most of his antics were designed to disguise his real nature. So that people would underestimate him.'

At her side, Lord Becconsall shifted in his seat, as though embarrassed.

'More to the point,' said Lord Becconsall, 'I have learned a lot about the habits of criminals from the men under my command. Not all of them, but rather a lot of them had cheated the gallows by joining up. And hardly a one of them reformed. Instead, they recreated the kind of network they'd been involved with in whatever town they'd come from. And set about flouting every rule ever devised by their superiors. They would have one man doing the thieving, another one watching out, another passing the goods to a fence—that is a receiver and handler of stolen goods. There were forgers and coiners, and confidence tricksters…'

'Oh! Forgers! Do you think that reference…?'

Lord Becconsall smiled at her. 'It is possible. Very possible.'

Lord Rawcliffe coughed. 'I hate to interrupt you, but the rest of us in this room have no idea what you are talking about.'

'I beg your pardon,' said Harriet. 'It is just that the girl suspected of being the jewel thief in our household was given a reference by an elderly lady who never sets foot from her home in Dorset. And the girl herself came from Norfolk. So how could they possibly have met?'

'Not in itself conclusive evidence a forgery has been employed.'

'No, but…' She sighed in exasperation. 'I am not explaining this very clearly. You see, at first, when I started asking the servants what they knew, they all got very annoyed with me. But then, when Lord Tarbrook had me shut in my room, they began to relent.'

At her side, on the sofa, she was aware of Lord Becconsall stiffening. If it was because she'd just said Lord Tarbrook had shut her in her room, then he wasn't as bright as everyone thought, for she'd told him, by way of her story, about being shut in. She glanced at him to see he was gazing at her with what looked like admiration, though why on earth he should do any such thing, at this point in her narrative, she couldn't imagine.

'Anyway,' she continued informing the others, 'by the time he threw us out—me and Mama, that is—they were beginning to see that all I wanted was to clear Aunt Susan's name, not send one of them, wrongfully, to the gallows. And they'd all been talking amongst themselves, and remembered this girl who'd worked for Lady Tarbrook for only a few weeks, a couple of years ago.'

'Two years ago? Then…the criminals must have been running this rig—which is what they call deceiving their victims,' Lord Becconsall explained, 'for some considerable time.'

'My grandmother,' put in Archie, 'died six months ago.'

'I wonder how many other thefts there have been in the interim,' Lord Becconsall pondered. 'Because I cannot see them leaving a great gap between one operation and the next, not if the method had such a successful outcome.'

'You are assuming the theft of the Kellett rubies took place only six months ago,' pointed out Lord Rawcliffe. 'Your jewel thief may have taken them at the same time as she took the Tarbrook parure. Each theft was only discovered upon the event of an impending betrothal, or burial,' he said, as though either fate was an equally horrid one.

'Well, I don't suppose we'll ever know,' Harriet answered. 'Because nobody will talk about the copying of jewels, will they? Because they will think that it means someone in their family is concealing debts.'

'My word, but whoever thought this up must be brilliant,' said Lord Becconsall. 'First they have the jewels copied, to delay discovery, and then they relied on the people concerned bickering amongst themselves about who may be responsible, rather than reporting it as theft at all. Hiding their crime under two layers of concealment.'

'They might have been doing this for years...' breathed Harriet.

'Until you believed in the innocence of one of their victims,' said Lord Becconsall with a look in his eyes that she could not mistake this time. He really did look as though he admired her.

'Come,' he said. 'Tell us everything you have managed to discover.'

'Well, not much more than I've already told you. Maud only had the time it took us to pack my things to tell me what the servants suspected, because Lord Tarbrook wanted us out of his house almost as quickly as Mama wished to leave. Maud only managed to tell me that they became suspicious about this one particular girl because although she said she was leaving because she'd got a better place, to their knowledge she wasn't actually in service anywhere any longer.'

'The better offer might have come from a man,' Lord Rawcliffe put in.

'I suppose it might,' Harriet conceded. 'Except that even in that case, somebody would have caught sight of her, wouldn't they? Parading about the park in her new finery? And also, she wasn't very attractive. Nor flirtatious. A little mouse, was the way Maud described her. Which makes her sound like the perfect person to creep into my aunt's house and sneak out again as soon as she'd accomplished what she'd set out to do. Oh, dear,' she added. 'I sound as if I've found her guilty already.

Just because she didn't fit in with the other servants and she didn't bother to tell any of them where she intended to go when she left. For whatever reason.'

'Well, isn't that another reason not to employ Bow Street Runners? They would be more concerned about appearing to apprehend a culprit, than finding out the truth.'

Harriet sighed. 'Yes, I suppose so. I certainly want to find her and make her answer a few questions. Even if she isn't involved, directly, she might know something…'

'We shall find her, Lady Harriet,' said Lord Becconsall gently. 'But we won't apprehend her unless we are sure she is guilty. You have my word.'

'And how are we to find her,' said Lord Rawcliffe witheringly, 'when the servants claim to have no idea where she has gone?'

'Well, we could start looking in the village where she came from. It's called Bogholt—'

Lord Rawcliffe let out a bark of laughter. 'If there is really any such place I shall be very surprised.'

'Well, be surprised then,' Harriet retorted, 'because I found it on a map. Somebody there is bound to know of her, if she really came from there, because it is only a tiny hamlet. In the Forest of Thetford.'

Lord Rawcliffe inclined his head in her direction. 'I stand corrected. Please, do tell us what else you believe you know.'

Harriet glared at him. And then proceeded to tell the others what she knew.

'Her name is Jenny Wren—'

'An alias if ever I heard one,' muttered Lord Rawcliffe.

'And she was given the job on the recommendation of the Dowager Lady Buntingford.'

'Lady B-B...' Archie began.

'Buntingford,' Lord Rawcliffe finished on his behalf. 'Why, is there some special significance to that name, in your case as well?'

'Yes. She was one of Grandmama's friends. C-Came out together, wrote to each other all the time. Asked her to b-be my own mother's godmother. Lives in Lesser Peeving, now, as I recall.'

'Is that in Dorset?'

'Y-yes.'

'Then there we have a clear connection.'

'Do you seriously mean to tell me,' said Harriet in disbelief, 'that you suspect this elderly lady of persuading her former friends to employ a jewel thief in the guise of a lady's maid? So that she can...hoard them all up like some kind of elderly demented magpie?'

'Perhaps that is why she has become a recluse,' suggested Lord Rawcliffe. 'Perhaps her family have her safely locked away on one of their estates so that she cannot wander about in society embarrassing everyone by helping herself to other people's gewgaws.'

'But she is thwarting them all by sending out an experienced jewel thief in her stead? No, I don't think that will fadge,' said Lord Becconsall. 'For one thing, how did she meet the thief? If she is being kept locked away?'

'What about forgery?' said Captain Bretherton, making Harriet jump because he'd been so quiet since he'd slumped down on his chair that she'd suspected he'd dozed off. 'Probably easy enough to forge the writing of an elderly lady. I've seen men forge my own signature,' he said bitterly, 'in such a convincing manner that I was half-persuaded I'd signed the docket myself.'

'I suppose,' said Lord Becconsall, 'that if a criminal gang can employ a girl to slip into houses under the guise of a maid and make her disappear afterwards, and can think of a crime that is damn near unnoticeable, then they would be bound to have access to a forger. And a fence.'

'But that doesn't explain why it's always rubies,' said Harriet. 'I mean, I can see a demented elderly lady wanting to pile them all up, in secret. But not for a professional criminal to only steal one kind of jewels. Why didn't he go for the Tarbrook diamonds? They must be worth a lot more than that old set of rubies that hardly anyone ever wore.'

'We have no evidence that the thieves have only ever stolen rubies,' said Lord Rawcliffe. 'We only know of two cases, after all. It may be coincidence that both crimes feature rubies.'

'According to my men,' said Lord Becconsall, 'some thefts are done to order.'

'You mean,' said Harriet incredulously, 'people say, I'd like a ruby necklace, and a thief just goes out and steals one?'

'Not quite that cut and dried, but someone with a particular demand will let it be known in certain quarters that a suitable reward will be offered for the right kind of goods. That sort of thing.'

'Goodness.'

'Yes, but I think you have also given us another very good reason why this particular criminal has targeted the jewels in question. The Tarbrook diamonds are famous and popular. The rubies were not.'

'That's true. Aunt Susan kept them shut away and nobody wore them except on special occasions because they were so hideous.'

'Another layer of insurance to ensure the theft wasn't detected. The gang only stole jewels that were not going to be missed in a hurry. Though they might well have had a specific buyer in mind, all the same,' said Lord Becconsall, as though reluctant to relinquish his theory about why there were two sets of rubies that had been copied.

'It m-makes you w-wonder how a thief w-would know ab-bout them, then. If the ladies hardly ever wore them.'

There was a beat of silence. 'They do appear in several portraits, apparently,' said Harriet. 'Painted whenever one of the Tarbrook ladies became betrothed. There is one hanging in the London house, of Lord Tarbrook's sister, done many years ago. Kitty pointed it out to me to prove how hideous they were.'

'Ah! It's the same with the K-Kellett Set. Show up in p-portraits going back hundreds of years. Starting in Elizab-bethan t-times. Only reason I knew a-bout them as I've never seen my mother actually wear them. C-couldn't have done, of c-course,' he added with a frown, 'since they were in m-my g-grandmother's p-possession until she d-died.'

Lord Becconsall whistled low. 'Whoever is running this particular rig must have had access to the homes of families from the *haut ton* and seen the jewels he planned to steal depicted in portraits, since the ladies in both these cases were reluctant to actually wear them in public.'

'Or she,' pointed out Lord Rawcliffe. 'There is some

merit in Lady Harriet's theory of the elderly demented magpie, in my opinion.'

Harriet would have preened had she not detected a hint of cynicism in Lord Rawcliffe's voice that made her fear he was actually mocking her.

'It would be much simpler to assume that she sent a lady's maid into the houses to steal jewels she had her eye on, rather than to have someone go to all the trouble of employing a forger to fake those references. She also knows the families intimately and would therefore have known that it would be possible to steal and copy jewels that weren't very often on show. And given the maid clear instructions as to how to go about it.'

'Oh, that's a very good point,' said Harriet, grudgingly, for she wasn't at all sure she wanted to be thinking along the same lines as Lord Rawcliffe. 'For Maud said none of the servants could see how a burglar could have got in and stolen the jewels, then replaced them with copies before anyone noticed they'd even gone missing. Which made me think that there must have been somebody who knew the family, and their habits, and all about the jewels, too.'

'It would also explain,' said Lord Becconsall, 'as you said earlier, Rawcliffe, why her family keep her shut away, nowadays, if she is in the habit of helping herself to shiny things that don't belong to her.'

'Lesser Peeving,' said Lord Rawcliffe, as though he hadn't been paying attention to the last few moments of conversation. 'Why does that place sound familiar? I am certain I can never have visited the place. But I have heard it mentioned. Somewhere.'

'It will come to you,' said Lord Becconsall. 'Probably when you are thinking about something else.'

'I feel sure you must be right,' he said in such a condescending tone that Harriet felt a bit indignant on Lord Becconsall's behalf.

'Well, then,' said Lord Becconsall, without appearing to have taken the slightest bit of offence. 'Now all we have to do is come up with a plan of campaign.' He got to his feet, as though eager to get started.

'I have already told Lady Harriet that I am willing to go to this Bogholt place to find out what I can about the servant girl,' he said, 'under pretext of attending the next meeting at Newmarket.'

'Do you not think it would be better,' said Lord Rawcliffe, 'if I were to do that? I attend the races regularly. Whereas you do not have the reputation of being much of a gamester.'

'Except when it comes to cream buns, apparently,' Harriet couldn't resist saying.

Lord Rawcliffe gave her a cold stare.

'I hope I am not going to regret admitting you into my confidence.'

'Never mind the cream buns,' said Lord Becconsall, planting his fists on his hips. 'We need to focus on the rubies. And finding out who took them. And I already have things all planned out in my head regarding the trip to Bogholt. I can mingle with the locals and win their trust far more easily than you, Zeus. You'll go striding in there as though you are God and set up everyone's backs, I shouldn't wonder.'

Lord Rawcliffe raised one eyebrow. 'You are seriously considering leaving Town, just when Lady Harriet is beginning to soften towards you?'

Lord Becconsall turned to look at Harriet, who felt as if she'd just been stripped naked by that percipient remark. Which wasn't a very helpful feeling to have, just when Lord Becconsall was looking at her so intently.

For a moment, they just stood there, staring at each other. And though Harriet was blushing, she couldn't drag her eyes from Lord Becconsall's face. Because it bore such a look of wonder, and hope, that her initial feeling of vulnerability faded with each breath she took.

'I have something to prove to Lady Harriet,' said Lord Becconsall to Lord Rawcliffe, though he hadn't taken his eyes off her. 'My trip to Bogholt will be in the nature of a quest.'

'I don't think that will be necessary,' Lord Rawcliffe drawled. 'Or advisable. You would do far better to stay here and court her in form. As she deserves. Ladies, so I have found, prefer a man to be near them, dancing attendance, not haring off on ridiculous quests which they will decide you have undertaken as much for your own amusement as to impress them.'

'Is that so?' Again, although he was speaking to Lord Rawcliffe, he was looking intently at her face. 'Lady Harriet?' He took a half-step closer to her and gazed down into her face. Whatever he saw there appeared to help him come to a decision.

'You go to Bogholt, then,' he said to Lord Rawcliffe airily, 'and find out what you can. I will stay here with Lady Harriet and—'

'Give her daily reports of progress with the investigation,' said Lord Rawcliffe smoothly.

'And I will go to Lesser P-Peeving,' said Archie. 'P-pay a visit to my mother's g-godmother. See if she is hoarding rubies in her chamber p-pot, or something of that nature.'

'Or if she's taken a skilled forger into her employ,'

put in Captain Bretherton, who appeared to have forgers on the brain. Not surprising if he'd had his own signature faked, she supposed. 'Do you happen to have a role mapped out for me?'

'I should think Ulysses will, in due course, be in need of a groomsman. And who better to stand up with him than you?'

Both Captain Bretherton and Lord Becconsall shot Lord Rawcliffe identical looks of indignation. And Harriet was pretty certain a similar sort of expression showed on her own face. It was all very well his friends calling him Zeus, and letting him manage their lives, but he had no right to subject her to the same kind of treatment.

'Ah. It has just come to me,' he said, as though oblivious to the hostile glances being aimed in his direction. 'Lesser Peeving. Oh, lord, how ironic,' he said with a shake of his head.

'Are you going to enlighten us?'

Lord Rawcliffe regarded the head of his cane for a moment or two. 'I do not think it has any bearing on the case. At least, I hope it does not have any bearing on the case. It is just that I happen to know of a clergyman who was sent to a parish there, a few years ago. His father is the incumbent of the parish nearest to Kelsham Park, so naturally I hear news of his offspring, from time to time.'

'Well, that's one mystery solved,' said Lord Becconsall, with heavy irony.

'Which, gentlemen, brings the proceedings here to a conclusion. I will take my leave of you, Lady Harriet,' said Lord Rawcliffe, bowing over her hand and kissing it. And darting her a look from a pair of heavy-lidded eyes that would, she was sure, have made the hearts of many society misses skip a beat.

Apart from one whose heart had already been given to another.

'Come, Atlas, Archie,' he said, jerking his head to the other two men, who immediately sprang to their feet.

Only Lord Becconsall remained exactly where he was. Even when his friends had left the room, shutting the door behind them.

And he was looking at her in such a way that her heart began to thump against her chest. For she was alone, in a virtually empty house, with a man who was gazing at her as though he wanted to devour her.

Chapter Twenty-Two

'**Y**our hands are absolutely freezing,' said Lord Bec-consall.

She looked down to discover that at some point he'd taken hold of them in his own.

He cleared his throat. 'At least the fire is beginning to put out a little heat now, along with the smoke.'

Harriet could not believe her ears. He'd led her to believe he was about to propose, but now all he could talk about was the smoking fire.

'I…we…that is…' He took a deep breath. And she suddenly perceived he was as nervous as she was. 'Hang it, you know we should not really be alone like this.'

'No.' She looked up at him shyly. 'It is highly improper.'

Whatever he saw in her face must have reassured him, for he grinned.

'What I am about to do next is even more improper,' he said. 'At least, people would say so, if they ever found out, but you were the one to point out that it was something I should have done already.'

She could tell from the burning look in his eyes that

he was going to kiss her. That was what he meant. She supposed a properly brought-up young lady should have protested. Laid her hand upon his chest as he loomed closer, as though to prevent him having his way.

But Harriet hadn't been 'properly' brought up. So she clung on to his hands very tightly and lifted her face to make it easier for him to gain access to her lips.

She'd expected him to kiss her the way he'd kissed her in the park, since he'd told her he wanted to find out if it really had been as splendid as he'd thought. But instead, he gently touched his lips to hers, with what felt almost like reverence.

And yet that scarcely-there brush of his mouth sent rivers of pleasure cascading through her body all the same. And made her utter a little hum of pleasure.

'Zeus was right, wasn't he?' he said, breaking off to gaze down into her face. 'You are softening towards me.'

'If I wasn't, I'd have reached for the poker long before this,' she said, looping her arms round his neck. 'And brained you with it.'

His breath hitched. He leaned in and kissed her again, this time with more confidence, and for considerably longer. By the time he broke off, they were both breathing heavily and Harriet's heart was pounding thickly, making her blood course hotly through her veins.

'I have been longing to do that ever since that morning in the park. I have dreamed of your lips. Your hair,' he said, reaching up one hand to stroke an errant strand that had come untucked from its pins. 'The feel of you…' he breathed, sliding one arm round her waist and pulling her closer.

'It wasn't just the park, though, was it? Or the blow to the head, or—'

He stopped her mouth with another kiss. Pulled her tight to his body, so that they were melded together from breast to knee.

'It was you, Harriet...' he breathed. 'The magic all came from you. How did I get to be so lucky?' He gazed down at her as though he'd never seen anything quite so lovely.

'You mean, if you hadn't fallen off that horse at my feet...'

'No. That was just how we met. I meant that I cannot believe I have been lucky enough to be here, with you in my arms like this, after doing everything wrong. I should have courted you, instead of teasing and tormenting you. Only...'

'Only what?'

'It was too important, that was what it was,' he said reflectively. 'If you hadn't liked me as much as I liked you, to start with, then it would have hurt. Very much.'

'Much safer to test the waters, first?'

'Something like that. God, what a coward I am.'

'No. Not you,' she said, twirling a strand of his hair between her fingers. 'You are just...a bit like me, I think. And that is why I understand the way you've behaved, better than another woman would. You have never had anyone love you very much, have you? Which has left you feeling as if perhaps you are not very lovable.'

He started. 'You feel the same way?'

She pressed her lips together in a rueful way. 'Most girls, I have observed, seem to find it easy to let men know when advances would be welcome. They have the confidence to believe that it is worthwhile giving their favourite a hint, you see. Only I always thought that if I did something like that, I would just be making a fool of myself...'

'We are a matched pair, are we not?' He gripped her hands again, as though what he was about to say was really important. 'I felt that, you know, right from the start. As though I recognised you, somehow. Does that sound very foolish?'

She shook her head. Nothing he was saying sounded foolish to her eager ears.

'I sometimes felt as though you saw me as well. The real me. The one who hides beneath all the layers of artifice and jocularity. The only other person who has ever appeared to see anything of value in me has been Zeus. It is largely because he believed in me at a time when I was at my most vulnerable that I forgive him so much else... Lord, listen to me! These are not exactly words of courtship, are they?'

'Actually, I feel as though they are,' she said. 'Because you are allowing me to see your very deepest self. The part of you that you conceal from everyone else.'

'I never want to be anything but totally honest with you, Harriet. I wish I had been from the start. That I'd laid my feelings bare and courted you properly.'

'I probably wouldn't have believed you were in earnest, anyway. I'm not exactly the kind of girl men fall in love with at first sight, am I?'

'Who has made you feel like that,' he said indignantly. 'Your aunt?'

She shook her head.

'Your uncle? Hauling you out of the drawing room

in front of everyone the way he did and locking you in your room…'

'No, no, I don't care what he thinks of me.'

'Hmmph,' he said. 'So if it wasn't them, then who was it? Your mother? That's it, isn't it? I have often wondered why she isn't the one bringing you out.'

'It isn't because she thinks I'm not marriageable. It's more because—oh, dear, this isn't very easy to explain. Especially as for years and years I thought she simply didn't care about me at all.'

'Why is that?'

'Well, she has some very…er…modern ideas about educating females, apparently. But also, well, to be perfectly frank, she is one of the most self-absorbed people you are ever likely to meet. And Papa is a dear, but…'

'But?'

'Well, I'm not a boy.'

'I had noticed,' he said with a wicked grin. 'And I thank God for it.'

She blushed, but persisted. 'Yes, but you see, Papa has always had to spend a lot of time with my oldest brother, Charles.'

'His heir,' he said, with a tinge of bitterness.

'Yes, his heir.'

'And they spend all day, riding round the estates. So that he can teach him all about the land he will one day have to manage.'

'Yes. That's only natural.' She looked up into his face with concern.

'Oh, yes, it's natural, right enough. One day Charles will have to fill your father's shoes. And should something happen to him, he still has the magnificent George ready to take up the reins.'

'And also, there is William. He takes after Mama in his mania for the natural sciences. Papa is proud of him for being so intrepid—he's off in South America, hunting for plants. And Mama dotes on him, too, because of all the fascinating things he writes to her about from his travels.'

'Ah. Your father has some pride in *his* youngest son, does he?'

'Did not yours?' she asked, finally understanding the source of his bitterness as they were discussing her older brothers.

'No. I told you, did I not, that I was always regarded as the runt of the litter.'

'At least I was just…merely a girl,' said Harriet with feeling. 'And an afterthought. I always thought nobody quite knew what to do with me, but they never made me feel…'

'Oh, I think they did, though, didn't they? That is why, at bottom, we understand each other so well.'

'Oh, oh…' She pulled up short. 'I cannot keep calling you Lord Becconsall. And I absolutely will not call you Ulysses.'

He grinned. 'My name is Jack. When we are making love, you can call me that.'

'Oh, Jack.' She sighed, raising her face hopefully.

And, since he wasn't a stupid man, he did exactly as she hoped. He kissed her, long and thoroughly.

And somehow, whilst doing so, he managed to direct both of them to the sofa and get them both sitting down. And then almost lying down, with him half over her. And her hands found their way under his waistcoat. And his hands traced the shape of her legs through her thin cotton gown.

'We should stop this,' said Jack, rearing back and sucking in a ragged breath.

'Must we? I have never felt like this before. Never so good.'

'Yes, I know, but we shouldn't. Not before we are married.'

'Oh. Are we going to be married then?'

'Yes. Definitely.'

'But I thought you didn't want to get married.'

'I didn't. Not until I met you, anyway,' he growled.

'Don't you think you should ask me, then?'

'No. If I'm going to do the thing correctly, the person I should ask is your father.'

She thumped him.

He laughed.

And then he kissed her some more.

'Mmm…no…' he breathed. 'Really must stop. I was about to say something important when you distracted me.'

'*I* distracted *you*? I didn't do anything!'

'Yes, you did. You looked at me all dewy-eyed and breathed my name as though it was a prayer.'

It had felt like one.

'No, now, don't start looking at me like that again,' he said. 'I have remembered, I was going to make all sorts of promises, about mending my ways and such.'

'Oh. Do you have to?' She ran one finger round his top waistcoat button. Pushed at it, experimentally. And smiled when it popped through the buttonhole.

'Yes, I do,' he said, catching hold of her hand. 'And it isn't going to help if you start undressing me.'

'Oh, very well,' she said, lying back and raising both arms above her head, as though in surrender.

'You...' His eyes flicked down over her body, to where their legs were tangled together in a muddle of holland covers. 'Now, see here, Harriet, I mean to do better with my life than I have done of late. I told you about my father not sparing me a thought, didn't I? Well, what I didn't tell you was that he wept when he knew it was I who would take his title and not one of my far more magnificent brothers.'

'Oh, Jack!' She stopped trying to be seductive. Reached up and laid one palm against his cheek. 'How horrid for you.'

'Yes, well...' He shifted position slightly. So that she could sit up. Which she did.

'And how very stupid of him,' she continued.

'What do you mean?'

'Well, for heaven's sake, you'd been a major in the army. There is a huge amount of work to do, running a brigade. Or so George is always saying. Mountains of paperwork, as well as handling the men under your command. And Papa is always telling *him* that there's hardly any better training for running a large estate.'

'No wonder I love you,' he breathed. 'But,' he said, his expression turning serious, 'it wasn't just him. The others, the trustees and so forth, advised me to come to Town and find a wife. As if they thought all I was good for was passing on the name to the next generation.'

'Then—oh! That's why you behaved so badly that even Aunt Susan warned me that you weren't good marriage material.'

'Did she? And yet you still lit up like a candle whenever I walked into the room.'

'Well,' she said, darting him a look from under her eyelashes, 'you'd already kissed me, hadn't you? So nothing anyone could say could influence the way you made me feel.'

His face fell again. 'Are you hinting that I should not have been influenced by what the trustees said? That I should have stayed in Shropshire and made everyone take me seriously, rather than coming to London and living down to their expectations of me?'

'No, of course not, I never meant—'

'It wasn't just that, you know. It was the memories that leapt out at me from behind every bush, every damn locked door...' He hung his head, his eyes briefly closed. 'I felt like a small, scared boy too often for my peace of mind.'

'Do you want to stay in London then, after we're married?'

He lifted his head, a grin spreading slowly across his face.

'I haven't asked you yet, you forward wench.'

'Yes, but you will do. *Eventually*,' she said drily. 'So, if you want to carry on living in London, living down to everyone's expectations, I shan't mind,' she said stoically.

'That's very noble of you, but, no. That is what I have been trying to tell you. It is high time I went and claimed my estates. Started running them the way I wish. Unless...do you prefer to stay in Town?' She could see him struggling to be generous as he made the offer. 'I know a lot of ladies like all the social whirl. The balls and picnics and such.'

'No.' She shook her head. 'I thought I would love all that sort of thing. Aunt Susan and Kitty made it sound so exciting. But I wasn't here long before I discovered that I *much* prefer the country, Jack. Which you know, really, deep down, don't you? Else why would I have been galloping about the park, at dawn, when it isn't the done thing?'

He smiled at her with evident relief.

'And while we are talking about going to your estates, and laying claim to them, may I make a suggestion?'

'Of course!' His eyes flew wide as though surprised. 'I don't want you to feel you have to tiptoe round me.'

She smiled. He clearly wasn't going to be the kind of husband who would stop her saying, or doing, whatever she wished.

'Well, when you *eventually* get round to going to visit my father and asking permission to pay your addresses to me...'

He chuckled.

'...why don't you ask him to visit your estates with you and give his advice? He lives and breathes land management. And...actually, he is very well respected in certain farming circles.'

'So...if I were to get him on my side, you mean, then I won't have any more trouble with my steward?'

She nodded, hoping he wouldn't take offence at her suggestion.

He looked thoughtful. 'Do you think he would be willing to do that? And...if he did, would he cut up rough if I were to ignore everything he said and did it my own way?'

'I think he would be delighted to have a son-in-law who had a mind of his own. He copes splendidly with Mama, after all, who very rarely agrees with *any*-one. But, seriously, he would also love to go exploring round someone else's estates and give them the benefit of his own opinion. He does it all the time. The only thing is...'

'Mmm?'

'Well, if he enjoys himself too much, we might never get rid of him. I have been the one to keep Stone Court running smoothly, you see, because Mama is simply not interested.'

'So he does value you, then?'

'He certainly values my housekeeping skills. But the moment Charles marries and brings another woman in to take over my duties, he will be perfectly happy to never see me again.'

Jack frowned and looked as though he was about to say something derogatory about her father. But then he bit it back. 'Then I fervently hope Charles marries very soon, so that I may have you, and your excellent housewifely skills, all to myself.'

'That was exactly the right thing to say,' she said. 'You clever, clever man.'

'And do I deserve a reward?'

'Oh, yes,' she said. And took his dear face between her hands and kissed him, just to prove she could understand what he wanted of her as cleverly as he'd just understood her need for him not to criticise Papa.

She was just starting to gently subside beneath the pressure of his answering kiss when the door flew open, causing them to spring guiltily apart. In the doorway stood her mother, the strings of her bonnet untied and half the buttons of her coat undone.

'Harriet,' she said. 'Do you know where my set of Napier's bones may be? I know I had them in my trunk when I came to Town, but in the move from your Aunt Susan's house they seem to have gone astray.'

At her side, Jack sat frozen, as though, if he kept still enough, his presence might go unnoticed.

'And I must have them,' Mama was complaining. 'The calculations Mr Swann put up on the blackboard tonight made no sense whatever. I need to go over them again, myself.'

'I placed them in the top drawer of your desk when I unpacked, Mama,' said Harriet, surreptitiously encouraging her skirts, which seemed to have risen up her legs, back to their proper place.

'Whatever did you put them there for?'

'Well, I thought you might need them.'

'Then you should have placed them on top of my desk, not hidden them away in a drawer. Honestly, Harriet, I despair of you sometimes, I really do.' Then she turned and flounced out of the room, slamming the door behind her.

Jack made a low growling noise. 'Did she even notice that I was here?'

'Probably not. She has just come in from some talk or other that clearly has her all fired up.'

'I couldn't really believe it when you said they wouldn't miss you, but that...' he pointed to the door through which Mama had just gone. '...that does it. Even if I hadn't decided to make an honest woman of you, I'd have to marry you now.'

'Because my mother found us together in a compromising position?'

'Because the blasted woman didn't even notice. She should be taking far better care of you. But she never has done, has she?'

'No, but only think, Jack. If she'd been a strict parent, then we would never have met, would we? Because she would have taught me to behave properly and I would never have gone riding in the park.'

'Yes, there is that,' he conceded. 'But...to leave you alone in the room, with me just now. I mean, I could be anybody. I could be a...an evil seducer, intent on having my wicked way with you!'

'I was rather hoping you were.'

He gave her a stern frown. Which didn't fool her one bit, since he hadn't managed to prevent his eyes from twinkling. 'Young lady, if you cannot tell the difference between a rake who is intent only upon his own pleasure and a man who is making love to the woman he intends to marry and spend the rest of his life with, then...'

'Then?'

'Then I had better show you.'

'Ooh...' She sighed. 'Please do.'

Epilogue

'But, Harriet, I really don't understand…' Aunt Susan twisted the strings of her reticule. 'I thought you wished me to help you purchase bride clothes, not—'

'Well, yes, I do want your help with that.' And it had been the one thing guaranteed to soften Uncle Hugo's stance on their associating with each other. When Harriet had written to tell him she had become engaged and needed her aunt's help with shopping for the wedding, his reply had been swift, and tinged, predictably, with a touch of gloating that she felt obliged to ask her aunt to perform that office, rather than be able to rely on her own mother. 'Just not today,' Harriet explained. 'Or perhaps, later on. After,' she said, wriggling across the seat of the carriage in preparation for getting out, 'we have finished with Lord Rawcliffe.'

Getting out of the carriage did the trick. Her aunt, who'd been displaying such reluctance to be seen anywhere near the house which took up such a large slice of Grosvenor Square, girded up her mental loins and set out after her niece.

'It is most inappropriate for you to be calling upon

such a man,' she said in an urgent undertone. 'Even if he is a close friend of your betrothed.'

Her curiosity piqued, Harriet delayed informing her aunt that her betrothed would also be at the meeting he'd arranged. She'd always wondered what it was about Lord Rawcliffe that set her aunt against him as a matrimonial prospect for Kitty. And there was no better time to find out than now.

'What do you mean, *such a man*? He seems perfectly respectable to me.'

'Oh, it is not a question of that,' said Aunt Susan, panting up the front steps after her. 'It is just that he has a reputation with…that is, I have lost count of the number of hopeful females who have dashed themselves to pieces against the hardness of his heart.'

'You mean, women throw themselves at him? Whatever for?'

'Because he is a matrimonial prize. Or at least, he was considered so, when he was younger. And he still is, in many respects,' said Aunt Susan, jerking her head at the imposing façade of his house in a meaningful way. 'It is just that careful mothers keep their daughters away from him. He won't marry anyone who looks the slightest bit…'

'Desperate?' When her aunt merely pursed her lips and shook her head as though words failed her, Harriet tried another one. 'Fast?'

'I think,' said Aunt Susan slowly, as though choosing her words with care, 'it is more likely that when he does marry, it will be a woman of his own choosing, rather than one who has thrown herself at him. Well, you saw the way Lord Lensborough reacted when those silly girls threw themselves at his head, at the picnic.'

'At his feet, don't you mean?'

'Harriet,' Aunt Susan said repressively. 'The point is, men who are as high in the instep as Lensborough, or Rawcliffe, only ever marry girls of good character, with an impeccable lineage and a fortune to match their own.'

He would remain a bachelor for the rest of his life then. Not that she could say as much, when the front door was being opened by exactly the kind of butler she would guess a man as full of his own consequence as *Zeus* would employ.

In spite of telling Harriet that setting foot inside Lord Rawcliffe's house was tantamount to committing some sort of social faux pas, Aunt Susan's eyes flicked round, taking in every inch of the immense hall, the portraits on the walls, the moulding round the doors, the little tables set at strategic points to display their collection of probably priceless urns and dishes, during the short walk across the hall behind the butler.

'Lady Tarbrook, Lady Harriet Inskip,' said the butler, as he opened the door, before stepping aside and making the slightest inclination of his head to let them know they should go in.

'Harriet!' Jack had been lounging against the mantelpiece, but the moment he saw her, his face lit up with such obvious pleasure it was impossible not to smile back. Especially since he flew to her side and seized her hands as though he meant to haul her close and kiss her.

She squeezed his hands back, then tilted her head sideways, to remind him that her aunt was standing right there.

'And Lady Tarbrook,' said Jack, finally recalling his manners. 'Thank you both for coming.'

'I…well, not at all,' said Aunt Susan, clearly bewildered, but determined not to let on that Harriet had virtually ambushed her.

'Please, do take a seat,' said Lord Rawcliffe, gesturing to a sofa set at a slight angle to the fireplace. He had been standing right next to Jack, Harriet realised, though she hadn't really noticed him before. As Aunt Susan did as she'd been told, Harriet dropped a brief curtsy to acknowledge her host, then she and Jack gravitated to the sofa opposite her aunt's and sat down together, still holding hands.

'You know Mr Kellett,' said Lord Rawcliffe, indicating Archie, who was sitting on a chair by one of the windows overlooking the rear to the house, his hands clasped in his lap.

Aunt Susan accorded him a regal nod.

'Then, I shall ring for tea,' said Lord Rawcliffe, going across to the bell pull by the fireplace.

There then followed a short interlude, during which Lord Rawcliffe kept the conversation at the most banal of levels, whilst they ordered, then waited for the refreshments to arrive. Aunt Susan did her best to look as though it was perfectly normal to pay a morning call upon an unmarried gentleman. But Harriet noticed how uneasy she was from the way she twined the strings of her reticule round her fingers so tightly that when it came time to remove her gloves, she was hard pressed to untangle them.

But at length, the moment that Harriet had been waiting for finally arrived. Just as they were all on their second cup of tea and the cakes had been reduced to crumbs, she heard the sound of the final, and most important guest of all, knock on the front door.

Only seconds later, Lord Rawcliffe's butler opened the door again, and, as all eyes swung to look at him, he announced, 'Lord Tarbrook.'

Aunt Susan started and dropped her teaspoon into her saucer with a tinkle. Fortunately, nobody but Harriet noticed this, because at the exact same moment, Lord Tarbrook was saying, 'Cannot imagine what business you have with me that you consider so urgent, Rawcliffe. Good God. Susan!'

By now, Aunt Susan had composed herself and was able to greet his incredulity at finding her there with the mere raising of one eyebrow, as if to convey she had every right to be there.

'What the devil is going on here?' said Lord Tarbrook, darting dagger glances round the room.

'Would you care for some tea?' Lord Rawcliffe asked mildly.

'The devil take your tea. What I want is an explanation.'

'And you shall have it,' said Lord Rawcliffe, waving a slender hand to another chair, inviting the latest arrival to sit on it.

Lord Tarbrook drew his brows down and leaned on his cane, as though declaring his refusal to accept the hospitality of a man who had engineered a meeting with his wife in such an underhand manner.

'As you wish,' said Lord Rawcliffe as though he perfectly understood. 'Becconsall, perhaps you would like to conduct the next part of this meeting?'

'Yes. Absolutely,' said Jack, getting to his feet. 'It's like this, my lord. Harriet, that is, Lady Harriet, my betrothed, has naturally confided in me about the rift that occurred between you over the matter of the missing jewels.'

'She did what?' Lord Tarbrook turned his attention to her. And threw her his most repressive glare.

'And it turns out that there has been a similar case in the family of our mutual friend, Mr Kellett,' said Jack, drawing Lord Tarbrook's attention to the figure sitting mute by the window.

'What?' Lord Tarbrook looked from one man to the other in confusion.

'Yes,' said Archie, finally getting to his feet. 'When my g-grandmother died, my father found that some of her jewels were not the genuine article. C-couldn't find any trace of gambling debts. Thought it must have been a private wager. Had them c-copied to raise the blunt. Hushed it up.'

'What!'

'Then, when we heard about the same thing happening in your own family, started wondering if…'

'You heard about… How did you… Harriet!' Lord Tarbrook whirled on her, his fury pouring off him in waves.

'Started asking a few qu-questions,' carried on Archie, ignoring Lord Tarbrook's outburst. 'T-turned out she had a maid with her during her last illness who matched the description of one employed by Lady Tarbrook.'

'What?' Now it was Lady Tarbrook's turn to express shock.

'More to the point, she'd c-come to my g-grandmother's notice through an old friend of hers. Lady B-Buntingford.'

'Oh!' Aunt Susan clapped a hand to her chest. 'I took

on a girl recommended to me by Lady Buntingford. As a favour. But that must have been...well, it was a few years ago.'

'We believe,' said Jack, 'that is when the switch of your rubies must have taken place.'

'You mean...' Aunt Susan was heaving for breath.

'Yes. We believe you have been the victim of a very cleverly orchestrated crime.'

'Lady Buntingford?' Aunt Susan was shaking her head. 'No. I cannot believe it. She would not...'

'All we know so far,' said Jack, 'is that she has been the link between the families who have had jewels switched and the girl who appears to have done the switching. We will need to investigate further to discover—'

'No!' Uncle Hugo thumped his cane on the floor. 'No investigation. I will not have my family's reputation dragged through the mire.'

'There will be no need for that,' said Lord Rawcliffe repressively. 'Archie will be going to Dorset on a visit to Lady Buntingford, who is his mother's godmother, to discreetly ask her a few questions. It won't arouse any suspicion outside our own circle. Nothing more natural for a man in his position to spend part of his holidays visiting such a woman. Particularly not when she happens to live in such a beautiful part of the country.'

'And what part, pray, do you play in all of this? What makes you think you have the right to become so busy in my family affairs?'

'I will be pursuing the girl who appears to have done the actual thieving,' said Lord Rawcliffe. 'Since I plan to go to the area from which we have reason to believe she hales, in a few days in any case, my own movements should not alert anyone to the fact that there is an investigation taking place.'

'I don't like it,' grumbled Uncle Hugo.

'That is what the thieves want, though, isn't it?' put in Harriet. 'For everyone to be so determined to cover up the crime that they get away with it. And we can't let them get away with it. We can't!'

'You don't seriously expect to apprehend the culprits, do you? After all this time? And as for thinking you will ever be able to recover the jewels…' He shook his head.

'It isn't a question of recovering the jewels,' said Harriet. 'But of seeing justice done. Of clearing Aunt Susan's name. Proving her innocent!'

'Hugo,' said Aunt Susan. 'What these gentlemen have just told us…the lengths to which they are prepared to go…well, you know what this means, don't you?' She got to her feet.

'What does it mean?' he replied testily.

'It means,' she said coldly, 'that you owe me an apology.'

Everyone in the room held their breath, or at least that was how it seemed to Harriet. Everyone except Uncle Hugo, who was glaring down at the head of his cane and heaving in great heavy breaths as though they were all sorely trying his patience. He rapped the cane on the floor once or twice, his face working.

Harriet braced herself for an explosion.

But then he sighed. Raised his head to look at Aunt Susan. 'Yes,' he said. 'Yes, I do.'

Aunt Susan, who clearly hadn't expected him to admit any such thing, especially not so quickly, sat down rather abruptly.

'I…overreacted, I suppose that is what you all think.

But...' he glared defiantly round the room '...I saw it as evidence.'

'Evidence?' Aunt Susan was glaring right back at him. 'Of what?'

He sighed again. And shrugged, in a rather sulky sort of way. 'Well, you only married me because our parents pushed you into it. And you never gave me any sign that...' He trailed off, going rather red about the ears.

'That what?'

'No matter what I did you never...cared.' He straightened up, almost defiantly, and focused intently on his wife. 'You never gave any indication that you returned my feelings.'

'Your feelings?'

As the middle-aged couple stared at each other, Harriet could see a maelstrom of emotion playing across their faces. And she recalled the list of grievances her aunt had poured forth about Uncle Hugo's behaviour, over the breakfast table.

And wondered if he'd been doing exactly what Jack had done to her. Acted badly, to try to get her attention.

Well, Uncle Hugo had certainly got Aunt Susan's attention now. The pair of them were looking at each other as though they'd completely forgotten anyone else was in the room.

Lord Rawcliffe cleared his throat, and, when Harriet looked his way, saw that he was gesturing to the door.

With a smile tugging at her lips, Harriet took Jack's arm, and followed Lord Rawcliffe and Archie out. Neither her aunt nor her uncle appeared to notice they were leaving, though neither of them had said anything, yet. Not that they needed to. Everything they were thinking was plain for anyone to see.

'I wonder,' said Jack, as Lord Rawcliffe shut the door behind them, 'which of them will be the first to break down and admit they've been secretly in love with the other for years.'

'I think it might well be Uncle Hugo,' said Harriet. 'After all, he almost went too far this time, the way he treated my aunt. He has a lot of apologising to do, and I dare say even he will have worked out, by now, that the best way to gain forgiveness is to admit that he loves her. And after that, she will admit that she loves him, too, and then—'

'Please, no more,' said Lord Rawcliffe with a shudder. 'I may never be able to look at that particular sofa with anything but revulsion again. In fact,' he said, pushing open the door to another room, which looked as though it might be his private study, 'I may well simply throw it out and get a new one.'

The thought of what he suspected Uncle Hugo and Aunt Susan of being about to get up to on his sofa, that would make him wish to destroy it, seemed to amuse Jack no end.

But Harriet thought it was rather sweet.

'I hope,' she whispered up to Jack, while Lord Rawcliffe was busy pouring himself a drink from a decanter that stood on a side table, 'that we are still as much in love as they are, when we reach their age.'

'You can count on it,' Jack replied, giving her waist a squeeze. 'Though I shan't be such a nodcock as to leave you ignorant of my own feelings for so many years.'

'No?'

'No. I plan to tell you, at least once every day, that you are the light of my life and that I love you more than...'

'More than what?'

'More than anything, of course.'

Harriet sighed with pure contentment. At last, she mattered to someone.

More than anything.

* * * * *

THE MARQUESS
TAMES HIS BRIDE

To Louise Marley – because she says
it's about time!

Thanks for persistently tweeting, sending me
congratulation cards every publication day, and
generally cheering from the sidelines.

Chapter One

'Well, well…what have we here?'

Clare's heart sank. It was just typical of Lord Rawcliffe to take it into his head to travel through Bedfordshire on the very same day as her. Trust him to stroll in through the back door of the inn where she was changing stages, looking so expensive and elegant, at the very moment she was on her way out to visit the necessary, wearing a coat she'd dyed very inexpertly in the scullery. How did he do it? How was it that whenever she was at her lowest, or caught in some humiliating predicament, he always managed to be there to witness it?

And laugh at her.

'No, don't tell me,' he drawled, taking off his gloves with provokingly deliberate slowness. 'A missionary visit to the raff and scaff of Biggleswade.'

And this was the way he always spoke to her. Every time their paths crossed, he would mock her beliefs and she would retaliate by denouncing his morals and informing him that just because he had a worldly title higher than most, and was rolling in filthy lucre, it did not give him the right to assume he was better than everyone else.

But today, she had no time for his games. Nor was she in the mood.

'Don't be ridiculous' was therefore all she said, lifting her chin and attempting to dodge past him.

She might have known he wouldn't permit her to do so. Instead of stepping aside politely, the way any other man would have done, he raised his arm, creating a barrier across the narrow passage, under which she'd have to duck to get past him.

In years past she might have attempted it. But she wasn't a child any longer. And she'd learned the folly of trying to dodge him when he didn't wish to be dodged.

'Will you excuse me?' she said in her most frigidly polite, grown-up voice.

'Not until you tell me what you are doing here,' he said, curving his thin lips into a mocking smile. 'Preaching sobriety to the parishioners of Watling Minor lost its appeal, has it? Need to spread your gospel farther afield?'

She winced. Why did he always have to make her sound as though she was some sort of religious maniac?

'Surely you, of all people, must know why I have so much sympathy for the message preached by the Methodists,' she retorted, reacting the way she invariably did when he addressed her in that sarcastic tone. 'Not,' she added hastily, when his smile hardened, presaging an escalation in hostilities, 'that I am here to preach at *any*body for *any* reason.'

'Joan,' he said, shaking his head. 'You cannot help yourself. Your whole life is one long sermon. You even manage to preach hell and damnation by the very way you look down that sanctimonious little nose of yours at the entire human race.'

She knew she shouldn't have mentioned his mother's

fatal weakness for alcohol. Not even indirectly. It was the equivalent of poking him in the eye.

But when it came to the Marquess of Rawcliffe, she just couldn't help herself. He was so infuriating that no matter how sternly she lectured herself about keeping her tongue between her teeth, he only had to half-lower those lazy lids of his over his ice-cold eyes and utter some puerile taunt, and reason flew out of the window.

'You should know,' she heard herself saying. 'Since you look down your own, arrogant, *big* nose at the whole world and everything in it.' Blast it. That wasn't what she'd meant to say. And now she was even *thinking* in profanities. 'And how many times do I have to tell you not to call me Joan?'

'As many times as you like and I shall still do so, since it is what your father should have called you.'

'No, he shouldn't.'

'Yes, he should. Since he named all your brothers after popes, then he should have done the same for you. But then consistency,' he said with a curl to his upper lip, 'has never been his strongest suit, has it?'

'There was no such person as Pope Joan, as you very well know,' she snapped, falling into the same argument they'd had countless times over the years. 'She was a myth. And would you please just leave my father out of it for once?' Did he have no compassion? At all?

'Absolutely not,' he said, his eyes hardening to chips of ice. 'For one thing, I cannot believe even he would approve of you frequenting places of this sort. If he were any longer in a fit state to know where you were or what you were about.'

The beast! How could he rub her nose in it like this? Oh! She'd always known he was the hardest-hearted person she'd ever met, but this? This was too much.

All the frustrations and hurts of recent weeks played through her mind in rapid succession and crystallised in the mocking smile on the handsome face of the last man she wished to witness her degradation.

There was nothing she could do about her brothers. Nothing she could do about her father, or her future. But right now, there was one thing she could do.

She could knock that sneering, cruel, infuriating smile off the Marquess of Rawcliffe's face.

Before she had time to weigh up the consequences, her fingers had curled into a fist. And all her grief, and anger, and confusion, and sense of betrayal hurled along her arm and exploded into movement.

She'd meant to punch him on the jaw. But just as she was letting fly, he moved and somehow her fist caught him right on the nose.

It was like hitting a brick wall.

If she hadn't seen his head snap back, she wouldn't have known she'd had any effect upon him at all.

Until a thin stream of blood began to trickle from his left nostril.

For a moment they just stood there, staring at each other in stunned silence. As if neither of them could credit what she'd just done.

'A fight, a fight!'

The excited voice came from somewhere behind her, reminding her that they were in a corridor of a public inn. And that other people travelling on the stage, or in their own vehicles, had a perfect right to be walking along this same corridor.

'It's a woman,' came a second voice.

'And stap me if it ain't Lord Rawcliffe,' said the first.

Lord Rawcliffe delved into a pocket and produced a handkerchief, which he balled up and pressed to his nose. But she could still see his eyes, boring into her with an expression that boded very ill. He was plotting his revenge. For he was not the sort of man to let anybody, but especially not a female, get away with striking him.

Her stomach plunged. The way it had when she'd almost fallen out of Farmer Westthorpe's oak tree... and would have done if a strap of her pinafore hadn't snagged on the branch she'd just been sitting on. And left her dangling, three feet from the ground, her dress rucked up round her neck. If Lord Rawcliffe—or rather Robert Walmer, as he'd been in those days—hadn't found her, she might still be dangling there to this day. Only of course he *had* found her. And freed her.

Though not before he'd had a jolly good laugh at her expense.

He wasn't laughing now. But she was as unable to move as she'd been that day. Unable to do anything but stare up at him helplessly, her stomach writhing with regret and humiliation and resentment.

She could hear the sound of tankards slamming down onto tables, chairs scraping across a stone floor and booted feet stampeding in their direction.

But she couldn't drag her horrified eyes from Lord Rawcliffe's face. Or at least his cold, vengeful grey eyes, which was all she could see from over the top of his handkerchief.

'What do ye think he'll do?'

Something terrible, she was sure.

'Have her taken in charge? Should someone send for the constable?'

'My lord,' said someone right behind her, just as a meaty hand descended on her shoulder. 'I do most humbly apologise. Such a thing has never happened in my establishment before. But the public stage, you know. Brings all sorts of people through the place.' She finally managed to tear her gaze from Lord Rawcliffe, only to see the landlord, who'd not long since been standing behind a counter directing operations, scowling down at her as though she was some sort of criminal.

'Remove your hand,' said Lord Rawcliffe at his most freezing as he lowered his handkerchief, 'from my fiancée's shoulder.'

'Fiancée?' The word whooshed through the assembled throng like an autumn gale through a forest. But not one of the bystanders sounded more stunned by Lord Rawcliffe's use of the word than she felt herself.

Fiancée?

'No,' she began, 'I'm not—'

'I know you are angry with me, sweetheart,' he said, clenching his teeth in the most terrifying smile she'd ever seen. 'But this is not the place to break off our betrothal.'

'Betrothal? What do you—?'

But before she could say another word, he swooped.

Got one arm round her waist and one hand to the back of her bonnet to hold her in place.

And smashed his mouth down hard on her lips.

'Whuh!' It was all that she managed to say when, as abruptly as he'd started the kiss, he left off. Her mouth felt branded. Her legs were shaking. Her heart was pounding as though she was being chased by Farmer Westthorpe's bull. Which would have been her fate if she'd fallen into the field, rather than become stuck on one of the lower branches.

'The rumours,' he said in a silky voice, 'about my affair with...well, you know who...are exactly that. Merely rumours.'

'Affair?' What business did he have discussing his affairs with her?

'It is over. Never started. Hang it, sweetheart,' he growled. 'How could I ever marry anyone but you? Landlord,' he said, giving her waist an uncomfortably hard squeeze, which she took as a warning not to say another word, 'my fiancée and I would like some privacy in which to continue our...discussion.'

And naturally, since he was the almighty Marquess of Rawcliffe, the landlord bowed deeply, and said that of course he had a private room, which he would be delighted to place entirely at their disposal. And then he waved his arm to indicate they should follow him.

Back into the interior of the building she'd just been about to vacate.

Chapter Two

Lord Rawcliffe kept his arm round her waist, effectively clamping her to his side.

'Not another word,' he growled into her ear as he turned her to follow the landlord. 'Not until there is no fear of us being overheard.'

She almost protested that she hadn't been going to say anything. She had no wish to have their quarrel witnessed by the other passengers from her coach, or those two drunken bucks who'd staggered out of the tap at the exact moment she'd punched the Marquess on the nose, or even the landlord.

'This will do,' said Lord Rawcliffe to the very landlord she'd been thinking about, as they entered a small room containing a table with several plain chairs standing round it and a couple of upholstered ones drawn up before a grate in which a fire blazed even though it was a full week into June.

'You will be wanting refreshments, my lord?'

'Yes. A pot of tea for my fiancée,' he said, giving her another warning squeeze. 'Ale for me. And some bread and cheese, too. Oh,' he said, dabbing at his bleeding nose, 'and a bowl of ice, or, at least, very cold water and some clean cloths.'

'Of course, my lord,' said the landlord, shooting her a look loaded with censure as he bowed himself out of the door.

'And one other thing,' said Lord Rawcliffe, letting go of her in order to give the landlord his full attention. Clare didn't bother to listen to what the one other thing might be. She was too busy getting to the far side of the room and putting the table between them for good measure.

'Look,' she said, as soon as the landlord had gone. 'I know I shouldn't have hit you and I—' she drew a deep breath '—I apologise.' She looked longingly at the door. Rawcliffe might have all the time in the world, but she had a stage to catch. 'And thank you for the offer of tea, but I don't have time to—'

He was nearer the door than she was, and, following the direction of her gaze, he promptly stepped in front of it, leaned his back against it and folded his arms across his chest.

'What,' she said, 'do you think you are doing?'

'Clearly, I am preventing you from leaving.'

'Yes, I can see that, I'm not an idiot. But why?'

'Because I am not going to permit you to walk into a scandal.'

'I am not going to walk into a scandal.'

'You think you can strike a marquess, in a public inn, and get away with it?'

'I don't see why not. You might be notorious, but nobody knows who *I* am.'

His mouth twisted into a sneer. 'You flew here on angel's wings, did you?'

'Of course not. I came on the stage.'

'Precisely. A stagecoach, crammed, if I know anything about it, with plenty of other passengers.'

'Yes, but none of them took much notice of me...'

'That was before you indulged in a bout of fisticuffs with a peer of the realm. Now they will all want to know who you are. And it won't take them long to find out.'

She thought of her trunk, sitting out in the yard awaiting her connecting coach. The label, bearing her name, tied to the handle. And then, with a sinking heart, the ostler who'd wrested it from the luggage rack and the withering look he'd given her after she'd dropped her tip into his hand. A tip so meagre he'd clearly regarded it in the nature of an insult.

She swallowed.

'It...it cannot really matter though, can it? At least, it wouldn't have,' she added resentfully, 'if you had not claimed I was your fiancée.'

'You think people would have been less interested in a random woman assaulting me in a public inn? Do you have any idea of the story they would have concocted had I not given them a far better one? You would have been a cast-off mistress, at the very least. Or possibly the mother of a brood of my illegitimate offspring. Or perhaps even a secret wife.'

'Well, I don't see how any of that would have been any worse than for them now to believe you have a fiancée nobody knew anything about.'

'You cannot just say thank you, can you? For rescuing you from the consequences of your own folly?'

She lowered her gaze. Studied her scuffed boots for a moment or two, weighing his words. She supposed she did ought to thank him. After all, she'd hit him and he hadn't done anything in retaliation. On the contrary, he'd covered for her behaviour by making up a story about her being an insanely jealous fiancée, so that everyone would believe she was perfectly entitled to waylay him in a corridor and bloody his nose.

'Very well.' She sighed. 'Thank you for attempting to rescue me from myself. And now—'

He let out a bark of laughter. 'Good God! An apology and an acknowledgement that I have actually managed to do something decent, in your opinion, in the space of five minutes. From you, that is nothing short of a miracle. If you continue at this rate you will become a model wife. Within about fifty years,' he finished on a sneer.

'You and I both know I am never going to be your wife—'

'But I have just announced our betrothal.'

'Yes, well, I know you didn't mean anything by that.' Just as he hadn't meant anything by it the last time he'd spoken to her of marriage. She gave an involuntary shiver as that particular episode came to remembrance, since it was not exactly her finest hour. She'd been emerging from the duck pond, covered in slime and with ribbons of weed tangled in her hair. And with the sack full of drowned puppies clutched to her chest. She'd been distraught, because she'd taken far too long to find them. Only later did she discover that the reason the sack into which they'd been tied had sunk deep into the mud was because it was weighted down with rocks. She'd been horrified by the cruelty of the wretch who'd thrown those poor innocent little creatures into the pond and there he'd been, bowed over with laughter, holding himself up by propping his hands on his knees at the sight of her. And then to make matters worse, she'd lost her footing as she'd been clambering out and fallen back into the water. To set the seal on her humiliation, her sense of failure, he'd extended his hand and laughingly said something to the effect of having to marry her if this was what she sank to the moment he took his eyes off her.

And her heart had fluttered. Even though she should have known better, should have known that a man as handsome, and wealthy, and elevated in rank as him could never seriously consider marrying a diminutive, red-haired, penniless vicar's daughter, some pathetic, lovesick part of her had dared to hope. For a moment or two. Which had been the height of absurdity. Because, deep down, she couldn't imagine any man losing his heart to her, let alone the one man in the county who could have any woman he wanted for the clicking of his fingers—and very probably had.

Which had, thankfully, prevented her from making any sort of reply apart from a haughty toss of her head—which had made him laugh all over again since in doing so it had dislodged a clump of weed—and stalking off with her nose in the air. Leaving her with at least one tiny shred of pride still intact. Because of course it turned out he had merely been teasing her. For if he'd been in earnest, he would have come calling on Father to make a formal offer. Or at least ask if he could start to pay his addresses, until such time as she was old enough to consider marriage.

But he hadn't.

Because he hadn't meant a word of it.

Any more than he meant what he'd just said about her becoming a model wife, even if he had put in the bit about it taking fifty years. Men like him didn't marry girls like her.

It was ridiculous.

'Did you indeed?' He pushed himself off the door, and sort of loomed over her. 'Then why did I say it? Why tell the world you are my fiancée?'

'I don't know!' She backed away. There was something so overwhelming about him. So dangerous. And now that he'd kissed her, she knew what that danger was. A danger to her self-respect which would shrivel away to nothing should she permit the attraction she felt for him to govern her actions. And right now, self-respect was all she had left.

But, oh, how tempting it was to latch on to his carelessly spoken words and make him stick to them, for once. It would serve him right...

But, no. Though the temptation surged swift and strong, she must thrust it aside. She couldn't marry a man simply to get revenge on him for all the hurts he'd inadvertently caused her over the years. What sort of marriage would that be? Not the kind she read about in the bible...not that she'd ever actually seen anyone in real life attain the state of being an image of Christ and his church. But if she ever did marry, she would at least hope the man would regard the estate as holy and make an effort to be *faithful*, if not actually be ready to lay down his life for her.

Oh, but she might as well wish for a castle and a chest full of jewels and an army of servants to see to her slightest whim while she was at it.

'Why do you ever say anything? And anyway, it's not as if it was to anyone who matters, is it? They didn't look to me like anybody you knew.'

'One of those bucks is a member of one of my clubs.

The news of my betrothal to a short, red-haired shrew will be all over town within hours.'

'I am not a shrew!' He just brought out the worst in her. Deliberately.

'Only a shrew would have punched me in a public inn, when all I'd done was tease you, the way I have always teased you.'

'*Not* the way you have always teased me,' she seethed. 'What you said was unforgivable!'

A frown flickered across his brow. 'I said nothing that I have not said before.'

'Only now, to say such things about Father, when he is gone, that, that, that…' She shuddered to a halt as her emotions almost got the better of her.

'Gone? What do you mean, gone?'

'Don't pretend you don't know!'

'I am not pretending,' he said, taking her by both shoulders and looking into her eyes as though searching for the truth. 'Where has he gone?'

She swatted his hands from the patchily dyed shoulders of her coat and took a step back, before she gave in to the temptation to lean into him and sob her heart out.

'I was not surprised that you did not attend his funeral. I know you are far too busy and important to bother with—'

'Funeral? He died? When? Good God, Clare,' he said, advancing and taking hold of her shoulders once again. 'You cannot think that I knew? Would have spoken of him in that way if I…' His fingers tightened almost painfully on her before he abruptly released her with a bitter laugh. 'You did, in fact, believe that I knew. And, knowing, that I would be cruel enough to taunt you...' He whirled away from her, strode across to the rather grubby window and stood gazing out.

Now that he wasn't trying to prevent her from leaving, Clare found herself strangely reluctant to walk through the unguarded door. There was something about the set of his back that, in any other man, would have looked...almost defeated. Weary.

'If you really did not know...'

His back stiffened.

'Then I am sorry for thinking that you would deliberately taunt me with...with...well...' She faltered. He'd never been cruel. Not *deliberately* cruel. Oh, he might have hurt her time after time, but he'd never been aware, not really, how much power he had to hurt her. He just thought she was funny. A joke. Because, although she tried her hardest to live up to the precepts set down in the gospels, her temper kept on overruling her better judgement. Time after time she fell into scrapes. And somehow he always heard about them and mocked her for them when next he crossed her path.

Unless he actually happened to be present when she was in one, when the chances were he was at the root of it, like today.

'I suppose...' she began, on a flood of remorse. But was prevented from making another apology by the return to the room of the landlord and a waiter. Between them they'd brought all the items Lord Rawcliffe had requested. Not that he acknowledged them. He just stood there, with his back to the room, in stony silence while the men set everything on the table.

While she stood by the door, shifting from one foot to the other.

Why were they taking so long to set out a few dishes?

Why couldn't they take the hint that both she and Lord Rawcliffe wanted them to go away?

Because, even though it was highly improper to remain in the room with only Lord Rawcliffe for company, she had too much pride to make her apology to him in front of witnesses.

And too highly developed a conscience to leave without making it.

Chapter Three

'**Y**ou had better remove your gloves,' he said, once the landlord and the waiter had bowed their way backward out of the room.

'My gloves? Why? I am not staying. My coach is due in any moment and I—'

With an expression of impatience he strode across the room and seized her wrist. 'You need to get some ice on your hand,' he said, wrenching the buttons undone and tugging at her fingers.

Oh, good heavens. He was removing an item of her clothing. True, it was only a glove and he was doing it as though she were a naughty child, but still it was making her insides go all gooey.

Until something he said jolted her out of that pathetic state.

'Ice?' The bowl of ice he'd ordered, while he was standing there staunching the blood flowing from his nose, was for her hand? She'd assumed it was for his nose.

'Yes, ice,' he repeated, drawing her over to the table. 'It is the best thing for injuries sustained when boxing,' he said, thrusting her on to a chair. 'I know how painful it must be.' He took some chunks of ice and wrapped them in one of the cloths the waiter had brought. 'It is just fortunate that your hand connected with my nose, rather than my jaw, at which,' he said as he placed the cloth over her knuckles and held it there, 'I believe you were aiming.'

'Are you saying you deliberately moved your face so that it was your nose I struck, rather than your jaw?'

He shrugged one shoulder. 'You don't seriously think you could have landed a blow unless I permitted it, do you?'

'Well, now you come to mention it, I was a bit surprised you didn't try to block me.'

He gave her one of those withering looks that made people say he was insufferably arrogant.

'There are a lot of little bones in the hand,' he said, looking at hers as he dabbed at it with the napkin full of ice. 'And not one of them, as you should know, as strong as the jawbone.'

'What do you mean, *as I should know*?' Did he think she went round punching people on a regular basis? And had he really, deliberately, put his nose in the way of her fist, rather than letting her injure herself on him?

'Judges 15, of course,' he replied scathingly. 'How do you think Samuel managed to slay all those Philistines with the jawbone of an ass, if it wasn't harder than all their skulls?'

Oh, that was more like him. To quote scripture at her in order to make her feel stupid. And yet…he was taking care of her. Tending so gently to her hand, which did hurt rather a lot. When never, as far back as she could recall, had anyone ever tended to any of her hurts.

She had always been the one tending to others. She'd started learning to care for her brothers, and her father, well before Mama had died and left the task of running the bustling vicarage entirely in her ten-year-old hands.

'There,' he said, giving her hand one last gentle pat. 'Does that feel better?'

She nodded. Because she couldn't have spoken even if she'd been able to think of the right words to describe how she felt. The ice did indeed feel soothing. But the fact that he'd sent for it, that he'd made it into a compress, that he was applying it...*that* was what was bringing a lump to her throat.

Oh, this was why Lord Rawcliffe was so dangerous. Why she'd always stayed well away from him. Because he made her want things she had no right to want. Feel things she had no right to feel.

Eventually she pulled herself together sufficiently to lift her chin and look straight into his face, and even give him a tremulous smile.

'Thank you for tending to my hand. And accepting my apology. And...and even for dodging so that I got your nose rather than your jaw.' She got to her feet. 'But I really must be going now. My coach is due in any minute and—'

His face hardened.

'I have *not* accepted your apology.'

'What? But—'

'Sit down,' he said sternly. 'You are not going anywhere until you have given me a full explanation. Besides, have you forgotten?' He gave her a cold smile. 'You are my fiancée. Do you really think I am going to permit you to go jauntering off all over the countryside, on your own?'

'Don't be ridiculous. I am not your fiancée. And I don't need your permission to do anything or go anywhere!'

'That's better,' he said, leaning back in his chair, an infuriatingly satisfied smile playing about the lips that had so recently kissed her. 'You were beginning to droop. Now you are on fighting form again, we can have a proper discussion.'

'I don't want to have a discussion with you,' she said, barely managing to prevent herself from stamping her foot. 'Besides, oh, listen, can't you hear it?' It was the sound of a guard blowing on his horn to announce the arrival of the stage. The stage she needed to get on. 'I have a seat booked on that coach.'

'Nevertheless,' he said, striding over to the door and blocking her exit once again, 'you will not be getting on it.'

'Don't be absurd. Of course I am going to get on it.'

'You are mistaken. And if you don't acquiesce to your fate, quietly, then I am going to have to take desperate measures.'

'Oh, yes? And just what sort of measures,' she said, marching up to him and planting her hands on her hips, 'do you intend to take?'

He smiled. That wicked, knowing smile of his. Took her face in both hands. And kissed her.

'Mmph,' she protested, raising her hands to his chest to ward him off. He paid no attention. He just wrapped his arms round her and kept right on kissing her.

'*Mbrrrhgh!*' She wriggled in his hold. To no avail. His arms were like bars of iron. Besides, she wasn't only fighting him. She was also having to fight the stupid, crazy urge to push herself up against him, to open her mouth and kiss him back.

And just as she was starting to forget exactly why she ought to be fighting him at all, he gentled the kiss. Gentled his hold. Changed the nature of his kiss from hard and masterful, to coaxing and…oh, his clever mouth. It knew just how to translate her fury into a sort of wild, pulsing ache. She ached all over. She began to tremble with what he was making her feel. Grew weaker by the second.

As if he knew her legs were on the verge of giving way, he scooped her up into his arms and carried her over to one of the upholstered chairs by the fire. Sat down without breaking his hold, so that she landed on his lap.

And instead of struggling to break free, she subsided on to his chest, burying her face in his neck. Because she could see absolutely no point in struggling to escape from the one place she'd always wanted to be: in his arms, the focus of his whole attention.

'Now,' he growled into the crown of her bonnet, 'you will tell me why you are in this godforsaken spot, trying to get on a coach, when you should be snug and safe at home in the vicarage.'

'The vicarage is not my home anymore, as you very well know,' she said, jerking upright under the impact of a dose of that bleak truth. 'Now that Father has died.'

'The vicarage *is* your home,' he said. 'Even,' he laid one finger to her lips when she took a breath to protest, 'even when the vicar is no longer living. There was no need for you to leave, the moment you buried him.'

'But the curate—'

'The curate should have damn well contacted me before evicting you and presuming to move in, which is what I have to assume he did?'

'Well, yes, but he did contact you. At least, I mean, he tried to. And when you didn't respond, he—' Well, everyone in Watling Minor believed that Lord Rawcliffe knew everything. Which meant that if he hadn't responded in the negative, then he simply didn't care what arrangements had been made for the late vicar's daughter.

'Assumed I would be happy to have you evicted?' His eyes narrowed. 'I shall have to have words with the Reverend Cobbet.'

'No, no, it wasn't like that.' She laid one hand on his chest. 'It wasn't him. I just… There didn't seem any point in me hanging on there. Not when Clement had arranged everything for me so…so…kindly.'

'Clement? Kind?'

'Yes, well, it *was* kind of him to go to so much trouble on my behalf.' He'd told her so. 'He didn't have to make *any* arrangements.' As Lord Rawcliffe raised one cynical eyebrow, Clare hastened to add, 'I mean, I would have thought if anyone had the duty to provide for me it would have been Constantine.'

He made a scoffing noise, expressing his opinion of her oldest brother. Since it pretty much coincided with her own, after the way he'd behaved lately, she made no objection.

'And what form did this kindness of Clement's take, dare I ask?'

'He found me work. A good, honest job. One I am well qualified to take up.'

'You are going to be housekeeper for another family of ungrateful, lazy, hypocritical, sanctimonious prigs, are you?'

'Don't speak of my brothers like that.'

He closed his mouth. Gave her a look.

Which somehow had the effect of reminding her that she was still sitting on his lap, with her arms about his neck, though she couldn't recall the moment she'd put them there. And that he was running his big hands up and down her back, as though to soothe her. And that, although she had just, out of habit, leapt to defend her brothers, right at this moment she couldn't help agreeing with him. For she'd spent years keeping house for them. Then nursing their father, while they'd all left and got on with their own lives. But when she'd needed them, all they'd had to offer her were excuses. Constantine's wife was due to give birth to their third child at any moment, he'd written, and couldn't be expected to house an indigent sister. It was asking too much.

Cornelius had no room for her, either. Though, since he lived in bachelor quarters in the bishop's palace he hadn't really hoped for anything from him apart from sympathy. But even that had been in short supply. Instead of acknowledging how hard it was going to be for her to leave the vicarage, the only home she'd ever had, he had, instead, congratulated Clement on his foresight in arranging for her removal so swiftly, so that the curate, a man who had a wife and a baby on the way, could move out of the cramped cottage where he'd been living before. He'd even gone so far as to shake Reverend Cobbet by the hand and say how pleased he was for him to finally be moving into a house where he and his family would be comfortable.

It had felt as though he'd stabbed her in the back.

At which point in her bitter ruminations she heard the sound of wheels rattling across the cobbles.

'Oh, the coach, the coach!' Finally she did what she should have done in the first place—she made an attempt to get off his lap. But he tightened his hold, keeping her firmly in place.

'Too late,' he said smugly. 'It has gone without you.'

'But my luggage! Everything I own is in my trunk...'

'Which has been conveyed to my chaise.'

'What? How can you know that?'

'Because I told the landlord to have it done when I ordered the tea and ice. Did you not hear?' He widened his eyes as though in innocence, when he must know very well she had heard no such thing. That he must have mumbled it while she'd been busy getting the table in between them. Which had worked really well, hadn't it? Since she'd somehow ended up not just in his arms, but also on his lap just the same.

'Well, you shouldn't have.'

'Of course I should,' he said with a touch of impatience. 'If I hadn't had the foresight to do so, you would have just lost everything you own.'

'Instead of which, I have fallen into the hands of a...a... Why, you are so high-handed, ordering people about and...and forcing people into fake betrothals that you... Why, you are little better than a kidnapper!'

Chapter Four

Rawcliffe drew in a deep breath and started counting to ten.

Just as he got to two, he realised he wasn't angry enough to need to resort to his usual method of dealing with Clare. He was still far too pleased with the ease with which he'd finally got her on to his lap, and into his arms, to care very much about what she had to say about it.

He smiled down into her furious little face.

'Far from kidnapping you,' he pointed out, 'I have rescued you from the consequences of your own folly. However,' he interjected swiftly when she drew a breath to object, 'I concede you must have been at the end of your tether, to hit me when all I did was tease you the way I have always done.'

And it hadn't hurt that much. Not as much as discovering she thought him capable of such casual cruelty that she'd ended up being evicted from her home before her father was even cold in his grave. When she'd said he'd gone, he'd just assumed she meant that he'd managed to get on to a coach when she wasn't watching and that she was searching for him. Reverend Cottam's behaviour had been getting increasingly erratic of late after all. And his sarcasm had been mainly aimed at her brothers, who'd left her with a burden she should no longer have to shoulder all on her own. He'd never dreamed the irascible old preacher could actually have died.

'But you cannot deny,' he continued when she drew her ginger brows together into a thwarted little frown, 'that had I not announced you were my fiancée, you would have been ruined.'

'I don't see that it would have been as bad as that,' she said, defiant to the last.

'Johnny Bruton, the man who is a member of my club, is a dedicated gossip. He would have left no stone unturned in his quest to discover your name and station in life.'

She shifted on his lap, giving him a delicious experience of her softly rounded bottom.

'That was why I instructed the landlord to have your belongings placed in my own chaise. So that he would not be able to read your luggage label with, no doubt, its destination thereon. Not for any nefarious notion of abduction.'

'Well, if you've prevented him from discovering my name, there is no need to carry on with this deception, is there?'

Need? No, it wasn't a question of need. But it was so deliciously satisfying to have the proud, pious little madam so completely at his mercy for once. True, she was still spitting insults at him, but they lacked the conviction they might have had if she wasn't sitting on his lap. If she hadn't put her arms round his neck instead of slapping his face when he'd kissed her.

Not only that, but she'd actually apologised to him. And thanked him, though the words had very nearly choked her as she'd forced them through her teeth.

Oh, no, he wasn't finished with Clare just yet. There were just too many intriguing possibilities left to explore.

'That depends,' he said, as though considering her point of view.

'On what?'

Hmmm. She'd stopped scowling. It was worth noting that pretending to be taking her opinion into account made her sheathe her claws. He would have to bear that in mind.

'On where you were planning to go. I presume, to the home of your new employer?'

'Yes, I told you, Clement arranged for me to begin work as a companion to an elderly lady.'

'No, you didn't tell me that.'

'Oh. Well, he did. You see, he is involved in all sorts of charitable work. And one of his causes is to find honest work for...er...fallen women.'

Something like an alarm went off inside him. Because he'd just spent the better part of a month searching for a girl who might have criminal connections. A girl who'd disappeared after the elderly, vulnerable woman she'd been working for had been robbed. And Clement's name had come up then, as well.

'He finds work for fallen women, does he?' He only just prevented himself from asking if he also found work for professional thieves. Just because he was on the trail of a group of criminals who'd been systematically robbing elderly ladies, it did not necessarily mean that Clare's brother was behind it. It could be just a coincidence that one of the people he'd questioned had mentioned Clement Cottam's name.

'What sort of work? And, more to the point, how does this affect you?' Because he couldn't see Clement being fool enough to ask Clare to rob an elderly lady she was supposed to be looking after, even if he was involved in the crimes Rawcliffe was currently investigating. She was too conscientious. 'Are you not insulted?'

'No, no, he… It is just that he has a sort of network, I suppose, of elderly ladies with charitable dispositions, who are willing to give that sort of woman a chance to reform. At least, that is how he explained it to me when I couldn't credit how swiftly he'd managed to find me a post.'

'That does sound hard to credit,' he agreed. So, Clement had a network of elderly ladies who would agree to take in servants with a shady past, on his recommendation, did he? Even though that could be a coincidence as well, two coincidences regarding a man he already suspected of being up to no good, coming in such rapid succession, were hard to ignore.

'You had better explain how it came about.'

'Well, I wrote to him, naturally, to inform him of Father's passing.'

'Naturally.' And somebody must have written to him, as well. What a time for him to be trying to stay beyond the reach of anyone who might have been able to reveal his identity.

'And within two days he was back, helping to arrange the funeral. And, say what you like about him, I cannot deny that I was very grateful for his help. He is very, very good at organising things. Keeps a cool head, you know, when I…'

He reached up and tapped the end of her nose with the tip of his forefinger. 'You feel things too deeply. You don't need to explain it to me.'

She jerked her head back, out of his reach. And he let her do so.

For now.

'No, and you don't need to bring up the curse of my red hair, either,' she said mutinously.

'It would, patently, be absurd to do so, when Clement has hair of almost exactly the same shade as yours.' His features were similar, too, so that nobody looking at the pair of them together could doubt they were siblings. Yet Clare's sharp little features and pale gold eyes made her look like some kind of sprite, or a woodland nymph, whereas Clement's face just reminded him of a fox. A fox that was contemplating a raid on the nearest hen coop.

'But do, pray, continue to explain how the saintly Clement provided you with employment.'

'Oh, well, as I said, he has this network of elderly ladies willing to employ girls on his recommendation. So he just sent a letter to one of them recommending me as her companion. And she accepted me by return of post. So, you see, before the funeral was over, I had work and somewhere to live, whereas before that I...'

She didn't need to say more. She'd had nothing. Believed she had no options. As she bit down on her lower lip, which had started to tremble, a strange feeling came over him. A feeling compounded of admiration for her bravery in the face of such adversity, coupled with a very strong urge to protect her from ever having to go through anything like it again.

Who would have thought he'd ever consider that the crusading Clare needed anyone to protect her from anything? But then who would have thought she could ever look so vulnerable as she did, sitting there trying not to give way to tears? Having just spoken of what must have been a horribly lonely experience in such a matter-of-fact way?

It made him want to hold her tighter. Tell her she was not alone anymore. That he would look after her...

'And I am sure,' she said, removing her arms from about his neck, reminding him that he was the last person she'd willingly accept help from, 'she will still take me, if only you will arrange for me to get on the next coach.'

'I am sure she will not,' he said, tightening his own hold round her waist in instinctive reaction to her attempt to escape him. She was going nowhere until he was ready to let her go. Until he'd wrung every last drop of satisfaction from this encounter. She hadn't anything like begun to repay him for the insults she'd heaped on him over the years. If he couldn't make her eat her words, precisely, then he could at least rub her nose in the fact that she was where she was because she'd fallen so very far short of the exacting standards she'd always been waving under his nose. 'Nobody wants to employ the kind of girl who gets into fist fights in public inns.'

'I didn't!' She glanced guiltily at his nose. 'That is, she isn't likely to find out about it.'

'Oh, but she is. Things like this get out. People like Johnny Bruton make sure of it.'

'But she lives so far away from London...'

'If she is part of a network of elderly women, who have little better to do with their time than write letters, somebody is bound to write and inform her of your part in this fracas.'

Clare's mouth turned down at the corners as the truth of his observation struck home. Oh, but revenge could be sweet.

'Even if she does not know anything about it to start with,' he persisted, 'the fear of discovery will hang over your head from the moment you inveigle your way into her household.'

'I would not be inveigling my way anywhere!'

'Oh, but you would. No doubt Clement promised her, and her family, the companionship of a gently reared, caring, competent young lady. Once they hear about this little escapade, they will think you have deliberately deceived them. That your *brother* deliberately deceived them.'

'No, no. You are making it sound far worse than it was!'

'And how do you think the likes of Johnny Bruton will make it sound? And how much do you think the tale will be embellished every time it is repeated? Why, the gossips will probably have the pair of us repairing to one of the bedrooms in this establishment and making up our quarrel in the most uninhibited fashion.' Which would, now he came to mention it, be the way he'd rather like this interlude to progress. The taste of her lips had been every bit as sweet as he'd once dreamed it would. And, though she'd fought her response, there was no hiding the fact that she had responded to him. If this were any other woman, they'd be negotiating terms by now.

But Clare, being Clare, was looking wildly round the perfectly respectable coffee room, then wrinkling her nose in disgust.

'You are probably right,' she said gloomily. 'Particularly given your reputation.'

And even though he'd been thinking along the very same lines, to hear her estimation of his character come out of her lips in such a disdainful manner was like a slap to the face.

He tried not to tense. He was not a rake or a libertine, but Clare had never managed to comprehend that a young man, with tolerable looks and plenty of money, was bound to make the most of the opportunities that came his way. In her opinion, men and women should never yield to the temptations of the flesh, outside the marriage bed.

'Exactly,' he purred, injecting every ounce of lasciviousness into his voice that he could muster. Living right down to her low expectations of him, the way he always did.

'Nobody will ever believe that I could take a young woman into a private room, particularly not one to whom I have declared myself to be betrothed, and allow her to walk away with her virtue unsullied.'

'Oh, dear.' She buried her face in her hands and bowed over as though trying to curl up into a ball.

And hang it if another surge of protectiveness didn't choose that very moment to sweep away his urge to needle her. Causing him to start rubbing his hands up and down the curve of her back.

'Never mind,' he said, wondering why humbling Clare wasn't making him feel like the victor. 'I am sure there are worse fates than marrying a marquess.'

She made a strangled little squeal as if of half-swallowed outrage. Bringing any inclination to show mercy grinding to a juddering halt.

Last time she'd acted as though his proposal was an insult, he'd had to walk away, licking his wounds. He'd been smarting under the insulting manner of that rejection ever since. So that every time their paths had crossed, he'd felt he had to make a point of demonstrating that he was over it. Over her. That he didn't give a rap what she thought of him. In fact, on occasion, he'd gone so far out of his way to show her how unimportant she was that he'd even disgusted himself.

Yet she could still wound him by shuddering in genuine horror at the prospect of marrying him.

And suddenly, he couldn't think of any sweeter form of revenge than actually doing it.

Marrying her.

Because, for the rest of their lives, if ever she felt inclined to look down her nose at him, or complain about his lax morals, or...*anything*...he'd be able to point out that it was entirely her own fault she was shackled to such a reprobate.

His lips quirked. He couldn't help it. She could be his, now. For as long as they both would live, if he dug in his heels. And she would have nobody to blame but herself.

Because she'd lost her temper and swung that punch a split second before he'd made his own move. Since, he'd reasoned, she couldn't think any less of him than she clearly did, since he hadn't thought he had anything to lose, he'd decided he might as well kiss her. It would, he'd thought, have taken the wind out of her sails. Taken her down a peg or two.

Thank God for her temper. Because now *she* was the instigator of the scene which had fatally compromised her and he was the magnanimous one, stepping in to save the day. Rather than playing the role of villain for the rest of their lives, the villain who'd ruined her reputation by kissing her in the corridor of a public inn, he would always be able to claim the moral high ground.

He could hardly wait.

Chapter Five

⊶⊷⊶⊷⊶⊷⊶⊷

'You don't really mean that, do you?' She lifted a tragic face to his.

He hadn't. Not to begin with. Announcing she was his fiancée had simply been the only thing he could think of, on the spur of the moment, that would both extricate her from her immediate difficulty and thoroughly annoy her at one and the same time. But now that he'd considered carrying through on his threat, the advantages were becoming clearer by the second.

Especially since he'd kissed her.

Because he'd been longing to get her into his bed for years. Even after she'd rejected him, she'd continued to fascinate him. He'd watched, with mounting frustration, as she'd blossomed from captivating girl to alluring woman. Always dancing just beyond his reach.

But now she was sitting on his lap. And once he got that ring on her finger, she'd have no excuse for refusing him. Not considering the vows she was going to make, in church. Vows which she, with her heightened religious conscience, would consider binding.

'Don't I?'

She peered at him as though trying to understand

him. *Really* understand him, rather than jumping to conclusions based on the lies and half-truths fed to her by the likes of Clement.

'Well, I rather thought,' she said, 'that you only said it because it was the one thing that would guarantee getting me out of hot water. And while I appreciate the, um, brilliance of your quick thinking—'

'Trying to turn me up sweet?'

'No,' she said with exasperation. 'I was *trying* to give credit where it is due. But since I know you cannot really wish to marry me—'

'Can't I? And just why would that be?'

'You are going to make me spell it out?' She narrowed her eyes. 'Very well, then. Since you seem determined to amuse yourself at my expense today, then I will freely admit that you ought to marry someone who is all the things I am not. Someone beautiful, for a start.'

And Clare was not beautiful, not in the conventional sense.

'Someone with all the social graces.'

She certainly didn't have any of those.

'Someone with a title and money, and, oh, all the things I haven't got. But because of my temper, my awful temper, you have told people you are going to marry me.' Her eyes swam with regret and penitence. 'But I'm sure, if we put our heads together, we can come up with another plan, an even better plan, to stop you from having to go through with it. We could perhaps tell everyone that we discovered we do not suit, for example, or—'

'Put our heads together?' Everything in him rose up in revolt. If he thought she could wriggle out of this, she had another think coming. There was only one way he wanted their heads close together. 'Do you mean, like this?' he said, before closing the gap between their mouths and stopping her foolish objections with a kiss.

She made a wholly feminine sound of surrender and fell into his kiss as though she was starving for the taste of his lips. With a sort of desperation that made him suspect she intended it as a farewell. As though she was giving in to the temptation to sample what she considered forbidden fruit just one last time.

At length, she pulled away and turned her face into his neck. She was panting. Her cheeks were flushed.

But when she eventually sat up, her face wore an expression of resolve.

'That was not what I had in mind,' she said, unnecessarily. Though it was pretty much all that was in his mind and had been from the moment he'd pulled her onto his lap.

'Poor Clare,' he murmured, without a shred of sympathy. 'So determined to escape my evil clutches...'

She went rigid, as though his words reminded her she'd been making precious little attempt to escape him from the moment he'd taken her in his arms. And bit down on her lower lip, the lip he'd been enjoying kissing so much not a moment before. And with which she'd kissed him back.

Her expression of chagrin made him want to laugh. She nearly always made him want to laugh.

It was a large part of why he'd proposed to her that first time. He'd just endured one of those days that were such a factor of life in Kelsham Park. His mother barricaded in her room. His father out shooting. The staff tiptoeing around as though scared of rousing a sleeping beast. Life had seemed so bleak. And then there she'd been, so full of life, and zeal, and all the things that were lacking in his. And she'd made him laugh. When he'd thought there was nothing of joy to be found anywhere in his life.

And he'd wanted to capture it. Capture her. So that he could…warm himself at the flame that was her spirit.

The proposal had burst from his lips before he'd thought it through. But then, as now, the moment he'd spoken he'd wanted it to become real. Wanted her by his side. In his life. Keeping the chill of Kelsham Park at bay.

He cleared away the lump that came to his throat, so that his voice would not betray the swell of emotion which had just taken him unawares.

'So determined to escape me. Yet you are the only woman to whom I have ever made an honourable proposal.'

'What?' She looked completely flummoxed by that.

'Yes. All the others,' he put in swiftly, before the conversation could turn to that first proposal and all the hurt that had ensued, 'were quite happy to receive *dis*honourable ones.'

Her puzzled frown turned to a veritable scowl. And she made her first real attempt to get off his lap.

Since he'd already decided they'd been starting to venture rather too close to territory he would rather not revisit, he let her go. All the way to the table where she seized the teapot with what looked like relief.

But the expression faded as she set the pot down after pouring herself a cup of tea, as if she'd realised that, although she'd scored one point in escaping his lap, there was still a major battle to fight. And the look she darted him as he got to his feet and followed her to the table was one of outright desperation.

'I, um, should thank you, then, for doing me the

honour of…though actually, you didn't propose, did you? You just informed the world that I was your fiancée.'

'Nevertheless,' he said, pouring himself a glass of ale, 'you will become my wife.'

'I—'

'And you will make the best of it. In public, at least,' he added grimly. Even his own parents had managed that. 'In private—'

'There isn't going to be any *in private*.'

'You mean, you wish me to make love to you in public?'

'Don't be…oh! You provoking man! You know very well what I mean. That there isn't going to be *any* making love, *any*where, since we are *not* getting married. You know we are not.'

'But, Clare, what will become of you if I don't make an honest woman of you?'

She flung up her chin. 'I will be fine. I will…well… I will work something out.'

He couldn't help admiring her stance, even though he still felt rather insulted by her determination to survive without his help. She was so brave. So determined to stand on her own two feet. No matter what life flung at her.

'There is no need to work anything out. This solution will do as well as any other either of us could come up with. And it saves us the bother of racking our brains for an alternative.'

'But—'

'Really, Clare, this is getting tiresome. I am offering you a position amongst the highest in the land. Wealth you have never been able to imagine.'

'I don't care about your money, or your position,'

she retorted. 'Worldly vanity, that is all you have to offer me—'

'Have you never considered how much good you could do, as a marchioness? You will be mixing with the people responsible for making the law. You will be able to preach your beliefs to their faces, whenever they eat at our table. You will be able to use your wealth to make a difference to the lives of very many of the poorest and most deserving, should you care to do so.'

She froze. Like a hound scenting prey. 'You would let me spend your money however I wish?'

'I will give you a generous allowance,' he corrected her, 'which you may spend however you wish.'

Her eyes went round and she stared right through him, as though she was imagining all the ways she could spend that allowance. For a moment or two. Before she lowered them to the table and bit down on her lower lip, as though chastising herself for indulging in some extremely mercenary daydreams.

Time to put some steel in her spine again.

'However,' he said sternly, 'I shall expect you to look the part whenever you appear at my side in public. I most certainly do not wish to see you out and about wearing garments that make you look like a bedraggled crow.'

Which served to put the mutinous look back on her face.

'How dare you! I am in mourning for my father—'

'Which is no excuse for looking shabby.'

Her eyes flashed. She took a deep breath. He cut in, swiftly.

'I can see I shall have to engage one of those abigails who do nothing but take care of clothes. A top-notch one,' he said, running a deliberately disparaging look over her complete outfit.

'You don't need to—'

'I always expected whomever I married to cost me a pretty penny,' he cut in again, deliberately misconstruing whatever objection she'd been about to make. 'Though unlike most husbands, instead of dreading the bills flooding in from the modistes, I may have to curb your enthusiasm for supporting beggars and cripples.'

'Now, look here...' she began, indignantly. And then petered out. Lowered her head again. Fiddled with her teacup.

'Damn me for being right?'

She nodded. 'It's terrible of me, isn't it? But, the thought of being able to do some good, *real* good, for once. It is so terribly tempting...'

Clare Cottam must be the only woman alive who would regard the opportunity to do good in the world as a *temptation*. It was all he could do to keep a straight face.

'Then let it be a consolation to you. For the terrible fate,' he said drily, 'of having to marry me in order to be able to do so.'

'Look, I never said it would be a terrible fate to marry you. You mustn't think that. It's just...it doesn't seem fair you have to marry the likes of me just because I...'

'Struck me?'

She hunched her shoulders. Lifted her teacup and took a large gulp, as though hoping it could wash away a nasty taste.

'It is true,' he said, provocatively, 'that you are obliging me to enter a state I would not willingly have walked into for some considerable time—'

'I am not! I am trying to think of a way out for you. While all you are doing is—'

He cut through her latest objection. 'But I would have had to marry somebody, some day. Because I must produce an heir.'

For a moment it looked as though Clare's tea was in danger of going down the wrong way.

'Yes,' he drawled. 'That is one very real function you could fulfil just as well as a titled, wealthy, beautiful woman.' He reached across the table and stroked the back of her wrist, where it lay beside the plate of bread and butter.

'Oh!' She snatched her hand away.

'Yes, Clare, you could be the mother of my child.' And what a mother she would be. He couldn't see her taking to drink when she didn't get her own way. Nor taking lovers, nor only visiting the nursery when she wanted to complain about his behaviour and telling her child that he was the spawn of his father and that the sight of his face made her sick to her stomach.

'Oh,' she said again in a rather softer voice, her eyes taking on a faraway look as though she, too, was imaging a child they could create together.

And then her face turned an even deeper shade of red and she began squirming so much he decided it was time to give her thoughts another direction.

'Possibly, I *should* have looked for a woman with all the qualities you listed. And a very tedious business,' he said, with a grimace of genuine distaste, 'it would have been making my choice from all the many candidates for the privilege.'

She gasped. 'How can you be so arrogant?'

He raised one eyebrow at her. 'You yourself have already pointed out that I could have had my pick of society's finest specimens of feminine perfection. I was only agreeing with you.'

'You—how typical of you to turn my own words against me like that.'

'Indeed,' he said affably. 'And you should have expected it, knowing me as well as you do. I have no shame, have I?' He'd added that last when she opened her mouth as if to say it. 'But never mind. There is no point in us quarrelling over this. Just accept that I am relieved that you have saved me a great deal of bother.'

'You…you…'

'Yes, and now I come to think of it,' he said, leaning back in his chair and looking her up and down speculatively, 'I may as well tell you that I don't mind having to marry you as much as you seem to think.' Not at all, to be truthful. But whenever had being truthful got him anywhere with Clare?

'Rubbish,' she said. 'I know full well that I am not fit to become your marchioness.'

'Why not? You are the daughter of a gentleman. Besides, I have known you all my life.'

'Exactly! You know we are not at all suited.'

That was only *her* opinion. 'On the contrary. With you there will be no surprises. You could never fool me into thinking you would be a compliant wife by being all sweet and syrupy whenever we meet, then turning into a shrew the minute I got the ring on your finger. Which could happen with any woman I got to know during a London Season. No,' he said, smiling at her in a challenging way as her little mouth pursed up in the way it always did when she was attempting to hold back a scathing retort. 'I already know that you are a shrew. That the last thing anyone could accuse you of being is compliant.'

Her hand tightened on the handle of her teacup.

'Are you planning on throwing that at my head?'

She deliberately unclenched her fingers and tucked her hands into her lap.

'Good, then, if we are finished here, may I suggest we get on our way?'

'Our...our way?' Once again, she looked slightly lost and bewildered. 'Where to?'

'London, of course. It is where I was going when I stopped here for a change of horses. I have pressing business there.' He had to report back to his friends on the progress he'd made so far with investigating the disappearance of some jewellery from not only Lady Harriet Inskip's aunt, but also from the family of his chaplain, Thomas Kellet.

'Oh, but...' She twisted her hands in her lap. 'I thought you were trying to avoid scandal. If you take me to London and parade me about the streets...'

'I have no intention of doing anything so fat-headed,' he said, 'since I know full well that nobody could parade you anywhere you did not wish to go.'

She shot him a narrow-eyed look, one with which he was all too familiar when attempting to pay her a compliment. As though she suspected him of concealing an insult behind his comment, one that she hadn't immediately perceived, but would discover on further reflection.

'I shall, instead, take you directly to the house of a respectable female, where you will stay while I arrange our wedding.'

She frowned. 'A respectable female?'

'Yes. A lady who has recently become...a friend.'

'I see,' she said, glowering at him. And bristling all over.

If he didn't know better, he'd think she was jealous. The irony was, that Lady Harriet, the lady to whom he was referring, would probably have applauded if she'd seen Clare punch him on the nose, since she'd often shown signs she'd like to do something very similar.

They would, when Clare had climbed down off her high horse and realised Lady Harriet was indeed respectable, get on like a house on fire.

Chapter Six

Clare couldn't believe she was getting into Lord Rawcliffe's luxurious chaise to travel to London, when not half an hour since she'd been planning to get on to the public stage and head in the opposite direction.

She couldn't believe she'd let him sweet-talk her into going along with his ridiculous proposition, either.

He couldn't possibly really want to marry her.

In spite of the outrageous claims he'd made about saving him the bother of choosing one from among the hordes of females who practically swooned whenever he walked into the room.

They were too far apart. Socially, to begin with. And morally, which was more important. He was a rake and a libertine, and a…well, no, she could not accuse him of being a drunkard.

Nor, if she was being completely honest, did he deserve the label of rake. He had never littered the countryside with his by-blows, nor taken any woman against her will.

No, because he didn't need to. Women had been throwing themselves at him since he'd first started sprouting whiskers on his arrogant chin and he hadn't thought twice about enjoying what they had to offer. He only had to smile at them, in that certain sort of melting way he had, and they'd…well, melted.

All except her. On the contrary, she'd lifted her chin and told him exactly what she thought of his promiscuity whenever he'd smiled at her in that lascivious way. Had kept all the melting she'd done hidden, deep down. Concealed it behind a smokescreen of invective. Told him he should be ashamed of attempting to corrupt a vicar's daughter. Informed him she would never become yet another victim of his dubious charms. And when all else failed, simply hidden if she'd seen him coming.

Not that she'd had to resort to such measures all that often. Thankfully. She cringed as her mind flew back, for about the third or fourth time that day, to the time she'd almost fallen out of the tree into the field where Farmer Westthorpe kept his bull. She'd climbed the dratted tree in the first place because she'd seen him coming down the lane. Shinned up it fast, so that she wouldn't have to bid him good day, or face the sniggers of Betsy Woodly, who was clinging on to his arm. And the innkeeper's daughter *would* have sniggered, because there could only be one reason why she was strolling along the lane on Lord Rawcliffe's arm. Which was that they were looking for a convenient place to…*urgh*.

Unfortunately, it was directly after they'd passed the tree whose leafy branches were doing such an admirable job of concealing her that Betsy had pulled him behind a hedge and flung her arms round his neck. Clare had squeezed her eyes shut so she wouldn't have to witness the unspeakable things they proceeded to do to each other. Which was why she'd lost her footing and almost tumbled to her doom.

Of course Lord Rawcliffe had found it hilarious. Had

taunted her with getting her just deserts for spying on him. And she'd been too mortified to offer a coherent explanation as to what, precisely, she had been doing up that particular tree at that precise moment. So that every time their paths crossed, for several months after that, he'd smile at her in a knowing way and offer to satisfy her curiosity.

She'd always managed to escape with her dignity intact. Until today, when he had proved that he was every bit as devastating as she'd always feared. His skilful kisses had not only melted her, it was as if they'd lit a fire in her blood and scrambled her brains. How else to account for the fact she'd ceased trying to find a way out of their predicament and agreed to marry him, instead? Yes, now she looked back over the past hour or so, it seemed to her that every time she'd almost come up with a rational alternative, he'd kissed her again and reduced her to a quivering heap of jelly on his lap.

On his lap!

She shifted on the seat.

'Trying to keep your face averted from my corrupting presence is clearly giving you a crick in your neck,' he said provokingly. 'Why don't you just turn your head and stare out of the other window? Pretend you cannot see me.'

She didn't need to see him to be aware that he was sitting right next to her. Even though he didn't allow a single part of his body to touch any part of hers. He was so…*there*. So vital and male, and sure of himself. Dominating the whole carriage just by the act of sitting in it.

How did he do that? Dominate whatever place he happened to be, just by breathing in and out?

'Have you ever been to London? I am not aware that you have done so, but you might have sneaked up to town in secret, on some mission you wished to conceal from me.'

She gritted her teeth. How could he accuse her of being sneaky, when she could not tell a lie to save her life? Everything she thought was always written on her face, or so he kept telling her.

Although—she darted a sideways glance at him under her lids—he'd never discerned the one secret she would die rather than have him discover. Which was the way she felt about him, in spite of herself. The way her heart pounded and her insides melted when he turned that lazy smile of his in her direction. The way her insides knotted with feelings she couldn't name or even fully understand whenever she'd heard about his latest conquest.

'You mean you don't know?' she said with mock astonishment. 'I thought you were infallible.'

His face hardened. 'No. As we have both discovered today, I do not know everything that occurs even within my own sphere of influence. Clare, you still cannot think that I would have stayed away had I known of your father's death?'

'Yes, I can think that,' she retorted. There had been no love lost between the two men she cared about the most and she could easily believe he would prefer not to attend the funeral. 'But,' she put in hastily when his lips thinned and his eyes hardened to chips of ice, 'I do acquit you of deliberately hurting me earlier. I do believe, now, that you just fell into the way you always have of teasing me.'

'How magnanimous of you,' he drawled, looking far from pleased.

They fell into an uneasy silence for some considerable time. Such a long time that she began to wonder if he was ever going to speak to her again. How could he think a marriage would work between two people who couldn't even conduct a civil conversation?

Perhaps, she reflected darkly, he didn't consider conversation important. His own mother and father never seemed to speak to each other. Whenever they were out in public, it was as if there was a wall of frost separating them. She almost shivered at the memory. Surely he wouldn't be as cold a husband as his father had been to his mother? Although…they'd still managed to produce him, hadn't they?

A strange feeling twisted her insides at the thought of conceiving his child. Under such circumstances. Though a pang of yearning swiftly swept it aside. That had been what had silenced her very last objection, the prospect of becoming a mother. To his child. She'd have had to be an idiot to carry on insisting she'd rather spend the rest of her life tending to an unfamiliar and probably cantankerous old lady.

She'd actually seen it. The child. Seen herself rocking it in her arms, holding it to her breast. Imagined what it would feel like to belong to someone. And have someone belong to her in a way she'd never truly known.

'We are now crossing the section of the Heath,' he suddenly said, jolting her out of her daydream which now featured not just one baby but three little boys of varying ages, 'where once a serving girl, armed only with a hammer, fought off a highwayman with such vigour she left him dying in the road.'

'Why on earth,' she said, half-turning in her seat to gape at him, 'would you think I would be interested in hearing that?'

He gave a half-shrug. 'I thought you would find her behaviour admirable.'

'What, clubbing a man to death? With a hammer?' She caught a glint in his eye. 'Do you take me for a complete idiot?'

'I do not take you for any kind of idiot.'

'Then kindly cease making up such outrageous tales. As if a maidservant would have been wandering around with a hammer in her hand, indeed. Let alone have the strength to fell a fully grown man with it.'

His lips twitched. 'I beg your pardon. No more tales of grisly crimes.'

He fell silent for only a few moments, before pointing out a ditch into which he claimed an eloping couple had met their grisly end when the gig in which they'd been fleeing to Gretna had overturned.

'I thought you were not going to regale me with tales of grisly crimes.'

'It was not a crime. It was an accident,' he pointed out pedantically.

'Well, I don't want to hear about grisly accidents, either.'

'No? What, then, shall we discuss?'

He was asking her? She swallowed. Then noted what looked like a mischievous glint in his eye.

He was trying, in his own inimitable fashion, to break through the wall of silence that she'd thrown up between them by being so ungracious. It made her want to reach out and take hold of his hand.

Rather than do anything so spineless, she said, instead, 'You could...point out the landmarks as we pass them. Explain what they are.'

'I could,' he said. And proceeded to do so. So that the ensuing miles passed in a far more pleasant manner. Especially once they reached streets thronged with traffic and bounded on either side by tall buildings. She was actually sorry when, at length, the chaise drew up outside a white house with at least three storeys that she could make out, in the corner of a very grand square.

'Is this your house?'

'No. This is not Grosvenor, but St James's Square. This is the home of that friend I was telling you about. The one who will be looking after you until we can be married.'

'If you can make her,' Clare mumbled as one of the postilions came to open the door.

He shot her one of his impenetrable looks. 'She will be an ally for you, in society, if she takes to you, so I hope you will make an effort to be agreeable to her.'

Which set her back up all over again. How dared he assume she would be anything but agreeable to a woman who was going to be her hostess?

She avoided taking his hand as they alighted and even managed to evade the hand he would have put to the small of her back as he ushered her into the portico that sheltered the front door.

A smart butler admitted them and took Lord Rawcliffe's coat and hat as a matter of course.

'Lady Harriet is in the drawing room, my lord, Miss…'

'Miss Clare Cottam,' said Lord Rawcliffe in answer to the butler's unspoken question.

For some reason, the butler's demeanour squashed any lingering suspicion that Lord Rawcliffe might be bringing her to the home of his mistress. Which made her slightly less annoyed with him. Which, she decided the moment they entered the most opulent drawing room she'd ever seen, was probably a mistake. Because it was only her anger which was shoring her up. Without it, she felt rather insecure and out of her depth. And had to fight the temptation to grab his hand and cling to it. Or the sleeve of his coat.

'Oh, Zeus, thank heavens,' said a young woman getting to her feet and coming over to them, rather than staying in her chair by the fire. She had nondescript hair and a rather square face. Not a bit like the kind of woman she could see Lord Rawcliffe taking for a mistress. At all.

'I am so glad to see you. Is this Jenny?'

Jenny? She looked up at Lord Rawcliffe's impassive profile. Why on earth would this woman think he was going to bring someone called Jenny into her front parlour?

'Ah, no, I am afraid not. Allow me to intro—'

'Then it was a wild goose chase? Just as you predicted?' Lady Harriet wrung her hands. 'Oh, this is dreadful. Dreadful. You see—'

'This is neither the time nor the place,' began Lord Rawcliffe, only to be interrupted almost at once.

'It most certainly is the time,' said Lady Harriet indignantly. 'Past time, you see, Archie—'

'We will not discuss that matter now, if you please,' he said sternly, jerking his head slightly in Clare's direction.

'You mean…you don't wish this person to know?'

'Astute of you,' he said sarcastically.

'Oh, well, then, perhaps we can leave her here and go into the kitchen to—'

'We are not leaving her here alone while we go off to discuss anything,' he bit out. 'And will you stop referring to her as *this person*. Clare is my fiancée!'

'Your fiancée?' Lady Harriet stared at her with all the shock Clare had felt last time he'd announced their betrothal. 'Good heavens. But she looks…'

'Be careful, very careful, what you say next,' he growled.

'I was only going to say she looks quite sensible. Whatever came over her to agree to marry you?'

'She has been recently bereaved. She was distraught. She had nowhere else to go—'

'Excuse me,' said Clare, goaded beyond patience by being talked about as though she wasn't there. 'But I had a very good place to go. And I was not distraught until you decided to taunt me with my misfortunes.'

'I thought we had already agreed that was an oversight.'

'Yes, we had. Which is why I cannot permit you to go about telling people it was anything other than it was. I think we've had quite enough economies with the truth for one day.'

Lady Harriet turned to gape at her. 'If what he said wasn't true, then how come you are going to marry him?'

'She hit me,' said Lord Rawcliffe, 'if you must know. In front of several witnesses who would have torn her reputation to shreds had I not made them believe it was a…lovers' tiff. She would not have been able to gain respectable employment, if word got out, which it was bound to do. Which left us with no alternative.'

'You hit him,' said Lady Harriet, ignoring all the rest.

'Well, yes, but—' Clare meant to explain that he could have blocked her, easily, if he'd been in the mood to do so. She didn't want this lady, in whose home she was going to have to stay until she could come up with a better plan, to think she was violent.

But Lady Harriet was smiling. 'I know, you don't have to explain how it was. I have very often wanted to hit him myself.'

'I am so glad,' Lord Rawcliffe interjected sarcastically, 'that you are hitting it off...'

'Nice pun,' said Lady Harriet.

'Since,' he continued as though she'd said nothing, 'I am going to have to leave her in your care while I go and procure a marriage licence.'

'Oh! Yes, of course. Only, well, you won't mind, will you,' said Lady Harriet turning to Clare, 'that this household is a little, um, disorganised at present? You see, I am getting married in a day or so myself and you wouldn't believe the amount of work and upheaval it creates.'

Clare turned to Lord Rawcliffe. 'It clearly isn't going to be convenient for me to stay here. Can't you take me to a hotel, or something?'

'My wife does not stay in hotels,' he said implacably.

'I am not your wife. Yet.'

He waved his hand as though dismissing her remark as irrelevant. 'I can see no difficulty about your staying here. You are a most capable woman. I am sure that you will be able to help Lady Harriet with whatever tasks *she*,' he said with a distinct sneer, 'is finding so onerous.'

Oh. Had he just intimated that he thought she was better, in some respects, than Lady Harriet? He'd called her capable. Had suggested that Lady Harriet wasn't coping as well as she ought.

And Lady Harriet was wearing the exact expression on her face that Clare was sure *she'd* worn on many occasions, when crossing swords with his lordship.

'I am not finding arranging my own wedding onerous in the slightest,' she said through gritted teeth. 'I was just explaining that I might not have time to...to entertain in the manner to which she might be accustomed.'

'Please,' said Clare, stepping forward and laying a hand on Lady Harriet's arm. 'Do not let him annoy you. I am perfectly happy to give you any help I may, since you are being so kind as to have me stay with you at what anyone with a modicum of sensitivity—' she shot Lord Rawcliffe a look loaded with reproach '—would know is a very difficult time to entertain strangers.'

'Besides, Clare isn't used to being entertained in any manner whatever,' he said coldly. 'She is far more used to being a drudge. Put her to work and she will immediately feel at home.'

She whirled on him. 'What a beastly thing to say!'

He shrugged. 'The truth? I thought you had been exhorting me to tell the truth. And not to be economical with it.'

'Yes, but that is quite different from wielding it like a weapon!'

'I think I'd better ring for some tea,' said Lady Harriet, darting across the room to a bell pull and yanking on it with a slight air of desperation.

'You have somebody to bring it now, do you? When last I came here,' he said to Clare, as though they had not just been on the verge of yet another quarrel, 'I had to come in by the back door because she had neither butler nor footmen to answer the front.'

'Clearly, I have rectified my lack of staff,' said Lady Harriet, 'since Stobbins let you in and announced you. Oh,' she said, clasping her hands together in agitation. 'What kind of hostess am I? Please, Miss... I forget your name, but it is Clare something, isn't it?'

'Cottam,' supplied Lord Rawcliffe.

'Please, won't you sit down? You must be exhausted if you've travelled up to town today.'

'And it was such a long way,' said Lord Rawcliffe sarcastically.

'I am sure it felt like it, if she was shut up in a coach with you the entire time,' shot back Lady Harriet.

'Fortunately,' said Lord Rawcliffe, turning to subject her to one of his lazy-lidded, stomach-melting smiles, 'Clare is not you. Clare and I have known each other practically all our lives, you see. And we…understand each other.'

He took her hand. Kissed it.

And her heart soared.

Because he'd declared he preferred her to another woman. True, he'd only implied he thought she was more capable that Lady Harriet and that he was glad she'd been the one in the coach with him, but for the first time, he'd made it sound as though she wasn't a total disaster.

And he wasn't laughing at her. Or mocking her. Or provoking her into an argument.

Suddenly she had to sit down. Because her knees were buckling. Oh, dear, whatever was she going to do? She was used to sparring with him. But if he started paying her compliments and kissing her whenever he felt like it, however was she going to resist him?

Because she had to.

Or he would, one day, casually break her heart without even noticing.

Chapter Seven

'**W**ell, this is all very romantic, I'm sure,' said Lady
Harriet tartly, eyeing the way Clare had just practically
swooned on to the nearest chair just because Lord Rawcliffe had kissed her hand. 'But I need to tell you what
happened to Archie. Because I cannot believe even you
could indulge in some sort of elopement, or abduction,
or whatever this is—' she waved her hand indiscrimi-
nately between them both '—if you knew.'

'Knew what?' Lord Rawcliffe dropped her hand and
turned his head to fix Lady Harriet with one of his chill-
ier looks. 'What has happened to Archie?'

'He…oh, dear, there is no easy way to break it to you.
I'm so sorry, Zeus,' she said, going over to him and laying one hand on his arm. 'He's…he's dead.'

Zeus? Why was she addressing him by that name?
Last time she'd thought it was some fashionable sort of
oath she'd uttered.

He flinched and drew back a step, effectively shaking Lady Harriet's hand from his arm.

'Dead?' He was looking at Lady Harriet as though
she'd been personally responsible for it. If he'd looked
at her that way, Clare thought she would be begging

his forgiveness, even if she was completely innocent. Of anything.

'How? When?'

'He…he drowned.'

Lord Rawcliffe went white.

'I'm so sorry.' Lady Harriet clasped her hands together at her waist. 'It was only a day or so after you went to—' she darted a glance in Clare's direction '—to Thetford Forest.'

'He's been dead all this time.' Lord Rawcliffe stood as though rooted to the spot. 'While I have been pursuing a woman who doesn't exist…' His hand curled into a fist.

'We tried to reach you, but nobody could find you…'

He flinched. 'The one time I abandon my responsibilities and travel incognito, everything goes to hell in a handcart.'

Clare had never seen him look so utterly devastated. Her heart went out to him.

'I'm sure there was nothing you could have done,' Clare began.

His head whipped in her direction, his pain so intense she could almost feel it like a physical blow.

'That is your considered opinion,' he snarled, 'is it?'

'Well,' she said, determined not to quail just because he was lashing out at her. It was what people did when they were grieving. She'd had enough experience visiting the recently bereaved to know that it was best to just absorb their hurt, rather than react as though they were angry with her, personally. 'There was certainly nothing you could have done to prevent Father dying. When it is time for someone to…to go…'

'Archie was not an old man. He was young. And talented, dammit. He had a brilliant future ahead of him. And I should not have let him out of my sight. He wasn't equipped to deal with the likes of—' He broke off, his jaw working.

'Death always comes as a shock, no matter what age the person was. And those left behind often feel guilty, but...'

'But nothing! I *am* guilty. I might as well have—' He stopped short again, this time with a shudder of what looked like self-loathing.

Lady Harriet stepped forward. 'Jack and Atlas re-acted in pretty much the same way when they heard, Zeus. They both feel responsible, too. But, the thing is, none of us could have foreseen—' She was the one to stop mid-sentence this time, with the addition of a guilty glance in Clare's direction that made her feel as though *she* was the one who ought to go to the kitchen and give them the privacy to speak to each other freely.

'Would you like me to leave you alone? I can see you are both terribly upset and—'

'No!' Lord Rawcliffe seized her hand as she made for the door. 'No. It is...' He looked down at her hand with a touch of bewilderment. Then he let it go. As he did so, she could see him pulling himself together. 'I am the one who should go,' he said in a voice that was far more like the Lord Rawcliffe she knew. Cool. Slightly disdainful.

'Do you happen to know,' he said, turning to Lady Harriet, 'where I might find Ulysses and Atlas?'

The transformation was astonishing. He sounded as though he was merely asking the time of day. If she hadn't seen how upset he really was, she would never have guessed it from his demeanour now.

Lady Harriet glanced at the clock on the mantelshelf.

'Probably at Jack's town house. Atlas has moved in there with him for now.'

He gave one brief nod. 'More discreet. Using the excuse that he is acting as groomsman?'

Clare was becoming increasingly bewildered by the rapid-fire questions and answers, but decided that to interrupt and demand an explanation, when both of them were so upset, would be highly insensitive.

'Yes,' said Lady Harriet.

'Then that is where I shall go. Clare,' he said, turning to her, though it didn't look as though he was really seeing her. 'Clare, I will bid you goodnight. I have much to attend to, as you can probably gather.' Even so, he had collected himself enough to remember his manners. 'I shall call tomorrow.'

'Very well. And, oh—' she took his hand and pressed it '—I am so sorry for your loss. And that I expressed my condolences so clumsily.' No wonder he was always accusing her of being sanctimonious and preachy. Instead of just offering him the sympathy he'd so clearly needed, she'd, well, *preached* at him.

He blinked. 'Another apology? My goodness,' he said in the sarcastic tone with which he usually addressed her. 'At this rate you will make a decent wife in merely a decade or so.'

He lifted her hand to his lips. Bestowed a brief kiss upon it, then set it firmly aside. Effectively dismissing her.

'We shall be married the day after tomorrow.'

'Oh,' said Lady Harriet. 'But that is the day I am to marry Jack. He will want you to be there.'

'And I shall be,' he said over his shoulder as he made for the door. 'We will make it a double wedding.'

'Oh, how lovely,' cried Lady Harriet.

The look he gave her could have curdled milk. 'Efficient, rather. Since you will have already booked the church, the minister and ordered the wedding breakfast. And the guests at both events would have been more or less the same. It will save me, and my own bride, no end of bother.'

'Oh,' cried Lady Harriet again as he left the room, closing the door behind him. Only this time she didn't look at all pleased. 'What a beast! Oh, I do beg your pardon,' she said, looking contrite. 'I know you are going to marry him, but—'

'No need to apologise,' said Clare. 'That was a beastly thing for him to say.' And just typical of him.

'Yes, but,' said Lady Harriet, coming over to the chair where she sat, 'it will be rather lovely having a double wedding. What with Jack and Zeus being so close.'

'Zeus?'

'I mean to say Lord Rawcliffe, of course. Only I have got used to calling him that because that is how Jack always refers to him. It started when they were at school together. Since he acted as though he was above most mere mortals.'

'Oh, I see.' And she did. Especially after this little scene. She could just see him looking down his nose at the other boys, setting them all at a distance, to disguise his hurt and bewilderment at his banishment. His father had put the word out that he'd sent him to school to learn how ordinary people thought and behaved, so that he would be a better judge of men when he came into the title. Though local gossip had it that he'd really done it to get him away from his mother's influence. Anyway, whichever it had been, he would have hated all the speculation about his sudden banishment. Was that when he'd started erecting defences behind which to hide? Because that was what he did, she perceived. He'd just done it before her very eyes. Pulled a cold, aloof demeanour round him like some kind of armour.

She didn't know why she hadn't understood it sooner. Because he hadn't been icy or aloof before he'd gone away to school. He'd even played with her brothers, occasionally. The vicar's sons and the young viscount, who was one day going to be a marquess, had fought King John's men with toy bows and arrows through the woods, swum together in the lake in Kelsham Park, flicked paper pellets across the aisle at each other in church and traded jokes in basic Latin and Greek.

While she had watched them wistfully, wishing they'd let her join in. Until her mother had died and she no longer had the leisure to trail after them. After that, she'd pretended she didn't care that she was stuck indoors, running the house while they carried on exactly as they'd always done. Acted as though she was too high-minded to even wish to descend to their level.

No wonder Lord Rawcliffe had started to tease her about her puritanical attitude. She taken on the airs of an early Christian martyr.

While he…he'd hidden his own hurts and resentments behind a shield of icy sarcasm.

'Perhaps I should explain,' said Lady Harriet, 'that Jack, the man I am going to marry, has the nickname of Ulysses, though his title is Lord Becconsall. But of course I always call him Jack.'

'Of course,' said Clare, trying to smile. Though she couldn't imagine Lord Rawcliffe ever letting her close enough to permit her to call him Robert. The boy he'd once been hadn't minded her doing so, but the man?

Good grief, she wouldn't be a bit surprised if he didn't insist she address him by his title.

Which was what many people of his class did, she believed.

Oh, well, if he did insist she call him Rawcliffe, it was at least marginally better than Zeus, which, to her way of thinking, bordered on the blasphemous.

'And Atlas,' Lady Harriet was saying, 'that is Jack's groomsman, he is really Captain Bretherton, who was also at school with them and quite their hero, on account of him being so tall and so defensive of the smaller boys who were prone to being bullied. And Archie...' She trailed off. 'Oh, dear, I don't know how much I'm allowed to tell you about all that.' She twisted her hands together. 'And you must be beside yourself with curiosity.'

Funnily enough, Clare wasn't all that curious. She felt as if she had enough on her plate with everything that had happened the last few days.

'I would not want you to feel you were breaking any sort of promise you have made.'

Lady Harriet sat down on the nearest sofa to where she'd been standing. Frowned. Shook her head. 'I haven't made any sort of promise, actually, have I? He just sort of shook his head to show he didn't want to tell you about what he's been up to of late...'

'Which wasn't surprising, since it sounds as if he was in pursuit of some female. I suppose that is his idea of being tactful.'

'Oh, no, it wasn't anything like that! It was...' She wrung her hands.

'Perhaps, instead, you could tell me a little about the man who died? I admit, I am curious about him, since I have never seen Lord Rawcliffe so utterly...' Yes, she wouldn't mind learning something about the person whose death had upset Lord Rawcliffe so much that he'd let his true feelings show, even if it had only been for a moment or two. Especially since she'd done such a poor job of offering him comfort.

'Yes,' said Lady Harriet with what looked like relief. 'There is no reason I may not tell you about poor Archie. He was another friend from Jack's schooldays. And later he worked for your Lord Rawcliffe as his chaplain...'

'Chaplain? No, he couldn't have. I mean, the chaplain at Kelsham Park was Mr Kellet.'

'Yes, that's him. Archie was the nickname they gave him. On account of his being so clever. After Archimedes, the Greek chap who did a lot of inventing. And mathematics.'

'Thomas Kellet? He is dead?' She could hardly believe it. 'And drowned? But...last I heard, he was coming to London to attend some lectures and consulting some scientific chaps who were working in the same area as him.'

'You knew him?'

'Of course I knew him. He was Lord Rawcliffe's tame scientist. I mean,' she added hastily, 'that is the way everyone in Watling Minor referred to him.'

'Oh. I see. Zeus said you had known each other for a long time. You live near Kelsham Park?'

'Yes. My father was the vicar of Watling Minor. That is the nearest parish. I used to see Mr Kellet occasionally. He didn't leave the grounds of the manor very often. Oh, dear. No wonder Lord Rawcliffe was so upset.'

'Yes, and it was all my fault,' said Lady Harriet, pulling a handkerchief out of a concealed pocket in her dress and blowing her nose.

Clare went to sit next to her and patted her hand. 'I don't see how it can possibly be your fault.'

'But it was,' wailed Lady Harriet. 'If only I... I could tell you...' She bit down on her lower lip, looking absolutely torn.

'But you cannot break your word, I understand. Besides, it sounded to me as though Lord Rawcliffe feels responsible. So I don't see how it can be your fault, as well.'

'Because I was the one who sent Lord Rawcliffe to... to Norfolk. If he hadn't gone there, Archie would never have gone to Dorset to confront his great-godmother and he wouldn't have drowned.'

'You *sent* Lord Rawcliffe to Norfolk?' She shook her head. 'Surely not. Knowing Lord Rawcliffe as I do, I could not see anyone being able to persuade him to do anything he didn't wish to do.'

As soon as the words had left her lips, it was as if she was hearing somebody else reminding her of that fact. Lord Rawcliffe never did anything he did not wish to do.

Did that mean he *wanted* to marry her?

No...no, that couldn't be possible.

Although...he'd said all that about not wanting to go through the bother of choosing a suitable bride. And him knowing her so well that he wouldn't be getting any unpleasant surprises, after he'd put the ring on her finger.

So...did that mean...?

Lady Harriet blew her nose very loudly and in a most unladylike fashion, jerking Clare out of her rather nebulous train of thought.

'I suppose I know that really. And Archie was like a dog with two tails at the prospect of searching his great-godmother's house for any signs of the missing jewels. He was so determined to prove that Lady Buntingford…' She slammed her mouth shut. 'I shouldn't have said that…'

Clare reached out her hand and touched Lady Harriet's.

'You are very upset. I can see that this has been a terrible thing to happen and right before your wedding, too.'

'Yes, I'm positively distracted. And with having so much to do, too, since Mama is rather…' She waved her hand in an agitated fashion.

'Well, perhaps it is a good thing I am here, then.' Hadn't her father been fond of saying that God moved in mysterious ways? Perhaps this was why her day had gone the way it had. He'd known Lady Harriet needed a friend, right now. And that she needed…well, to be useful. 'As Lord Rawcliffe said, I am used to hard work. And I will feel much more comfortable about being foisted upon you if I can make myself useful.'

And as Lord Rawcliffe had said, she was a very capable, practical sort of person.

Growing up in the vicarage, without a mother and with three brothers and a father to keep house for, she'd had to be.

Chapter Eight

'I should never have let him go down to Dorset,' said Lord Rawcliffe, taking the glass of brandy Lord Becconsall held out to him.

'You couldn't have stopped him.'

'Yes, I could. I am his employer. Was his employer,' he corrected himself. 'I could have forbidden him…'

Jack took him by the upper arms and gave him a little shake. 'Damn it, Zeus, don't you think we all feel guilty? I could have gone down to Dorset in his stead. Or to Thetford, while you went to Dorset. But the truth was we all saw how blue-devilled Archie had been lately and thought it would do him good to prove himself.'

'It was his family that had been robbed, don't forget,' put in Atlas, from the chair in which he was slouched, clearly having got on the outside of a fair quantity of brandy already. 'It was his right to be the one to investigate.'

'I was responsible for him, though…'

'It wasn't your fault,' said Ulysses firmly. 'It was the fault of whoever is behind the jewel thefts. Because you can depend upon it that is why Archie was killed. Because he was getting close to the truth.'

'You are right,' said Rawcliffe. 'I know you are right. The trouble is, the moment he told us his great-godmother lived in Lesser Peeving, I smelled a rat.' He downed his drink, which had the effect of flinging Lord Becconsall's hand from his arm, as well as giving him the hit of alcohol he sorely needed after the day he'd had.

'What do you mean?' Atlas raised his head and peered at him, blearily, across the room. 'You *knew* there was something fishy going on down there?'

'Not for certain.' Lord Rawcliffe stared into the bottom of his empty glass. 'Though I do know of someone with a…shady past, who was sent there to…' He shook his head in frustration.

'Who?'

That was the worst part of it. 'One Reverend Cottam.' Clare's brother. Clement. The one who'd given her a reference for a post with an elderly lady with suspicious swiftness. The one who'd been so good at organising that she'd been glad when he'd arrived to supervise their father's funeral.

'A *vicar*? A vicar with a shady past?'

Rawcliffe nodded and held out his glass for a refill. The tale wasn't going to be an easy one to tell. 'He lost his post in a parish in Exeter after the bank began to complain about the amount of counterfeit coins being handed in to them from the collection plate. The young Clement Cottam was the one responsible for counting the money and taking it to the bank.'

Ulysses whistled. 'So, how did he end up in Lesser Peeving?'

'Partially as punishment. The parish is poor, inhabited mostly by fishermen and quarrymen. Positively infested by smugglers, too. Not the kind of place where he'd have the opportunity to enrich himself by stealing from the collection plate. And also…' He got a bitter taste in his mouth, which he washed away with another gulp of purifying brandy. 'Well, you do not think the church is willing to advertise the fact that one of its clerics is a thief, do you?'

'They wanted to hush it up?'

'That's about the size of it. Also, as I think I mentioned to you before I left for Norfolk, his father held the living in the parish close to Kelsham Park. He probably used what influence he had to get clemency for… Clement.' He glanced into his empty glass, wondering if draining it so swiftly had been responsible for him speaking so clumsily.

'Which reminds me,' said Ulysses. 'Did you discover anything about the girl from Norfolk, while you were *in* Norfolk?'

'It wasn't her,' he said, setting down his glass and walking away from it before he was tempted to ask for another refill. 'That is, there *was* a girl called Jenny Wren, who came from that hamlet.'

'Bogholt,' supplied Ulysses.

'Yes. And a more aptly named place I have yet to discover,' he said with a sneer as he recalled the extreme simplicity of the place and all its inhabitants. 'However, by casting out lures, which mostly involved inventing a brother with a dubious talent for compromising innocent young females and insinuating that I had heard of a child who must be provided for by my family, I did track down a girl of that name. Who bore no resemblance whatever to the description given of the person who worked as a maid for both Lady Tarbrook and Mrs Kellet. However,' he continued, when both Ulysses and Atlas groaned in disappointment, 'it turned out that she had spent some time in a charitable home where they hoped to reform unmarried mothers. Find them respectable work. And it was run by a group of ladies filled with evangelical zeal, who had a most understanding young cleric come in to hear their confessions and offer absolution on a regular basis.'

'Not...'

'Yes. One Reverend Cottam. The trouble is...' the words stuck in his throat '...I have just, this very day, become betrothed to his sister.'

'Good God! How did that come about?' That was Atlas.

Ulysses, however, gave him a knowing look. 'You already have a plan, don't you? Damn it, but as usual you are one step ahead of us.'

Rawcliffe toyed, for a fraction of a second, with admitting that it had been a total coincidence that he'd stopped for a change of horses at the very same inn where Clare had been waiting for her connecting coach. But it would take too long to explain the history between them which had resulted in her bloodying his nose. 'I came across Clare in an inn, just as she was about to take the stage to employment which her brother had organised for her. And...effectively compromised her,' was all he was willing to say. Especially since he still couldn't quite believe he'd practically forced her to marry him, in spite of all her objections.

'My God,' said Ulysses, giving him a hard stare, 'that's cold, even for you. Using the family connection as the perfect excuse for going down to Lesser Peeving and carrying on the investigation Archie started.'

Rawcliffe thought about protesting that he'd never considered that aspect of things, but then, to be honest, Ulysses had a point. Clare's relationship to Clement *was* a factor he could exploit in regard to their investigation.

'We are dealing with a man who has murdered,' he pondered out loud, 'or perhaps has caused to have murdered one of my oldest, closest friends. Do you think there is anything I should not do to see him brought to justice?'

'You cannot know, for certain, that this Cottam person is responsible,' Atlas pointed out. 'Don't forget Lady Buntingford's part in it all. She was the one who provided the references that got those girls into the houses where they stole the jewels.'

'Now that I know Clement Cottam has connections to a group of women with dubious morals, and a network of elderly ladies intent on helping reform such women, and has, moreover, taken up residence in an area renowned for harbouring smugglers who would know exactly how to get stolen jewels into the hands of buyers, I think it is fairly certain that he is the one who has been organising the whole enterprise. All I need to do is find some proof. Some concrete proof that will expose one of the most godless, devious, sanctimonious hypocrites it has ever been my misfortune to know.'

'And to that end, you'd even go to the length of marrying his sister,' said Ulysses, shaking his head.

That wasn't why he was marrying Clare. The thought had never entered his head until Ulysses had planted it there.

Not that he was going to admit any such thing. Not even to these men.

'I would have had to marry and beget heirs at some stage,' he said with a shrug, using the same excuse he'd given Clare. 'As well her as another.'

Atlas gave him a reproachful look. Ulysses appeared

more sympathetic. 'It isn't going to be easy, marrying a woman whose brother you will be dragging off to prison. Possibly even the gallows.'

He got a vision of large golden eyes looking at him as though he'd betrayed her. And bade farewell to his dream of being able to occupy the moral high ground throughout their marriage. Instead of featuring as her benefactor, she'd regard him as a monster.

'Then I had better get her with child quickly,' he said with a sinking feeling. 'Before she discovers what I am about. And to that end, I had better inform you that I have told her we will be marrying the day after tomorrow.'

'What? The same day as Harriet and me?'

'The same ceremony. I have already put the matter to Lady Harriet and she has seen the wisdom of having a double wedding.'

'Harriet has? When did you see her?'

'Well, where do you think Clare is staying? She has no family in London. And I had no intention of leaving her in a hotel, where she might have been able to… contact her brother and seek to escape me.'

'You think she could be in league with her brother?'

'No!' His whole being revolted at the notion she could have anything to do with anything the slightest bit shady. 'She is so puritanical that were this the sixteen hundreds she would probably have become a prophetess in one of those outlandish sects that sprang up all over the place. No, the trouble with Clare is that she can believe no ill of any of her family. Even when evidence is thrust right under her nose.'

He'd tried to explain, a number of times, why he could no longer consider any of her brothers his friends.

But she wouldn't countenance a word of criticism against any of them. Not from his lips, anyway.

'If she were to get wind of my suspicions about Clement, she would be so incensed that she would probably tell him. And alert him to the fact that we are on to him.'

'Archie probably did just that,' said Ulysses thoughtfully. 'He would have trusted a fellow cleric, wouldn't he?'

'Yes. Also, he knew Clement, slightly, from when he first took up his post at Kelsham Park. Knew, and respected, his father, too.'

'Then the chances are that Clement already knows we're on to him. If you go down there, you aren't going to be able to poke around and find out enough to bring him to justice. Especially not with his sister in tow.'

'Actually, I rather think that Clare might be a very effective weapon to use against him. He is fond of her, in his own way.'

'You think you can use her as a sort of...hostage?'

'I might be able to make him believe I would do so. At the very least, I think he would think twice before making an attempt on my life while she is with me. Since it would be extremely difficult to do away with me without her suspecting who is behind it.'

'You do realise, then, that going down to Lesser Peeving will be dangerous?'

'Dealing with Clement Cottam was never without its dangers,' he said, recalling the many instances of the vicar's son's malice and cunning he'd witnessed as a boy and young man. 'The difference between me and Archie, though, is that I am up to his weight. And I know what I am walking into. Whereas Archie did not.'

'So, you seriously mean to take your bride to Lesser Peeving, the moment you've signed the marriage lines?'

'No. Not straight away. I am as keen to avenge Archie as either of you,' he said, raising one hand to prevent either of them from interrupting. 'But as Ulysses has already pointed out, once I bring Clement to justice, it is going to take my bride some time to forgive me. If she ever does. So I need a little time, before then, to... see to the matter of an heir.'

Both men looked into their glasses, rather than at him. Which was probably as well. He wasn't sure he could have looked them square in the face. Not after outlining what sounded, even to his own ears, like a most dastardly way of treating any woman. Let alone a woman who deserved so much better.

'Then we are in agreement,' he said with determination. 'I will marry Clare, and bed her before I take our investigation any further.'

Both men nodded, although Atlas was now looking at him as though he was some kind of monster.

He let it go. Because Atlas couldn't possibly think any worse of him than he did of himself, right at that moment.

Chapter Nine

The church was packed with a lot of people Clare had never seen before and all of them there to witness Lady Harriet's marriage to Lord Becconsall. It didn't look as if any of them had any idea Lord Rawcliffe was getting married in the same ceremony, to judge from the curious stares people were giving her as she walked up the aisle on the arm of Lady Harriet's father.

And oh, how glad she was now that he'd been thoughtful enough to make the suggestion.

'Don't seem right,' he'd said as they'd all been gathering in the hall before setting off for St George's, 'for you to have to walk down the aisle on your own behind me and Harriet. Bad enough you've just lost your own father, without having your nose rubbed in it. And I have two arms,' he'd finished gruffly. 'You don't mind sharing, do you, Harriet?'

Lady Harriet didn't. But then she was so full of love for her groom, so happy to be marrying him, that Clare didn't think anything would have dimmed her joy. Besides, Lady Harriet had a very generous disposition. It was entirely thanks to her that Clare was wearing the most beautiful gown she'd ever *seen*, let alone owned.

'I have more clothes than I know what to do with,' Lady Harriet had said airily when they'd started discussing the tricky question of what she ought to wear for her wedding, since she was in mourning. And to prove it, she'd flung open the lid of a trunk absolutely crammed with clothes. 'And it will be much quicker to have something of mine altered to fit you than attempting to get a dressmaker to create something in the scant time his High and Mightiness has agreed you may have,' she'd finished acidly, 'before he screws his ring on to your finger.'

Which was true, since Clare was much shorter than Lady Harriet. It had been fairly straightforward to remove a couple of rows of flounces from the hem and put a few darts into the bodice of the one she'd chosen, and substitute a black sash for the green one. Black gloves and a black ribbon to tie up her posy would suffice, Lady Harriet had assured her, to satisfy conventions.

So that now Clare was walking up the aisle on the arm of Lady Harriet's father, a belted earl no less, wearing a gown of shimmering white satin, embroidered here and there with a tasteful motif of ivy leaves, under a delicate overdress of black lace.

But instead of feeling like a glowing bride, the way people were craning their necks to stare and then whispering about her behind their prayer books made her very conscious it was a borrowed dress she was wearing and someone else's father upon whose arm she was leaning. And that she was heading toward a groom who was marrying her for all the wrong reasons.

She kept her head held high, but she could feel her cheeks heating and knew they must be bright red. For nobody could be saying anything worse about her than what she was feeling about herself. She'd spent the last day or so keeping the kindly Lady Harriet at arm's length by talking of nothing but clothes. Of speaking to her future husband of nothing but trivialities.

Because she couldn't help fearing that if she mentioned any of her fears, everyone might see she was correct and would call off the wedding. And then she'd be facing a lifetime of servitude to an elderly and probably cantankerous old lady instead of marrying the man who'd featured in far too many of her girlish dreams and having his child. And she knew it was selfish, but the prospect of having her own baby was just too precious to risk. In spite of knowing she was not fit to take Rawcliffe's title, she'd stopped arguing when he'd pointed out that she could give him the heir he needed. And had avoided any sort of conversation that might prompt him to think of a way out of the proposal he'd fabricated on the spur of the moment.

So that now, here she was, standing beside him at the altar as he drawled vows he couldn't possibly mean. *Forsaking all other* indeed? She would wager not a single person in the entire congregation believed he had any intention of doing any such thing. Particularly not her.

Which made her want to fling her own responses back at him like a challenge. Because she would, of course, stick to vows made in church. They were sacred.

But just as she was opening her mouth to speak she made the mistake of glancing at the other couple who were gazing at each other in a sort of smug mutual adoration. And her heart contracted painfully. Because Lord Rawcliffe was only marrying her on sufferance. And instead of sounding defiant and brave, her voice quavered with all the fears and doubts that she was struggling to control.

As though he knew exactly how she felt, and sympathised with her, Lord Rawcliffe kept hold of her hand after he'd slid the ring on to her finger. Which meant they stood hand in hand while the vicar intoned the blessing. The warmth and strength of his hand clasping hers was strangely comforting, so that she made no attempt to shake it free until the moment the vicar ought to have been joining their right hands together to symbolise their union before God.

But Lord Rawcliffe would not let go. Instead he gave the vicar a very haughty look, as though declaring he'd already taken her to wife, thank you very much, and nothing the vicar could say or do would make any difference.

And once again, Clare was ready to sink through the floor.

After an awkward pause, the vicar turned to the other couple, who allowed him to join their hands in the prescribed manner, while she stood there fuming. What gave Lord Rawcliffe the right to think he didn't need to observe the traditions that had been laid down by the church and adhered to for hundreds of years?

By the time they all turned to process down the aisle, as two married couples, she had worked herself up into such a state of righteous indignation that she scarcely noticed the rude stares and the wave of shocked, thrilled whispers foaming in their wake.

Until they were almost at the door. At which point she was glad he'd tucked her hand into his arm so possessively because it spared her the necessity of having to cling to him for support.

Because she couldn't really blame anyone for being shocked at this mésalliance. If she'd been a guest at Lady Harriet's wedding, she might have been speculating as to why on earth Lord Rawcliffe was getting married at all, let alone to a complete unknown. And in a double wedding to boot. The whole thing reeked of scandal.

As they stepped out into the colonnaded portico, she heaved a sigh of relief. Just before Lord Rawcliffe leaned down and put his mouth close to her ear. 'Well done,' he murmured.

'What? What for?' She blinked up at him in a mixture of confusion and reaction to coming into such a bright light after the gloom of the interior.

'For bearing up so splendidly through the ordeal,' he said in a tone she could only interpret as withering.

'You mean the very opposite, I suppose. You think I should have skipped down the aisle, looking as radiant as Lady Harriet. And said my vows as though I believed I was the luckiest woman on earth.'

'I should not like being married to a woman who thought it permissible to skip in church,' he replied caustically, 'no matter what the ceremony she was attending.'

Oh. Well, it ought not to matter, but she was still rather glad she'd managed to do *something* of which he approved.

And then she recalled how comforting it had been when he'd held her hand when she hadn't been able to disguise how nervous she'd felt. Even though the vicar had disapproved. And she wondered if perhaps he wasn't taunting her. If perhaps he might truly be attempting to support her through what he termed *the ordeal*.

She darted him a look, but could see nothing on his face but a sort of weary contempt for the crowds gathering on the steps and the air of gaiety surrounding the other newly married couple.

'We shall have to attend the festivities organised by Lady Harriet's family,' he said. 'I hope you can continue to behave as bravely as you have just done in church.'

She frowned. Did he mean that as a compliment or a criticism? Well, whatever it was, marriage to a man like Lord Rawcliffe was going to be hard enough without fretting herself to flinders trying to work out what he meant by every casually uttered caustic comment.

She'd do better to give as good as she got.

'I can endure it,' she therefore declared, 'if you can.'

He turned to look at her. And gave her the benefit of one of his most penetrating stares. And then suddenly, the corner of his mouth kicked up in an ironic smile.

'I shall find it easier to endure than you, I suspect.'

'Yes, since all these people are your friends.'

Whereas she'd only known most of them for a couple of days. She did recall seeing Lord Becconsall visit Kelsham Park once or twice, during the long vacation from school, and later, when he'd been on furlough from his military service. Not that she'd ever spoken to him, or known that he answered to the name of Ulysses. But she'd paid close attention to everything Lord Rawcliffe did every time he returned from school. And suffered agonies of mortification when people had gossiped about his conquests, with a kind of salacious glee, whether he made them in the villages surrounding Kelsham Park, or London, or anywhere else.

'Some of them, yes,' he replied cryptically. 'But most of them are mere acquaintances.' Just then his carriage drew up at the foot of the steps and he urged her in its direction. Not that she needed much prompting. She was jolly glad to climb inside and shut out all the people who were looking at her as though she was some kind of fairground sideshow.

He said nothing during the short ride back to Lady Harriet's house, where the wedding breakfast was being held. She'd been told that just the bridal parties and close family would be invited. But as they alighted, it felt as if an awful lot of people were converging on the enormous mansion. It was one good thing about having such a massive house, she supposed. You could sit thirty to dinner and not feel cramped.

You could, however, feel small and lonely and out of your depth, she reflected. Especially as both Lord Becconsall and Captain Bretherton, who were her new husband's closest friends, kept giving her most peculiar looks. Halfway between pity and suspicion.

If she'd had any confidence in him, she'd have asked Lord Rawcliffe what he'd told them about her. But she didn't think she'd be able to look them in the face if she knew for a fact that he'd described the way she'd hit him, and the steps he'd taken to salvage her reputation. If he *had* told them, it would definitely account for their air of disapproval.

And the pity? Well, anyone who knew him well would expect him to make any woman a devil of a husband. Why, even she had almost said *hah!* when he'd come to the part of the vows about staying faithful.

Practically any other woman would be able to bear that better than her. The kind of woman who'd been brought up to expect a fashionable sort of marriage might have expected nothing else. But Clare wasn't fashionable, or brought up to expect to contract a fashionable marriage. So she could foresee him hurting her on a regular basis. And not only by being unfaithful. It was the fact he didn't love her, would never love her... and probably wouldn't even be able to consider her as a companion, let alone a partner in life. He had too much pride to consider *anyone* his equal.

Not that she believed a wife should think herself *equal* to her husband. A husband represented Christ and the woman the church. Which was why she'd promised to obey him.

But couldn't he just glance at her, from time to time, even if he couldn't think of anything to say to her? He didn't even meet her eyes when he handed her into her chair before sitting down at table beside her. It wasn't that she expected him to act like Lord Becconsall, who was fawning all over his bride in the most revolting manner. But did he really have to make her feel about as attractive as somebody's maiden aunt?

She reached for her wineglass, which a footman had obligingly filled. And reminded herself it wasn't Lord Rawcliffe's fault her feelings were all over the place like this. He was being remarkably affable, all things considered. He *had* held her hand and he *had* spoken a word or two of encouragement. She'd got to stop comparing his behaviour with that of Lord Becconsall. Stop hankering for the impossible. Stop being so ridiculously sensitive.

Besides, a man who took his bride's hand for himself, rather than allowing the vicar to join them, was declaring that the marriage would be entirely of his own design. He'd conduct himself the way he wished, no matter what was written in the prayer book.

And she was just going to have to accept it.

She got through the meal by keeping her eyes fixed firmly on her plate, or her lap, and since nobody attempted to converse with her, she didn't need to come up with any kind of response. But, oh, how glad she was when Lord Becconsall eventually got to his feet and made a short speech. It made everyone else laugh, with its allusions to how he'd fallen at Lady Harriet's feet, but only served to make her feel a bit apprehensive. For what could Lord Rawcliffe say about his own bride when it came to his turn to make a toast? Not that she could believe he would really relate how she'd shouted at him like a shrew, then punched him on the nose. Or that he'd had to marry her, or she would have ended up without a shred of reputation and without a job or a home, as well. Because he'd done all that to *prevent* gossip. He might share some things with his closest friends, but he would never broadcast his private business to all and sundry.

Nevertheless, when Lord Rawcliffe got to his feet, she gripped her hands together in her lap, bracing herself for whatever might come next.

'I thank you all for coming,' he said, just as if it was his own house they were sitting down to dine in. 'And for all your good wishes for my future happiness.' Though to her knowledge, nobody had actually given him any. 'But now my wife and I must bid you farewell. As you probably know, she has recently been bereaved and feels that it would not be appropriate to stay for the dancing.'

She laid her napkin carefully on the table next to her plate, hoping that her fingers did not resemble those of a woman who could cheerfully wring her husband's neck. How dare he use her father's death as an excuse to leave a gathering he had not wished to attend in the first place? Let alone make everyone believe it was *her* wish? Not that she did want to stay and dance, because she couldn't, anyway, what with her father having so recently died…

Oh…*swear words and profanities!* He might at least

have asked her what she was thinking before informing everyone else what it was.

'But before we go, I invite you to raise your glasses to absent friends.'

"Absent friends," went the sombre echo around the table. The contrast between his toast and the cheerful one Lord Becconsall had made could not have been more stark. Which hurt and angered her in about equal measure.

'Come.' He held out an imperious hand to hers, which he clearly expected her to take like a meek little biddable...*serf.*

It was the last straw. She might have just promised to obey him, but that didn't give him the right to speak for her as though she had no mind of her own. And it was all very well telling herself she must expect a man like him to go into marriage on his own terms and make it what he wanted, but if she didn't make a stand at some point, he'd trample all over her, the way he appeared to trample all over everyone else.

'I must just bid Lady Harriet farewell,' she said. 'She has been so very kind to me over the last couple of days.'

His mouth thinned. And he gripped her elbow as she walked to the chair upon which Lady Harriet was sitting, as though he didn't trust her to get there and back to him on her own.

Lady Harriet got to her feet as they approached and flung her arms about Clare's shoulders in a fierce, brief hug.

'Good luck,' she whispered, under cover of the hug, then darted a glance in Lord Rawcliffe's direction and one back to her, full of sympathy. Suddenly, Clare had had enough. No matter what she thought of him, Lord

Rawcliffe was her husband now and part of her duty as a wife was to support him. She'd always despised those women who did nothing but complain about every single little flaw their husband possessed. It was so disloyal.

So she lifted her chin. Patted her husband's hand where it lay on her arm.

'Thank you for your good wishes, Lady Harriet. And for your generosity to me.'

And then, with her head held high, she walked out of the room on her husband's arm, determined not to look back.

Chapter Ten

❧❧❧

His heart was beating so fast it was making his hands shake. She'd clung to his arm. Recoiled from the way Lady Harriet had practically invited her to bemoan her lot and walked out with her nose in the air as though she felt offended.

The way a wife *ought* to behave.

He wasn't sure what it meant, but whatever it was, he was not a man to look a gift horse in the mouth. He kept her hand clamped to his arm until the very last moment, handing her into his carriage himself rather than allowing his footman the pleasure.

By the time he climbed in she was sitting bolt upright, her hands folded primly on her lap.

'Are you comfortable?'

'Yes, thank you,' she replied, looking anything but.

Still, he acknowledged her statement with a nod before thumping on the roof with his silver-topped cane.

Her eyes widened as the coach lurched forward. As though she couldn't believe that he'd consulted her before giving the driver the office to depart. As if he was incapable of thinking of anyone but himself and his own comfort.

Which was much more like her. For this was the woman who had never believed him capable of doing *anything* good. Even today, even after all he'd done for her, her little mouth had pursed up with scepticism as he'd repeated his marriage vows. And when he'd tried to offer her some comfort by holding her hand, when he'd seen how nervous she was, to demonstrate that at least he could fulfil the cherishing part, all he'd got was a dirty look for defying the vicar.

He'd been sorely tempted to show her exactly how a man behaved who didn't give a rap for his marriage vows, on the way to their wedding breakfast. He'd had to grit his teeth and recite whole chunks of Ovid under his breath to prevent her from arriving with bruised lips and rumpled clothing, rather than with her dignity intact.

He'd been the very model of propriety. And what was his reward?

There wasn't one.

'Don't look so surprised,' he drawled, leaning back in his seat as though her total lack of faith in him didn't matter in the slightest. 'It is only good manners to ensure that any passenger in my coach is ready before signalling to the driver to depart. I wouldn't want anyone flung from their seat and landing on the floor with broken knees.'

'Not even me?'

She had that look on her face. The one that showed she was spoiling for a fight.

'Especially not you,' he flung back at her. 'Since I have so recently vowed to cherish you.'

'Yes, well…'

There! He knew it. She thought him the kind of man

who would make vows, in public, he had no intention of keeping.

'But then, you surprised me, too,' he continued. 'When you resisted the temptation to join Lady Harriet in bemoaning your fate.'

'I have never approved of wives,' she retorted, 'who behave as if their husband was a cross they had to bear.'

It felt like a slap. He should have known it would be something to do with her principles, or her pride, that had made her refuse to stoop to Lady Harriet's level, rather than any tender feelings she might be developing towards him.

'Not even the ones,' he bit out, determined to force her to see how absurd she was being, 'whose husbands come home intoxicated and beat them?'

'Oh, well, yes, those ones may have some excuse for complaining, but ironically those are the ones who rarely do. In my experience, that is. In the parish of Watling Minor, anyway. I cannot speak for wives of violent men in general.'

'What a little pedant you are,' he drawled in the most mocking tone he could muster.

Up went her chin. 'Would you prefer it, then, if I was to make sweeping generalisations about topics I am in complete ignorance of? Or take every opportunity that presents itself to let everyone know our marriage is not a happy one?'

Not a happy marriage? How could she tell? It had been less than two hours since he'd put his ring on her finger. She had no notion whether they were going to make each other happy or not.

As usual, she'd judged him and found him wanting without giving him any chance to put his side of the case.

'It would certainly make you seem more like a normal woman,' he said out of bitterness, 'and less like a plaster saint.'

'Oh!' After throwing him one look of searing reproach, she turned her back on him and spent the rest of the short journey to Grosvenor Square staring out of the window.

And so they arrived at his town house in a state of silently eloquent resentment. Though she placed her hand upon his arm as he led her into the house, she managed to do it without even glancing at him. And she stalked up the front steps and into his house with her nose in the air.

Looking, ironically, every inch a marchioness.

Ponsonby, the man who'd served as butler both here and at Kelsham Park for as long as he could remember, raised one eyebrow at the dignified little creature standing at his side. Hardly surprising. The man had known her as the threadbare firebrand of a vicar's daughter and couldn't have expected her to alter so much simply because she was now draped in satin and lace. But after only that brief and barely perceptible start, the butler inclined his bald head deferentially. 'Welcome to your new home, my lady,' he said. 'May I present Mrs Chivers, your housekeeper? She will make known to you the members of staff who serve you here in London.'

It was just as well Chivers was ready to do so, since Ponsonby had staged this introduction, *en masse*, of every person who lived and worked here, because he was pretty certain he'd never clapped eyes on about half of them. They probably inhabited the nether regions of the house and never crept up to his level during his waking hours.

Mrs Chivers confirmed that conjecture when she told

his new bride that the skinny little girl who bobbed a clumsy curtsy with eyes round with awe was the one who went round lighting all the fires first thing in the mornings.

'I shall conduct you to your rooms,' said Mrs Chivers once she'd accounted for the very last person in line, a rather idiotish-looking boy described as the boots, though he was sure Cadogan, his valet, would never permit someone like that to lay so much as one greasy finger on his gleaming Hessians. 'I hope they meet with your approval,' she finished, folding her hands at her waist.

'I am sure they will do very well,' said Clare, 'since I know you did not have much time to prepare them.'

She couldn't have said anything more likely to impress them all. Mrs Chivers was appeased by the acknowledgement that she would have done better had she had more warning, whilst put on notice that Clare had such exacting standards that she would find something that needed improving.

Clare would be good with the staff, who had been without a proper mistress for far too long. Since well before his mother had died. In fact, all the previous Lady Rawcliffe had achieved when she'd been in charge of things was to create chaos. Clare, on the contrary, would find out all about them and know, within days, which of them were good workers and which needed a swift kick up the backside. And she'd administer it, too— metaphorically, of course. She'd run her own father's house on a shoestring, from what he could gather, and had still managed to make charitable donations to the really needy in the parish.

He watched the sway of her own backside as she began to mount the stairs, following Mrs Chivers to her bedroom. Where he had half a mind to go himself, right now, so that he could sink his hands, if not his teeth, into those tempting little mounds of flesh. After all, it was his right now. At long last, there was not a single excuse she could make for keeping him at bay.

Except...if he appeared too keen, she might assume...

No, she wouldn't be able to assume anything. She was too innocent. But she *would* be shocked if he went straight upstairs and pounced on her. She'd accuse him of being an animal, driven by base lusts. A rake. A fiend.

So he'd better leave her for a while to settle into her new room before making what she'd probably consider his beastly demands upon her.

With a grimace of distaste at the prospect of such a response, he took himself off to his study.

His hands shook as he unstoppered the heavy decanter and lifted it. Damn it! He slammed the crystal decanter back down on the table, picturing the way Clare's nose would wrinkle if she smelled brandy on his breath. Held his trembling hands before him, imagining the scorn in her eyes if she assumed he was nervous. Not that he didn't have a right to be nervous. So much rested on the outcome of his performance this night. He *had* to break down Clare's dislike and distrust of him enough to get her to relax, so that she could enjoy her initiation into married life.

Though it wasn't nerves. It was anticipation that was making him tremble. The thought of finally having her in his bed was enough to make him drop to his knees and give thanks to the God he wasn't at all sure he believed in anymore.

Though, ironically, that was a gesture she might approve of—her husband dropping to his knees beside their bridal bed and offering up thanks to the deity who'd brought them there. A wry smile touched his mouth at the image—her sitting in her bed, piously approving while he knelt on the rug, ranting like a dissenter.

Ah, Clare, poor Clare. He shook his head. Chained for ever to a confirmed sinner, when all she wanted was to rise above every temptation the world had to offer.

Well, tonight, he was the one who was going to rise to the challenge. And she was going to sin.

And enjoy every damned second of it.

He had the skill. He had the experience.

And tonight he was going to unleash it all on her.

With a mirthless smile, he left his study, crossed the hall and mounted the stairs two at a time.

Chapter Eleven

There was a short, imperious rap on the door before Lord Rawcliffe strode in, claiming the room.

'You…that is, I…that is, I hadn't expected you to come to me so soon,' she stammered.

She'd thought he would at least have given her time to get out of her wedding dress and into her nightgown. She was hoping she'd even have time to down the glass of wine she'd just sent for.

But, no. There he was, standing in the doorway, looking all harsh and determined and handsome and wicked.

Temptation in the flesh. And what flesh. He was so tall and muscular, and the way his lids drooped ever so slightly as he ran his smoky eyes over her with a look that made her insides melt…

She swallowed.

She'd always thought that marriage was a sacrament. That joining with a husband ought to be a holy occasion.

But the man she'd married was the walking embodiment of sin.

Her stomach flipped.

'I am not ready.' Her heart started pounding. Parts

of her that never ought to be mentioned were throbbing. Because of him.

He strolled across the room, going straight to the bed, across the foot of which lay the nightgown Lady Harriet had insisted she wear tonight. He picked it up and let the fine lawn sift through his long, supple fingers. Then held it to the light, which shone right through it.

He shook his head as though in disbelief. 'I take it Lady Harriet procured this scandalous piece of frippery?'

She flinched at his implication she was not the kind of woman who could get away with wearing anything so sensuous.

'Yes, well,' she said, flinging up her chin, 'she thought she was being kind. She went right through my clothes and threw up her hands in horror when she saw the patches on my nightgown. Said it was not what a bride should wear for her husband on their wedding night. And that I shouldn't allow your servants to see it, or they might think I wasn't worthy of you. And there just wasn't time to do any shopping for the kind of thing that would have suited me and make it look as if I was the kind of woman you *should* have married, and...' She faltered to a standstill as he tossed the flimsy bit of nothing aside and stalked towards her.

She swallowed. Again.

'And I, um...' She didn't get to finish what she'd been going to say about not wanting to let him down and how she would do her best to be a good wife to him, even though he wouldn't have chosen her in a million years, for he took her in his arms and kissed her. Full on the mouth. As though he couldn't stand listening to another single word of the nonsense she was babbling.

Or...no...better to pretend he was showing the eagerness of an impatient bridegroom. Yes, yes, that was better. For her self-esteem. It also gave her the courage to yield to the temptation to slide her arms up his muscular body and round to the back of his broad shoulders. After all she was his wife now and so this was no longer a sin. On the contrary, it was positively her *duty* to appreciate her husband's caresses and return them. With fervour.

'You are shaking,' he observed huskily after a few deliciously fevered moments of doing what she'd always wanted to do. At which point she made a startling discovery.

'So are you!'

'It is merely lust,' he said dismissively. 'In *my* case, that is. Though I dare say you are trembling with nerves.'

'Umm…' She felt her cheeks heat with shame. At the fact that she was, apparently, as responsive to his kisses as any of the other women he'd bedded. And also at her reluctance to admit it. Because to let him think she was trembling with *nerves* was a sort of a lie. And surely no marriage founded on lies, or half-truths, could possibly prosper. Could it?

'Which is why I decided not to wait,' he said, stroking one finger along her jaw line. 'I could see you working yourself up to such a pitch that making you mine tonight would have become impossible.'

'Oh.' That was actually rather thoughtful of him. He could be considerate, in his own fashion. No, no, considerate by *anyone*'s standards. Only think of the way he'd sent for ice after she'd punched him, knowing her knuckles would be sore.

And…he was trembling, too. With lust, he'd said. For her. When he was such a connoisseur of women.

'Oh,' she said again. Or rather, sighed. For his admission he was so filled with lust he was shaking with it made her feel desirable for the first time in her life.

Womanly.

'Turn around,' he growled.

'Wh-what?'

Instead of repeating his order, he spun her round in his arms and his intent became clear as he began to tug open the fastenings at the back of the gown Lady Harriet had given her for her wedding. She'd wondered how she was going to manage it, tonight, without the help of a maid. All her own gowns fastened at the front, or under the arms since she'd never had a personal maid to help her dress and undress.

Though it looked as though she wasn't going to need one now. Her husband was amazingly efficient. He had her gown and stays undone before she could say Jack Robinson. Had slid them down her arms, and kicked them away, and spun her back to him and was kissing her again as though he needed to have his lips upon hers without wasting one second.

Which was fine by her. After all, she'd longed, for years, to know what it would feel like to have him kiss her. And, oh, it was everything she'd dreamed. Exciting, and pleasurable and…golly! He was picking her up and carrying her over to the bed.

He set her down with deliberation on top of the counterpane, before straightening up and removing his neckcloth. Jacket. Waistcoat. Shirt.

She lay still, licking her lips and breathing rather fast. My, but he had a beautiful body. Lean and muscular. With just a smattering of hair in the centre of his chest. Which formed an arrow, pointing down to where his hands were impatiently tugging at the fall of his breeches. Oh, dear. That was just a bit much.

She squeezed her eyes shut before she caught sight of anything too…masculine.

She heard him chuckle. Heard the noise of fabric rustling, the thud of a garment landing on the floor. Felt the bed depress as he climbed on to it.

She might not be ready to look at him, naked, but she didn't want him to think she was too prudish to make love with her own husband. So she reached for him blindly. And he let her catch him before drawing her close to his firm, naked body and kissing her.

'Clare,' he murmured, drawing back and trailing hot kisses down the length of her neck.

'R—' She bit back the name she'd been about to use. His given name of Robert. For he hadn't granted her permission to do that. And the last thing she wanted was to offend him when, so far, everything seemed to be going well. Swiftly, she substituted his title. 'Rawcliffe.' She sighed.

'Mmm…' He groaned in a way that sounded appreciative as his lips closed over one breast, through the fabric of her shift. She didn't know whether it was the hum of his voice against her, or the wetness of his tongue, or whether it was because he was paying attention to her *there*, but she became so excited she simply couldn't keep still. She ran her hands up and down the satin expanse of his back, revelling in the feel of his muscles flexing and bunching under the skin. Ran her leg up and down his, stroking the springy hairs with the sole of her foot.

Lifted herself when he began to push her chemise out of his way, so that they could be together, skin on skin, from breast to thigh.

And then it was like nothing she had ever experienced. As though she'd been lit on fire and had become one great conflagration of need. She was aching, hollowed out by needy fire. Needed him to fill that aching hollow that sprang to life between her legs, where he was stroking, and probing, and teasing with his fingers.

'Oh, please,' she sobbed, 'don't tease me any longer. I can't bear it. I need… I need…'

'I know what you need,' he growled and came over her fully, thrusting her legs apart with his own, and probing at her with something that wasn't his fingers any longer. His…his manhood. She blushed as he began nudging at her with it. She knew it was coming, of course, but the way he was opening her with his fingers so that he could thrust it inside was so…so…

'Oh!'

Painful. That was what it was. And she hadn't expected that. Not from him. He was so experienced. And she'd never heard even the faintest suggestion that he'd ever given any woman anything but pleasure.

Why was it so different for her?

He stilled, stroked her hair back from her face, kissed her brow. 'There, that's the worst bit over with,' he said.

'Is it?' She opened one eye to squint up at him.

He ground his hips provocatively against hers.

And to her surprise, and relief, the pain turned into the achy wanting feeling again. He half-lowered his eyelids in a satisfied, knowing way, as though he knew exactly how he was affecting her.

Well, of course he did. He'd done this before. With lots of other women.

She shut her eyes again on a wave of hurt that was not the slightest bit physical and turned her head to one side in an attempt to conceal it from him.

And he kissed her neck. Fastened his lips to a point just beneath her ear as his lower half pushed slowly in and out. And then made a throaty, growling sort of noise that reverberated right through her. Right down to the tips of her toes. And somehow made her forget about all those other women. Forget everything but him, and her, together *now.*

And suddenly, almost out of nowhere, she caught fire all over again. She was all flame. Slick, burning, incandescence.

Which he stoked into a crescendo of burning, pulsing rapture. It was so consuming that for a few seconds she was aware of nothing else. But when it started to fade, it was to the discovery that Rawcliffe was panting into her ear, his own body slack over hers. As though he, too, had reached that place where she'd just gone.

It made her feel strangely close to him. Made her want to hug him, with her arms and her legs. And kiss him again. Like a besotted little fool.

Deliberately, so that he'd never guess how vulnerable she was to him, she uncurled her fingers, which were clinging into the skin of his shoulders, and began to run them down his sweat-slick back instead.

He reared back. Gave her one of his half-smiles.

'That went remarkably well, considering,' he said.

And just like that, the feeling of intimacy, of tender closeness, shattered. For his casual remark had reminded her that this hadn't been anything special, for him. She was just the latest in a long line of his conquests.

'Considering what, exactly?' Her lack of experience? Her lack of allure? She cringed to recall the way she'd writhed with pleasure when he'd sucked at her breasts— her tiny, almost non-existent breasts. In comparison with women like Betsy Woodly, that was, whose bosom resembled a cow's udders.

'Considering your so-called virtue.'

'My *so-called*…'

'Yes,' he said, disengaging and rolling to one side. 'I had half-expected you to lie there with your eyes closed as rigid as a board. Instead of participating with such enthusiasm.'

He might as well have slapped her. It hurt so much, to hear him speak so mockingly of an experience that had been so sublime that she very nearly slapped him back.

'Oh, don't take it like that,' he said, running one forefinger over the fist she'd made in her effort to prevent her wedding night from descending into another fight. 'I am pleased with you for responding so beautifully.' He sat up and turned his back on her. Which was covered in claw marks. Which she'd made. And worse, she was able to see them clearly because it was *still light.*

'My delight in you will be reflected by the generosity of my morning gift,' he said, reaching for his shirt.

'Your…what?'

'A tradition in my family. The groom always gives his bride a gift after their first night together, to signify his approval. Or gratitude, or whatever you wish to call it,' he said with an insouciant half-shrug. 'I think your response, just now, deserves something very special.' He stood up, and went in search of his breeches. 'The traditional gift of a diamond parure seems a little inappropriate, considering your views. I shall keep the set I bought yesterday, for the birth of our first son. In the meantime…'

He got no further. From somewhere she gained the

energy, and the agility, to roll across the bed and seize a water jug she hadn't been aware of until she'd started needing to have something to throw at him.

He must have caught sight of her movement because he dodged to one side, so that the jug shattered harmlessly against the wall.

'You don't want to wait until the birth of our first son for the diamonds,' he said, with raised eyebrows. 'Really, Clare, you only had to say…'

With a shriek, she seized the basin and hurled that after the jug.

He raised his hands as if in surrender. 'My presence is obviously unsettling you. I shall withdraw and leave you to calm…'

There was a candlestick and a set of brushes, and a small porcelain soap dish on the wash stand, all of which went the same way as the jug and basin.

None of which actually hit him. Her aim grew steadily more erratic in direct proportion to her fury.

He was actually smiling, in a maddeningly superior manner by the time he shut the door firmly behind him. At the very same moment she ran out of missiles.

Clare sank to her knees on the floor beside the bed, surveying in turn the wreckage strewn across the floor and the rumpled bedding, and the blood smeared down the inside of her leg. And couldn't stand the sight of any of it. So she buried her face in her hands, but that only made it worse, somehow. Because she could still feel his hands all over her body. And the echoes of the glorious state he'd induced with them, before bringing her crashing back down to earth with those few cutting, callous remarks.

Oh, lord, how was she going to survive being married to him, if he could toss her from one extreme to

the other with such ease? If he could walk away from
her with a smile on his face when she was…*distraught*?

She leaned forward, pressing her forehead against
the cool silk of the counterpane. And prayed the prayer
so many wives had done, she reckoned, since the beginning of time.

Lord, give me strength…

Chapter Twelve

She was sitting up in bed, taking breakfast, when Rawcliffe strolled into the room next morning wearing only, as far as she could see, an oriental-looking sort of dressing gown.

He was her husband, she reminded herself as he approached the bed, barefoot. And this was his house. Of course he thought he could go wherever he liked, dressed however he wished.

'I trust you slept well,' he said, then bent over to give her a kiss on the cheek. As though nothing untoward had occurred.

She struggled with her answer. Should she be truthful and tell him that she'd passed a wretched night? Wrestling with her conscience for hours before finally drifting off into a fitful doze. And that only after getting down on her hands and knees, and clearing up all the broken crockery, and blotting up the water with a towel so that his staff would not guess what she'd done.

Or should she take her lead from him and pretend nothing had happened?

'I cannot say it was the best night's sleep I've ever had,' she finally decided to say. Honesty had always been important to her. And she wasn't prepared to abandon all her principles the minute she ran into difficulties as a married woman. 'I was…so…'

He sat on the chair beside her bed, crossed his legs and gave her an indecipherable look.

'So…?'

Oh. So he was determined to exact his pound of flesh, was he?

'Ashamed of myself.' There, she'd admitted it.

'Indeed,' he said coolly, raising one brow. 'For what, precisely?'

'For losing my temper with you! I don't know why it should be, but you only have to raise your brow, the way you are doing now, and I want to…scream and throw things, and…'

'Is that your notion of an apology? Dear me, it seems to fall short in so very many ways.'

'I…' She took a breath. Counted to three. 'Yes, I…' She drew on every reserve of self-control she possessed. 'That is, you are right, I *should* be apologising.'

'Your response did seem a little extreme,' he said, looking down his nose disdainfully. 'If I had known you had such a partiality for diamonds, I should not have dreamed of withholding them from you—'

'It wasn't the diamonds! And don't pretend you think it was about them. You know perfectly well you made me feel…cheap. Used. As though you had to pay me for services rendered.'

'No, no, I am sure I explained it was a family tradition—'

'I don't give a fig for your family tradition. All I wanted was for you to…' to hold her in his arms as though she mattered '…to let me know I wasn't a disappointment.'

'I believe I did exactly that.'

By saying it had gone *remarkably well, considering her so-called virtue?*

'You did it,' she said from between clenched teeth, 'in such a way that you made a mockery of my values and comparing me to all the other women you've had...'

'I did no such thing—'

'Oh, not out loud. But you did in your mind.'

'So you think you know what I'm thinking, do you?'

'Yes. You—'

But then, as if to prove she could have no idea what he was thinking, he leaned over and stopped her mouth with a kiss. It surprised her so much that she promptly forgot whatever it was she'd been about to say in the sheer delight of having his mouth on hers again when she'd been so certain, from the caustic comments he was making, that he was never going to forgive or forget the way she'd brought their wedding night to a close. She was so relieved he could still bring himself to kiss her that she put her arms round his neck and tugged him closer.

In the dim reaches of her consciousness, she was half-aware of the breakfast tray sliding to the floor, accompanied by the sound of more breaking crockery, as he threw back the covers so that he could climb in beside her. But she didn't care. He must have decided to draw a veil over her temper tantrum now he'd made her apologise, to judge from the way his hands were all over her. Not that she could keep her hands off him, either. Which was easy to do, since the dressing gown *was* all he was wearing.

Much later, when he'd taken her to the heights she'd experienced the night before, only without giving her even the slightest twinge of discomfort, he tucked her into the crook of his arm as he rolled on to his back.

'I almost forgot,' he said, reaching for his gown and drawing a square of card from a pocket. 'Your bride gift.'

She took it from him and held it up to the light filtering in through the lace curtains at the window.

'It is a voucher for Almack's,' he explained when she frowned.

'Almack's?'

'Yes. Even you must have heard of the place. Vouchers to gain admittance are highly prized by most debutantes. They will do whatever it takes to get their hands on one.'

'I am not,' she said with sinking heart, 'a debutante.'

'Nevertheless, you need to make an appearance there. You will find your future as my wife will go much more smoothly once you show that you have the approval of the patronesses. Which is why I asked them to call and look you over.'

'Oh,' she said, recalling the visit from two rather nosy women when she'd been staying with Lady Harriet. 'I thought they were interviewing Lady Harriet. They promised to send *her* vouchers for Almack's, but they never said anything to me.'

'Do you not wish to attend?'

She would rather crawl over broken crockery all the way to…to Walsingham!

'Would you have preferred,' he said, turning to his side and raising himself up on to one elbow so that he could look down into her face, 'the diamonds after all?'

She almost said something very rude about the diamonds.

'I know I ought to feel grateful that you went to so much trouble for me—'

'It was no trouble. Just had a word with one or two people…'

'And it was as much for your dear friend Lady Harriet as for me, wasn't it?' she snapped.

'You have no need to be jealous,' he said in what she could only think of as an extremely patronising tone.

'Jealous? The very idea! You seem to forget that I know that Lady Harriet dislikes you intensely.'

'Besides which, it was not for Lady Harriet that I obtained vouchers, but for the sake of her husband. My friend, Lord Becconsall. I do not want his marriage to be a cause for regrets. Unsuitable though, in many people's eyes, she may be.'

'Unsuitable? She's the daughter of an earl!'

'Rank is not everything, my dear.'

'Well, no, it can't be, or they wouldn't have given me a voucher, would they?'

He shook his head as though in disbelief at her stupidity. 'What do you think you are, now?'

'What do you mean? I am a nobody.'

'No, you little goose, you are a marchioness. Now that you are my wife, you are Lady Rawcliffe.'

'Good grief, so I am.'

He gave her a withering look. 'You must be the only woman in England who could forget the little matter of becoming a marchioness, upon marriage to a marquess.'

'Are you saying I'm stupid?'

'No,' he said, tapping her on the tip of her nose with the end of his forefinger. 'Just very, very unworldly.'

'Hmmph,' she said. And would have crossed her arms across her chest if they weren't still linked as far round his body as she could reach.

'I know that you don't possess the clothes you would need to attend such an exclusive club, if that is what is bothering you. But that is a matter which can easily be rectified.'

'It isn't the clothes! Well, not only the clothes.'

'What, then?'

Dear me. When he looked at her like that, as though he was really interested in hearing what she had to say, he was even more dangerous to her peace of mind than when he was kissing her.

'I'm just…not…ready. Perhaps I never will be. I'm not… I wasn't brought up to take a place in society. I'm just a vicar's daughter. And it's no use,' she carried on hastily when he took a breath as if to make an objection, 'saying that now I am your wife I have a title. I have absolutely not the first idea of how to be a marchioness. I wasn't brought up to be anything but possibly a housekeeper or companion to some elderly invalid. I have no idea how to be a grand lady.'

'First of all,' he said silkily, sliding his foot up and down her leg in a most suggestive way, 'you have already proved to be the ideal marchioness, for me, by your response to me in this bed.'

She wasn't sure whether to be flattered, or offended. After all, very many women had responded to him in his bed, she had no doubt. And he hadn't been obliged to marry any of them to prevent a scandal, either.

'And second?'

One side of his mouth hitched up in amusement. 'Second, my pedantic little bride, if you are so intent on glossing over the most basic reason any man marries any woman, you do not need to *learn* how to be a marchioness. You *are* one already, by virtue of marrying me. And you will find that there are no rules to govern the behaviour of such a high-ranking lady. You may behave however you wish and nobody will dare criticise you. Not,' he added more seriously, 'that I fear you are ever likely to do anything that might give any-one cause to criticise you, let alone bring disgrace to my family name.'

She was just starting to glow with pleasure at his praise when he ruined it all by adding, 'You are far too pious.'

How could he manage to make what ought to have felt like a compliment sound like a criticism just by in-jecting a certain tone to his voice?

'But—'

He stopped her next protest by the simple expedient of leaning in and kissing her again. And though she strove to hold on to her annoyance she found it impos-sible to do anything but melt.

'Perhaps it *is* too soon for you to face the tabbies,' he said, smoothing her hair back from her face once he'd reduced her to a pliant puddle. 'Perhaps it would be easier for you if you were more at ease with me. With your new station.'

'Oh.' Goodness, sometimes he could be so... understanding.

When he wasn't being infuriating, that was.

And since he was clearly trying very hard, by his standards, she couldn't very well do anything but meet him halfway.

'Well, yes,' she therefore admitted. 'It has all been rather sudden. One minute I was all set to start a new life as a companion to an elderly invalid and the next...'

'We shall go away for a while. Get right away from London and spend some time getting to know each other, as husband and wife. Once you have gained more confidence, I have no doubt that you will excel in your role.'

'Really? You really mean that?'

'Yes.' He frowned. 'I must warn you, however, that I will not be able to relinquish all my duties. I have been…out of touch for some time and there are some matters which need urgent attention.'

'I would never expect you to dance attendance on me. I know you are a very important man, with a great many calls upon your time.'

'You see? You are proving to be an excellent marchioness already.'

This time, there was no sting to the compliment that she could discern. Apart from the message that she would only be a rather small part of his life. Which was all any woman he married could hope for.

She lay back and watched him through her lashes as he retrieved his dressing gown and knotted the belt loosely round his waist.

She might only be able to inhabit a very small corner of his life, but by heaven she would fill that place to the very best of her ability. He would never have cause to complain about her behaviour, or her appearance, or… she glanced guiltily at the broken breakfast dishes littering the rug…*any*thing.

Chapter Thirteen

'You look very well in that outfit,' said Lord Raw-cliffe as he handed Clare into his travelling carriage. Actually, she looked utterly divine in her new carriage dress. She'd always managed to make the best of what came to hand. But now she had access to almost limitless funds he wouldn't be a bit surprised if she soon became a leader of fashion.

Clare blushed as she took her seat. Then surreptitiously smiled down at her fine leather gloves.

'You have outdone Lady Harriet already,' he added as he took the facing seat.

'Oh?' Clare looked puzzled. Suspicious. As though she expected him to say something unkind now, to rob her of her pleasure in his compliment. 'In what way?'

'Until her husband took her in hand, Lady Harriet had no idea what suited her and went about in some extremely unflattering outfits.' Which was one of the reasons he'd hired an extremely experienced dresser to oversee Clare's purchases. Lord Becconsall might not care what people said about his wife behind her back, but he was not going to leave Clare exposed to the same kind of gossip.

'Yes, I know, she told me as much,' said Clare, with a little sniff. 'I suspect,' she added sadly, 'that is why she was so keen to let me have so many of her old gowns.'

He stiffened. 'I do hope that your trunks are not full of another woman's cast-offs. Did I not give you enough time to kit yourself out, properly, for a trip to the country?' One week. Just one week had he kept her entirely to himself. He'd refused all invitations to socialise and insisted that modistes and what-have-you came to her rather than let her venture out into the streets without him. Until he'd caught her gazing wistfully out of the window and suspected she was starting to feel like a prisoner.

And so here they were, setting off for Lesser Peeving and talking about clothes as if they were all that mattered.

'They are not *full* of Lady Harriet's cast-offs,' she was saying waspishly. 'But I saw no reason to throw away any clothing that I was able to make use of.'

'That carriage dress you have on is never one of hers.'

'No. This is new.'

'I thought so.' He sat back with a feeling of satisfaction. He couldn't expect Clare to abandon her habits of thrift overnight. But at least she could treat herself to new clothing now, whenever the mood did take her. He'd done that much for her. No more dyeing coats because she couldn't afford decent mourning garments.

He'd taught her how much pleasure her body could give her, too. Although she wasn't at all comfortable with that new knowledge. Not when the pleasure came at the hands of a man she despised so heartily.

Not that she'd said as much. But then he hadn't given

her the opportunity to do so. Every time she'd started to stiffen up, in his arms, and he'd seen the waves of guilt and regret wash across her expressive little face, he'd given her thoughts another direction. Had deliberately goaded her into an argument about something else, so that they wouldn't have to confront the issue which he dreaded hearing coming from her lips.

Her true feelings about him. About marrying him.

She'd never made any secret about the way she felt about him when they'd been growing up. She'd called him a libertine, a profligate care-for-nobody, a ne'er-do-well, an arrogant, unfeeling, miserly, harsh landlord... oh, there had been no end to the insults she'd flung at him.

Although to be fair, she'd only done so in retaliation to his teasing. Because teasing her had been the only way he'd been able to get her to make any sort of reply to him at all. Goading her into flying into the boughs had always been one of his greatest pleasures. She looked so funny, spitting fire and practically hopping up and down on the spot. And whenever he'd prodded her down off her high horse, forced her to lose control with him when what she most wanted to do was treat him with haughty disdain, it had felt like a victory.

Not the best way to conduct relations with one's own wife, perhaps, but then that was the way they'd always interacted and it wasn't as easy to get out of a habit, he was finding, as it had been to fall into it.

Though he could see she was trying to. He shifted guiltily in his seat as she darted him a tentative smile. Since she'd given vent to her feelings in that initial orgy of crockery-smashing, she'd been doing her utmost to keep her temper in check. He could see her wrestling with it right now, as his secretary finally clambered into the coach, his satchel of papers slung over one shoulder and his portable writing desk clutched under one arm.

'You won't mind, my dear,' he said to Clare, who clearly did to judge from the way she narrowed her eyes, 'if I spend some time attending to my correspondence? I often spend the time it takes travelling from one place to another in this manner.'

Any newly married woman would be insulted to find her husband was bringing a secretary along on her bride trip. Clare was no exception. But after sitting up very straight, she said, 'Of course not,' with a determined smile. 'I know you are a very important man and must have a great deal of work to attend to. You know, I have never travelled very far from Watling Minor before so I will be quite content watching the passing scenery out of the window.'

Dear lord, but Saint Paul had it right when he talked about heaping coals of fire upon your enemy's head. He felt downright scalded by Clare's dogged determination to enjoy the journey, so as not to be a nuisance. Especially since he'd only invited Slater along to create a barrier between them. The last thing he wanted to do was talk to her for any length of time. Because she would probably start to thank him for taking her out of town rather than forcing her to go to Almack's, where she'd have taken her place in society as his bride. And he wasn't sure how long he would be able to let her think he was being a caring, thoughtful husband when the truth was he'd deliberately manipulated her into taking this trip. First of all, he'd reduced her to a state of boneless satiation, and then, when her judgement was clouded, he'd scared her with that threat of parading her before the town's tabbies at Almack's. If he'd suggested a trip to the country to start with, she'd have been so offended at the implication she wasn't up to snuff that he'd have had to drag her into this carriage kicking and screaming.

What was worse, though, was leading her to think that they were taking this trip solely to benefit her, whereas nothing could be further from the truth.

Slater began to pull documents from the case and arrange them on the portable desk which he balanced upon his knee. At least the man had no idea anything was out of the ordinary. Not on this leg of the journey, at any rate. It might well be different after they'd been to visit Clement, particularly if Clare found out that he suspected her darling brother of being involved in not only the disappearance of a large amount of jewellery, but also of the suspicious death of his friend Archie. She wouldn't be able to pretend she wasn't angry with him after that. And she would be. So angry that he wouldn't be able to manipulate her into a state of smiling compliance with his skills in the bedroom. Bedroom? She'd never let him anywhere near a bedroom ever again. In fact, if she ever *spoke* to him again it would be nothing short of a miracle.

And two miracles in one lifetime were more than any man deserved. He'd had his when he'd walked into that inn and she'd fallen into his clutches like a ripe peach.

Actually, make that two miracles. The second had occurred on his wedding night, when she'd not merely yielded to his lovemaking, but responded with an untutored enthusiasm that had stunned him. For a moment or two, he'd experienced such a strong surge of emotion that it had almost leaked from his eyes. He'd almost told her...

He pulled a face. Thank heavens, his fit of lunacy

had only lasted a second or two before he'd pulled himself together sufficiently to take steps to ensure things didn't start getting...*sentimental.*

He'd managed to extricate himself from her arms, and then her room, with his own dignity intact. That he'd done it by goading her into a state where she'd found relief in throwing a selection of breakables at him also ensured she didn't notice how shaken he'd been by their encounter. And then the next morning, before she could launch into a discussion about what had happened the night before, he'd distracted her by deliberately seducing her again.

And that was the way he would continue to handle her. Handle his own weakness for her. And stop it getting out of hand.

Lord Rawcliffe was acting exactly the way a newly married man should, tenderly handing her out of the carriage at every halt, making solicitous enquiries as to her comfort and seeing to all her wants, be it delicately sliced bread to go with a cup of tea, or directions to the necessary.

The only hint that all was not as it should be was the presence of Slater and his bag of *extremely important documents.* Most newly married men would surely have consigned his secretary to one of the coaches containing all the other members of staff her husband seemed to think necessary for a trip to...wherever it was they were going. He hadn't deigned to inform her. And she was too proud to give in to her curiosity and beg him to tell her. Or to ask any of his staff, either, because that would expose the fact that he hadn't seen fit to share his plans with her.

And as the day wore on it became harder and harder

to keep her feelings in check. Because none of the topics Slater and her husband discussed sounded as important as all that. Not that she supposed they would discuss state secrets with her sitting right there, she conceded. Perhaps it was just the *amount* of business her husband had to deal with that was the issue. Perhaps he just wanted to catch up with all the things that had escaped his attention while he'd been searching for the mysterious 'Jenny' Lady Harriet had mentioned before he'd made it clear she was supposed to be a secret.

He certainly hadn't liked being kept in ignorance of her father's death. And he'd been downright shaken by the news of his chaplain's horrible fate.

She let her eyes drift in his direction. And sighed. He was, in spite of all the accusations she'd flung at him over the years, a very conscientious landlord. At least he didn't regard his tenants as merely a source of income, the way so many others of his class did. Though he lived well, extremely well, actually, he never neglected repairs on the cottages of his estate workers. And he generally took such a keen interest in everything that was going on, at all his estates from what she could gather, that he had the reputation of knowing *everything*. Perhaps this was how he did it. By paying such meticulous attention to all his correspondence, no matter how trivial it appeared.

She promptly decided to give him the benefit of the doubt upon that issue. Because apart from anything else, it was a good way to argue herself out of being offended by Mr Slater's mere presence, when Rawcliffe had led her to believe this was going to be a time for them to get to know each other as husband and wife.

Though, actually, wasn't this a sort of getting to know him? She was certainly learning that he wasn't the kind of man to neglect his duties to his estates, not even when on a bride trip.

Which made his jaunt into the wilds of Norfolk in pursuit of that Jenny person all the more remarkable. He'd put himself beyond the reach of even his secretary, never mind his friends. So he must have considered it a very important matter.

Which he didn't want her to know anything about.

Even though she was his wife!

A wife who didn't feel she had the right to question him about his movements *now*, let alone before they'd married.

She sighed as they approached another coaching inn.

'Tired?'

Even though his carriage was very comfortable and she'd been regaled with all sorts of treats at every stop they'd made, she was growing rather weary of travelling.

'A little,' she admitted.

'Then you will be pleased to hear we are going to break our journey here, overnight.'

She wondered where *here* was, precisely. And wondered if now would be a good time to finally break down and ask him. Not in front of Slater, though. But later, surely he couldn't think she was being demanding, if she raised the topic...over dinner perhaps?

Yes, that was when she would ask him, over dinner. Because apart from anything else it would give them something to talk about, which wouldn't lead to an argument, the way most of their encounters did.

Unless, of course, he invited Slater to dine with them, to prevent them from descending into the kind of childish bickering that nearly always developed whenever they were alone. Except when they were in bed, of course, in which case they didn't do any talking at all. Not anymore. She just let him leave when he'd done, rather than demand more than he seemed willing to give her. It was better, she'd found, to feel a slight resentment over his behaviour than to behave badly herself.

Clare was glad to see Slater scuttle off to the nether regions of the inn while the landlord bowed and scraped her and Rawcliffe to a suite of rooms upstairs. Although it depressed her a bit to note that her husband would rather pay for two bedrooms than to have to share a bed with her all night.

'Are the rooms not to your liking?'

She lifted her gaze from an inspection of the table upon which she guessed they would be dining in due course to find Rawcliffe inspecting her sardonically.

'The rooms are lovely,' she countered.

'Then what has put that frown upon your face?'

She blushed. And decided that she wasn't going to tell him that she'd been thinking about their sleeping arrangements and wishing that after taking her to the heights of pleasure, he wouldn't always wreck it all by displaying such determination to get as far away from her as possible as swiftly as he could.

'Um…' She reached for something she might say to explain her thoughtful mien. 'Actually, it has just occurred to me that I have no idea where we are going.' Or where they were right now, come to that, not that it mattered.

It didn't matter. She blinked at the revelation. She no longer cared where she was, all that much, or where she was going. Because…she trusted him.

For so many years, she'd been the one upon whom others depended. But now, within less than a week of becoming his wife, she had a deep and abiding faith that he was going to look after her.

She went to the nearest chair and sat down upon it. He'd sown the seeds of that faith by tending to her hand after she'd punched him. Had watered it by insisting on marrying her, even though she must be the last person he'd ever have considered, had he actually been considering marriage. And it had steadily grown every time he'd greeted her outbursts of temper by walking away and giving her time to calm down. He had never responded to her with anger, or rebuked her for losing control—not even the time she'd thrown all that crockery at him—but with patience and tolerance.

'Is something amiss? Do you feel unwell?'

The look of concern on his face was almost her undoing. She lowered her head, rummaged in her reticule and pulled out a handkerchief with which to blow her nose and dab at her eyes.

Oh, dear. She'd been half in love with the handsome Robert Walmer for most of her life. Now that she was living in close proximity to him, was it any wonder that she was falling all the way?

And now he was kneeling at her feet, looking up into her face with a frown.

'I am just, I have to admit,' she gulped, dabbing at her eyes, 'rather overwhelmed by all...' she waved her damp handkerchief vaguely '...all this.'

'This inn?'

'Don't be absurd,' she said tartly. 'The inn is...just an inn. I mean, my circumstances. Us.'

His face shuttered. He got to his feet and went over to the window.

'You will feel better once you have had a cup of tea,

I should think. I have rung for some. It should be here shortly.'

Which meant, *do not become sentimental, or expect more of me than I am prepared to give.*

Well, she wasn't stupid. She could take a hint.

'Thank you,' she said meekly. And bit down on the acid retort that sprang to mind—that if he though a cup of tea was going to cure a painful case of unrequited love then he was all about in his head. Because the last thing he'd want to hear was that the bride he'd taken on sufferance was falling deeper in love with him with every day that passed.

Chapter Fourteen

And then a chambermaid bustled in with a tray of tea things, closely followed by Nancy, the maid her husband had insisted on hiring.

'I shall leave you to freshen up and calm yourself down,' he said sternly. And then headed for the door which led to his room, through which she glimpsed his own valet, Cadogan, laying out clothes into which she assumed he meant to change for the evening. Which meant he expected her to do the same. Which was why Nancy had come.

She screwed her handkerchief into a twist, the way she'd wring the neck of a chicken before plucking it and popping into the pot. How could she be falling so hard for a man who was so...*infuriating*? So oblivious to her?

Because, in so many ways, he'd been so tolerant, considerate and patient.

If he did speak to her sternly from time to time, was it any wonder? She had a terrible temper herself and knew how easily she could lose it.

Perhaps he'd thought those tears were a prelude to another crockery-throwing scene, and had withdrawn before she had the chance to behave badly.

She supposed she couldn't blame him. Besides, she did need to regain some composure. She drew in a deep breath. She could be calm. She was sure she could be calm. And, actually, having the chambermaid and her own rather toplofty maid bustling about the room did help her to control herself. She couldn't give vent to any sort of feelings when servants were about, he'd warned her. *It just isn't done, in this level of society*, he'd said, as though she'd been in the habit of discussing everything in front of servants her entire life.

Which had, of course, made her itch to slap his face right then. And, she now saw, was one reason his talking-to had been so infuriating. Because he'd initiated it in front of Nancy. After warning her she needed to watch her behaviour when servants were watching.

If she didn't know better she'd think he was deliberately provoking her. Only, why on earth would he do anything of the sort?

No, no, she was imagining things. She was tired from the journey and drained from the effort of keeping her temper in check, and unsettled by the strength of feelings she was developing for a man everyone knew had a lump of ice where his heart ought to be.

'I'll press the apricot silk for this evening, shall I, my lady?'

Clare lifted her cup of tea to her lips and took a long, soothing sip before answering her maid. Because Nancy was not actually asking her opinion. Nancy was telling her which dress was appropriate for her to wear to dine with her husband, in an inn. It was the reason her husband had hired the girl, he'd told her. So that she wouldn't make the same mistakes as Lady Harriet had. He *did not have the same level of tolerance*, he'd added, unnecessarily to her way of thinking. He *was not prepared to permit her* to go around town looking a fright. Because it would reflect badly upon his taste.

His taste.

She set the cup down on the saucer with a snap.

'Apricot silk? Do you think that is appropriate?'

'The trimmings are all black. There is no harm in wearing just a touch of colour, when dining in private, on what is, after all, your honeymoon,' replied Nancy with exaggerated patience.

'Very well,' she said through gritted teeth. 'By all means, bring me the apricot silk.'

'Shall I just help you off with your carriage dress?'

The carriage dress he'd complimented her upon. Telling her she'd outdone Lady Harriet. Which had pleased her no end, at the time he'd said it.

She supposed she ought to be grateful to Nancy. Left to herself, Clare would have purchased far cheaper, more hard-wearing clothing which he would not, she'd discovered earlier, have approved of at all. Nor would she ever have thought of changing to eat dinner in a private inn room, either, let alone into a silk gown.

'Yes, thank you, Nancy,' she said, trying to inject the gratitude into her tone of voice which she was striving to feel.

'I shall have hot water brought up directly, your ladyship,' put in the chambermaid.

Because of course she would have to wash off the grime of travelling, before donning the silk. And, yes, she did want to have a wash. It was just that afterwards she would much rather have curled up on the window seat and gazed down at the bustling inn yard. Or simply flung herself onto her bed, to rest. Neither of which she'd be able to do in the apricot gown, which was cut far lower than she was used to and therefore required the kind of underpinning that not only kept her decent, but meant there would be no flinging herself onto beds, or lounging upon comfy seats, or, if she ate too much, breathing too deeply, either.

She sighed. It was harder work being a marchioness than she would ever have imagined.

'You look very appetising in that confection,' said Lord Rawcliffe as he handed her to her chair at the table set for two. From this position, leaning over her from behind as she settled on to her seat, he had a very intriguing view down the front of it.

It made him want to slide his hands down and cup the delicate white mounds and squeeze the raspberry-pink nipples between his fingers.

Which would shock her. And be highly disrespectful, considering the waiter was still in the room, fussing over the chafing dishes on the sideboard.

And so, while the fellow's back was turned, it was exactly what he did, swiftly delving down her bodice, locating the tightly furled bud, pinching it and withdrawing his hand in the time it took her to stiffen and gasp in disbelief.

Hopefully she would now be too angry to remember whatever it was she'd been thinking of discussing with him over supper. Whatever it was that had made her look wistful, before rendering her teary-eyed. And too aware of the waiter to launch into a tirade upon his manners, either.

She was certainly angry enough to grasp the handle of the gravy boat in a very threatening manner. He had a hunch that his dignity was only spared because the waiter turned round at the very moment she lifted it from its stand. So that instead of throwing it in his face, she poured it over her plate. But she then started sawing at her food with such savagery he could easily interpret what she would rather be doing with her knife and fork.

Her ill humour was so thinly disguised that even the waiter began to grow nervous and made a strategic retreat far sooner than Lord Rawcliffe would have liked.

Still, he had not played his last card. Not by any means.

'Did you not like the food?' he enquired politely, eyeing the mangled remains of what had once been a perfectly innocent slice of steak and ale pie on her plate. 'I chose this inn particularly because the cook has a sterling reputation…'

'I have no complaints about the *food*,' she retorted.

He leaned back in his seat and put on his most patient, enquiring, innocent expression.

'Then you do have some form of complaint?'

She almost hissed with fury. 'You know very well I do.'

'And are you going to tell me what it is?'

'I shouldn't have to! The way you…' She glanced down at the front of her bodice. Went bright red.

'Ah,' he said and smiled. 'Forgive me, my dear, that I did not have time to meet your needs before supper. But with the waiter hovering…'

'Meet *my* needs?' She gripped her napkin between the fingers of her right hand as though she was hanging on to it, and her temper, for all she was worth.

'Yes,' he said, getting to his feet. 'But you have no need to be ashamed of them,' he continued provocatively, as he made his way round the table.

'Ashamed? I am not ashamed! Because—'

'Tut-tut,' he said, shaking his head. 'You are blushing so deep a shade of crimson that there is no point trying to deny it. So don't. Instead take comfort from the fact that I have been just as impatient for that waiter to take his leave as you have been,' he said, leaning down to take the hand that wasn't employed in strangling her napkin.

Her eyes narrowed. And then, as he brought her hand to the front of his breeches and pressed it very firmly against his hot, hard length, they flew wide.

'Yes,' he said mildly. 'You have the same effect upon me as I do upon you.'

'I do not… That is, I am…'

'If I were to lift your skirts now and run my hand up your thigh,' he growled provocatively, 'I would find you swollen and wet.' He noted with satisfaction the way her eyes darkened. Her breath hitched.

Yes, this was the way to play it. Keep their interactions firmly rooted in the carnal. Never let her suspect that his feelings were anything other than lustful. Never permit the more tender feelings that he seemed to be developing for her to take hold, come to that. That was how he would survive when she discovered his true motives for bringing her on this trip. By not allowing himself to feel, to hope, for anything more than what he'd get from a torrid *affaire*.

He guided her hand up the length of him and down again. Taught her how he would like her to stroke him.

She swallowed. Kept her eyes fixed firmly on his face, though she must have been able to feel him growing under the ministrations of her hot little hand.

'That's it,' he growled, letting go of her hand. 'Keep on doing that.'

But she didn't, of course. The moment he told her to

keep stroking him, she stopped, even though she hadn't whipped her hand away the moment he'd let it go.

'You are…you are…'

'Beastly?' He bent over her and fixed his mouth to the point where her neck joined her shoulder, a spot where she was particularly sensitive. And growled. She shuddered, as he'd known she would, and let her head loll to one side to give him better access.

'Shall I ravish you across the table? Sweep all the dishes to the floor, and push up your skirts, and take you, fast and hard?'

She whimpered. Reached up and grabbed hold of his shoulders.

'N-no,' she panted, kneading at his shoulders and writhing in her seat.

'No? The idea excites you, but you would deny us the pleasure of doing exactly as we please?'

'No, it… I mean, yes.' Her face flamed. She bit down on her lower lip. Her eyes filled up. 'I can't deny it. What you said…it did make me…' She glanced at the table with a sort of sick fascination. 'But we can't—'

'We can do whatever we like. Nothing is wrong between a man and a woman, if it gives them both pleasure.'

'But it wouldn't, that's just the problem.'

'Don't claim you are too shy, my little hypocrite.'

'I'm not a hypocrite! It's just that…and I won't claim it's because I'm too shy, either, when you know perfectly well that you make me too…that is, I forget about everything I ought to hold dear when you start to…work on me!'

A dark, twisted sort of satisfaction flared as she confessed he could rob her of her every principle, just by *working* on her. That she resented him for it he knew all too well. But to hear her confess how very helpless he could render her made him feel, for the first time in relation to her, as though he was starting to gain the upper hand.

'I know it ought to be that, but to my shame, it isn't. It's...' She gave a little sob that sounded, somehow, resentful. 'It's my corsets.'

'Your corsets?' He straightened up a little, to inspect the rather rigid outline of the front of her gown.

'Yes,' she bit out. 'They are so tight, and so cumbersome, that I cannot even lounge comfortably in a chair, never mind disport myself amidst the crockery.'

And she wanted to. She'd as good as admitted she wanted to. For a moment, the knowledge brought him to a standstill.

'Then I had better get you out of them,' he said, just about regaining enough presence of mind to drop one swift kiss on the tip of her pert little nose, as though he was in full control of the situation. 'Before they do you an injury.'

She looked so relieved, and then so embarrassed, and then so guiltily excited that he changed his mind about laying her across the table like a delicacy for him to sample. Because, no matter how much she would have enjoyed it, afterwards she would have felt ashamed of herself. And though sometimes he had deliberately made her angry, he never wanted her to feel ashamed of her natural, and so far uninhibited, response to their lovemaking.

So he picked her up and carried her to her room. Set her on her feet and turned her round so that he could undo the lacings of her gown, and her ridiculously constructed corset, whilst pressing open-mouthed kisses to the nape of her neck. By the time he had her naked apart from her shift and stockings, she was moaning and rubbing her bottom against him in a way that was highly provocative, all the more so because he was certain she had no idea what it was doing to him. It was all instinct with her. In spite of all her much-vaunted religious beliefs, her rigid moral viewpoint, she simply couldn't help herself.

And nor could he. He was so hot for her by now, so hard, that he didn't think he was going to be able to wait much longer.

But was she ready for him? He ran his hands down her stomach, reached between her legs and delved into her moist, slick heat.

She cried out and reached behind her, running her hands down his flanks.

Oh, yes. She was ready. He'd only have to stroke into her, once or twice, and she'd explode around him. She was so passionate. So wild in his arms. Exceeding every fantasy he'd ever had about her. And there had been many, over the years. Far too many…

So, now that he had her, what was to stop him indulging in one or two of them? Where was the harm? When he was going to make sure she enjoyed them as much as he was going to?

And so he held her trembling, responsive little body up with one arm while he brought her to a quivering, sobbing, climax with his other hand.

And then he pushed her face down on to the bed, undid his breeches, and pounded into her from behind until he reached his own release.

And then, because he wasn't sure he was going to

be able to stop himself from saying something he'd regret, about how perfect she was, or how much more wonderful it felt to have her than he'd ever imagined, he pulled up his breeches and fled to the relative safety of his own room.

Chapter Fifteen

It was a good job, Clare thought as she took her break-fast in bed, that he didn't seem very keen to see her first thing this morning. She wouldn't have known how to face him, not after what they'd done last night. It was hard enough attempting any sort of conversation at the best of times, but when she thought of where he'd made her put her hand…

She went hot all over just thinking about it. And that had only been the start of what, in hindsight, she could only regard as a rapid descent into an act that had been like…like…the behaviour of two rutting animals.

Fortunately, her first sight of him was as she was climbing into the carriage to set off. And since Slater was there before her, she could hope that Rawcliffe would assume that was why she was being so stiffly polite.

Once again, the secretary was armed with an im-mense stack of letters and documents, and, the moment they set out, the pair of them took up where they'd left off the night before.

The coach had barely left the inn yard before grow-ing resentment started nudging her shyness aside. He might have bid her good morning. Asked her how she'd slept. But, no. Just a curt nod was all he'd afforded her as she'd taken her seat facing him.

With a huff, she jerked her eyes away from the space he occupied and stared determinedly out of the window.

And it wasn't merely because he hadn't bid her good morning just now. It was the way he'd got up and walked out on her the night before. Leaving her sprawled face down on the bed. As soon as he'd got what he wanted.

Ooh, men were so *selfish!* She was sick, utterly sick of having to live her life on a man's terms. Her only function in the vicarage had been to make sure her brothers and her father were free to pursue their own ambitions. To smooth their way. Make life easy for them. Nobody ever asked her what she would have liked to do with her day. With her life. Not even when Father died and she could have…could have…well, she didn't know what she could have done, there had been no time to think. But she certainly hadn't deserved to be swept to one side without even being *asked* whether she wanted to go and look after an elderly invalid.

Although she wasn't going to have to do that now, was she? Thanks to Rawcliffe. She shot him a repentant look from beneath her eyelashes, for bracketing him with her male relatives. He was holding a document between his forefinger and thumb, an expression of irritation on his face. Slater muttered something in an apologetic tone and scribbled something down in the book he had open on his portable desk. And Rawcliffe put the offending document to one side and reached for the next one in the pile that lay between them.

And just like that, she got a searing, vivid memory of him plunging that very same hand down her bodice while the waiter was busy arranging the chafing dishes on the sideboard.

Her face heating, she turned to look out of the window again. She really shouldn't have accused him of being selfish, even if she had only done so in her head. For he hadn't been totally selfish last night, had he? No, he'd made sure she'd got a great deal of pleasure from that encounter as well.

Which had, ironically, made her writhe with shame the moment he'd left. For he'd made her glory in a swift, hard, animalistic coupling, when she'd always dreamed that what a man shared with his wife would be an almost spiritual union.

Why did he always have to drag their encounters in the bedroom down to such a…well, it was almost as if he was determined to keep their encounters as basic, and brutal as he could. Even the position in which he'd taken her, on her knees, from behind, was positively *degrading*. Why, when she thought of the way he used to smile and flirt with Betsy Woodly, the charm she'd seen him exerting on a variety of females at local assemblies, she could…

Oh, she didn't know what she could do, she was so jealous of all his other conquests. Well, she always had been. Which was why she'd always vowed never to appear eager to join their ranks. And she hadn't. Except that now she was his wife, she just wished…

No. There was no point in wishing for what she didn't have. In fact, it was contrary to scripture. The bible taught that, in everything, she should give thanks. And wasn't that an attitude which had kept her going through some of her darkest moments? She'd only had to think of the things she could be grateful for and her lot had always become easier to bear.

So that was what she ought to do now.

She bowed her head, as if in prayer, and clasped her hands in her lap. And as she did so she began to rub her thumb over the ridge in her glove where she wore her wedding ring. Which was the first thing she could be thankful for. That he had married her *at all*. If he hadn't, she'd have been pitched into a household full of strangers, to care for that elderly lady about whom she knew nothing. After spending the last few years enduring that backbreaking, depressing role for her own father, whilst colluding with the curate to conceal the worst of his decline from the parishioners.

And there had been no real need for Rawcliffe to have done anything so chivalrous. It was far more than most men would have done for a woman they'd denounced, for most of their lives, as a termagant.

She supposed he felt entitled to have some reward for performing an act of such outstanding selflessness. He was a man, after all. And all men seemed to think a lot more about carnal things than women. She glanced across the coach where her eyes lit on the firm muscles of his thighs, which were lovingly outlined by the fabric of his breeches…

Which reminded her what those thighs had felt like, straining between her own, the night before.

She shut her eyes with a grimace of annoyance as her thoughts drifted back towards the things she resented about him, rather than counting her blessings.

She took a deep breath, clasped her hands tightly again and determinedly sought for something else to be thankful for today.

Once again, it was the supple material of her gloves that inspired her. And the glossy sheen of her carriage dress upon which they were now resting. It was terribly,

terribly worldly of her to count shopping for clothes as something for which to give thanks to God, but truly, it had been like a sort of fantasy for her to send for dressmakers, who brought samples of the most glorious and costly fabrics, and know she could choose any of them and have them made up in whatever style she wished. Even if they did have to be predominantly black. It was such a contrast to the hours she'd had to spend mending and darning, and making over old gowns to disguise the most worn areas, that she'd gone a little mad.

To assuage her guilt over what had felt, after a day or so, like the most reckless extravagance and self-indulgence, she'd vowed to donate a tithe of her allowance to worthy causes before she went anywhere near a dressmaker in future. To charities that supported girls who couldn't afford to buy whatever they wanted, for example. Girls who were as destitute and friendless as she'd been, or at least had felt before Lord Rawcliffe had swept into that inn and transformed her life with one wave of his magical wand.

No. Not his *wand*. His wand was not magical.

Oh, dear. How very easy it was, now she was married to such an earthy, carnal sort of man, for her thoughts to turn in a carnal direction. She ground her teeth in frustration. It must have taken all of five minutes for her to descend from her ambition to apply spiritual principles to her state of mind, to recalling how it had felt to stroking and fondling his...his wand. To realise that she was the one causing it to...

Oh, dear. How she wished she had a fan in her reticule. Or had the excuse that it was unseasonably warm to explain her suddenly overheated face.

But that would make him look at her. And he'd discern somehow what she was thinking about. And he'd smile that lazy, knowing smile and half-lower his eyelids and she'd know he was now thinking about it, too. And…

Oh.

He would be thinking about it, too. Because he wanted her. Just about all the time. In the most inappropriate places. And whether there was anyone else in the room or not. It might not be the least bit romantic, let alone spiritual, but did she have any right to complain that he didn't want her in *exactly* the way she'd hoped he would? Or feel cheated because he hadn't even courted her? For here she was, married to him. As married as it was possible to be. And she was always going to be his wife.

Which was something she could be truly thankful for.

As was the prospect of one day having a baby. A baby to love. Which would grow into a child that would love her back. Even if her husband didn't.

And why would he, considering the fact she wasn't the wife he'd have chosen, if he'd actually been looking for a wife?

Perhaps she'd do better to start trying to learn how to be the kind of wife he wanted her to be, rather than complaining that he wasn't being a perfect husband. Why should he be a perfect husband when he hadn't wanted to be any kind of husband at all? In his eyes, he was probably already going the second mile.

Very well, then, from now on she would…

'Oh!' She leaned forward in her seat as she glimpsed what looked like a body of water, in the gap between two hills. A large body of water, ending at the horizon.

'Is that…?' She turned to Rawcliffe, her confused thoughts tumbling to the back of her mind in the need to ask him if that water was what she thought it was. 'Is that the sea?'

'Yes.'

She pressed her nose to the window in her eagerness to look at it. 'The sea! Oh! Are you taking me to the seaside?' She turned to look at him properly for the first time that day, no longer struggling to think grateful thoughts, so genuinely thrilled was she by this unexpected, and completely unearned, treat. 'I have never seen the sea.'

'I would never have guessed,' he replied drily.

She pressed her nose to the window again, but the carriage was rounding the foot of another hill, which obliterated her view of the sea. Almost in the same way his sarcastic attitude had blotted out her pleasure.

Why did he do that? Put her down in that odious manner? When, sometimes, he could be so kind? For instance, he'd been so gentle and tender with her when he'd bathed her injured hand with ice. But now he seemed to be deliberately going out of his way to prevent her believing there was any good in him, as if he regretted letting her see he had a streak of decency within him.

'But, yes,' he said in a voice that was no longer harsh and impatient. 'We are indeed going to the seaside.'

She turned to look at him in the vain hope he regretted speaking to her the way he had.

'We are going to spend a week in a small fishing village. Which is situated,' he said drily, 'of necessity, at the seaside.'

'It might be nothing special to you,' she said, her hurt at his attitude once again sweeping aside all her good intentions. 'But going to the seaside is the most exciting thing that has ever happened to me.' If you discounted marrying the man she'd been dreaming about ever since she'd grown old enough to know that lips were made for kissing, that was.

It felt like an age before the carriage finally drew up in front of a row of cottages, clinging to the side of a hill in a position that gave them an unobstructed view of a most picturesque little bay.

'I do hope the accommodation meets with your approval, my lord,' said Slater, pulling down the window and letting in the sounds of gulls and waves on a tide of the freshest air she'd ever breathed.

'The middle cottage is for your use exclusively,' said Slater, 'yours and her ladyship's, that is. The rest of us will take the cottages to either side.'

The rest of us were just rolling up in the three carriages that had been trundling along behind them all the way from London. Apparently a marquess could not enjoy a holiday by the sea without his French chef, who required an army of scullions, as well as his valet, a couple of housemaids, a brace of footmen, and Ponsonby to preside over them all. Not to mention Nancy, who was riding in the coach containing, to her chagrin, the other female members of staff.

Lord Rawcliffe inspected the whitewashed front of the row of cottages with faint disdain. 'I am sure,' he said witheringly, 'that you did your best, in the short space of time I gave you to procure something. Shall we inspect our lodgings?' He held out his arm to help her from the carriage and led her to the middle of the three blue-painted front doors.

It opened into a small hall, from which a staircase ran straight to the upper floor. There were chipped and dented doors to both right and left, leading to small reception rooms, one of which contained armchairs and a sofa, the other one being fitted up as a dining room. Both of them had views straight down the hill to the bay.

Upstairs there were two more rooms. But unlike the layout downstairs, where the rooms were on either side of the stairs, up here, one faced the front, and one the back. She paced to the window of the front bedroom from which she could see little boats dotted about a harbour. Men bending over fishing nets, which were spread out in all directions. Cliffs, which spread out like arms protecting the bay from harm. And beyond that, in a great, grey, sparkling silken sheet, the sea.

'I take it,' said Rawcliffe in that dry, sarcastic tone he'd been employing ever since she'd betrayed how excited she was to be coming to the seaside for the very first time, 'you would prefer to have the use of this bedroom?'

She would prefer them to share this room. To lie all night in his arms and wake up feeling...cherished.

But it was no use wanting the impossible.

So she smiled. 'Yes, please.'

He shrugged. 'As you wish, my dear.'

She watched the stiff set of his shoulders as he strolled out of the room. And wondered, which was the real Lord Rawcliffe. The one who spoke so cuttingly? Or the one who did such kind, unselfish things?

Chapter Sixteen

'Well, now that is settled, shall we go and explore and see if we can discover what passes for entertainment in this hamlet?' Rawcliffe was already out on the landing, holding out his arm, practically demanding she place her hand upon it and follow him.

But for once, she had no desire to argue with him. She *wanted* to go and explore this quaint little town, especially the parts which bordered the sea. And, since Nancy was starting to show signs of regarding her wardrobe the way a dragon did its hoard, she was going to be better off getting out of the way while the maid unpacked and arranged her room anyway.

First of all they went down the lane which led from practically their front door to the harbour. When they reached the harbour wall, Lord Rawcliffe surprised Clare by placing his hands round her waist and swinging her on to its roughened lip, which was broad enough to stand on.

'You will get a better view from up here,' he said prosaically as he climbed up beside her. And, while she wrestled to conceal the way his touch had made her pulse flutter, she noted that what he'd said was true.

From this vantage point she did have a splendid view of the many boats moored beneath them, as well as a small, pebbled beach which featured a few large rocks draped with seaweed.

'I believe,' said Lord Rawcliffe, whipping out a handkerchief and pressing it to his nose, 'that fishing boats, and all that appertains to them, are more agreeable from a distance.'

Clare giggled. And reached over to squeeze his free arm. Nothing was going to dim her pleasure in this experience, certainly not her husband's fastidious manners.

He stiffened. Looked down at her with an inscrutable expression on his face. After a moment or two of studying her, appearing perplexed by her good humour in the face of his own displeasure, he leapt down from the wall and held out his hand to her. 'Come,' he said, inviting her to scramble down to the road. 'Let us walk up the hill and explore the rest of the hamlet. I believe that the air up there will be less malodorous, since there appears to be a land breeze.'

'Very well,' she said, smiling up at him. 'Though it looks as though it's a bit more than a hamlet to me.'

'It was merely a fishing village until quite recently,' he said, turning his back on the picturesque little harbour, 'when the craze for sea bathing, and exploring scenic, wild parts of the countryside, gripped the minds of those with money to spend.'

It was proving far harder to climb back up the hill in the direction of their lodgings than it had been to go down. Yet her husband was managing to carry on talking as though he was just out for an afternoon stroll. He must be incredibly strong. Well, she knew he was, since she'd had the privilege of running her hands all over his muscular body on several occasions. 'I am told,' he continued in a dry tone that showed he was completely oblivious to the direction of her thoughts, 'that the place now boasts an inn with pretensions to being a hotel, in that it has an assembly room, library, reading room and what-have-you.'

'An assembly room? Does that mean there might be balls? Or,' she hastily added, in case he thought she was becoming flighty, 'or concerts?'

'In what they consider their high season, yes to both,' he said with a grimace of distaste. 'Fortunately for us,' he said as he turned into a street which ran parallel to the coast, rather than continuing any farther up the hill, 'that season does not commence until July.'

'Oh.' Not for another week or so. She darted him a glance. He'd got that cold, forbidding expression on his face again. And was ignoring everyone who happened to be in what appeared to be the main street. Plenty of whom, she suddenly noticed, were openly staring at them. She'd been able to understand the townsfolk's curiosity when their cavalcade had driven through this same street earlier, but it seemed rather rude of them to stare now that they were on foot.

'You'd think they'd never seen holiday makers be-fore, from the way they are gawking at us,' she said.

He gave her a bitter smile. 'This, my dear, is what it is like to be a peer of the realm in an out-of-the-way place such as this. We are providing entertainment for the rustics who are normally starved of the sight of any-one more interesting.'

She blushed as one of the rustics, who happened to be passing, clearly heard what he was saying and scowled. Not that her husband was making any attempt to keep his voice down.

'I am sure there are plenty of interesting people who visit such a beautiful town,' she said, in an effort to counteract his insult by praising the town, 'especially in high season. Why, I'm sure it must be extremely popular.'

'Only with people from the merchant classes,' he said witheringly. 'Or so I am reliably informed. This is not, by any means, a fashionable resort.'

She grew a little indignant at his dismissal of what appeared, to her, to be a perfectly charming little place. 'So, why have you brought me here? Oh.' She flinched as one reason struck her very forcibly. She wasn't up to snuff. She wasn't fit to be seen upon his arm anywhere like Almack's, for example.

Although…no, that couldn't be right. He'd wanted her to step straight into London society and ignore whatever anyone might say or think about her. He'd only relented because she'd asked him—no, thrown a tantrum at the prospect of mingling with titled people.

Was this his idea of the kind of place where she'd be content? Mingling with the merchant classes? Or, at least, the kind of people who relied on the merchant classes in the high season?

He glanced down at her.

'I don't know what you are thinking, but to judge from the various expressions flitting across your face, you have not as yet correctly deduced why we are here, precisely.'

'Well, no, I can't say that I have. Though it is a very lovely town,' she said, waving with her free arm at the street along which they were strolling and the bow windows of the various shops they were passing. 'It appears to have more, and better, shops than Watling Minor.'

'That is hardly difficult,' he said scathingly.

'No, but even if the harbour is a bit pungent, I am sure I shall enjoy sitting and watching the comings and goings from my window. I noticed someone had set a chair there. I expect other visitors have done the same as I plan to do.'

'Yes,' he said shortly. 'The fact is…' he said and then took a breath. His hesitation was so uncharacteristic that she darted a look at his face and caught what appeared to be a troubled frown on his brow. 'The reason I picked this particular fishing village, out of all the others I might have taken you to, is that,' he said, pausing to clench his jaw, 'it is so very close to Lesser Peeving.'

'What?' Lesser Peeving? The village where Clement now lived? The place her brother had described as the back of beyond?

'Yes,' he continued in a lazy drawl. 'I thought you would be pleased. I have already made arrangements for us to visit your brother, in a day or so.'

'But, but, you…you…' He disliked Clement. And the feeling was mutual. 'Why?'

He gave a shrug with one shoulder, as though the animosity which had festered between the two men for so many years was of no account.

'He is the only one of your brothers who actually did anything for you, when you were left in such a vulnerable position, after your father's demise. For that reason, do you not think that I ought to make an attempt to… ah…go and thank him? On your behalf? And explain why it is that you have not, in fact, taken up the post he arranged for you? I am sure that there were questions arising from your apparent disappearance.'

'Oh, I thought of that and wrote to explain what had happened straight away, so that he wouldn't worry.'

'You did?' He went very still. 'When, precisely?'

'Oh, as soon as Lady Harriet could spare me and I could get my hands on some paper.'

'Has he replied to that missive?'

'Well, no, but then none of my brothers is very good at replying to any of the letters I write to them. They are all very busy men.' She paused, as a vision of her husband wading through his immense pile of correspondence flashed into her mind, along with the certainty that none of her brothers ever had to deal with a fraction of the amount of work he did. 'And besides, he may very well be...' She trailed off, biting her lip. Knowing Clement, he would be mad as fire with her for getting into such a serious scrape she had ended up having to get married. And, what was worse, to a man he heartily detested.

'You expect him to be displeased with you.'

She nodded.

'Then it is as well I have taken steps to...mend fences with him, is it not?'

'You...you have truly come all the way down here, just so that we can...' Her vision blurred as emotion moistened her eyes. 'You have deliberately exposed yourself to...the kind of attention you particularly dislike, from people you consider vulgar, for...for my sake?' She recalled the way he'd wrinkled his nose before pressing the handkerchief to it, the disdain in his eyes as she'd rhapsodised about the shops, the assembly rooms, the chances of hearing a concert. 'Oh, R-Rawcliffe, that is, truly, the most...' And then words failed her. This proud, proud man had taken the first step to restoring links to her brothers which had looked precariously as though they might have been sundered completely, given the way they felt about him. A huge rush of emotion flattened her inhibitions. She couldn't help flinging her arms about him and giving him a hug.

'Oh, thank you, thank you,' she breathed into his chest. 'You cannot know what this means to me. I had quite accepted the fact that I would probably never have anything to do with any of them again, but now…'

She stopped as he gripped both her arms and set her back, quite forcibly.

'Don't,' he barked.

'I b-beg pardon,' she began, looking up into his face, expecting to see an expression of censure blazing from his eyes.

Instead, she caught a look of what appeared to be anguish. Or guilt.

No, she must be mistaken. He must be angry with her for making a scene in a public street, when everyone was already looking at them as though they were some sort of sideshow, that was what it was.

The expression only lasted for a fraction of a second, anyway. For now his face was a mask that could have been carved from ice.

'Calm yourself,' he said sternly. 'My wife should not make an exhibition of herself in a public street.'

'Not even if she has just discovered something wonderful?'

'Especially not then,' he bit out. 'Because far from doing anything the slightest bit wonderful, I have—' He shut his mouth with a snap. 'Just remember your station in life. You are not some vicar's daughter, for whom nobody cares, any longer. You are *my wife*. And as such, should make more of an effort to maintain a dignified appearance.'

She recoiled.

'Dignified,' she repeated. 'Yes, I see. You want me to try to behave in a more dignified manner.'

'Precisely.' He gave her a cold look. 'Now, do you think we might continue on our way? I should like to look in at the reading rooms and take a cup of coffee. Since you were so fired up to come out and explore, you did not give me any chance of taking any refreshment in our own lodgings.'

'I do beg your pardon,' she said stiffly, all her pleasure leeching away as though he'd just tipped a bucket of icy water all over her. 'By all means, let us go and take a cup of coffee, my lord,' she said. And then stuck her nose in the air and stalked off in the direction they'd been headed before.

Chapter Seventeen

◈◈◈◈◈

It wasn't long before they reached a market square. The Three Tuns took up one entire side of it. A rather inexpert layer of stucco had been pasted over extensions to the original building and if she hadn't been so annoyed by the way he'd just spoken to her, she would have agreed that it did look rather pretentious.

But nothing, now, would force her to agree with his opinion, about *any*thing. There was no need for him to speak to her in that odiously condescending manner. She needed to be dignified, indeed! Why, for two pins she'd…

Hang on a minute, though. Earlier on, when she'd told him she wasn't ready to go into society because she didn't know enough about the proper etiquette, he'd told her that he wanted her to be *herself*. That she had no need to worry about what anyone else thought. So why was he now saying exactly the opposite?

She ran over the content of both conversations as they crossed the market square. During the one about Almack's he'd been trying to comfort her when she'd confessed to feelings of inadequacy. But just now, he'd acted as though she was letting him down by hugging him in the street. Which was inconsistent, to say the least.

It made her feel as if she'd tried his patience to the limit. That so far, he'd been remarkably forbearing, considering, but that hugging him in the street had been the last straw.

Although, he hadn't minded when Betsy Woodly had hung off his arm, had he? What was it—different rules for wives than mistresses?

She got a sudden, vivid image of him holding a naked Betsy in an affectionate embrace. It brought such a sharp pang to her chest that she almost gasped out loud.

'Is something amiss? Have you turned your ankle?'

She realised she'd stumbled slightly under the weight of her jealous image of how he'd been with Betsy, or how she imagined he'd been, all those years ago.

'No, I…' He was looking at her with concern. Genuine concern.

Which confused her. How could he have been so patient and kind when she'd punched him, then act so cold and cutting when she hugged him?

Was this really how marriage was going to be? Tiptoeing round her husband the way she'd had to tiptoe round her own father's increasingly erratic temper? At least she'd been able to see her father's moods brewing, and had known, for the most part, how to deflect them. But Rawcliffe's behaviour made no sense to her at all.

'It's nothing,' she said. 'The cobbles are a bit uneven, just here, that's all.'

'Hmm,' he replied, looking unconvinced.

But he didn't pursue the matter.

Well, he wouldn't. Because he would understand her need to guard her own thoughts, since he guarded his own so carefully.

She glanced up at his face as they mounted the single step and passed into the portico of the Three Tuns. It was set in the expression he normally wore. Shuttered. As though determined to keep everyone from guessing what he was thinking, or feeling.

As though determined to keep everyone at arm's length. Instead of being open and friendly, he would put on a disdainful look and use a mocking tone of voice, and give anyone who tried to encroach upon him the most severe put-downs.

Which made many people think he was a horrible person. But he wasn't. A horrible person would not have married a woman who'd punched him, nor made any attempt to reconcile with her brother, which could only be for her sake, because Rawcliffe detested Clement and made no secret of it.

No, he was not horrible, he was just…guarded. He wrapped his dignity and consequence round him like some kind of protective shield. As though he couldn't bear to let anyone close to him these days.

And he *was* consistent in that.

When he'd heard that Mr Kellet had died, he sort of withdrew into himself, after that one, brief moment when she'd seen he'd really been devastated by the news.

From there, it was but a small step to see that it was whenever she'd started to act affectionate towards him, that he'd done something, or said something, to make her fly into the boughs, effectively re-establishing some distance between them and also enabling him to retreat with his dignity intact.

Even having Mr Slater ride with them in the carriage on what should have been their bride trip had been a way to preserve some distance from her.

And that fit in with the way he got up immediately after they'd had conjugal relations. At the very moment when she felt as if they'd really become one flesh, one person, and wanted to hug him and get closer in an emotional way.

But why? Why did he need to go to such lengths to keep her at arm's length? What did he think he had to fear from *her*? From drawing close to her?

She sighed. It was becoming increasingly obvious that she was going to have to be the sensible one in this relationship. Men were such babies when it came to their emotions. She ought to know, having had to nurse the tender sensibilities of three brothers and a father, who all threw tantrums over the most ridiculous and imagined slights on a regular basis.

Although, to be fair, so far she was the one who'd done the tantrum throwing in this relationship. Whenever he made her feel shut out, she'd practically flung herself at the barriers and tried to batter them down. She'd flung herself at him in the street just now, too, though for a different reason.

Well, she'd just have to stop doing that if it made him uncomfortable. And accept it when he pulled away with such vehemence that it felt like a slap in the face. And then, perhaps, once he began to realise she wasn't going to demand anything he wasn't prepared or able to give, she decided as they passed through the open door into an airy hallway, he might not feel the need to be quite so nasty.

'Welcome to the Three Tuns, sir, madam,' said a man she guessed must be the landlord. He was extremely neatly dressed. In fact, he looked more like a butler than the keeper of a large inn.

Ah, yes, but hadn't Rawcliffe told her that they

wanted visitors to think of the place as a hotel nowadays? That was why he'd tacked on a reading room and an assembly room, and, according to a sign hanging over a doorway to the right of the hall, a library and gift shop, too. And that was why this man was dressed the way she suspected managers of hotels dressed.

'Would you care to sign the visitors' book?' he said, indicating an immense leather-bound ledger, situated on a waist-high shelf under the stairs. 'We do like to know who is staying in Peacombe, so that we can apprise you all of the events planned during your stay and facilitate your enjoyment of all that Peacombe has to offer.'

Clare winced. If there was one thing Rawcliffe disliked it was drawing attention to his movements so that 'vulgar' persons could come and stare. At least, that was the reason he'd given her for not putting an announcement of their marriage in the papers.

So it came as a shock when he calmly followed the manager across to the stairs and added his name to the list of previous visitors, rather than giving him a sharp set-down.

The manager, too, appeared to have sustained a shock when he read her husband's name.

'My lord,' he wheezed, as though all the breath had just left his lungs in a rush. 'I am afraid we have very few notable people staying at present. Nobody suitable for introductions…'

Which immediately put her out of charity with him. For she knew very well that nobody notable *ever* stayed in Peacombe. It simply wasn't fashionable enough.

'And the season has not really begun. The first concert is not planned for several weeks, and as for dancing…'

'It is of no consequence,' said Rawcliffe dismissively.

'We have not come here to attend balls or concerts, but to enjoy the walks and the views.'

Had they? Well, that was news to her. Especially since he'd told her he'd chosen Peacombe because of its proximity to Clement. But then, he wouldn't want to share that bit of information with a virtual stranger, would he?

'The walks and the views are indeed excellent,' said the manager with evident relief. 'This part of the coastline, with its rugged cliffs and sweeping moorlands, has vistas second to none. The cliffs, angled as they are, also shelter Peacombe from the most intemperate weather. And of course,' he cleared his throat, 'the Three Tuns is open to serve refreshments whenever you desire. Please, do come and see the facilities we have to offer the discerning traveller,' he said, bowing and making a sweeping gesture with one hand. As Rawcliffe nodded in acceptance of the invitation, the man set off along a corridor that led them deeper into the bowels of his architectural abomination.

'We take the London newspapers,' said the manager over his shoulder, 'and a selection of all the best periodicals for the edification and amusement of our visitors.' With a triumphant sort of flourish, he flung open the door of what looked to Clare exactly the way she imagined the interior of a gentleman's club would look. It was all leather chairs and little tables piled with various periodicals, and a hearth containing a gently smouldering fire which made her want to remove her coat and bonnet straight away.

'Coffee, tea, chocolate?' The manager looked from one to the other as he ran through the beverages on offer.

'Ale, for myself,' said Rawcliffe, strolling over to one

of the tables and flicking open the topmost newspaper as though he couldn't wait to start reading it.

'My lady?'

'He means you, my dear,' said Rawcliffe after a short interval.

'Oh, yes, um, tea would be lovely,' she said, her cheeks burning. She made for the fire which gave her the opportunity to give her prickly husband the distance he so obviously needed to preserve, pulled off her gloves and held out her hands to the fire as though warming them was the sole reason she'd gone there.

But she could feel him, watching her. Waiting, no doubt, for her to turn round and launch into a barrage of complaints about the way he'd just rebuffed her, in the street.

Well, for once, she wasn't going to do any such thing. He wanted to keep her at a safe distance, physically as well as emotionally? Fine!

She'd give him distance.

And plenty of it.

Rawcliffe kept on mechanically turning the pages of the day-old newspaper, though he wasn't taking in a single word printed below the date. He was aware of nothing but Clare. Clare, who'd stalked across the room to the fire so that she could stand with her back to him, under the pretext of warming her hands.

Clare.

He could still feel the imprint her arms had seared into his treacherous back when she'd flung them round him. Because he'd told her a pack of lies about his reasons for coming to Peacombe.

If she knew, if she only knew...

But she didn't. Nor did she understand why he'd

flung her from him with such horror. She couldn't know that, once again, she'd rewarded him when he least deserved it.

And now she was standing on the other side of the room, with her back to him, confused and hurt, and desperately trying to hang on to that fiery temper of hers, because he'd just told her he wanted her to behave in a *dignified* manner.

When what he wanted... He sucked in a deep breath as a stunning truth blazed into his awareness.

She was trying to behave the way he'd said he wanted.

And she'd flung her arms round him, with every indication of feeling some affection for him.

Even though he'd treated her worse than a whore, bedding her with all the finesse of a sailor on shore leave, then leaving her sprawled naked in her bed as he stalked off to his own. Night after night.

When all he wanted to do was roll her to his side and hold her. Tight. All night long. And wake up with her. So that she would be the first thing he saw every morning.

And then she sniffed.

He glanced over his shoulder to see her furtively brushing something away from her cheek.

Dammit, he'd made her cry.

Which was unforgivable.

'Clare,' he said. 'Don't cry.'

'I'm not crying,' she said defiantly.

'Of course not.' He abandoned any pretence of being interested in the newspaper and walked across to where she stood, her back resolutely turned in his direction.

What was he doing? Pushing her away in an effort to prevent himself from being hurt when she eventually spurned him? Which meant that *she* was the one being hurt.

And then she sniffed again and the decision was made for him. Whatever the outcome for himself, she deserved better. Much better. And, anyway, hadn't he survived the last time she'd spurned him? And he was no longer a callow youth with delusions that he could find true love. He was a man.

A man who couldn't stay away from his wife for one second longer.

Chapter Eighteen

'Clare,' he said, laying one hand tentatively on her shoulder. 'I…that is…there was no need for me to have been so brusque with you just now.'

She turned to face him and lifted her chin. 'Well, I should not have…flung myself at you in the street like that, should I? I am not surprised you lost your temper with me. I know I am not the wife you would have chosen, but I do want to be the best wife I can be and, if you do not like me to—'

He couldn't stand there letting her try to shoulder the blame when absolutely nothing that had happened was in any way her fault. But nor was he ready to explain that she was the one who'd been forced into a marriage she hadn't wanted, not him. So he took the simple expedient of stopping her mouth with a kiss.

She gasped, but then melted into his embrace. Though she didn't respond with the kind of eagerness he'd become used to. She didn't put her arms round him, for a start. Because his reaction to her hugging him had made her think he didn't want her to. And she was trying to be the best wife she could be. Because she was that kind of girl. Giving and brave, and loyal to those she believed deserved her loyalty. He only had to think of how loyal she'd been to her selfish father and spendthrift brothers. Their father's income had nearly all gone on providing them with an education, while he knew for a fact she didn't even have a dowry worth mentioning. And even though they now all had decent livelihoods, not one of them had come to her aid when she'd needed it, apart from Clement. And all he'd done was arrange for the kind of post that only a truly indigent female should have to endure. Yet not one word had she ever said against them. Even when he'd caught her travelling on the public stage, in a coat she'd clearly dyed herself because they hadn't given her the funds to obtain decent mourning garments.

She wouldn't ever utter a word of complaint against him, either, no matter what he did. It would go against the grain.

'Clare,' he murmured ruefully, closing his eyes and leaning his forehead against hers. 'What am I to do with you?' He'd tried to prevent her from falling in love with him. Because he hadn't wanted her to give him her heart. He didn't deserve it. And he'd only break it when she found out what he was doing with her. He hadn't wanted to live with that on his conscience.

But that hug, just now, told him that she might already be starting to think she was falling in love with him. She wasn't one to do anything in a half-hearted fashion. Many women imagined themselves in love with a man once she'd gone to bed with him. Besides which Clare had such strong religious beliefs about the sanctity of marriage, she was bound to try to convince herself it was love driving her, rather than lust. It would be the only way her conscience would be able to deal with it.

He groaned. She was the one who was trying to do

her best, while he kept on hanging back, like a coward. The least he could do was match her. So he finally did what he should have done earlier. He hugged her, hard. It felt like total surrender. But he was done wrestling with his conscience. From this moment on, he was just going to live with her the way he wanted to be able to live. As though they had chosen to marry each other because it was what they both wanted, with all their hearts.

It wouldn't last, of course. But he might have one day, or possibly two before it all came crashing down round his ears. Then at least when it all went sour, when this affection she was starting to feel for him turned back to antipathy, when she routinely performed her wifely duties with the air of a martyr rather than with startled pleasure, he could look back on this short interlude and be able to treasure the taste he'd had of what marriage to her could have been like. If only...

'Wh-what do you want to do with me?' She was staring up at him, confusion pleating her brow.

'Poor love, I haven't been much of a husband to you, up to now, have I?'

'Well, you didn't wish to be one, did you?'

He sighed. It was about time he owned up to some aspects of the truth. Aspects that might stand him in good stead when she learned the rest of it.

'I have wanted to marry you since you were about sixteen.'

Her mouth dropped open. 'No.'

'Yes. Did it mean so little to you, my first proposal, that you have forgotten it entirely?'

A frown flitted across her face. 'That day at the duck pond, you mean?'

'Yes. Not the most propitious of times to ask you, I admit. I am not surprised you turned me down.'

'Turned you down? That was…you were…serious?'

He nodded.

'But you were laughing your head off. I thought you were making fun of me.'

'No…' He'd never considered that might be a factor in her total rejection of him. 'Is that what you thought? Is that why you refused to let me court you?'

'Let you court…?' She frowned in evident confusion. 'What are you talking about? You never came near me again, during that visit to Kelsham Park.'

'Because I had been told you found my proposal offensive. That you would never lower yourself to receive addresses from a man with such lax morals. That—'

She gasped. 'No. I didn't. I mean, I might have thought it, but who could have told you that without even asking me first?'

'That response did not come from your lips? From your heart?'

'No! I thought you—'

He was doomed not to discover what she thought he'd done, because the landlord chose that moment to return with a waiter bearing a tray of refreshments. And Clare, predictably, took a step away from him, disengaging herself from his arms, her cheeks flushing pink.

He let her have her space. Even though what he wanted was to haul her back into his arms and smother her face with grateful kisses.

She hadn't rejected his proposal in that offensive manner. She hadn't even known he'd proposed, not in earnest. She'd thought he'd been mocking her…

Oh, good lord, what a coil.

He ran his fingers through his hair as he watched the landlord and waiter make a production of setting out Clare's tea things and a tankard and jug for him, along with a selection of delicately cut sandwiches and tiny cakes on a low table before the fire.

'While the weather is fine, my lord, my lady,' said the landlord obsequiously, 'might I suggest taking a walk along the newly laid gravel path which extends from the town end of the harbour along the shore-line...'

And as for this time, now he came to think of it, not one of the reasons she'd given for trying to evade marrying him had to do with him or his morals. She'd kept saying she wasn't good enough. Hadn't got a title. Or any social address...

He half-heard the landlord wittering on about admission fees for various local attractions, while his mind was turning his whole life, since the day at the duck pond, upside down.

'You can drink from the source,' he suddenly heard the landlord saying, very clearly, 'for only a ha'penny a cup. The waters are, if I do say so, as beneficial to the health as anything you could procure from any of the more fashionable resorts.'

He grimaced. What the man meant, of course, was that they tasted as foul.

Though the landlord must have noticed his lack of interest, he would not stop.

'Another very good reason for making the climb is the ice house whose entrance lies there. You can descend via man-made steps into a series of caves which stay at a constant temperature all year round. Round these parts, many such caves are used to mature cheese...'

Cheese! Good God, what did he care for cheese? He'd just discovered Clare hadn't rebuffed him. That she had never believed the proposal had been made in earnest.

It explained so clearly why, after that, she behaved as though he'd been guilty of insulting her. Because she'd thought he'd been mocking her.

'...but due to a unique combination of factors, our caves keep at a very low temperature and are therefore used to store snow, which is brought down from the moorlands in winter and naturally compacts into ice.'

Just as his heart had compacted into ice once he'd sworn he didn't need Clare, nor the comfort and warmth she represented.

'It sounds like an extremely unpleasant experience,' he said when the landlord paused to draw breath. 'Grubbing about in some dark and dingy caves.'

And he should know. All his encounters with women, after Clare's rejection, had become grubby, sordid little affairs. His expectations of the entire female sex sinking to such depths he'd even treated Lady Harriet, on their first meeting, with such disdain she'd lashed out at him with her riding crop.

'Well, since it is such a splendid day you might naturally prefer to visit the beach to the far side of the cliff gardens. It contains what I am told by experts is a most fascinating selection of shells and fossils. You may descend to the beach by means of steps, provided by our town council—'

'On payment of a fee?'

'The price is included in your ticket to the gravel walk,' said the landlord, oblivious to his sarcasm. Though Clare darted him a reproachful look.

'There is no sea bathing, unfortunately, because the beach shelves so steeply. And the large pebbles would hinder the progress of bathing machines. Besides which there are strong currents close in to the shore which make swimming inadvisable—'

Rawcliffe flinched. Mentioning those currents only brought his reason for coming here to the forefront of his mind. Archie's drowning. And the need to discover what the hell he'd been doing in the water when he couldn't swim. At all.

'If we had been interested in sea bathing,' put in Clare hastily, 'we would have gone to one of the resorts where it is advertised. Isn't that so, my lord?'

She was my lording him now? When before he'd rebuked her for hugging him she'd at least ventured as far as using his title.

'Well, then, you might like to know that you can obtain a spectacular view, over both ours and the neighbouring bay, from the cliffs which you can reach by walking across a short stretch of moorland which you can easily access from a track that runs behind the cottages you are renting. It is the kind of view any artist would wish to capture on canvas.'

'Should one happen to be staying nearby,' he said curtly, hoping that the fellow would understand his total lack of interest in art from the tone of his voice and cease pestering them.

'It sounds lovely,' said Clare, shooting him a dagger glance from behind the landlord's back. 'Thank you so much for telling us. A walk up to the cliff tops sounds just the thing.'

The landlord turned and bowed to her.

'And thank you so much for the lovely plate of cakes,' she continued, waving her hand in the direction of the table upon which the waiter had deposited them. 'And the tea.' She smiled. 'Just what I was wanting.'

'Shall I pour for you, my lady?'

'Oh, no, thank you. I prefer to let it steep for a minute or two. And I am sure you must be far too busy to be kept waiting upon us.'

And with one smile, and a polite little speech, Clare obtained the result he'd been unable to produce by glowering and being rude. The landlord bowed himself out of the room and left them to pour their own drinks.

'So,' he said, as she took a seat by the table and lifted the lid of the teapot to peer inside, 'where were we?'

She glanced at him as he took the seat opposite, her cheeks turning pink again.

'You were telling me that when you saw me emerging from the duck pond, dripping with slime and holding a bag of dead puppies in my arms, you were not in fact mocking my predicament, but actually making a genuine proposal of marriage.'

Put like that, it did sound unbelievable.

'Dead puppies? Was that what you'd been doing in the pond? Trying to fish them out?'

'You surely did not think I had been wading in it for my own amusement,' she replied snippily, replacing the teapot lid with a resounding clink.

'I… I did not really think of that aspect of it at all. You just looked so…'

'Ridiculous.'

'Adorable.'

'Covered in pond slime?'

He shrugged. 'To my eyes, all I could see was a naiad come to life.'

'A naiad,' she repeated with a scornful sniff. 'Had you, perchance, just emerged from a tavern?'

'I was not foxed! You were so…'

'Wet.'

'I was going to say beautiful.'

She pulled her lips into a flat line. 'You don't have

to say things like that,' she said, averting her gaze as she reached for the milk jug.

He reached out across the table and stayed her hand.

'Somebody needs to say them. And who better than your husband?'

'I don't hold with the telling of falsehoods,' she said vehemently.

'I am not telling falsehoods. You are an extremely attractive woman, Clare.'

'Fustian!'

'It is no such thing.'

'But you never... I mean, the kind of women you took up with... I mean...' She glanced down at the front of her coat. And went an even deeper shade of pink.

'You don't have the more obvious attributes that attract the notice of young men who are just beginning to notice the difference between males and females, no. But you have something of far greater merit.'

'Oh? And what's that?' She lifted her chin in what looked like a combination of defiance and hope. As though she wanted him to pay her a compliment, but was braced to receive whatever else might come from his mouth next.

'You have character. You have integrity. You have—' he shrugged with one shoulder '—passion. You never hesitated to wade in on the side of anyone you thought was enduring persecutions or tribulations, no matter what anyone else did.'

'I...what do you mean? How could you know...?'

'I have always made it my business to know everything that occurs within all the estates for which I am responsible. And your name was always coming up in connection with good works of one sort or another.'

'You cannot have wanted to marry me because of my good works,' she said with a touch of scorn.

'No, I confess, I did not think of it until that morning I saw you emerging from the pond, your gown plastered to your figure, leaving nothing to the imagination, your eyes flashing defiance, your hair escaping its proper arrangement and snaking round your shoulders like damp flames.'

'You thought of marriage, because my dress was wet? And proposed on the spot?'

'I think,' he said, feeling a creeping impatience with her flat refusal to see the romantic aspect of what had, to him, felt like the fabled *coup de foudre*, 'that we have exhausted all there is to say upon this topic.'

'Oh, no, we haven't.' She sloshed some milk into her cup and slammed the jug down on the tray. 'You said you were in earnest about that marriage proposal when I've always believed you'd been making fun of me. And what's more, that you believed I'd turned you down, which means you must have spoken to somebody about it...'

Her father. But it wouldn't do to bring up that particular conversation now. She wouldn't appreciate him speaking his mind about the old buzzard. Not so soon after his demise. He'd learned his lesson on that score in Biggleswade.

He rubbed his nose. 'That, too, is a subject perhaps best left in the past. We are married now. Let us be content with that.'

She opened her mouth to make another protest. Thought better of it. Threw a couple of lumps of sugar into her teacup instead, her brow knotted in deep thought.

Dammit, had all the men in her life done nothing but abuse her trust? Even him? Hah—especially him.

Well, it was about time somebody made it up to her. Time he made it up to her.

'I have decided to give Slater the rest of the day off,' he said, as he poured himself a measure of the local ale. 'From now on, I am entirely at your disposal.'

She darted him a suspicious glance over the rim of her teacup.

'Would you like to take that walk the landlord recommended? Or, we could just take a leisurely stroll through the streets of this town and see what the shops have to offer.'

'Which would you prefer?'

'I should prefer it if you would tell me what would please you.'

She shifted in her seat, as though struggling with the notion that she could express her own wishes and he would abide by them. As though it was an entirely novel experience to have anyone ask her what she would like to do.

'If you wouldn't mind,' she said hesitantly, 'I think I should like to climb up through the moorland above our house and see if we can find that view he was telling us about.'

'Then that is what we shall do. As soon as we have done justice to these sandwiches. I would not like you to faint away with hunger in such a remote spot.'

Her face lit up as though he'd just presented her with a rare gift. Which pierced him to the core. A walk through rugged terrain to enjoy a view, that was all he'd promised her. And she was looking at him as though he'd done something generous.

When it wasn't generous in the least. It was nothing. Less than nothing.

And when she found out what they were really doing in Dorset, she'd no doubt say the same thing.

But still, he could give her today. Small compensation for all the grief he would soon be bringing her, but today was all he had.

He downed his ale with a deep sense of foreboding.

Chapter Nineteen

'Are you quite sure,' said Rawcliffe in apparent earnest, as they trudged up the steep track which started at the end of the lane that ran past their lodgings, 'that you would not prefer to part with a penny and clamber up through the enhanced series of terraces to drink, for a further ha'penny, a cup of turgid spring water?'

'No, no,' she replied with equal seriousness, though she was almost sure he was teasing. 'I am determined to enjoy the vista from the cliff top and dream of one day being able to capture it in oils.'

'Can you paint in oils?'

'I can barely paint in watercolour. My upbringing was not of the kind where idle pursuits were encouraged. However, from the way this turf is so closely cut down, and from the number of scrapes visible, I would say that there is a large population of rabbit up here.'

'The tunnels into the gorse bushes would tend to uphold your theory. Though what has that to do with painting the scenery?'

'Not a thing. I was just going to point out that I am more the sort of girl who would be able to dress a brace of rabbit, should anyone decide to snare them for me, and turn them into a savoury dinner.'

'Pierre would be extremely upset if you were to attempt to oust him from his kitchen.'

'Oh, I didn't mean I *wanted* to cook you a rabbit stew, particularly. Just that I could, if I had to.'

'You will never have to resort to skinning rabbits again,' he said firmly. 'Besides, I am not partial to rabbit stew. All those little bones.'

'I shall bear that in mind,' she said as he held out his hand to help her clamber over a particularly rugged jumble of boulders which lay in their path. As she took it, she couldn't help thinking about that remarkable statement he'd made. Had he really wanted to marry her when she'd been a mere sixteen years old? It was extremely hard to believe. Especially as he'd said he'd reached that decision because he'd seen her wading waist deep in muddy pond water with her hair coming down in rats' tails.

But if he hadn't meant it, why had he said it?

And why had he said all that about someone telling him that she would not countenance such a proposal? If he'd really approached Father, she could imagine him claiming that a betrothal was out of the question because she was too young. And counselling the young Robert Walmer, as he'd been then, to return, if he was truly in earnest, in a year or so at which time he might, possibly, consider granting him permission to pay his addresses. Or, if he hadn't approved of the match under any circumstances, simply telling him in no uncertain terms to take himself off.

What she couldn't believe was that Father would have

claimed she'd asked him to turn the proposal down on her behalf.

Yet Rawcliffe's demeanour had changed since he'd told her that was what had happened. As if, having admitted he'd been...well, smitten with her, back then, he'd been able to lower part of the defensive barrier behind which he habitually hid himself.

But all her jumbled thoughts came skidding to a halt as they crested the last of the jagged boulders. It was as if the land ended, not ten yards farther on. From that point onward, it was just the sea, extending as far as the horizon.

'My goodness, but the sea is big,' she said, reaching up one hand to hold on to her bonnet, which was making a bid to escape. Rawcliffe's hat, which did not have the additional security of being held in place by ribbons, leapt from his head as though flicked off by some invisible, mischievous sprite and went dancing gaily off into the blue.

'I believe,' he said sardonically, watching his hat make one sally up into the air, before tumbling end over end over the edge of the cliff, 'that this is what is described in the guide books as a bracing sea breeze.'

She giggled.

'There appears to be a sort of hollow over there,' he said, indicating a natural grassy amphitheatre with his ebony cane, 'that might be sheltered from the wind. Where we could sit and admire the view. If you like,' he added as though it was an afterthought. Although he knew full well that she wanted to admire the view. Was it really so hard for him to just admit he was trying to make her day as pleasant as it could be?

'What...' She faltered to a halt. She had no wish, really, to shatter his current affable mood and revert to their more normal habit of squabbling by asking him any one of the many questions she had teeming in her brain. 'What a lot of ships,' she finished, inanely, gesturing out to sea, at the dozens of craft of all varieties, their sails sprinkling the grey backdrop with white, mirroring the tiny white clouds scudding across the sky above.

'I believe that just offshore, there is what is known as a road. Ships sailing from places such as Portsmouth, heading out to the Atlantic Ocean, will of necessity pass by this section of the coastline.'

'And all the little boats, bobbing about nearer the shore?'

'Local fishermen, at a guess. Checking their lobster pots and so forth. I do hope they are successful, since Pierre has promised me buttered lobster for dinner.'

'No wonder you turned your nose up at my offer of rabbit stew.'

One corner of his mouth twitched up in the semblance of a smile. It was a jerky movement, as though the muscles he used for the purpose had gone rusty.

'I suppose,' she said, heartened by the way he appeared to be relaxing in her company, 'that we ought now to turn our attention to the harbour, since that is the view the landlord of the Three Tuns recommended.'

They both turned slightly to their left. She could, indeed, see the way Peacombe curved round the bay, at one end of which the locals had constructed a harbour wall. Farther away she could also see a waterfall tumbling down a cliff and, beyond that, another curve of steeply shelving pebbled beach.

'The harbour is definitely more agreeable from this distance,' he observed drily.

She breathed in deeply. 'The air up here smells like nothing I've ever smelled before. There is a tang to it, but it's not unpleasant. Though it still reminds me a bit of what we could smell down in the harbour.'

'It is the smell of the sea, I would guess. Or perhaps seaweed.'

'Well, whatever it is, I like it,' she declared. 'I could stay here all day, just breathing it in and watching the big ships out there, and the little ones closer in, and... just be.'

'If we are to stay up here for any length of time,' he said, 'then I suggest that we make ourselves comfortable in that hollow I pointed out to you before.' Once again, he indicated the grassy amphitheatre.

She laid her hand upon the arm he held out to her and they walked the short distance to the hollow.

'If I remove my coat, we can both sit upon the ground,' he said and promptly stripped it off, spread it out, sat down upon it, and held out his hand to invite her to join him.

'Thank you.' She couldn't help smiling at him as she took his hand for help to lower herself to the ground, where she arranged her legs as decorously as she could.

For a moment or two, it felt very awkward, sitting side by side, with him in his shirtsleeves.

'You are right,' she said, feeling a need to break down the walls she could almost feel him rebuilding round himself, brick by brick, the longer the silence continued. 'It is more sheltered here. And the view is still stunning.'

He made a sort of grunt, which she took to indicate agreement, since he was gazing fixedly out to sea as though he found the ships and the waves, and the few gulls battling against the invisible currents of air, utterly fascinating.

When for her, the most fascinating thing up here was him. Oh, how she wished she could just lean her head on his shoulder and slide her arm round his waist.

'The sound of the waves,' she said in a tone that even to her own ears sounded slightly panicked, 'sighing against the shore, over and over again, is really... soothing, isn't it?'

He turned to give her one of his enigmatic looks. She bit down on her lower lip and turned away. It was so galling that he could look at her as though he could see right down into the depths of her soul, somehow, whereas she could never tell what he was thinking. Ever. Even when he'd told her he'd been in earnest about proposing to her, all those years ago, she wasn't sure if she could believe it.

And coupled with their position, on top of the cliffs, with only the sky above them, and all that expanse of sea below, she felt very small. And insignificant. Just a tiny speck of humanity perched upon the very edge of the vastness of nature.

Which made her want to snuggle up against him even more. For comfort. And reassurance.

So naturally she sat up even straighter.

'The sound of the waves *is* very soothing,' he agreed with what looked like a glint of amusement in his eyes. 'In fact, it is so soothing, I scarcely know how to keep my eyes open.' So saying, he shifted round, then startled her by spreading out his legs in one direction and settling his head on her lap. 'You won't mind if I take a nap.' He sighed, closing his eyes.

Goodness.

'You…you are missing the view.'

'I have seen it,' he murmured drowsily. 'And now I am enjoying the sensation of feeling the breeze caressing my face and the sun beating down on my body, and the softness of your thighs beneath my head…'

'Stop that! You shouldn't mention my…'

'Thighs? Why not? They are very lovely thighs,' he said, reaching round to run the back of one hand over the curve of her bottom. Sending a surge of warmth and wetness to that place between her legs that seemed to belong to him in a very special way.

She didn't know what to do. They were outside. In broad daylight. Her mind flew back to his tryst under the hedge with Betsy. *She* hadn't felt the slightest bit inhibited by either the daylight or the venue. *She'd* bared her breasts for him. Hitched up her skirts, too.

She glanced over her shoulder. From where she was sitting she could see the upper windows of their lodging house. Which meant that anyone looking out could see them, too. If they had opera glasses trained in that direction.

What was wrong with her? How could she be thinking of doing…wickedness, out in the open, just because he'd laid his head in her lap and given her bottom a casual caress?

No, she couldn't possibly…

But perhaps she could just permit herself to run her fingers through his hair. It was something she'd wanted to do for a very long time. And she'd never quite dared to do anything so bold, not even when they'd been in bed together. But perhaps he wouldn't even notice out here. Now that his hat had blown away, he might think, if she stroked it very gently, that it was the wind ruffling his hair, nothing more.

Tentatively, she lifted her hand and just touched the crown of his head. His hair was springy, yet soft. He half-opened one eye and peered up at her quizzically. She held her breath, bracing herself against a caustic comment. For he never seemed to want to indulge in any behaviour she would regard as affectionate. And stroking a man's hair, as he lay with his head in her lap, most definitely came under that category.

'That would feel much better,' he said, eventually, 'if you were to remove your gloves.'

And then he closed his eyes again, freeing her to breathe out and then to remove her gloves and put them down on the grass at her side.

Stroking his hair with her bared fingers did indeed feel much better. And, since he'd pretty much given her permission to do it, she not only ran her fingers over his hair, but plunged them through the thick, springy softness.

After a while, he reached up and caught her hand, but only to kiss her fingers, one by one. Which sent lightning bolts of excitement winging all over her body.

Making her wish she could be as bold as Betsy Woodly. Because thanks to that afternoon she'd spent stuck halfway up Farmer Westthorpe's oak tree, she knew that he enjoyed, um, *sporting* with females in the open air. And now he'd brought her down to the ground, in this sheltered little spot, with the birds mewing overhead and the waves shushing dozens of feet below, she was starting to think she could see the attraction. It would certainly be a most elemental experience to feel the sun, and wind, upon naked skin.

She snatched her hand from his and pressed it to her mouth. Good lord, what was happening to her? Thinking such wicked thoughts?

Such tempting thoughts.

'I have changed my mind,' she said. 'I think I would like to explore the walk and the gardens, and perhaps even the caves, as well.'

Chapter Twenty

It didn't help. Not even stumbling around in the chilly, gloomy caves had been able to damp down the feelings that he'd started up on the cliff top by laying his head in her lap. By telling her that he'd truly wanted to marry her so many years ago. Because that meant that all the snide things he'd said to her since, the way he'd mocked her and taunted her, hadn't stemmed from disdain, but thwarted desire.

By the time they returned to their lodgings her insides felt as though they were melting, and her blood was fizzing through her veins like champagne. She hadn't felt as ready for him, in a sexual way, since...

She shook her head. She'd never wanted him this much. Well, she'd never allowed herself to want him. At all. Not when she'd believed the attraction was one-sided. But now, oh, how she wished she could drag him into her room and tear off her clothes, and then his, and push him to the bed. Only Nancy was bound to be waiting in her room with a basin of water and her evening clothes laid out in readiness. As though she'd been watching out for her return. It wouldn't surprise her to learn that Nancy owned opera glasses which she used for just that purpose.

The thought of Nancy in possession of opera glasses acted on her like a glass of water to the face. She actually did splash her face with water some moments later, when she reached her room to find everything exactly as she'd foreseen. For Nancy was the kind of servant who prided herself on giving superlative service.

Clare washed herself briskly and went to the dressing table where she sat down with her back to the maid.

'You should have taken a parasol out with you,' said Nancy with a little shake of her head. 'Your cheeks have become quite pink in the sun.'

It wasn't the sun that was making her cheeks pink. Clare was pretty sure she was blushing all over.

'The wind would have blown a parasol away, if I'd taken one up to the cliffs,' she retorted, irritated by Nancy's determination to 'improve' her. 'In fact, it did blow his lordship's hat away.'

'No!' Nancy giggled. For the first time since coming to work for her. As though she was a friend, rather than a maid.

And Clare saw that, actually, Nancy wasn't that much older than her. It was just the severe way she styled her hair and the sombre hue of her clothes that made her look so strict and stuffy.

She decided there and then she was going to stop resenting Nancy, who was only doing her job, after all. And doing it to the best of her ability, for a mistress who had such a temper she'd even thrown a room full of breakables at her groom on her wedding night.

She discovered that getting ready for dinner was not such an ordeal when she was chatting with Nancy rather than glowering at her in resentful silence. That Nancy could be good company when given just a little encouragement.

She even plucked up courage to smile and tell Clare that she would *take his lordship's breath away* when Clare hesitated on the point of opening the bedroom door to go down for dinner.

Clare lifted her chin and flung open the door. She had no need to be nervous. So why was her stomach so full of butterflies? Why was she trembling so much she had to reach out and steady herself by using the banister rail as she went down the stairs?

Ponsonby was standing sentinel outside the battered door of the sitting room, so she knew Rawcliffe must be inside. As soon as she reached the hall, Ponsonby opened the door and, since the hallway was so narrow, stepped smartly to one side so that she could get past him.

Rawcliffe was standing by the fireplace, sipping a drink. He eyed her over the rim of his glass as she entered, in such a way that he made her feel as if he was considering having her for dinner, rather than buttered lobster. Which made her turn as pink as one. Which made him smile, in a slow, knowing kind of way that made her feel as if she was standing there stark naked.

Ponsonby cleared his throat. 'Dinner is ready, should you wish to take your places at table, my lord, my lady.'

'I suppose we better,' said Rawcliffe, setting his glass down on the mantelpiece and extending his arm to her, 'or Pierre would never forgive us. He has, so I believe, been labouring under extremely trying circumstances today.'

He had been talking to his chef? Or talking about his chef? She glanced up at him out of the corner of her eye. Perhaps she ought not to be surprised. He seemed to need to know exactly what was going on, in every corner of his dominion. No matter how trivial or insignificant the matter might appear to others.

The dining room was, in keeping with the rest of the cottage, not designed to accommodate two footmen and a butler, as well as tables and chairs. But rather than permitting them to dine informally, by setting all the dishes on the table at once and letting them serve themselves, Ponsonby received each dish at the door, returning emptied ones to the footmen who hovered there.

It really was a bit ridiculous, to have so many servants scurrying up and down the passage to the kitchen, with each remove, so that she and her husband could dine in state, in what amounted to a glorified fisherman's cottage.

And yet Rawcliffe appeared to think nothing of it.

'Is the sauce not to your liking?' he enquired politely, making her realise she had been frowning at the river of cream Ponsonby had just poured over her lobster.

'I do beg your pardon, my lady,' said Ponsonby. 'I shall remove it at once.'

'No, no need. The sauce smells delicious,' she said, grabbing hold of her plate with both hands to prevent the solicitous butler from whisking it away. 'I was just thinking how very much trouble you must have all gone to, to produce such a…lavish meal, in what is only a tiny cottage, after all.'

'Chef has had to make use of all three kitchens available,' said Ponsonby gravely.

'Have you not noticed the amount of running up and down the lane behind the lodgings that has been going on all evening?' Rawcliffe arched one eyebrow at her as he signalled Ponsonby to bring the sauceboat round to his side of the table.

'Oh, dear, has there?' She hadn't noticed. She'd been far too busy fussing over her clothes and hair, and making friends with Nancy to notice what had been going on outside. 'It does seem like an awful lot of effort. For just the two of us,' she finished guiltily.

Ponsonby drew himself up to his full height and seemed to swell to twice his normal size.

'There is no excuse for lowering our standards of service to his lordship, simply because we do not have the facilities available to us in the town house. His lordship may be taking a holiday, but we,' he said repressively, 'are not.'

'Nevertheless,' said Rawcliffe, leaning back and twirling his wineglass by the stem, 'I hope that each of you will be able to take some time off while we are down here.'

'That is very good of you, my lord,' said Ponsonby, unbending a touch. 'I shall inform the staff and organise their leisure hours so that there will be no inconvenience to you, or her ladyship.'

'I don't doubt it,' said Rawcliffe tersely, 'or I would not have made the suggestion.'

Which made Clare wonder whether Rawcliffe or Ponsonby was the one being hardest on the servants. However, to show her appreciation, she made sure she sampled a little of every dish and sauce Ponsonby brought to table, declaring each one more delicious than the last. She actually had no need to pretend to marvel over the little spun-sugar baskets filled with fresh strawberries. They were works of art.

She was just beginning to wonder if her stay laces could withstand any more strain, when Ponsonby set a plate of cheeses on the table. 'Chef thought you might like to sample some local cheeses to finish with,' he announced.

Oh, thank heaven.

Rawcliffe cut a small piece from two of the truckles and placed them on his plate. She simply shook her head. Her stays had survived this far, but she wasn't prepared to test them any further. 'I couldn't eat another bite.'

Rawcliffe gave her a heated look across the cheese board. 'All the exercise, climbing up over the moors today, must have made you tired. Perhaps you would like to go up to bed?'

Oh, yes, she would like to go up to bed. It was just that she hadn't dreamed for a minute that he'd announce the fact to his butler. Who was smiling at her in a positively avuncular fashion.

'Oh...er... I...' she stammered.

'I shan't be far behind you,' said Rawcliffe, with the kind of look in his eyes that made her think of that time he had entered her from behind with animalistic fervour.

Blushing feverishly, she laid her napkin down beside her plate and allowed Ponsonby to hold her chair out for her as she got to her feet.

'I...er...goodnight!' She fled from the room and went up the stairs in a far from dignified manner, shot into her bedroom and shut the door behind her, leaning on it for support. If he were to come in now, he could push her down on to her hands and knees, and find her ready to receive him. It was as if the whole day had been a slow, tortuous preparation for the moment when they could get to the bed.

There was a firm knock at the door which had her

leaping from it with a guilty start, as though she'd been caught napping in church.

She opened the door, to find Nancy on the landing, a jug of warm water in her hands and a towel over her arm.

But just mounting the stairs, with a slow, deliberate tread, was Rawcliffe. And he was looking at her as though he felt about the same as she did. As though, if they didn't get their clothes off, and their hands on each other soon, he would explode.

'Thank you, Nancy,' he said tersely, taking the jug, basin and towel from the maid. 'I believe my wife will have no need of you tonight.'

Nancy grinned and dipped her head. As Rawcliffe stepped into the room and kicked the door shut behind him, she could swear she could hear the maid giggling.

Which was awful.

'Your servants will all know what we're about to do,' she protested. 'You might as well have issued a proclamation!'

He raised one eyebrow, then went across to the wash stand where he deposited the items he'd taken from Nancy. 'We are doing nothing we have not done every other night since our marriage,' he pointed out calmly.

'That's different. You didn't oust Nancy from the room with such...'

'Impatience?'

He stalked towards her, shucking off his jacket. 'But I am impatient. I feel as if I have been waiting for this moment all day.'

She gulped. And far from making any further protest, when he kissed her she flung her arms about his waist and kissed him back for all she was worth.

She could never hang on to a single rational thought once he started kissing her. It was as if he turned her into a creature who was all passion. She needed to feel skin on skin and to that end she began to burrow under his shirt. Just as he was burrowing under her clothes and tearing at fastenings to make their progress towards nudity as swift as was humanly possible.

She panted and moaned, and pressed herself up against him whenever he wasn't removing another layer of material. Whenever she wasn't clawing away the clothes he was wearing. She was naked well before he was. But then he had far more experience at getting females out of their clothes than she did at undressing men.

For a moment, that reflection dimmed her pleasure. But as if he sensed her withdrawal, he set his mouth to her neck and suckled on the tender spot beneath her ear that always made her knees turn to jelly.

And then he lifted her and…

Instead of carrying her to the bed, he coaxed her legs about his waist and slammed her up against the bedroom door.

Goodness. Could he possibly mean to…?

Yes, he did. He cupped her bottom and slid into her with a shocking proficiency that made her gasp. In shock, she told herself as she grabbed his head and speared her fingers though her hair. Not excitement.

Not excitement.

Not…

'Oh!'

Her fingers clenched into his hair and her legs tightened round his waist, as pleasure ripped through her like an explosion.

He groaned. Thrust into her just once more and experienced his own explosion of pleasure.

No, no, it couldn't be all over so quickly. He was going to put her down and go back to his own room. And leave her alone.

And it wasn't even fully dark outside. She could have wept.

'Clare,' he breathed into her neck. 'Don't tell me you regretted that. Admit it, you needed it as much as I did.'

'I…' She swallowed. 'Yes, I did,' she admitted. 'I am just…'

'Was I too rough? I thought you came to a spend?' He leaned back a little and looked into her face with a touch of what looked very much like concern.

'You weren't too rough. And I did…' She faltered, completely unable to use the words he could employ so easily.

'Thought so,' he said, his expression of concern turning to one of smug satisfaction.

She turned her head away. She felt so exposed, having a conversation with him while he had her pinned to the door with her legs wrapped round his waist.

'Do you think you could put me down now?'

'Absolutely not,' he said, taking a step back and walking across to the bed, with her still wrapped round him like coat.

Where he manoeuvred them both down on to it, still locked together. 'There,' he said, flexing his hips against hers. 'Isn't this better?'

'I…' She felt a blush heating her cheeks. Because he was still quite firm. 'I thought you…'

'Oh, I did. But now I find I'm ready for more. Are you not?' He teasingly ground his hips against hers.

Well, she hadn't wanted him to leave. And if this was what it took to keep him in her bed, then…

Oh, who was she fooling? She wanted more, just as much as he did. Shutting her eyes, she ground back up against him and dug her heels into his bottom.

'I shall take that as a yes,' he growled.

And this time, he took it much more slowly.

Chapter Twenty-One

She fell asleep immediately. Which meant he didn't have to explain anything.

Which was perfect, as far as he was concerned.

He could just cradle her in his arms while she slept. Gaze down at her piquant little face and commit every plane, every curve and every freckle to memory.

She stirred in her sleep once or twice, and he let her wriggle round until she'd found a more comfortable position. And then, when she'd settled, he hooked one leg over her to prevent her sliding away from him should he happen to doze off himself.

But she didn't slide away while he slept. Instead, when he woke, it was to find she'd snuggled closer, as though unconsciously seeking his warmth, though it wasn't a cold night. He blessed the moonbeams that were streaming in through the window, since nobody had got round to drawing the curtains, for they'd woken him to a moment he would always treasure.

Her, snuggled trustingly against his chest as though…

The moment shattered. Something woke Clare, the moonlight striking their shared pillow, or some subtle movement of his, he couldn't tell.

What he did know was that she was now as tense as a plank within the circle of his arms. As though wondering what on earth he thought he was doing, holding her so tightly. And what she was going to do about it.

He held his breath as he awaited her verdict.

But when she sighed in what sounded to him like a very martyred fashion, he decided that if she wanted him to leave, tonight, then she was damned well going to have to tell him outright.

He waited for her to say something. When she didn't, he found he couldn't bear the suspense.

'Are you awake?' he murmured into her ear.

She still said nothing. Though he could almost hear her thoughts flitting through her head. Was she considering the correct way to dismiss a husband from her bed? Or...dammit! Never, in his whole life, had he wanted to know what a woman was thinking when she was in bed with him. But this was Clare. Who could tie him in knots with a sigh, a tilt to her shoulder and silence.

'You are awake,' he declared. 'So you may as well open your eyes and admit it.'

She turned her head then and by the light of the moon he could see a very determined expression settle over her features. As though she was steeling herself to face some kind of battle.

Which she wasn't, he promptly decided, going to win, not tonight. Not if it took every ounce of skill he possessed to seduce her into letting him be the husband he'd wanted to be all those years ago. Just for one night.

With what one of his conquests had termed his *I'm going to have my wicked way with you* smile, he gently tucked a stray tendril of hair behind her ear.

'I like your hair like this,' he said.

'What, in a mess?'

'Streaming across my pillow, rather than being confined in one of those braids you have insisted on adopting every night so far.'

'A braid is practical, at night.'

'It is not seductive, though. You should wear it loose, like this, in bed.'

Something nebulous flickered across her face. Something that looked...

'What thought has just crossed your mind?' he asked her. 'You got a very wicked look in your eyes. As though you were plotting mischief.'

'Perhaps,' she whispered, looping her arms round his neck, 'I was.'

'If it is the sort of mischief I am hoping it was,' he began, before pausing to kiss her, 'then I have to say...'

She turned in his arms and pressed her breasts into his chest. *She* pressed up against *him*. His heart started pounding so fast he felt dizzy with it. He swooped to her lips again and kissed her with all the finesse of a starving beggar falling upon a meat pie. He'd always known her fire would be able to warm the cold places in his soul. He'd never dreamed she'd be so hot they'd create steam.

After a few seconds, perhaps inevitably, she pulled away.

He braced himself for the recriminations.

'What,' she panted, 'were you about to say?'

'Say?' *She* wanted to know what *he* was thinking? 'Nothing of any consequence,' he replied. 'At least, it cannot have been because I have completely forgotten what it was.'

She wriggled against him, again, with a positively naughty look on her face.

No matter what else she thought of him, there was no denying she enjoyed doing this. And, it occurred to him, if he could take her to such heights that she fell asleep immediately after he finally finished with her, then he'd be able to remain in her bed without having to make any explanation at all about why he'd been so quick to leave it before tonight.

And so he paid great attention to detail. Kissing and caressing every inch of her alabaster skin. Running his tongue over the areas he'd already learned were particularly sensitive. Until she was moaning and writhing with need. At which point he honed in on the obvious target, flicking his tongue over her to tease her to the point where she was desperate for his penetration. Which he denied her. Not until she'd gasped out in surprised rapture. Not 'til he'd roused her to that same pitch all over again and she was almost sobbing with a mixture of exhaustion and frustrated need.

Only then did he slide up and into her, and give her all of himself.

His body, that was. He would never trust his heart to anyone, for them to stamp on and grind under their heels. The way she'd stamped on his when she'd...

Only she hadn't. Not intentionally.

Ah, what did it matter what had gone on between them before? When right now she was clinging to him, shuddering to her own completion in the same instant as him. Even when she slid almost immediately into oblivion, her arms and legs remained fastened round him as though she couldn't bear to let go. He buried his head in the crook of her neck, in the softness of her hair, breathing in the scent of her. Of their shared passion.

And wished it could always be like this.

* * *

Almost at once, it seemed to him, he woke to the cry of gulls. And the first rays of morning light drumming against his eyelids.

And the feel of her soft bottom pressed against his groin. And the dip of her waist, under his arm. And the fullness of her breast, cupped in his hand. It felt like heaven.

But how did she, prim little vicar's daughter, feel about waking to a man, with a man's most basic needs? When she didn't even want to let him keep a candle burning when he came to her bed at night? When she felt embarrassed and confused by the lust that flared between them in spite of all their years of antagonism for each other.

As if she was thinking along the very same lines, she stiffened in his arms.

He removed his offending hand from her breast and used it to brush her hair from her face, and tuck it behind her ear, so that he could kiss it.

'How are you this morning? I…' He faltered. It wasn't just her morals he'd violated, by forcing her into this marriage. He'd kept her body exercised practically all night long.

'I was abominably selfish last night,' he admitted. 'You must be quite…tender, after the way I used you.'

She stiffened even further, before turning in his arms to glare up at him.

'Used me? You did not use me,' she said fiercely. 'We shared a…that is—' she swallowed '—I enjoyed every moment of it.'

The reprieve was such a surprise it knocked the wind out of him. And then she surprised him even more, by putting her arms round him and hugging him. And planting a kiss on his bare chest.

'But I am grateful to you for being so considerate… in enquiring after my…that is, showing concern about me being…sore…when…honestly, I…'

She floundered to a halt on a fiery blush.

'You enjoyed *every* moment of it,' he couldn't resist teasing the top of her head, which was all he could see of her once she buried her blushing face in his chest.

She nodded.

'Even—' he ran one finger down the length of her spine until it reached the knot of nerve endings that had proved so sensitive to his explorations the night before '—even when I took you up against the door?'

There was a pause, as she squirmed with pleasure. But then she took a deep breath and nodded her head again.

'Hmmm…' Waking up with his wife wasn't proving to be as awkward as he'd anticipated, after all.

'What?'

'Well, perhaps now would be a good time to warn you that my appetite is…prodigious. And that I do like variety.'

Her head flew up. 'You mean, you want to have other women?'

'No.' His arms tightened round her. The thought of having any other woman, now he'd had Clare was almost abhorrent. 'I mean, I enjoy variety in…the way I…' Their eyes met. And, to his amazement, he was the one who was squirming now, in response to her wide-eyed look of incomprehension.

How on earth had she managed to make him…*shy*… of speaking to her about…earthly delights? Carnal appetites. Dammit, she was now even making him censor his own *thoughts*, when before he'd married her he'd had no trouble whatsoever in describing it exactly as it was. In good old Anglo-Saxon terms.

'You mean,' she asked him, with an innocent expression in her eyes, 'that sometimes you would like to take me up against a door. And sometimes you would like to take me from behind, while I am on my hands and knees?'

God, yes! But…he swallowed. Searched her face for signs of revulsion, or rejection. Instead, he perceived a glint of humour lurking in her eyes and making the corners of her mouth twitch with suppressed laughter. The little minx! She was teasing him. Almost daring him to try to shock her.

So he decided it was about time he took back control.

'Precisely,' he said in as clinical a voice as he could muster, given his very, very aroused state. 'And right now,' he declared, rolling to his back whilst keeping hold of her, so that she ended up lying on top of him, 'I would like you to ride me.'

'R-ride you?'

Ah. That had put her off balance again. As did the way he took hold of her thighs, arranging them on either side of his legs, before pushing her into an upright position, so she could have no doubt about what he meant.

'B-but that means…' She faltered, lifting her hands to cover her breasts. He took hold of them gently, but firmly, and moved them out of the way.

'Yes, it means that I can see you. All of you. And not just your breasts. But your face, as you enjoy me.'

'I… I…' Her face went bright red. She twisted her lower lip, biting down on it in delightful confusion.

But she was also wriggling her hips experimentally as he grew harder beneath her. He thought he actually saw the moment it occurred to her that in this position, she had a good deal more power than she'd had thus far, in bed with him. And that the possibilities intrigued her.

But before she had time to feel guilty for her very natural desire to explore those possibilities, he reminded her that he had chosen this. That he was only permitting her the illusion of being in charge.

By gripping her hips and encouraging her into movement.

'Like this,' he said, showing her what he meant.

She rocked against him, tentatively, but obligingly. 'That's it,' he said, letting go of her hips to stroke his way up her flanks. 'Take your pleasure of me...'

They slept again after that. At least, she did. She sort of dived off him after and buried her blushing face in the pillows so that she didn't have to look him in the eyes.

His shy bride. He caressed the length of her spine idly as he recalled the way she'd ridden him like a stallion. With her head flung back, her wild red hair tumbling all over her shoulders. And the cry she'd made, when she'd finally reached her peak.

'Ah, Clare,' he murmured, kissing the nape of her neck. She grumbled in her sleep and made a faint movement with one hand as though she was brushing off a pesky fly. He chuckled and slid across the bed so that he could press his whole body up against the entire length of hers.

And then slid into a light doze. Feeling like the luckiest man in the world.

It was somebody knocking on the bedroom door that shattered that feeling. A feeling he might have known wouldn't last.

But even so, he couldn't keep the irritation from his voice when he bid whoever it was who was knocking to enter.

It was his voice, rather than the knocking on the door, which roused Clare. But when Nancy came in, Clare gave a little squeak and pulled the covers up over her head. As though she had something to be ashamed of.

He ground his teeth.

'Begging your pardon, my lord, my lady,' said Nancy, keeping her gaze fixed firmly on the footboard, rather than the occupants of the bed, 'but there has been a man come to the house saying that if you still wish to take the trip in his boat you mentioned, then you won't find better conditions than what he expects today. And then he said a lot of things about wind direction and tides and so forth which none of us understood. But he was most insistent, he was, that if you wanted to take your trip, then you would need to be down by the harbour within the hour. And we did leave you as long as we could, but Slater said as how you'd gone to a lot of trouble to arrange this trip, so it must be important, and so...'

'Yes.' Yes, it was important. It was the whole reason they'd come to this benighted little hamlet rather than go somewhere with some real facilities, like Weymouth.

And it would spell the end of any more nights like last night.

But he had a duty to investigate the circumstances surrounding Archie's death. And to avenge him, if it turned out that foul play had been involved. No matter who was behind it.

'Yes, thank you, Nancy,' he said as calmly as he could, considering a part of him wanted to howl and pull the covers up the way Clare had done, and bury his face in all that soft hair and let the rest of the world, and all his responsibilities go to blazes.

But that wasn't who he was.

'We will get up now,' he told himself sternly, as well as informing the maid of his intentions. 'Bring her ladyship a can of water and get Cadogan to take some to my room. And have a light breakfast ready for us when we come down.'

Nancy bobbed a curtsy and left.

And since he wasn't the type of man to let the world know when he was hurting, he smacked Clare playfully on the bottom, before rolling out of bed.

'You heard, sleepyhead,' he said. 'We need to be down at the harbour to catch the tide within the hour.'

'Do we,' she replied crossly, sticking her head up above the covers, 'really want to catch the tide?'

'If you want to go and visit your brother, we do.' And then, because it might be the last time she would ever be this receptive to him, he bent down and kissed her, one last time, with every atom of his being. Bidding her farewell in the only way he could, without words.

And then, since the tide waited for no man, not even a marquess, he tore his lips from hers, and strode to the door.

To face whatever the day had in store.

Chapter Twenty-Two

Clare looked at the small ketch he'd hired to ferry them along the coastline to Peeving Cove as though she suspected it of plotting to leap out of the water and bite her at any moment. He was experiencing a similar feeling. Not about the boat itself, but what was going to happen once it had brought them to their destination.

'I regret the boat is only a simple craft,' he said. 'But I have been led to believe it is the most suitable one available.' The only one available, in point of fact. No other fisherman in the area was prepared to take strangers into the lair of 'The Gentlemen', which was the way they spoke of Peeving Cove. They were afraid of reprisals.

Only the captain of this boat, who was now standing on the deck wringing his cap between his gnarled and weather-beaten hands, had been willing to take the risk. And that only after having been paid one hundred pounds.

'For that amount,' he'd said, 'I c'n buy myself a new boat, if'n the gennlemen scupper this old wreck. So long's I'm not on it when they sink it,' he'd added gloomily. 'And as fer going fer me family, as a warning to others, well, I've only the wife and the lad left. And the lad's damn near useless and I'm sick on the owld shrew's nagging ways, anyhow.'

And so the deal had been struck.

'Won't find a better craft to take you up Peeving Cove, ma'am,' said the fisherman. Or at least, that was how Rawcliffe interpreted the assortment of strangulated vowels that emerged from the whiskers obliterating the entire lower half of the man's face.

Clare apparently thought so, too.

'Oh, I'm sure it is a very fine ship,' she said earnestly. 'It is just that I have never been on one before, and I am—' she gave a little laugh '—a bit nervous.'

'Aar,' said the captain, with a shake of his head. 'Have reason, I reckon. Warned his lordship 'ow it'd be, only he would hire 'un.'

The captain had actually warned Rawcliffe about the inadvisability of attempting to sail any sort of craft up the inlet which led to Peeving Cove, without first gaining permission from the smugglers whose lair it was. Clare, however, not knowing the first thing about the kind of company her brother was keeping these days, naturally assumed the captain had been talking about her own reaction to going on a ship.

Which annoyed her so much, she stopped dithering on the quayside, lifted her chin and stepped onto the gangplank. It bowed under her weight, the boat bobbed lower in the water and Clare shot forward, fetching up inelegantly in the captain's arms.

Which clearly made the old fellow's day, judging from the grin that slashed a gap through his whiskers and the length of time it was taking him to let go of her.

'Ooh,' she said, as he stepped into the boat behind her and relieved the captain of his post as chief propperup of his wife. 'It feels so peculiar! It's like...just as if I'm standing on the water itself.'

'T'will be better if you sit yourselves down,' said the captain. 'Over yonder—' he indicated, with a jerk of his head, a bench upon which Ponsonby had just finished strewing as many cushions as he'd been able to find in their lodgings '—while me and the lad cast off. That is, if you're still sure you want to sail today.'

He didn't want to sail in this old hulk today or any other day. But it was too late to draw back now.

'Indeed,' replied Rawcliffe tersely. 'Or I would not have paid you such an outrageous sum of money.'

'T'wouldn't have been worth the risk, for any less,' said the captain.

'What risk?' Clare grabbed hold of his sleeve. 'Is the boat not safe? Is it the currents that Jeavons was telling us about?'

No, the captain was not afraid of the currents and the craft itself was seaworthy. It was 'The Gentlemen' the captain feared, in spite of saying he didn't care what happened to his family.

Not that he was going to share any of that information with Clare. It would be better if she saw how Clement was living with her own eyes and made her own decisions about him. If he gave her any warning at all about his suspicions that he'd become embroiled with 'The Gentlemen', the chances were she'd think he was trying to poison her mind against her brother and she'd go into the meeting bearing him a grudge. Which Clement would then pounce upon, and work on, until he'd managed to turn her against him, somehow.

His stomach clenched.

'You have no need to be nervous,' he said as he ushered her down to sit on the cushioned bench. 'The captain is just trying to add a little touch of...the exotic to this trip, that is all. A little excitement.'

'Just being in a boat is excitement enough for me,' she said, looking about her keenly as the captain, and the lad who acted as his only crew, began looping ropes and hauling sails, and shouting completely indecipherable remarks at each other.

'Oooh,' she cried, as the boat dipped, and lurched under the auspices of a particularly playful gust of wind. She clung to his arm, her eyes wide as she watched the shore recede. She flinched when the sails made a loud cracking noise as the wind filled them completely and bore them out to the deeper waves of the Channel.

'Oooh,' she cried again, as the ketch plunged down the side of one wave, then soared up the crest of the next.

'It's...it's...' Her hand went up to the brim of her bonnet, which was making an attempt to escape from her head, dislodging a handful of hairpins in the process. 'I imagine this must be what it feels like to fly.'

'The sea is a touch rough,' he said as the ketch plunged through the crest of a wave, showering them both with salt spray, 'for you to be making your first trip.'

'I don't care,' she said, turning to beam at him. 'It's the most exhilarating experience I have ever had. Although—' her smile dimmed '—I must say, you don't look as though you are enjoying yourself. Are you not,' she said, searching his face with concern, 'a good sailor?'

How like Clare, to show concern for him when he was on the point of betraying her. Just like the way she'd tried to console him when he'd heard about Archie's death, even though he'd been in the process of exacting some petty revenge upon her.

His stomach, which had been so tense from the moment they'd awoken that he'd been unable to do justice to his breakfast, was now positively roiling.

'Look at the horizon,' said Clare, gesticulating out to sea. 'I believe that is supposed to help.'

It wouldn't. The thing that was making him sick to his stomach was the thought of losing her regard. The dread that after Clement had worked on her, she'd never look at him like this again. Never cling to his arm this way, let alone hug him in the street. He'd lose it all. And without her warmth, he'd go back to living in the cold isolation that had been his habitat since the day she'd spurned his first proposal of marriage.

Unless he explained...

Explained what? Even his two best friends had assumed he was so calculating that he'd marry his enemy's sister just to get close enough to him to find the proof they needed to bring him to justice.

Besides, he'd left it too late. If he'd only told her the truth in the first place, she might have listened. But now, if he told her that getting even with Clement hadn't even occurred to him when he'd pushed her into marriage, that it was only an additional benefit...

He groaned inwardly and shut his eyes. If it sounded that bad, even in his own head, how much worse would it sound if he said it out loud?

He should have told her how much she meant to him, that was what he should have done. The moment he'd got the ring on her finger. Or when they'd talked about his first proposal and he'd discovered she hadn't thought all those vile things that her father had told him were her reason for turning him down. She'd have listened to him then, as he told her...

Told her—his stomach constricted painfully—that he...loved her?

Did he? Was that why the prospect of losing her was making him feel so ill?

Good God. He did. His eyes flew open to stare at her. She was still clinging to his arm and looking at him with concern.

'Clare...'

His heart sped up. No. He couldn't tell her. Not now. Not just before she went to speak to Clement. Even if she believed him now, once she heard her brother's version of events, she'd look back on this moment and think he'd just been trying to *turn her up sweet*. So that she wouldn't believe what Clement had to say. They'd lived for too long in a state of mutual suspicion to easily believe anything good the other might say.

The time was not right. He passed a weary hand over his eyes. The time was never right for him and Clare. They'd both been too young when he'd made his first, impulsive and rather rash proposal. And now they were adults and free to govern their lives the way they wished, he was locked in what she'd consider a long-standing feud with her brother.

'There she is,' said the Captain suddenly. 'That be Peeving Cove. God 'elp us.'

'It's all right,' she said. 'You will be fine, soon. We are nearly there.'

He would never be fine again. Once again, Clare was going to slip through his fingers. Because he'd...he'd gone about this all wrong. He should have...

'See, the waves are less rough already,' she said, as they slipped through the gash in the cliff face that led into a narrow inlet. 'And the water in the harbour, further in, looks as flat as a mill pond.'

Even though the waves out at sea had been boister-

ous. It made the place a safe anchorage no matter what
storms might rage elsewhere, he suspected.

'Oh, what a charming little place,' she exclaimed,
straining forward now to admire the cluster of sturdy
houses, built of and tiled with local stone so that they
blended in with the cliffs backing the cove to the point
where they looked as if they had sprouted there entirely
naturally. They sat upon a sort of shelf projecting from
the cliff face, down which poured a continual torrent,
which was, he'd discovered by dint of studying maps
of the locality, the River Peever.

She might see only a charming little village, nestling
into the shelter of protective cliffs, but he was looking
at a virtually impregnable stronghold. The mouth of the
river, where it emerged into the sea between two massive, sheer cliffs, which provided the only access to the
village, was only just wide enough to admit their craft.
And the seabed there was festooned with rocks, so that
only those who knew the channel extremely well would
dare attempt to sail through the gap except at high tide.
Though, by some quirk of geology, the water remained
deep enough for craft to sail right up to a broad quayside. So that the inhabitants could sail their own craft
right up to their front doors, should they so desire, and
unload whatever contraband they had on board. And,
thanks to their guided tour of the caves the day before,
he'd learned that all the cliffs along this part of the coast
were riddled with tunnels and caves, due to extensive
quarrying. Tunnels and caves in which smugglers could
conceal no end of contraband.

He wondered if the smugglers had mounted guns
anywhere up on those cliffs, which surrounded the village like fortress walls. He could actually see one or
two ledges, which would give cover to the entire sweep

of the harbour. So that they could repel any potential invaders. Such as customs men.

'I wonder which house is Clement's,' said Clare, reminding him that her motives for coming here were at such odds with his own.

'I don't like the looks of that, yer lordship,' said the captain, sidling up to him and jerking his head in the direction of the quayside, which they were steadily approaching, upon which a group of tough-looking men was gathering.

'Allow me to handle them,' he said.

'Ar, that's easy for you to say,' grumbled the captain. 'But you don't have to live in these parts.'

'Good morning,' said Lord Rawcliffe, as the captain threw a rope in the direction of a wooden post and thrust his lad up out of the sides of the ship after it.

One of the men on the quayside caught the rope before the lad could get to it and tossed it back into the boat.

'You can't land here,' he barked. 'We don't have nothing for tourists,' he finished, eyeing Rawcliffe and Clare with contempt.

'Ah, but we are not tourists,' said Rawcliffe. 'We are here to visit the Reverend Cottam.'

The men on the quayside looked at each other. Their spokesman, a tall, rough-hewn individual with shoulders a couple of yards wide, stuck his meaty hands on his hips.

'You want to speak to the Reverend, you go to church on Sunday up at Lesser Peeving and wait for him after service. He don't like being bothered during the week.'

Clare gasped. And stood up. 'That cannot be true. He would never—' she paused to swipe a tendril of hair, which had escaped from her bonnet, from her

mouth '—neglect his calling by refusing to permit parishioners to come to him with their problems during
the week!'

Rawcliffe sighed at her misplaced faith in her brother.

'Ar, but you ain't one of his parishioners, are you?'
sneered the spokesman.

'No,' retorted Clare, lifting her chin. 'I am his sister!'

The spokesman peered at her intently. Tilted his head
to one side as he noted the colour of her hair which the
wind was still whipping across her face. And for once,
Rawcliffe was glad that she bore such a striking resemblance to her brother.

'He never said as you was coming,' said the spokesman resentfully.

'What difference does that make? Why should I not
visit my brother whenever I wish?' Clare had become
so annoyed that she did what she always did when provoked. Took to physical action. She bent to pick up
the rope which the captain's lad was too intimidated
to touch and threw it with remarkable accuracy at the
spokesman. 'You will tie this boat to that post, if you
please, and then take me straight to my brother!'

The spokesman gestured to one of the men at his
side, who took the rope and looped it round the nearest bollard.

Just as he'd suspected, Clare had become the key to
gaining entry to this supposedly impregnable stronghold. Not that it made him feel any better about how
she'd feel when she discovered he'd been using her.

The spokesman made a signal to a sturdy boy
who'd been standing on the outskirts of the group,
who promptly went running off in the direction of the
houses.

It took a few moments to get the gangplank in place and for him to help Clare cross it to gain solid ground.

'Oh, my word,' she said, clinging to his arm. 'It feels as if the land is pitching up and down. How peculiar.'

Just then, the boy who'd been sent away came running back and went straight to the spokesman, who bent down to hear what he had to say. Whatever it was had the spokesman straightening up sharply, whipping off his cap, and making a clumsy bow to Clare. His men followed suit.

'Beg your pardon, Miss Cottam. The reverend says as how we're to take you straight to him.'

And treat her with respect, too, by the looks of it. Interesting.

'I should jolly well think so,' she said. Not bothering, he noted with irritation, to correct their assumption that she was still a single lady.

'It's this way,' said the spokesman, indicating with a sweep of his arm that she should follow him. 'Not you,' he growled, as they set off, arm in arm.

'Not I?' Rawcliffe raised one eyebrow at the man, in his most imperious fashion.

'No. The rev said as how we was to bring his sister to him. *Only* his sister. Not nobody else, see?' To show he meant business, the man stuck his chin forward aggressively.

'How very tiresome of him,' he said mildly, though he wasn't at all surprised. Cottam would want to get Clare alone, so that he could present his own, twisted version of events, and no doubt try to convince her that whatever he'd done, he'd been acting from purely altruistic motives.

And if she believed him…

'I am so sorry,' said Clare, turning to him and plac-

ng one little hand upon his forearm. 'I cannot think
vhat has induced Clement to be so rude. You would
hink—'

'It does not matter,' he assured her, though a great
veight seemed to be pressing on his chest. 'You can-
iot think I actually wish to see him myself?' He gave a
heatrical shudder. 'This entire trip is entirely for your
›enefit, my dear.' My darling. My love, he wanted to
ay, but didn't. Because this wasn't the time.

'Well, perhaps it is as well. You don't look at all the
hing.' She stepped closer, stood on tiptoe and kissed
iim on the cheek. Sending a pang of...something, some-
hing he couldn't recognise but suspected was a nox-
ous cocktail of regret and guilt, and despair, searing
hrough him. 'I will try not to be long.'

However long she was away it would feel like an
ternity. While he sat, powerless to defend himself
gainst whatever lies Cottam chose to tell her.

He had never felt so helpless in his life.

'Make sure you don't, miss,' said the captain. 'We'll
eed to depart with the tide. You take too long and we'll
ever make it through the eye,' he said, waving to the
arrow entrance to the inlet.

'Oh. Well, perhaps somebody could send me word
›efore then?' She turned and smiled hopefully round
he semi-circle of 'gentlemen', who either stared ston-
y back, or looked to their spokesman for guidance.

'But what,' said Clare with concern, 'will you do
vhile I am gone?'

He would curse himself for being seven kinds of a
›ol. For not realising, until he was faced with losing her
egard, how very much it meant to him. For not treat-
ig her like the treasure she was, but instead taunting
er, abducting her, forcing her into marriage and then

treating her like a whore, night after night. And most of all, for using her like a jemmy to prise open Cottam's fortress.

He made a languid gesture to the pile of wicker hampers stowed at the front of the boat. 'Oh, I shall make inroads into the picnic and admire the scenery,' he said with a bland smile at the group of surly men on the quayside.

'Really? Your stomach has recovered that quickly?'

'There has never been anything the matter with my stomach. I do not suffer from seasickness.'

A frown flitted across her face. 'But then, what—'

'Go,' he said, giving her a little push. 'Go and make your peace with your brother.'

'Well, if you're sure.'

No. He wasn't sure of anything. Except that somehow, Clement would use this meeting to sow discord between him and Clare. And that the worst of it was that all he'd have to do, to achieve his aim, would be to tell her some cold, hard facts.

But Clare was giving him one last tremulous, grateful smile, and turning to follow the spokesman.

The rest of the smuggling gang stood still, glowering at him. Even when he got back into the ketch, sat down on his pile of cushions and ordered his captain to open the first of the picnic hampers.

Lord, but he hoped Ponsonby had provided something decent to drink. He could do with a bottle of brandy. Or two.

Chapter Twenty-Three

Clare followed the burly giant of a man who appeared to be the head man of Clement's latest gang.

Typical. Wherever he went he managed to surround himself with the roughest, meanest boys and make himself their leader.

And would spout scripture at her whenever she, or anyone else, tried to remonstrate with him about the importance of 'being all things to all men', or 'seeking after that which was lost'. Which sounded incredibly evangelical, if you didn't happen to know that he'd never, to her knowledge, ever managed to save the soul of any single one of the miscreants with whom he enjoyed consorting.

The burly man stopped outside the largest house in the village. He knocked on the door, whipped off his cap and smoothed down his hair.

'The reverend's sister,' he said to the tough-looking, swarthy woman who opened the door.

'Indeed,' said the woman, eyeing them both, but particularly Clare's red hair. 'Yes, I can see why you might think so,' she said to the burly man. 'Very well, you may go.'

He wasted no time in doing so. 'I suppose you'd best come in,' the woman said grudgingly. 'The reverend is in his study.' She turned on her heel and Clare stepped up into the hall, then into the room to the right. A room which had a very clear view all the way round the quayside and right down the inlet. There was a telescope on the windowsill, she noted. A telescope through which Clement could easily keep an eye on everything that happened in his little kingdom.

And there, sitting behind a desk piled high with books and papers, sat her brother. Who nodded at his dragon of a housekeeper, dismissing her.

'Clement,' said Clare, stepping into the room. 'I do hope—'

He held up his hand to silence her. 'Before you go any further, Clare, let me just inform you that there is no need to beg for my forgiveness,' he said graciously. 'It would not be Christian of me to withhold it.'

'Well, thank you, Clement,' she said, lowering her head as though concentrating on tugging off her gloves while she strove to keep her temper reined in. How did Clement always manage to make it sound as if he thought she was very much in the wrong and didn't deserve his forgiveness, even as he was bestowing it? Besides which, was there anything more provoking than having someone assume he knew what you were about to say and making his answer before you'd even realised you'd been about to say exactly that?

'I know how annoyed you must have been when I didn't reach the employer you found for me,' she conceded, 'after all the trouble you went to, in order to secure my future,' she finished, quoting as far as she was able to recall, the exact words he'd used on her at Father's funeral.

'Oh, I soon found another girl, a girl who was *genuinely* grateful for the chance to better herself, by doing honest work. The cities of England are full of the unfortunate wretches.'

'Yes, I'm sure they are, but—'

'And I was not annoyed with you. I was disappointed. Very disappointed,' he added with a doleful shake of his head.

'Yes, me, too...' If only she'd been able to control her wretched temper. But no amount of scolding or preaching from either Father or any of her brothers, or forming resolutions to do better, had ever had any effect.

'I simply cannot understand how you managed to fall into that man's clutches.'

'Clutches? I am not in his clutches. And as to how I came to marry him, I explained it all. In my letter.'

'Oh, this,' he said, pulling a sheet of paper from one of the piles on his desk. 'Yes, you say he planned to get up some sort of ceremony, to persuade you that you are married, but let me tell you—'

'No. We *are* married!'

The look in his eyes was full of sympathy. 'I am sure you believe that. I know that you would never succumb to his charms, the way so many other women have, unless you truly believed he had married you. But, Clare, don't you see? He knows that, too. Which is why he wants you to believe you are his wife, since it is the only way he could ever persuade you into his bed. But—'

Everything in her recoiled at Clement's foul suggestion. 'But nothing. We are married!'

'You are living in sin.'

'Clement, you are being ridiculous. Why ever do you think that my marriage is not legal?'

'There was no notice in the papers. Which shows

that this was a deliberate attempt to conceal his misdeed from the eyes of your family. If you had not written to inform me of the event, not one of us would have known of it.'

'That's... I... No, it isn't like that. Rawcliffe is the kind of man who simply doesn't care what people think.' And men of his rank rarely bothered to send notices of their marriage to the papers. They didn't think it was anyone else's business.

Clement gave a disapproving snort. 'Which we all know, to our cost.'

'Our cost? What do you mean? Honestly, Clement, I cannot think why you hold him in such dislike.'

'He may have been able to charm you into believing his smooth lies...'

Charm? The last thing Rawcliffe had been was charming, to begin with. And far from being smooth with her, at times he'd been brutally honest.

'...but I am a man of experience. I know his sort. I know that he would do anything, anything he can, to hurt and humiliate me.'

'You? What do you mean?' Why did Clement always assume everyone did things specifically to annoy him? When most of the time he never crossed her mind?

'To think that we used to be friends,' he said, with a shake of his head. 'When we were boys together. Until he found a class of people with whom he clearly felt he belonged. Young gentlemen with titles and money. He never had time for us after that.'

She was sure that couldn't be right. Oh, she knew Rawcliffe hadn't wanted much to do with her brothers from about the time he went away to school, but it wasn't anything to do with their rank or wealth. Why, Mr Kellet had been as poor as the proverbial church mouse and Captain Bretherton was merely a half-pay officer in the navy. But even though she opened her mouth to point out the flaw in Clement's logic, he just kept right on ranting.

'And he took to whoring and drinking. Not the sort of person Father wished us to associate with. His betrayal of his childhood playmates was thus twofold. He left us all behind without even a backward glance. That is the sort of man who has duped you into a semblance of a marriage. A man without conscience, without honour, or loyalty.'

'Well, first of all—' He did have a conscience, or he would never have made an honest woman of her.

And secondly, he was loyal. So loyal that he'd even given one of those friends he'd made at school a job so that he could continue with his experiments in peace, without feeling as though he was accepting charity. Everyone in Watling Minor knew it, too.

Though Clement had been furious, now she came to think of it, that Rawcliffe had made a school friend his chaplain, when he felt *he* ought to have been given the post.

Not that Clement gave her a chance to express a single one of her objections. 'No, Clare,' he said, holding up his hand to silence her the way their father had so often done when any of them had a view he hadn't wished to hear. 'You must listen to my warnings.'

Which was true. Just like their father, Clement was not going to let her get a word in edgeways until he'd said what he had to say.

She trod heavily to the chair by his desk and sat down, since she had no intention of remaining on her feet while he delivered his lecture. Father might have had the right to make her do so, but Clement was only her brother. Not even her oldest brother, come to that.

And what was more, now she was a married lady with a title, shouldn't he have got to *his* feet when she entered the room?

'I have not spoken out against Rawcliffe in the past,' Clement was saying, as Clare mentally chastised him for his bad manners, 'because I thought you had the sense to avoid such as he. A philanderer and a libertine,' he said with a curl to his lip. 'And a liar. Not only has he persuaded you that you are his lawful wife, rather than his…mistress,' he hissed the word, narrowing his eyes, 'but he has no doubt attempted to poison your mind against me.'

Far from doing any such thing, Rawcliffe had been careful never to mention him. But then she knew the two men hated each other. Why, she had no idea. It had started before Rawcliffe had appointed Mr Kellet, rather than Clement, as his chaplain, though that had certainly fanned the flames.

'No matter what he has told you, though, Clare, the fact that you have come here, to me proves that you have not yet lost complete control of your common sense. You need to hear the truth from my own lips, is that not so?'

She wouldn't mind learning why the two hated each other so much, actually. So, with a bit of a shrug, she nodded her head.

Clement's eyes gleamed with triumph.

'Good girl.'

Since she was neither particularly good, and well past the age when anyone could consider her to be a girl, she ground her teeth.

'I dare say he has told you I am embroiled in crimina

activities. That I have become, in spite of my calling, some kind of kingpin in all sorts of nefarious schemes.'

Rawcliffe had never said any such thing. Why on earth did Clement assume he had?

Oh, dear...

'You don't believe it, do you? You surely cannot believe that your own brother, brought up in the sacred sphere of a family given to the service of God, could possibly stoop to the things of which he accuses me?'

Clare got a sinking feeling. It was the bag of puppies all over again. He'd used almost the exact same words to deny having anything to do with it when she'd burst into the house, dripping wet, holding that gruesome bundle in her arms. And he'd said them in the exact same tone of voice he was using on her now. He'd sounded so convincing, that day, that, had she not seen him, with her own eyes, tossing the bag off the bridge into the pond, she would have believed him.

She clenched her fists. The fact that he was denying something, so vehemently, was the clearest sign she could possibly have that it was exactly what he *was* doing.

'He is the villain of the piece, Clare, not I.'

She hadn't been looking for a villain. She'd come here to try to apologise for embarrassing him in regard to the position she was supposed to have taken with that elderly invalid. To express her hope that the lady had found another, more suitable companion— because frankly she didn't think she had been right for that kind of job at all.

But now, with all his talk of villains and philandering, and lying, she couldn't help wondering why Rawcliffe had really brought her here.

From what Clement was saying, he must believe her

brother was up to no good. Which wouldn't surprise her. Not one bit.

She gazed across the desk at Clement with sadness and a sort of sick, disappointed feeling. At both of them. Clement for being up to his neck in some sort of mischief, by the sound of it. And Rawcliffe for not warning her about his suspicions. What had he thought she'd do if he'd told her? She got a fleeting image of her shying all the breakables at his head on their wedding night. And her spirit sank still further.

'Ah,' said Clement, leaning back in his chair with a look of mock concern. 'I see that you are starting to believe me, at last. The scales are falling from your eyes.'

They certainly were. But not in the way he thought.

'Look…' She squirmed in her chair. What kind of man could sit there, lying to his own sister so brazenly? As though she was some kind of idiot, who would swallow whatever he said. Although Rawcliffe hadn't been exactly honest with her, either, had he?

'You need not be afraid,' he said with that sickly smile he wielded whenever he was trying to convince her he was full of brotherly love. The one he'd worn when he'd told her he'd taken care of her future and pressed a letter of introduction and a ticket on the stage into her hands.

'I can help you to escape his clutches. I can make you disappear so completely that he will never be able to find you. Should he bother to look, that is,' he finished on a nasty laugh.

She shook her head. 'Whatever do you mean?'

He looked down his nose at her. 'What can you possibly think I mean?'

'I don't know,' she cried. 'You are not making any sense.'

'That is because he has completely addled your brains with all his smooth talk,' he sneered. 'By now, I suppose you even think you are *in love* with him.'

'I... I...' Well, that was the first thing Clement had said that was completely true. She did love Rawcliffe. She couldn't help it. Even though he didn't trust her enough to share his suspicions about Clement with her, let alone love her back.

Something must have shown in her face, because Clement got up and came round the desk, his face creased into a careful expression of unctuous sympathy.

'You poor girl. I should reprimand you, for being so foolish, but I know how cunning he is. He caught you when you were at your lowest, did he not? When you were alone and far from home, and probably fearing the change in your circumstances. He made you think you would be safe with him, didn't he? That you would always wear fine clothes, and jewels.'

She couldn't help wincing at just how inaccurate that statement was. Far from catching her at a weak moment, she'd punched Rawcliffe. And the only time he'd threatened her with jewels of any kind, it had been by way of an insult.

And because that argument had taken place in her bedroom, when she was naked, and because it surged to the front of her memory in vivid detail, she found herself blushing and lowering her head, completely unable to look her brother in the eye.

He took her embarrassment as a sign he'd hit the nail on the head, though, apparently, because he took her hand in his and gave it a brotherly pat.

'There, there. No need to take on so. You are here now. And here you may stay.'

'What?' Her head flew up, in shock.

'You don't think I will leave you in his power, do you?'

She withdrew her hand, and got to her feet. Since she and Clement were of a similar height, she was able to look him straight in the eye.

'I am not leaving him. How can you even suggest it? He is my husband!'

Clement shook his head.

'Dear me, he really does have you completely fooled, does he not? Well,' he added with a shrug, 'at least I have done my duty. I have warned you how things stand.'

'I don't…' She pressed her hands to her temple as he stalked back to the other side of his desk. She couldn't understand why Clement kept insisting that the marriage was a fake, that she ought to leave Rawcliffe. Why was it so important to him to separate them?

'You find it hard to believe in such villainy, even when it is staring you in the face, don't you, Clare? It is something I have often observed in gently reared females. You simply cannot see what is going on, right under your noses. However,' he went on, when she took a breath to object to his latest insult, 'I am still willing to provide you with a sanctuary, when the time comes.'

'The time?'

'When he reveals his true colours. What you must do is always keep enough money about your person for you to flee him, at a moment's notice.'

She let out a wild, strangled laugh. 'Clement, you cannot be serious.'

'Oh, I am,' he said, leaning both hands on the desk and jutting his head forward, as if to demonstrate how serious he was. 'Deadly serious.'

'But—'

'And if you cannot escape him, for any reason, you may write to me and I shall arrange for you to obtain your freedom.'

'Write to you? You don't suppose that if he is such an ogre,' she pointed out, 'he will permit me to write to you, do you?'

'He hasn't done so to date, has he?,' he pointed out. 'The only letter you wrote to me was not franked by him, but by some other person.'

Ah, yes. She'd sent her hastily scrawled explanation of why she hadn't reached her employer's house from Lady Harriet's home, the day before her wedding. And Lady Harriet had handed it to her father to frank, along with all the rest of the post.

'Could you employ the same methods to communicate with me, should you find the need to do so?'

'I hardly think it will be necessary…'

'No, I can see you do not. But should it become…of dire importance to get in touch with me, without your husband knowing of it, you can always send letters to Lady Buntingford, in Lesser Peeving. So that nobody will suspect you are communicating with me, rather than a female friend of yours.'

'Lady Buntingford?' Why did that name sound familiar?

'Yes. And you need not be afraid she will read it herself. Her eyes are…not what they used to be,' he said with a strange smile. 'Which is why I deal with all her correspondence, these days. As I am her…trusted spiritual advisor.'

She must be all about in the head, then. For nobody with an ounce of sense would trust Clement, with either spiritual or any other sort of matter.

But then he'd just told her that gently reared ladies could rarely see what was under their noses, hadn't he?

He was just taking a breath to say something else she probably didn't want to hear when there was a knock at the door and his housekeeper came in.

'Message from the harbour,' she said, without waiting for permission to speak. 'Tide's turning and that boat needs to leave, else it'll be stranded here.'

Clement frowned. Glanced at her. At the door.

Through which she suddenly felt the strongest compulsion to run. To run and not stop running until she was on the boat, in Rawcliffe's arms and sailing safely away.

And yet to do anything of the sort would be to alert him to the fact she now knew he was up to no good.

She swallowed.

'I suppose,' she said, pushing herself to her feet as slowly as she could, considering the fact that something was telling her she needed to get out of there while she still could, 'I had better go.'

'There is no need,' said Clement, leaning back as though it was of no great importance to him either way. Only, he was tapping his forefinger on the arm of his chair, a sure sign he was nowhere near as calm as he looked.

'No...but...' She gave what she hoped was a resigned shrug.

'You know how I feel about you consorting with that man. But since you clearly believe you are married to him—'

'Yes,' she said, seizing on the excuse he'd handed her. 'I made vows in church and—'

'Say no more.' He flicked his hand in a contemptuous gesture of dismissal. 'Just know that when you have repented of living as his whore, I shall be here to help you. Even should you find yourself with child...' His gaze flicked to her belly.

She laid a hand over it, in an instinctively defensive manner. Help her? He didn't want to *help* her. Or any child she might have. He wanted to...destroy her marriage, by the looks of it.

She stumbled to the door and out onto the cobbled street, putting up her hand to shield her eyes from the bright sunshine. And as she did so, it struck her that though the sunlight was half-blinding her, it wasn't anywhere near strong enough to warm the coldness that was making her innards clench.

She'd only gone a few paces before she started to shiver. And her legs felt so unsteady that she wasn't sure they'd carry her as far as the harbour. Though they had to. They had to.

Because if they didn't, if she collapsed on the street and one of Clement's...*gang* picked her up...they'd carry her back to him.

And she'd never see Rawcliffe again.

She just knew it.

Chapter Twenty-Four

Clare drew on every scrap of control she could muster, stuck out her chin and made herself walk down the hill at a decorous pace. And when she reached the quay-side, she allowed the captain to hand her into the boat, stepped carefully over to the cushions upon which Rawcliffe was lolling, his hat pulled over his eyes, sat down next to him and folded her hands in her lap.

He eyed her from under the rim of his hat with the cold expression he always adopted when trying to conceal what he was feeling. For once, it filled her with admiration. She'd never realised, until just now, how hard it was to prevent anyone knowing what you felt, or thought. And it was jolly hard work.

'Enjoy your visit with your brother?'

'Not really. And I am sorry, since you went to so much trouble to arrange it, but—' she spread her hands in a gesture of exasperation '—that is Clement for you.'

'What it Clement, exactly?'

'Impossible! He—' She broke off, glancing at the captain and his lad.

'They cannot hear us,' said Rawcliffe, sitting up and setting his hat to the correct angle. 'Besides which they are too busy concentrating on steering this craft out of the cove, without running on to any of the hidden rocks which present such a danger to the unwary.'

'Really.' He had clearly spent his time, while she had been enduring that painful interview with her brother, chatting with the crew about the nature of the cove.

'Yes. Besides—'

'*Another* besides?'

'Yes,' he said firmly. 'I need to know what he said to upset you so.'

She ground her teeth. Where to begin?

'Well, to start with, he tried to have me doubt the legality of our marriage.'

Rawcliffe stiffened. But before he could say anything, she carried on. 'Which is perfectly absurd. Because if you have made me go through some kind of bogus ceremony, then so have Lord Becconsall and Lady Harriet, who stood up before the same officiant in the same church. And the prospect of him tricking Lady Harriet is…ridiculous.'

'But not the thought I tricked you?' He spoke with such coldness that if she hadn't been so furious she might have tried to appease him. But her blood was up.

'Don't be absurd. The chances of a spate of fake marriages breaking out amongst the ranks of the *ton* is so unlikely it is laughable! Why would you all suddenly decide you want to live in sin, unless it is so that you can get rid of your wives at some later date, without having the bother of pushing a bill of divorce through Parliament?'

'Why indeed?'

'Exactly! And then, for him to suggest I stay with him, instead of returning to you, to avoid the shame of living in sin, as he put it…'

'Now that I would not have permitted,' he growled. 'You *are* my wife. And I would never let you go.'

And then, to cap all the shocks she'd received so far today, he took her by the scruff of the neck and kissed her. Rather savagely.

When he finally let her come up for air, she could do nothing but gulp and stare at him. And then raise her hand to her bonnet, at which the wind was whipping, because they'd emerged from the close confines of the cove and were now out at sea once more.

'Why are you looking at me like that?' he sneered. 'Did your estimable brother not warn you that I am a rake? Not safe to be alone with? Completely without morals?'

'More or less, yes,' she admitted.

'And yet you came back to me,' he said coldly.

'Well, of course I did,' she said, swatting his arm. 'Apart from the fact you are my husband, not a word of it is true.'

'You don't believe I am a rake? A libertine?'

'No. Or you wouldn't have bothered to even *pretend* to marry me. Besides, there was a huge great flaw in his argument. And I've just realised what it is.' She turned to him, her heart pounding with a sense of satisfaction in at last being able to put her finger on what it was about Clement's standpoint that hadn't added up. 'Why on earth would you *pretend* to marry me *and* try to prevent me from escaping? I mean, surely the whole point of arranging a fake ceremony is so that you can dispose of your unwanted bride when you grow bored? And also, why would you try to prevent me from writing to him, let alone fleeing to him if *I* wanted to end it? You would just wash your hands of me and think *good rid-*

dance, wouldn't you?' She shook her head. 'Sometimes I think Clement must be touched in the upper works.'

'You are a remarkable woman.'

'What?'

He ran the tip of one finger along the curve of her jaw. 'Remarkable, I said. And I mean it. To have been able to deduce so much, while you are clearly rattled by the way Clement spoke to you, is remarkable.'

'I cannot really take much credit,' she said, blushing under the intensity of his gaze. As well as struggling with the urge to lean into his one-fingered caress like a cat. 'He went on and on about how much you hated him and what dreadful things you must have been saying about him, when you hadn't said anything of the sort. Why, in spite of disliking him, you were even prepared to offer him a sort of olive branch, weren't you, by bringing me on this visit?'

His expression closed up.

'What dreadful things did he think I had been saying?'

'Oh, a lot of nonsense about being the kingpin of some criminal gang, or something of the sort. Honestly, it was all so ludicrous I hardly remember the half of it. Though the way those fishermen on the quayside behaved, it wouldn't be surprising if everyone did think he was up to no good.'

'Hmm?'

'Yes, you know. The way they all seemed to wait for his permission to so much as breathe. And that, coupled with the way he always did make up to the worst bullies in any area, and then compel them to respect him, or even follow him like as not, well…' She finished on a shrug. 'I know he only does it to make himself feel bigger. Or more powerful, or something.' She finished on a sigh. 'Oh, there is no point in dwelling on it. He and I are…well, now that I am married to you…' She darted a glance up at his stern profile.

He did not look back at her, but kept his gaze fixed intently out to sea.

'Would you mind very much,' she said boldly, 'if I asked you a few questions?'

He sighed, as if he thought she was being tiresome. 'What sort of questions?,' he said in a tone designed to warn her that he had the greatest reluctance to answer to her or anyone.

'Well, to start with, I'd like to hear your version of how you came to fall out with Clement…and actually now I come to think of it, my other brothers, too.'

'It wasn't a falling-out,' he said, turning his face, at last, to look at her. 'It was more a realisation that they were not the sort of boys with whom I wished to spend my time.'

That was more or less what Clement had said. Only he'd made it sound as if Rawcliffe had become very high in the instep once he'd gone away to school. Which was the thing about Clement's lies. There was always just a grain of truth embedded in them somewhere, that misled you into believing the rest of what he was dishing up along with it.

'In what way, precisely?'

'Precisely?' He raised one eyebrow at her to convey his displeasure. But then, after searching her face for a moment or two, he appeared to relent. 'I discovered that I would rather keep company with boys who resisted bullies and used their intelligence to try to improve the lot of others.'

By placing a slight emphasis on the words *resist*ed and *improve*, he'd just implied that her brothers preferred being bullies and tormenting those weaker or less intelligent than themselves.

She lowered her head and stared at her linked fingers for a second or two. There was no arguing with that. All the males in her family were of a despotic disposition. Even her father used to attempt to terrorise his congregation from the pulpit with threats of hellfire.

'No wonder you didn't mind practically being forbidden to set foot on shore,' she said with a rather desperate little laugh. Because she felt, and not for the first time, acutely embarrassed at being related to Clement. 'In fact, you probably preferred waiting in the boat, if it meant you didn't have to come face-to-face with Clement.'

'I did,' he said. 'Especially since the picnic Pierre provided was of such a high standard.'

'Oh, please tell me there is some left,' she said, placing one hand on her stomach which, she suddenly discovered, felt completely hollow.

He put his foot on the hamper, preventing her from checking inside. And gave her one of those looks, with his lids half-lowered, that always put her in mind of bedroom activities.

'Will you be very angry with me if I confess to being selfish enough to have devoured it all?'

'What?' Why would he say anything of the sort? Pierre would have prepared enough to feed not only Rawcliffe and herself, but also the crew of the ketch, like as not. And why was he looking at her in that particular manner? As though he was...flirting with her.

As though she was one of the women he'd pursued because he found them so irresistible, rather than the sister of a man he detested, who'd just been pestering him with a series of questions he'd clearly found impertinent.

And why start doing so now? How typical!

How vexing!

She'd always stopped him in his tracks whenever it had looked as though he'd been thinking of flirting with her, in the past. So that now she was actually of a mind to encourage him, she had no idea how to go about it.

'I... I...' She blushed and lowered her head.

'Would you like me to make a few suggestions,' he said, sliding closer and looping one arm about her waist, 'about how I could make it up to you?'

'Not while we are on this boat,' she said, going rigid within his hold. 'Not while those fishermen can overhear anything you might suggest.'

'When, then?' He nuzzled the word into her ear. 'When we land?'

That was almost as bad. Because she didn't need him to make any suggestions whatsoever. Her own imagination was supplying plenty of forfeits she would dearly love him to pay. Which made her blush all over and shake her head.

'Well, how about tonight, then?' he said, running his tongue round the outer edge of her ear. Which made her bones feel as if they were dissolving. If he hadn't still got his arm round her waist, she was sure she'd melt off the bench and all that would be left of her would be a puddle on the deck.

Thankfully, at that point, her stomach rumbled.

'Never mind what you mean to do later,' she said, lunging forward and pushing his foot off the hamper. 'As you can tell, all I can think about right now is having something to eat.' She flipped open the latch securing the lid. 'And drink. Because, do you know, Clement didn't even have the manners to offer me a cup of tea.'

'The true sign of a villain,' said Rawcliffe with a slight smile playing about his lips.

'Whereas you,' she said, finally flinging up the lid of the hamper, to find it still contained plenty of delicacies, 'are the perfect gentleman. At least, you would be perfect if you didn't try to make me believe you would actually eat an entire hamper full of food and not leave a single bite for me.'

She threw him a smile over her shoulder as she rummaged for a glass into which to pour herself a drink. And caught him looking at her bottom. In a lascivious manner.

'Perfect, eh?' He ran his gaze the length of her spine, finishing by skewering her with a look of such heat her mouth ran dry.

'Perhaps,' she said, dropping the lid of the hamper, wriggling backwards and putting herself within the circle of his arms once again, 'I was mistaken.'

'Mistaken? You? Surely not.'

'See? A *perfect* gentleman would never imply that I always think I'm right.'

'He wouldn't dare.'

'Why, you—'

She raised her fists to give him a playful punch. But she never got the chance. In one slick move, he had pinioned her arms to her sides.

And brought the conversation to an end, the way he so very often did.

By kissing her.

Chapter Twenty-Five

Thank the Lord, Cottam was such a sanctimonious little weasel. Because, by comparison, Rawcliffe appeared to Clare like a perfect gentleman.

And thank God—again—for her temper, which had propelled her away from her brother, fizzing with indignation, and right back into his arms.

He'd feared her anger would be aimed at him. Had spent the entire time she was ashore bracing himself for the confrontation which would put an end to such moments as this, filled with teasing, and hugs, and laughter.

But it sounded as if Cottam had completely mismanaged her.

Well, he wasn't about to make the same error. He was going to devote the rest of the day to keeping her off balance, to taking her mind off her brother's behaviour and directing it where he wanted it.

It wasn't going to be all that difficult. Her shy, flustered response to his gentle teasing betrayed her lack of experience in the game. Whilst also showing her eagerness to learn. So he reached for the picnic hamper and started selecting choice morsels to pop into her mouth.

Kissed the juice of peaches from her lips. Showered her, for the entire remainder of the boat ride, with compliments that were so outrageous she protested with giggles and blushes.

After they disembarked they walked back to the house arm in arm. He noted with satisfaction that her eyes, which had been so stormy when she'd left Peeving Cove, now sparkled.

Ponsonby opened the door when they were still a few yards from their cottage, and bowed them into the house. Clare put her hand to her bonnet.

'I suppose I had better go and tidy myself up. I must look a perfect fright.'

'You look adorable,' he said, kissing her fingers, rather than her nose as he'd have preferred to do, out of deference to her shyness around the servants. 'You always do.'

'Even when I'm waist-deep in muddy water, with pond weed all over my face?' She laughed up at him, though there was a trace of uncertainty in her lovely golden eyes.

'Especially then.' His mind flew back to the way he'd felt at that moment and, as he handed his hat and gloves to Ponsonby, he experienced an overwhelming urge to share it with her. 'That was the moment,' he said, turning back to her and taking hold of her hands again, 'when I fell in love with you.' And then, on a wave of panic, he added, 'In a boyish fashion.'

She blushed and flicked a nervous glance at Ponsonby.

'No, really, you couldn't have…'

And there it was. Doubt in her own ability to inspire love. How glad he was that he hadn't succumbed to the temptation to tell her he loved her now. She wouldn't have believed him. He would have to convince her she was worthy of love, before he risked using the words.

However long it took.

She had shaken her head, but she'd kept her gaze fixed intently upon him and appeared to be holding her breath.

'But I did,' he assured her. 'Because that was the moment I realised you were nothing like my mother. I looked at you and knew that I would never meet any woman more diametrically opposed to everything she stood for. Appearances didn't mean more to you than doing the right thing. Your own safety or dignity wasn't more important than trying to save anyone in trouble. And you were *sober*.' He squeezed her hand hard for a moment, raised them to his lips one after the other, then let them go.

There, that should give her plenty to think about while she was getting changed for dinner. Hopefully, he'd surprised her enough that she'd want to dwell on what he'd confessed, rather than whatever poisonous notions Cottam had tried to infect her with.

'Run along and get changed, then,' he said. 'But don't take too long.'

'Why, are you hungry?'

'No,' he growled, leaning in close. 'But I don't want to spend more time away from you than is absolutely necessary.'

She lit up with pleasure, before turning and bounding up the stairs.

Ponsonby cleared his throat. 'A word, my lord, if it is convenient?'

He'd been wondering why Ponsonby hadn't melted discreetly away the moment he'd started making verbal love to his wife. So he went into the little sitting room, with Ponsonby on his heels.

'It concerns Kendall,' said the butler, after carefully closing the door.

'The footman?'

Ponsonby nodded. 'I arranged for all the staff to enjoy some extra leisure hours, in accordance with her ladyship's wishes,' he said. 'Kendall appears to have made straight for a tavern down by the harbour where, he claims, he was befriended by two locals who plied him with drinks, and then, once they were convinced he was deeply under the influence, with questions. About your lordship. And her ladyship,' he finished, looking uneasy.

'I see.' It could just have been natural curiosity, but what if the locals plying his footman with drink were Cottam's minions? 'What did Kendall tell them?'

'Nothing of any importance. He was not as intoxicated as *that*. However, once the evening air cleared his brain, he became a touch concerned about whether he ought to return to that tavern. Or any other.'

'I see...' he said again. He turned to look out of the window while he considered both what Ponsonby had said and what he'd left out. Which was that this Kendall was conscientious enough to repeat what many footmen would have attempted to conceal. And appeared to be able to keep a clear head even when everyone else thought he should be drunk enough to become indiscreet.

Which could come in handy.

'I see no reason,' he said, turning back to Ponsonby, 'to curtail his enjoyment of the local amenities. Providing, of course, that he is able to carry out his duties when needed.'

'Thank you, my lord. I was unwilling to turn him off whilst we are so far from London...'

Rawcliffe raised one eyebrow. It was unlike Ponsonby to talk about the way he governed the staff, or to bring such concerns to him. Did this sudden outburst of familiarity stem from the fact that they were in a holiday resort? Or was this Clare's influence? He'd already noted that his staff all believed they owed their increased leisure time to her, rather than to him.

Ponsonby took the hint and left the room. Leaving Rawcliffe free to go upstairs and change for dinner. Over which he renewed his sensuous assault on Clare, turning the eating of food and the drinking of wine into a protracted form of foreplay, so that by the time they went upstairs Clare was as impatient as he was to get to the main course.

He just about had the finesse to get her to the bed before ravishing her for the first time, unlike the previous night.

When they'd finished, she kept her arms and legs round him, as though she couldn't bear to let him go.

'Stay with me again tonight,' she whispered. 'I... That is...'

He stopped her mouth with a kiss. There was nothing he wanted more than to hold her in his arms all night, telling her, and showing her, how much she meant to him.

But his conscience kept him silent. Reminded him he'd just spent all day manipulating her and using her, and withholding a great deal of information from her.

Somehow it didn't feel right to say he still loved her, had never stopped loving her, while he was deliberately keeping her in the dark about...so many things. Far better to show her. Didn't they say that actions spoke louder than words? If he worshipped her body, the way he'd vowed to do in church, stayed faithful, cherished her, eventually, there would come a time when he'd be able to tell her what was in his heart, with some chance of her believing him.

So he nipped at her ear lobe. 'You know what it will entail, don't you? Inviting me to stay in your bed is inviting me to…' He ground his pelvis against hers, just in case she hadn't got the message.

She nodded. 'I know. You told me you have a big… appetite. And that is fine.'

No, it wasn't! He'd deliberately made her think he had an immense appetite for the act itself. Whereas it was his appetite for *her* that was damn near insatiable. He slid off her to lie at her side.

'I wouldn't want you to feel used,' he ground out.

She rolled to face him and looped her arms round his neck. 'If you are using me, then I am using you right back.'

'Oh?'

'Yes. Because I need someone to hold me. Someone to make me feel…after today when Clement…'

He pressed one finger to her lips. 'I don't wish to hear his name, Clare. Not while we are in bed together, at least.'

'Sorry,' she said, giving him a hug. And resting her head on his chest with a sigh.

He stroked her hair until, after only a few moments, she fell asleep. In his arms. Though his guilty conscience would not grant him the same luxury. How was he ever going to get her to trust him, with the whole situation with Cottam lying between them? He ground his teeth, wondering how the hell Damocles ever got any sleep, with that ruddy great sword hanging over his head. He probably lay looking up at what was hanging over him, rather than down at the woman in his arms, but still...

The smile she gave him on waking the next morning did not make him feel glad to be winning her trust. Instead, it cut him to the quick. So did the ones she kept on darting him over the breakfast table.

Eventually, he couldn't take anymore.

'Much as I would love to spend another day entirely in your company,' he said, screwing up his napkin and setting it aside, 'Slater will be foaming at the mouth if I do not keep up to date with business matters.'

Her face fell. But she swiftly rallied. 'Of course,' she said brightly. Like the dutiful wife she was determined to be.

'I will be going to the cottage next door,' he told her. 'Slater has fitted out one of the rooms as a functioning study for me.'

'It's a great pity you have to work so hard on such a lovely day,' she said, her gaze turned in the direction of the window and the sea beyond it.

'There is no need for you to stay indoors.' Unless Cottam, or his henchmen, had some mischief planned. 'Though you must take Kendall with you if you do go out.'

'Kendall? Not...Nancy?'

Definitely not Nancy. Nancy would be no use in a fight. Whereas Kendall was over six feet tall and built of solid muscle.

'Kendall will be better able to keep up with you than Nancy, I should think. She does not strike me as the kind of female who would enjoy hiking across the moors should you take it into your head to do so. Nor be prepared to go scrambling over seaweed-strewn rocks if the beach is your destination.'

She smiled. Again. 'You are right.'

What? She wasn't going to kick up a fuss about having a guard?

'He can carry any purchases I might make if I go into town, or any other equipment I might decide to take with me.'

'Equipment?'

'Yes, you know, a blanket so that I can sit down without getting grass stains on my skirts, a small picnic, perhaps, if I walk a long way and get hungry.'

If she was going to have a picnic outside, he should be the man to share it with her, not his footman.

And if she intended to take a blanket with her, he could put it to far better use than merely using it to prevent grass stains.

Nevertheless, he couldn't alter the plans he'd announced, not right away. He would look weak and indecisive.

And there *would* be piles of correspondence awaiting his attention.

Ponsonby cleared his throat. 'Though the sun is shining, I have it on good authority that the wind has a sharp bite today. You might wish to take a warm shawl out with you, as well, my lady.'

'And a parasol,' she said, with a mischievous glint in her eyes. 'To protect my complexion. Yes, it is a good job you have already suggested I take Kendall with me. It is amazing how much more equipment I need to take out with me, now that I am a marchioness, than I used to need when I was merely Miss Cottam.'

If that was the extent of the fuss she was going to

make, he could let it pass. He didn't want to play the heavy with her.

He wanted…

No. He'd already decided how he was going to spend his day. He got to his feet and strode to the door.

Before he weakened and changed his mind.

Chapter Twenty-Six

Clare went upstairs to fetch the requisite pelisse, bonnet, parasol, gloves and shawl with a little smile playing round her lips. It was rather lovely being married to Rawcliffe. And not, she thought as she walked past the bed, just because of *that*. It was the way he, and all his servants, treated her. Reminding her to take a shawl in case there was a cold breeze and a parasol to protect her complexion, and a footman in case she took it into her head to purchase something that weighed more than half an ounce.

As though she mattered.

She picked up her bonnet and set it on her head, then went to the mirror to make sure her hair was all tucked up out of the way. It was a troubled face that looked back at her. For thinking about her hair escaping had led her mind straight back to her encounter with Clement the day before. He hadn't even invited her to take a seat, let alone offer her a cup of tea. He hadn't asked after her health, or if she was happy, but had just launched into a tirade. To him, she was still just the pesky little sister.

She lifted her eyes to the sun shining in through the window and the sea sparkling in the distance. She wasn't going to let thoughts of Clement creep in and spoil her day. She was at the seaside, for the first time in her life—and, come to think of it, Clement could have invited her to stay with him for a short time, since he lived by the sea, while she came to terms with losing her father and her home, but, no, he'd…

She pulled herself up short. She *was* at the seaside. Thanks to Rawcliffe. And he had given her leave to go out and do whatever she wished, provided she took a footman with her. A smile tugged at her lips again as she tied the ribbons of her bonnet into a secure knot. She wouldn't be a bit surprised if Rawcliffe had really wanted her to take a footman with her, in case she got into some sort of scrape. Now that she belonged to him, he wasn't going to leave her to deal with the consequences of her impulsive behaviour on her own. Though he'd been too diplomatic to actually say he didn't trust her out of his sight. Probably with an eye to the safety of the breakfast pots.

All the while she'd been tucking up stray strands of hair under her elegant little black silk bonnet, and comparing Rawcliffe's thoughtful protectiveness with Clement's self-centred attitude, she'd been aware of a bit of a commotion downstairs. Someone had come to the door, which had resulted in lots of running feet in the lane at the back of the house which linked all three of their holiday cottages. But now she heard Nancy's distinctive tread on the stair.

Nancy barely scarcely paused to knock on the bedroom door before poking her head round it.

'You have a visitor, my lady. At least…' Her face crinkled in thought. 'At least, she came with a message for his lordship. But she don't seem like the kind of lady who is just a messenger to me. So I've put her in the sitting room and ordered tea.'

Which meant Clare was going to have to receive her, or whoever it was would take it as a snub. Clare took one last look out of window and sighed. There would be plenty of day left to enjoy the delights of the seaside after dispensing hospitality to the person Nancy had deemed worthy of the sitting room.

'I shall come down,' said Clare, removing her bonnet. 'I just need a minute to take off my coat and so on.'

Nancy whisked off to inform the visitor straight away. Clare wasn't all that far behind her.

Today it was the footman, Kendall, who was standing in the hall, waiting to open the door for her. Ponsonby must be performing that office for Rawcliffe, in the neighbouring cottage.

She gave Kendall a little smile as they went through the pantomime of sidling round each other as he opened the door, which she could far more easily have done for herself. A smile which slipped when she smelled the unmistakable whiff of alcohol on his breath.

So she entered the room with a frown on her face, as she wondered whether she was going to have to have a word with Ponsonby about the footman's drinking. Surely, it wasn't acceptable for him to be performing his duties reeking of the tavern?

Or, worse, was that why Rawcliffe had practically insisted she take the footman out with her today? Because he needed to clear his head? Or he didn't have enough to do down here and needed to be kept from the lure of the taverns?

Her eyes lit on her visitor, a tall girl who was sitting on one of the fireside chairs, twisting the strings of a very large and lumpy reticule between gloved fingers.

She leapt to her feet, as though in alarm. And only just avoided striking her forehead on one of the beams supporting the ceiling. And then as she dropped into an awkward curtsy, the tip of one flailing elbow caught a spray of roses that somebody had put into a jug on a side table. There might have been no harm done if the girl had just left it, but instead, she whirled round to try to steady the flower arrangement. And succeeded only in knocking the whole lot, jug and all, into the hearth with an almighty crashing of breaking pottery and splashing of water, and sizzle of burning roses as a few of them landed on the embers.

'Oh, no!' The girl dropped to her knees by the fire and began plucking smouldering roses from the grate, scattering them over the hearthrug in the process.

Clare got the horrid feeling that if she didn't stop her visitor, the girl would end up setting the cottage on fire in her frantic efforts to undo the minimal damage she'd already caused.

'Kendall!' Better to summon a drunken footman than attempting to deal with such a large and highly strung visitor on her own.

Kendall flung open the door, sized up the situation in a heartbeat and strode into the room.

'Excuse me, miss,' he said, taking the girl by the elbows and lifting her aside as though she weighed no more than a feather pillow.

'I'm so sorry,' said the girl, peeping round Kendall's shoulder as he began stamping out the parts of the hearthrug that had begun smouldering. 'Things of this sort are always happening to me. I'm so clumsy. I am sure you wish me at Jericho. I… It was good of you to receive me, but considering the…' she waved at the charred hearthrug and the fragments of broken pottery, causing Kendall to duck as her reticule whooshed past his head '...I had better go.'

'No, please,' said Clare, as the girl made for the door. 'The hearth rug is of no consequence. At least, I suppose we will have to pay for the damage, since it is a rented house...' She quirked an eyebrow at Kendall.

'Mr Slater will see to it, my lady. And I shall have this cleaned up in a trice.'

'There, you see?' Her heart went out to the poor girl, who was wringing her hands and looking utterly woebegone. 'And it doesn't matter that the fire has gone out, either. It is a lovely day outside and I'm sure I have no idea why anyone thought it necessary to light it in the first place. Kendall will take no time to put all to rights and then we shall have some tea.'

'Oh, no, really, I only came on behalf of my grandfather, who wanted to speak with Lord Rawcliffe. Only then curiosity got the better of me. I... I have always wanted to see inside these little cottages, you see,' she finished apologetically. 'They look so quaint.'

'Yes, they are quaint,' she said above Kendall's bent back, as he deftly rolled up the charred hearth rug round the remains of the roses and fragments of pottery. 'Though charming. But you must tell me your name, you know.'

'Oh! Oh, of course. Yes, it's Miss Hutton, my lady,' she said, blushing and dropping into another equally inelegant curtsy. And knocking Kendall, who'd been on the point of getting to his feet, back to his hands and knees again.

'Oh, I am so sorry,' she said, holding out her hand as though intending to help the hapless footman to his feet.

'Think nothing of it, miss,' said Kendall, backing hastily away, the hearth rug clutched to his chest. 'I shall…just take the worst of the…that is… I shall take this lot to the kitchen and send Maggie in with the tea tray,' he babbled, backing away to the door.

'Oh, dear,' said the lanky girl, watching his hasty departure. 'I have scared him off. I have a tendency to do that to men,' she said wistfully. 'And as for tea,' she said, turning to Clare with a sad little smile, 'you had probably better not invite me to stay. I shall probably only spill it. Or worse.'

'I am sure you will not,' said Clare, her disappointment at missing a walk vanishing when weighed against the importance of comforting the lanky, awkward and utterly miserable young giantess. 'And if you do, what does it matter? It's not as if you can ruin the rug twice, is it? And whatever you do, don't worry about the footman. I probably shouldn't tell you this,' she said, going closer, and lowering her voice, 'but I have a suspicion that he drinks. I could smell it on his breath just now. So the fact that he was a bit unsteady probably had nothing to do with you at all. Now, won't you please sit down?' Clare waved to the chair on which the girl had been perched when she first saw her.

'Thank you,' she said, subsiding morosely. 'But… actually, I cannot stay long. Grandfather will be furious with me if I keep him waiting once he's finished his business with your husband.' Her forehead pleated into two anxious furrows. 'Oh, I say, you are the Marchioness of Rawcliffe, are you not?'

'I suppose I am,' said Clare. 'Though you don't have to tell me I don't look much like anyone's idea of a marchioness.'

'Oh, no, I didn't mean…' Miss Hutton blushed.

'That's quite all right. I don't really feel like a marchioness, either. I am only a vicar's daughter, by birth, you see, not a grand lady.'

'Oh?'

'And you don't have to tell me all about the tyranny of elderly gentlemen, either. My own father was an absolute tartar.'

'I thought you said he was a vicar.'

'He was. But he was also very, very demanding. And in his last years I was the only person who could handle him.'

'Ah,' said Miss Hutton. 'Yes, it's rather like that with my grandfather. He has a tendency to lash out with his walking stick when his gout is playing him up.'

'Is his gout playing him up today?' If so, she wondered how he would deal with Rawcliffe, who would probably have resented receiving what sounded like a summons.

'No, fortunately. Or I would not have been able to escape even for half an hour. Oh,' she said, looking stricken. 'I did not mean that he…that is, that I…'

'You have no need to explain how it is. I know only too well how tempting it is to try to escape, if only for a few precious minutes, from the demands of an erratic and demanding elderly relative.'

'Yes, and then, you know, Grandfather was a colonel, as well. So he has a tendency to bark orders and expect everyone to leap to attention and salute.'

Clare had a vision of this gawky girl doing so and sweeping a whole shelf full of china ornaments to the ground in the process. And couldn't help smiling.

'You say you have always wanted to see inside these cottages? You live locally, then?'

'Well, off and on. We used to…my brother and I that is, we used to come and stay here when Papa was alive very often. But then when he died, we moved in with Grandfather permanently.' Her face fell. 'It wasn't so bad when I was little...or comparatively little, because he just treated me like a boy and I ran wild with my brother. But when I grew up—'

And up, and up, thought Clare.

'And Lady Buntingford said I ought to learn how to be a lady.' Her shoulders slumped.

'Lady Buntingford?' There was that name again. Why did everyone keep bringing her into everything lately?

'Yes, she is about the only other person, locally, Grandfather considers suitable company for us. Everyone else, he says, are yokels or mushrooms.'

Clare laughed. 'No wonder he was so keen to send for my husband and talk with him. It must feel like a rare treat to have a genuine marquess come down here for his holiday.'

'Oh, no, it isn't like that,' said Miss Hutton. 'Grandfather is the magistrate, you see. And dealt with the case of that poor young man who came down here on the pretext of visiting Lady Buntingford and drowned.'

That was it! It all came flooding back to her now. Lady Buntingford was some relative of Mr Kellet's, which was why he'd been the one to come down here and search her house for...missing jewels, wasn't it?

'He has been brooding over it ever since. And he was so pleased when he read your husband's name in the visitors' book at the Three Tuns. Because your husband was his employer. Did you...did you know him? I am sorry if you did. He was such a nice young man.'

Clare was sure she heard a kind of clattering noise as all sorts of things that had been puzzling her fell neatly into place.

Her husband's uncharacteristically meek agreement to sign that visitors' book at all, for one thing. She should have known he had an ulterior motive for doing so. And now she knew what it was. He'd wanted the local magistrate to know he was in the vicinity. He'd wanted to be able to discuss Mr Kellet's drowning without appearing to be actively investigating it. And what better way to advertise his presence than to sign the visitors' book in the establishment of the thrusting, ambitious Mr Jeavons?

That was the reason he'd chosen this resort to visit, out of all the places he could have taken her. His dislike for Clement was so intense she should have known he would not have come within a hundred miles. And as for telling her he wanted her to be able to mend fences… Her mind flew back to the way he'd settled himself in the boat, with his hat tipped over his eyes to ward off the sun. As though he hadn't a care in the world.

Because he hadn't really cared. Not about what was going to pass between Clement and her, anyway. Whatever reason he'd had for taking her to Peeving Cove, she was absolutely certain he'd never expected them to *mend fences*.

She came back to the room with a start, realising that the clattering noise was real. And that it wasn't the facts falling into place at all, but the rattle of the tea tray as Maggie set it on the table before her. And now Clare was going to have to play hostess, while her mind, and her heart, was in complete turmoil. And her hands were shaking.

She wasn't sure how she got through the rest of the half hour that Miss Hutton stayed. But the moment the girl had gone, she darted out of the house, as well.

She didn't even bother going up to her room to fetch her bonnet and shawl, let alone wait for Kendall to get ready.

She had to think. And she couldn't do it in the cramped little rooms, surrounded by Rawcliffe's servants. Loyal servants. There was only one place she could think of going. Only one place where she could be free to think.

Chapter Twenty-Seven

'The Colonel is in the reading room, my lord,' said Jeavons with an unctuous smile. 'If you would care to follow me?'

'I remember the way,' said Rawcliffe curtly. 'Though I should be grateful if you would make sure we are not disturbed.'

'Of course, my lord, of course,' said Jeavons, bowing several times in a way that put Rawcliffe in mind of a jack-in-the-box with a slack spring.

There was only one person in the reading room. An elderly man with bushy white eyebrows.

'Ah,' he barked, lowering his newspaper. 'You must be Rawcliffe, eh?'

'As you say,' said Rawcliffe.

'Didn't take you long to get here,' said the Colonel in an approving manner. 'Good, good. Cannot abide time wasters.'

'No more,' said Rawcliffe, taking a chair facing the old man, and folding his hands over the top of his cane, 'can I.'

'Want me to get on with it, eh? Tell you straight out why I wanted to speak to you.'

'Precisely so.'

'Well, it's about that young feller that drowned. Employee of yours, I believe.' He crooked one eyebrow by way of query.

'That is so.'

'Nasty business,' said the Colonel with a shake of his head. 'Very nasty.'

The hairs on the back of Rawcliffe's neck stood on end. 'In what way?'

'Well, feller came down here trying to pester Lady Buntingford, or so he said. Most put out, he was, that he had to put up here—'

'Here? In the Three Tuns?'

'Yes,' snapped the Colonel, lowering his eyebrows into a scowl at the interruption. 'That's what I said—'

'But why on earth would he stay here, when Lady Buntingford is his great-godmother?'

'Makes no difference who anyone claims to be. The old girl won't let anyone in to see her these days apart from my granddaughter, to read her the latest rubbishy novels that come into the circulating library, and the vicar, to give her communion.'

'Is that so?'

'Just said so, didn't I?' The Colonel took a deep breath, as though wrestling with his temper. 'Anyway, back to your chaplain, or whatever he was.'

'He was my chaplain,' said Rawcliffe, defensively.

'Be that as it may, he had no business throwing himself off the cliff under my watch!'

'I beg your pardon?'

'Don't hold with suicide,' said the Colonel with a scowl. 'Especially not over a woman. Can understand a man taking a pistol to his head if it is a matter of honour, or—'

'He did not commit suicide,' said Rawcliffe firmly.

'Hmmph,' grunted the Colonel. 'Well, of course, I didn't put that down in my report. Thought it would be too upsetting for the family. Wouldn't have been able to give him a decent burial. Slur on his memory and so forth. Did I do wrong? Jeavons seems to think so. And I would have thought he'd rather the place *didn't* get a reputation for accidental drownings, when he wants to make his fortune turning Peacombe into a fashionable watering hole. Not that anyone *could* bathe here anyway, couldn't get the bathing machines down that beach—'

Rawcliffe cut in. 'Would you mind telling me your reasons for suspecting it was a suicide, rather than an accident?'

'Well, what else was I to make of it? He comes down here, asking questions about his young lady, not six months after she threw *her*self off a cliff...'

'I beg your pardon? Young lady?'

'Yes. Dreadful business that. Breaking her heart the way he did. Wouldn't think he had it in him to seduce and abandon a woman to look at him, would you?'

'Definitely not.' Archie could barely string two sentences together at the best of times, unless it was something to do with science. The notion of him suddenly becoming eloquent enough to seduce a young woman, let alone behave so contrary to his gentle nature as to abandon her, was utterly preposterous.

'Wouldn't have believed it myself,' said the Colonel, 'if I hadn't got it from Cottam.'

'Cottam?' Rawcliffe's hackles rose.

'Yes. Our latest vicar. Crusading sort of chap. Thinks he can tame the local smugglers by living cheek by jowl with them and holding regular prayer meetings, or some such rot,' he said scornfully. 'From your neck of the woods, by all accounts, so I dare say you know all about him.'

'Yes,' said Rawcliffe. Though it was beginning to look as though he'd underestimated him. 'You say the Reverend Cottam informed you as to Mr Kellet's state of mind? They…spent some time together, then?'

'Oh, yes, they were thick as thieves. Terribly upset, Cottam was, after the drowning. Presented himself to me, almost as soon as we found the body, to tell me all about it.'

'I see.' Though what he saw was that he should have warned Archie to be on his guard around Cottam. That he should have listened to his instinct to prevent Archie from coming down here at all. But then, everyone had urged him to let Archie undertake the quest as an aid to his flagging self-esteem. Nobody had thought there would be any danger attached to visiting an elderly lady, to find out what she might have to do with the theft of several sets of jewels. Nobody had thought it would have ended in murder.

But…Cottam had been upset. Perhaps it was the smugglers with whom he was now involved who had so brutally disposed of Archie. 'What, precisely,' he said, hoping that he might be able to exonerate Cottam from the charge of murder, if not the rest of it, for Clare's sake, 'did Cottam tell you?'

'Well, firstly, it was on account of his work with fallen women that he knew the girl at all. He thought he'd put her back on the straight and narrow, but I could have told him how it would be. A leopard doesn't change its spots, eh? Anyway, she came running to Cottam when this young Kellet feller broke her heart. And in spite of all his counselling, she gave way to despair. Threw herself off the cliffs. I suppose Kellet did show some remorse in the end, coming looking for her the way he did. And, when he heard what happened, followed her, in a fit of despair.'

'That is the story Cottam told you, is it?'

'That's the gist of it. Thought it best to hush it up, of course.'

'Was that Cottam's idea, too? No, never mind, it really doesn't matter.' The Colonel had taken Cottam's version of events at face value. Because Cottam was a man of the cloth. And there was no point in trying to explain what sort of man Cottam really was beneath his clerical guise. Nobody would believe it. Hell, he didn't want to believe it himself.

But it was becoming increasingly clear that whatever was going on, regarding the jewel thefts, and the drownings of both Archie and the girl he was supposed to have driven to suicide, Cottam was up to his scrawny neck in it.

And then, as if to prove the old adage about speaking of the devil, the Colonel tossed his paper to one side and smiled at someone just entering the room. In spite of Jeavons promising to admit no one.

'Ah, here he is now,' said the Colonel. 'Mr Cottam, you know the Marquess of Rawcliffe, I believe?'

Rawcliffe got to his feet and turned round, slowly, desperately resisting the urge to stride across the room and knock the corrupt little clergyman down. Never had he been so glad to have his cane to grip, because if he hadn't, he would have been hard pressed not to clench his fists into the weapons he so badly wanted to use.

'Know me?' Cottam strolled forward, an unctuous smile on his face. 'Why, hasn't he told you? The Marquess is married to my little sister. I hope you don't mind, Colonel, but I would like to have a word or two in private with my brother-in-law.'

'Hmmph? Harrumph.' The Colonel made as if to move from his chair and vacate the room, with exceedingly bad grace.

'No need to get up,' said Rawcliffe. 'I believe we have finished discussing our business, Colonel, so I shall bid you good day.'

'Oh? Ah!' The Colonel looked distinctly relieved.

'Cottam, you may walk with me back to my lodgings, if you wish.'

'How very gracious of you, my lord,' said Cottam with a bow that was practically a sneer.

They left the Three Tuns, navigated the shoals of the busy high street and turned into the lane leading to the lodgings before either of them said a word.

'My sister,' said Cottam with a strange smile, 'appears to be very smitten with you, at the moment.'

They walked on in silence for a few paces.

'It would be a pity, a very great pity, if she were to discover something that might lead her to work out your true reasons for marrying her, would it not?'

Rawcliffe ground his teeth. Though the weasel was quite right. He didn't want to upset Clare. And so they kept right on walking past the row of cottages and struck out for the track leading up to the moors.

'What reasons,' he said, once they were well out of earshot of any building, 'do you presume I had for marrying your sister?'

'Why, the very same ones that brought you down here. Your relentless need to persecute me. These... trumped-up charges you plan to bring against me, that you have sent your minions to try to pin on me...they are all figments of your imagination. And so I shall tell

Clare, if you pursue your enquiries. Then we shall see where her loyalties truly lie.'

He'd already factored that into his calculations and had counted the cost.

'If they are not figments of my imagination, but are, on the contrary, facts, I will make sure the whole world knows of it.'

Clement glared at him. 'If you dare to try to humiliate me, by making accusations in a court of law, I will inform Clare exactly why you married her. That it was merely a pretext to have an excuse for pursuing me down here, and trying to…discover what happened to your spy. Mr Kellet,' he finished on a sneer.

If the man had been innocent, there would have been no need to make threats. It was as good as an admission of guilt.

At that moment, Rawcliffe decided that Clare's brother really *was* the man behind the theft of the jewels, and the subsequent death of Archie, probably because he was getting too close to the truth. And as for the girl who drowned? Who was she and what part did she play in all this? Or had Cottam merely used her untimely death as something to pin on Archie?

'Ah, you have seen the wisdom of thinking twice,' said Clement, since Rawcliffe had made no reply to his last threat.

'If you are responsible for the death of my friend, Mr Kellet, I shall have no hesitation in having you sent to the gallows,' he breathed between clenched teeth.

'Ah, but how will you prove it?' Cottam smiled with evil glee. 'So hard to find reliable witnesses, in these parts. So hard, once a man has been buried, to prove what happened to him, one way or another.'

Rawcliffe had never felt closer to throttling someone.

'Besides, how do you think Clare would look at the man who attempted to send her favourite brother to the gallows? Do you think your marriage would succeed, under those circumstances?'

Cottam was a weasel. He'd thought it before and he thought it still. He had the uncanny knack of sending a direct hit to his victim's weakest point. And Clare's regard for him was it.

'I know you don't want her to find out what you are about, otherwise you would have been frank with her from the beginning. I have to say, as a man of the cloth, that lying to your bride is not the best foundation to a marriage.'

'Nevertheless,' said Rawcliffe, 'I cannot let you get away with it.'

'Dear, dear how very melodramatic you sound. Get away with what, exactly? Do you even have any idea?' Cottam laughed then. And never had Rawcliffe been so sure that a sound was evil.

'You never do have, do you? You look down your aristocratic nose at the rest of the world, believing yourself so superior, assuming you are in control of everyone and everything around you, but you are not. I have thwarted you once and I shall do it again.'

'Thwarted me? I very much doubt it.'

'You do not even know, do you? How I managed to foil your plans for Clare when she was still a sweet innocent.'

'What do you mean?'

Cottam turned to him, an evilly triumphant smile on his face. 'That day when she came home, dripping wet after her venture into the village pond, she told me what you had said. How you made a mocking proposal to her. She was so visibly upset that I had no trouble persuading Father *that* was at the root of her distress, rather than the fate of those stupid dogs. Because he never would listen to her once she'd reached the stage of screaming like a fishwife. He sent her to her room to calm down and put on clean, dry clothing, leaving me to relate what happened. So that by the time you came to call on Father to ask his permission to pay your addresses, he was so sure he needed to shield Clare from you, that she detested you, that nothing on earth would have persuaded him to listen to your proposal. Yes,' he breathed as Rawcliffe reeled. 'I made sure you couldn't get your hands on her then and, though I wasn't able to stop you bedding her this time round, I can make sure that any affection she might have started to feel for you will start curdling with distrust until eventually it turns into a festering mass of resentment.'

'What?' Clement had been the one who'd come between him and Clare all those years ago? And now he was going to try to do the same thing again?

No. Not while he had breath in his body.

Rawcliffe flung his cane aside before he succumbed to the urge to brain Cottam with it and grabbed him by the lapels of his jacket.

'I don't care,' he growled. Because persuading the rest of the world he didn't care about anything very much was the position he always adopted when he was hurting the most. And then, because he had to conceal his weakness from Cottam, or who knew what advantage he would try to take, he took the only course guaranteed to stop him interfering in his marriage any further.

'Do you think I care what she thinks of me? Do I look like a man who needs a woman to *love* him? All I need is for her to open her legs. The rest can—'

He heard a cry of distress. From behind a group of rocks, just up ahead of them, he saw Clare emerge. A devastated look on her face.

He let go of Cottam so abruptly that the cleric staggered and almost fell.

'Clare,' said Rawcliffe, taking a step in her direction. 'Clare, it isn't what you think…'

She backed away, shaking her head, her mouth quivering as she strove not to weep.

'Clare!'

She turned and ran, stumbling over the rough ground. Straight towards the cliff edge.

Chapter Twenty-Eight

Rawcliffe pounded over the close-cropped turf, steadily gaining on her. His legs were far longer and she was hampered by her skirts. Her bonnet tumbled from her head so that her hair streamed out behind her like flames from a rocket.

He caught up to her in the sheltered hollow, where they'd spent the afternoon before, in such bliss.

'Clare,' he said again, hauling her into his arms and crushing her to his chest. 'Don't, don't, don't…'

'Don't what?' She lifted her tear-stained face to look at him in confusion. 'Cry? I cannot help it. I am…' She waved her arms in agitation. 'You have…'

'I know, I know, but truly, Clare, I didn't mean what I said.'

'Didn't you?'

'No!' He looked into her eyes and then, fearing lest Cottam should still be lurking, and might overhear what he had to say next, he simply took her face between his hands and kissed her. Kissed her until, with a half-smothered little cry, she put her arms round his waist and kissed him back.

'I know, what I said was a betrayal of what we've

shared this last few days,' he breathed into her ear, since it was the only way he could be sure that only she heard his words. 'But when he admitted he was the one behind your father's decision to keep us apart, back then, and threatened to tear us apart again, I thought that if I could make him believe that I'd grown into a cynical, harsh bastard who would treat you like a whore, he might give up. I was desperate, Clare. I couldn't go back to the way I'd been for so many years. When everything felt like dust and ashes when I thought you meant all those horrible things you said when you turned down my proposal.'

'But I didn't say any of them.'

'Yes, yes,' he said, raining kisses on her face. 'I know that *now*. But that doesn't alter the fact that I was miserable for years. And so lonely.'

'Lonely! But you had so many other women—'

'But none of them were you. So how could any of them heal the hurt you dealt by rebuffing me, in such terms—'

'But I didn't.'

'I didn't know that, though, did I? I thought you despised me. And it changed everything. Before that day at the duck pond, I made the most of what women wanted to share with me. It was all just…like a game. But the game turned deadly when I started to believe I could never have you. And every encounter after that just felt empty and sordid. And I raged at you for ruining it for me—'

To his shock, this time she was the one to stop his mouth with a kiss. Which was no mean feat since she was so much shorter than him.

'I raged at you, too,' she said. 'Because you flaunted

your women under my nose. And made me feel small and unattractive, and unfeminine...'

'Ah, darling, I'm sorry. It was a terrible way to show you how much I loved you, wasn't it? And even now we're married, I've treated you abominably.'

'It doesn't matter.'

'Yes, I know. You believe that no wife should complain about the way her husband behaves, even if he beats her,' he reflected bitterly. 'That you must be loyal to me because of the vows you made in church.'

She reached up, grabbed him by the ears and kissed him again.

'It's because I love you, you idiot,' she said. 'Not because of the vows. Not altogether. And anyway, do you really think a woman who didn't love her husband would put up with being taken on a bride trip that was arranged purely for the purpose of investigating a crime?'

'You knew?' He felt as if someone had just punched him in the gut. 'How did you know? How long have you known?'

'I only worked it out today, really. Just now, as I was walking along the cliff tops. I started putting two and two together.'

'I will drop the investigation, Clare.'

'What? Why would you do any such thing?'

'Because he is your brother. He was right. You would not be able to live with the man who'd been responsible for sending your brother to the gallows.'

She pulled back from him and planted her hands on her hips. 'Have you thought about the other side of the coin? How *I* would feel, knowing you had let a man get away with murder, simply because he is my brother?'

'Murder? You know about that? How?'

'Two and two,' she said cryptically. 'It was Miss Hutton who helped me piece it all together.'

'Who the deuce,' said Rawcliffe, running his hands through his hair and wondering at what point he'd lost his hat, again, 'is Miss Hutton?'

'Colonel Hutton's granddaughter. The one he sent to fetch you to discuss the drowning of Mr Kellet.'

'Oh. She told you that was why he sent for me?'

'In a roundabout way, yes. And then I worked out that must have been why you were so amenable about signing that slimy Mr Jeavons's silly visitors' book. That it must have been a way of letting the local magistrate, who'd dealt with Mr Kellet's drowning, know that you were in the area, so that he would come looking for you, rather than for you to have to go and visit him, which would have told everyone exactly what you were really doing down here.'

'Clare,' he said, taking her by both arms and wishing that she wasn't quite so intelligent, 'you are correct, but—'

'No, let me finish. You've done enough to confuse and distract me to this point, but I...I can't take any more.'

There were tears in her eyes. Because he'd hurt her so badly.

And yet she'd kissed him. Grabbed him and kissed him, even though she said she thought she'd worked out what he was up to.

'If I tell you the truth...'

'You have *got* to tell me the truth,' she said, flinging up her chin. 'It is high time you stopped...distracting me by being...kind one moment, then cruel the next. Confusing me. Keeping me off balance. Because that is what you have been doing, isn't it? I didn't realise hat was the method you were employing with me until Clement did pretty much the same thing. When he cast doubt on the legality of our marriage and came up with so many contradictory theories which were so ludicrous hat I got too angry to think straight. Just the way you did. Time and time again.

'Why? No, don't answer that. I know why,' she said, slapping her hands on her hips. 'Because marrying me was a brilliant excuse to come down to this neck of the woods, under the pretext of letting me visit my brother, when all the time you were really trying to find out who'd killed Mr Kellet. Even the way we met in the inn was no coincidence, was it? Let alone the way you provoked me to throw that punch and made sure it landed on your nose, so that there was just sufficient blood to make me feel guilty enough to try to mend matters and flustered enough to let you lure me into that coffee room where you—'

'No. I won't have you thinking I engineered that meeting, or married you under any other pretext than the real one. It *was* a coincidence that I happened into the inn at the very moment you were walking along that corridor. And...' He shifted from one foot to the other. He had to tell her the truth. All of it, no matter what light it threw on his nature. 'And I didn't deliberately make sure that punch you threw landed on my nose, rather than my jaw.'

'Oh?' She searched his face keenly, as though looking into the depths of his soul. 'Really?'

'Yes, really. I was—' he took a deep breath '—I was moving in for a kiss.'

'A kiss?'

'Yes. And as for provoking you deliberately, you know that I didn't really know how hurtful my comments must have been. What I said about your father being inconsistent, it arose from seeing you looking so…threadbare. Because I would never, ever have allowed you to end up in such a state, if he'd permitted me to marry you. And all his words about my morality and exposing no child of his to my blighting influence came roaring back into my mind, when he'd neglected and used you for so long, well, that was what I meant. Though I never would have said any of it if I'd known he'd only just died.'

'Oh,' she said again. And continued to look at him expectantly. Waiting for him to make a full confession.

He took another deep breath.

'It wasn't until we reached London that I considered taking advantage of our marriage, with regard to the investigation I'd already begun. I know that sounds cold, but don't forget, at the time I thought you hated me. Had always hated me. So that there was no hope our marriage stood a chance anyway. And I knew somebody had murdered Archie. And the reason I kept you in the dark about it all was because I had no proof your brother was involved. Only suspicions. And I didn't want to put you in the position where you might be obliged to take sides.'

'Oh,' she said. And then nodded and stepped forward and slid her arms round his waist.

'He did it,' she mumbled into his chest.

'What?' He took her face between his hands and turned it up so he could look into her eyes. Eyes which were deeply troubled.

'Whatever it was you suspect him of doing. The first thing Clement said to me when I walked into his study was that he hadn't done it. Since I didn't know I was supposed to think he'd done anything, that put me on ny guard. Because he always protested his innocence, ven when I'd seen him do something beastly. Take... hose puppies, for instance. I *saw* him throw the sack nto the pond. And yet later, he shook his head over heir poor little bodies and said how terrible it was that eople could be so cruel, as though he was as shocked nd upset as I was.

'And then,' she said, drawing a huge gulp of breath, when Miss Hutton spoke of how Mr Kellet had rowned, my mind shot right back to those puppies. And I couldn't help remembering how Mr Kellet always id put me in mind of a spaniel, with his big brown eyes nd the eager way he used to follow you around. And recalled how Lady Harriet had let slip that he'd come own here to search for some missing jewels. And I new. I just knew...'

And then she went stiff and looked past him, to the umble of rocks behind which Clement could very well e lurking.

'I thought I saw something. Someone. Just a shadow, t might have been, but...'

Of one accord, they strode over to the rocks, to see f Clement was trying to overhear what they were dis-ussing. But he was halfway down the track to the cot-ages, his long clerical coat flapping out behind him ike the wings of some great crow.

'How much do you think he heard?'

'I don't think he could have heard much,' he said, atting her hand. 'He was further away from us than ou were when you heard my discussion with him. Be-ides, the wind and the roar of the surf and the crying f the gulls would have prevented much of our speech rom reaching him.'

'What do you think he plans to do? Where is he going?'

He slung his arm round her waist and tugged her to his side.

'It doesn't matter. Wherever he has gone, whatever he plans to do, I will not let him hurt you. Or damage us, I swear it.'

'Yes, but you cannot let him get away scot-free. He is…he has gone bad. He was always full of mischief was always inclined to be a bit of a bully, but…' She shook her head. 'And he would always blame everyone else. He'd sort of wind up his followers the way any other boy would wind up a top and set them off. He was always at the back of it, but nobody ever caught *him* only those who followed him. The village boys were far less organised once he went away to university. And now he's got a gang of smugglers to do his bidding. Oh,' she said, placing one hand to her forehead. 'I'm not telling you anything you don't already know, am I? *That* is why you stopped being friends with him. Because he was a bully and taunted the other boys until they felt they had to join him.'

He hung his head for a moment. 'I stayed out of his way. I did indeed know what he was, but instead of confronting him, I just…'

'Then do it now. Stop him, before he goes any further.'

'Somebody has to stop him, yes, I agree. But it will not be me. Just think—you might say you love me, but it will always be between us. Festering.'

'No, it won't!'

'How could it be otherwise? In one form or another You might be able to forgive me, but…there would be talk. Supposition. And I…you might not think it, but do have a conscience. I know it would cause you grief to see your own brother brought to trial as a common criminal. And if I were the man responsible...'

She flung her arms round his waist again and hugged him hard.

He hugged her back. Rested his cheek on the crown of her head and rocked her.

After a short while, she looked up at him, her forehead creased in anguish. 'Then he has won.'

'Oh, no,' he said grimly. 'I cannot be the man to pursue him any longer, but I shall make damn sure the investigation continues. I shall pass on everything I've learned to...' No, not Lord Becconsall. Not now he had a wife. A married man couldn't risk the welfare of the one he loved. And Cottam was just the sort of adversary to defend himself by attacking the weak and vulnerable. 'Someone else.' He'd find someone. Someone tough and fearless, and clever. Someone who wouldn't be fooled by Cottam's cunning, nor vulnerable to any threat he might try to make.

'Oh, thank goodness,' she said on a sigh of relief. 'I couldn't live with myself if I thought he'd got away with whatever it is he's done, because of your scruples on my account.'

'But it will be far easier on you if another person handles his arrest.'

'Yes.'

'Then, since we have accomplished all we are likely to do, down here, I suggest we return to London—'

'Before Clement can put any plan he might be hatching against us into action...'

'That had crossed my mind. And compile all the information we have gleaned, between us,' he said, squeezing her hand.

'It isn't going to be easy, is it, to prove he's guilty of Mr Kellet's murder?'

'No. But Ulysses...that is, Lord Becconsall, is bound to be able to come up with a plan to expose him. In the meantime...how about if we let Clement think that he has won?'

'What do you mean?'

'Well, if he thinks I am so worried about losing your regard that I will do nothing against him, he might...'

'Lower his guard! That would be brilliant.'

'How much did he see, I wonder? And what might he have made of it?'

Rawcliffe swiftly went over the last few minutes, considering how they might have looked to an outsider.

'If he really couldn't hear anything we said to one another, he would have seen your devastation when you overheard me speaking crudely about our relationship...'

'Then running straight for the edge of the cliffs...'

'And me running after you, reaching you only just in time to stop you throwing yourself off...'

'As if I'd do anything so melodramatic,' she said, wrinkling her nose in disgust. 'But, yes, for the purposes of hoodwinking Clement, I am willing to go along with the fabrication.'

'Would he swallow it, do you think?'

'Oh, yes. He doesn't have a very high opinion of women.'

'Very well, then. And once I'd pulled you back from the edge, he would have seen me kissing you, desperately...promising you anything?'

'Ah,' she said, catching on. 'And then he would have seen me kissing you, for promising me that anything.'

'So. All we have to do is...'

'Oh!' She pressed her hands to her cheeks. 'He told me that if ever I needed to write to him, I should do so, care of Lady Buntingford, because he handled all her correspondence, because she doesn't see as well as she used to.'

'So *that* is how he did it. He wrote all those fake references and just got her to put her signature at the bottom.'

'References?'

'We started becoming suspicious when each family that had jewels taken, and substituted with fakes, also took into their employ a girl who had impeccable references from Lady Buntingford. That was the angle Archie was looking into. Whether she was developing some kind of mania for rubies.'

'Oh,' said Clare, a touch wide-eyed. 'Yes, that makes sense. But actually, what just occurred to me was that the reason he told me about Lady Buntingford's being a safe address to write to was so that I could write and warn him, if you were about to make a move against him. It wasn't for my benefit at all,' she said indignantly, 'but his. *That* is why he made as if he was only letting me return to you against his better judgement—so that I'd be in a position to be able to warn him if you found some solid evidence against him.

'Right! Well, I can jolly well turn his scheme against him. I can write that you are so besotted with me you would promise me anything—'

'Which would be the perfect truth,' he said, catching her round the waist and hauling her close.

She blushed.

'And in the meantime, we can also drop a hint or two along those lines to the locals.'

'How could we do that?'

'Kendall.'

She wrinkled up her nose. 'I don't think we can put much faith in a footman who drinks so heavily.'

'On the contrary. He has demonstrated a remarkable amount of trust in me by admitting what goes on when he goes to the local taverns. And it seems that certain fellows who ply him with drinks are extremely interested in our doings.'

'That doesn't mean the tale we want told will get back to Clement.'

'I think it does. The man appears to have eyes and ears everywhere. Even in London. I still can't fathom how the deuce he knew about the Tarbrook rubies.'

'People do talk to clergymen,' she said thoughtfully. 'It is a sort of relic of the confessional, from the Church of Rome. Father was very keen on utilising it. Said it made people feel better to clear their conscience.'

Clare shivered.

'Cold? You shouldn't have come out without a coat or bonnet. What were you thinking?'

'I was thinking I wanted to get out of that stuffy cottage and think,' she said, rubbing her hands up and down her arms. 'Do you really think we can make Clement believe he has won?'

'Oh, yes. He has sufficient arrogance to believe he will triumph. And I will make sure that nobody makes a move against him for some time.'

'Lulling him into a false sense of security?'

'That's right. And then, when he least expects it—' he made a crushing motion with his fist '—we will make our move on him!'

'And…and what of us?' Clare gazed up at him with wide eyes.

'We,' he said, cupping her sweet little face between

is hands, 'are going to live happily ever after. I shall
do my utmost to make sure of it. No woman will ever
be so spoiled, so cosseted, so well loved...'

'Careful,' she said. 'If you carry on like that, people
will start to think you are a romantic.'

'No, they won't. For I am not a romantic. I am just
a man in love.'

She gasped.

'Clare,' he said, taking her sweet little face between
his hands. 'Surely you must have guessed that, as well?
You have worked out everything else I've tried to keep
from you.'

'You are in love? With...me?'

'Desperately.'

'But...no...you can't be...'

'Why do you think I was so green about the gills on
the way to Peeving Cove?'

She shook her head.

'Because I was sick to my stomach at the prospect
of Clement would do...exactly what he threatened to
do just now. Turn you against me.'

He saw her turn over that statement in her mind.
And accept it.

'But—' she began.

'Now, cast your mind back to the day you punched
me. Why do you think I refused to countenance any of
your objections to marrying me?'

She bit down on her lower lip. But at last, he could
see a spark of hope begin to gleam in her eyes.

'Yes, that's right. It was because I had finally seen a
way to make you mine. After all those years of thinking my goddess was unobtainable. Why do you think
I moved in for that kiss? I was attempting to compro-
mise you. Right there in that corridor.'

'And then I ruined it for you by punching you,' she said, aghast.

'No, actually, you didn't. You made my day. You'd just given me an excuse to…lord it over you for the rest of our lives. For I would always be able to remind you that it was entirely your own fault we'd had to get married. Because you'd lost your temper and behaved disgracefully. In a public inn.'

'You are the most despicable…'

But even though she was saying the same words she'd flung at him countless times over the years, this time there was a smile hovering about the edges of her mouth.

'Ruthless…'

And now she was positively beaming at him.

'Yes,' he confessed. 'There are no depths to which I would not sink to have you in my arms. In my bed. In my life.'

'You really mean it, don't you?' She looked at him in dawning wonder. 'You love me.'

And then, because there had been quite enough talking for one day, he decided to communicate with her in the way that worked the best.

With a kiss.

* * * * *

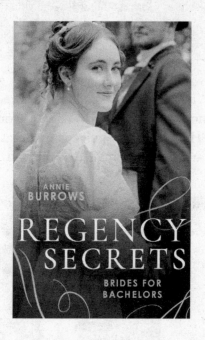

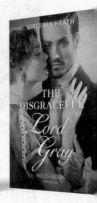